WHERE MAGIC RULES

Enchantment's Edge rested upon the very rim of the leagues-long escarpment from which it took its name, its scores of turrets and spires craning and clambering to seemingly impossible heights, like living things, the topmost limbs of colossal petrous trees, straining to taste the sunlight. Massive fortified walls of fused stone encircled it in its entirety, in places spilling over the lip onto the sheer face of the scarp. Over time, within these constantly expanding walls, a small city had come into being, burrowing deep into the scarp itself where lack of space denied expansion at ground-level, or alternatively edging upwards like tentative new shoots in the shadows of the hoary, venerable, petrified towers.

Its origins were lost in the intricate meander and blur of fargone history and legend, but written records testified to the great castle's having stood in some form or other throughout the centuries that the gods of Enchantment were known to have warred . . .

About the author

Philip G. Williamson was born in Worcestershire in 1955. He has worked in a wide variety of jobs in the UK and abroad, from A&R for major and independent music companies to shepherding in Greece. He now lives in North London with his wife and daughter. *Enchantment's Edge*, the first volume in a new fantasy trilogy, is his ninth novel.

Enchantment's Edge

Philip G. Williamson

Volume 1: The Orb and the Spectre

NEW ENGLISH LIBRARY
Hodder and Stoughton

First published in 1996
by Hodder and Stoughton

First published in paperback in 1997 by Hodder and Stoughton
A division of Hodder Headline PLC

A New English Library paperback

10 9 8 7 6 5 4 3 2 1

British Library Cataloguing in Publication Data
A CIP catalogue record for this title is available from the British Library.

ISBN 0 340 66669 2

Printed and bound in Great Britain by
Cox & Wyman Ltd, Reading, Berkshire

Hodder and Stoughton
A division of Hodder Headline PLC
338 Euston Road
London NW1 3BH

ENCHANTMENT'S EDGE

PART ONE

ONE

I

The child had been playing contentedly by the water's edge for some time, oblivious of the eyes that watched from the concealment of the surrounding forest. The day was warm, barely a breath of breeze stirring the early autumn air, and the child's warden, a bow-kneed man no longer in his prime, had seated himself upon the soft grass, his back propping the trunk of a huge ancient oak. His eyelids had grown heavy and his thoughts had begun to drift. He dozed now, his head tipped back, mouth agape, snoring as he wandered in his dreams.

'This is the one?' demanded the woman, Arene, in a curt whisper. She was old: her body was heavy and bent even when she was not crouched and hiding, but she was not without a kind of strength, and her eyes as they watched the infant beside the water were bright with a strange fever.

Her companion nodded a touch impatiently, for he had already answered the same question. 'Aye.'

'You are sure, Hal? There can be no doubt?'

He turned his eyes upwards. 'I have told you, Mistress, there is no other child of this age hereabouts, not with the background you have described.'

Her lips formed a tight, drooping smile. 'This is the one I have come for. And the moment offers itself. Look,' she nodded towards the sleeping man. 'Irresponsible to neglect his charge so. A child so young and trusting, unaware of the world's myriad dangers. So easy to slip there upon the bank, and the water, even at the edge, is deep for one so small. A child of such tender age . . . a terrible accident which might so easily have been avoided.'

She rose slightly from her uncomfortable position and made as if to move away. Hal had turned to her with a sagging jaw. 'Mistress?' He laid a hand upon her arm to stay her motion. 'Mistress, what are you saying? What do you intend? You cannot mean—'

Arene stiffened, turning an outraged stare to the hand that touched her. Hal withdrew it as though scalded.

'And what is it to you, Hal?'

'Mistress, I agreed to guide you to the child, but this . . . I had no . . . I cannot be party to infanticide!'

'What do you know, you fool!'

He gulped, dismayed by her venom, and achingly conscious that he could not defy her. 'I know nothing, Mistress. Only what you have told me. But—'

'Nothing, that is right! I take no pleasure in this, Hal. I am not by choice a murderess. But you truly can know nothing of what is at stake here. Let me tell you this, I act to avert a disaster the scale of which you cannot begin to imagine. That child, that innocent which you see playing so happily there, is not what it appears. Be sure of this, Hal. Be sure.'

Hal gaped at her, dumbly terrified. In her eyes there brimmed an intensity of emotion more complex than he could fathom. He recalled how she had come to him in his cottage in the forest, questioned him almost obsessively, and when satisfied that he had the information she sought, offered good coin for his co-operation. He had been nervous then, aware from the way in which she posed her questions and the tale they almost told, that he was being asked to embark upon a business he would have been wiser to stay ignorant of. But the money . . .

Arene made a contemptuous sound. 'You see, you do know nothing, yet you have the gall to try to judge me! Do not even dream of doing so, Hal, for I speak of matters that are far beyond your ability to judge or even comprehend.' She gave a sigh, as if relenting slightly, watching him. When she spoke again her tone, though still laden, was softer, and she looked suddenly weary. 'I act now only because I must. The child may look like an ordinary child, but it is not. It is Foulborn, a cursed thing, and it carries a dark destiny. If it is allowed to live it will in time bring incalculable suffering in this land and beyond. Foulborn: it has come from—' she broke off. Hal's expression told her all she needed to know.

Arene gave herself a moment to gather her thoughts. She had

said more than was necessary. It was a consequence of age and of the loneliness of her station that on those infrequent occasions when she found herself in the company of others her words tended to tumble forth more loosely and willingly than she intended. It was as if, in their eagerness to be gone from her and attract the attention of others, they possessed a will and volition of their own. She feared this tendency in her, aware that one day it could bring about her ruin.

And in this instance a minimum of words was all that was necessary. Hal was a simple man brought up amongst fearful folk. He had lived his entire life here in the wild, wooded, mountainous fringes of the land called Enchantment. His was a strange world, where the inexplicable was commonplace, where terrors and wonders abounded, where the fabulous and miraculous became almost a part of everyday life, never understood and best left unquestioned. The gods warred in Enchantment, and had done so for longer than any man knew. Weird and mighty beings whose bitter feuds ravaged the surrounding lands and brought havoc and, sometimes, strange gifts into the lives of humans. Arene needed only suggest the involvement of elements beyond Hal's ken. Imagination and his own experience would do the rest.

'You have done what I asked, Hal, and have been more than adequately rewarded,' she said. 'If your conscience or better judgement bids, you may go now with my thanks. Perhaps it is preferable that way.'

Without waiting to see whether he heeded her she turned and slid from the bushes. She crept near-silently to the edge of the glade and paused, appraising the child, then its slumbering warden, then the narrow path along which they had come, which meandered away into the depths of the forest. She listened. A crow cawed in the high trees, some small woodland creature shifted in the undergrowth, the man snored and a fly hovered above his open mouth; a bee hummed across the glade, the child burbled quietly to itself. Arene stole forward noiselessly, with a lightfootedness that belied her age and bulk.

Her quarry had its back to her and had no inkling of her presence. Arene looked down at the small fair head, crowned with a floppy blue cap of stained cloth, and the little muddied hands. A dragonfly, iridescent in the bright sunlight, glided past. The child cooed and leaned forward to investigate this wonder as it settled upon a nearby frond of creeping willow.

Arene's eyes went to the dark, silent water which reflected the overhanging trees, barely more than an arm's length away. It was so simple: a swift movement – the Foulborn would be too surprised to cry out – then hold the head and body still beneath the water so that its small thrashings did not rouse the sleeping warden. It would be done in moments; none would be the wiser.

But could she be certain? She experienced a sudden jolt, a spasm of doubt. A torrent of emotions shook her. Truly she wanted no part of this deed. *Must it be this way?*

Her hand went to her cheek; tears brimmed suddenly and spilled from her eyes. She swayed, felt the aches of her joints, a weakness in her limbs.

I am not a murderess!

But there was no other course, she knew it. She had been set this task, with the absolute certainty that she could not allow herself to fail. With a terrible effort she stilled her thoughts and gathered herself, taking the final step, lowering herself, hands extended, for the small, perfect body.

There was a crashing in the undergrowth. She glimpsed a movement across the water.

'Ho there!'

Arene spun, stepping back.

'Ho, Mother! Don't be alarmed.'

On the other side of the pool a figure had appeared from beneath the trees. He was a young man, perhaps eighteen years young, twenty at most. His limbs were long and lean, not yet hardened or moulded with the blows of true manhood. His hair was the colour of tow and he was garbed in grey hose, a loose blouse of pale olive, a leather jerkin and wide, calf-high boots. A shortsword in a leather scabbard was buckled at his waist.

'You – you made me jump,' accused Arene, struggling for composure. Her skin tingled, suddenly clammy, and her heart hammered so hard it almost choked her. *What had he seen?*

The newcomer was smiling. Possibly he had perceived nothing sinister in her actions – but if he had come a moment later! Arene glanced aside. The child's warden was sitting up, roused by the voices, blinking and rubbing his chin, gazing blearily at her, then at the newcomer, and scrambling erect. She noticed, ridiculously, the silence now that his snoring had ceased. The child looked up from beside her feet, mild bewilderment on its face as it took in the two intruders upon its play.

Addressing the young man, Arene feigned indignation, though her voice quavered. 'Crashing out of the wood like that; for all I knew you could have been a boggart or a grullag come to carry me away.'

'And for all I knew, Mother, you might have been a witch or a harridan intent on doing harm to this fair child. But naturally I assume otherwise.'

Arene caught her breath, shocked to muteness. But still his blithe demeanour revealed nothing to heighten her alarm. Could it have been only a chance remark?

'Mother, you are pale,' the young man observed, picking his way around the edge of the pool, carefully avoiding the water. 'Plainly I have given you a fright. Please accept my sincere apology. It was unintentional, but I did not know anyone was here.' Standing before her he offered her his hand. 'Let me assist you, Mother. Here, sit before you fall.'

'I need no assistance,' snapped Arene. '*And I am not your mother!*'

He stepped back as if stung, proffering two open palms in appeasement, but the corners of his wide mouth quivered, his head tilted slightly to one side, and a wry humour lit his eyes. 'I have offended you. Let me make good, then, I shall drown myself now. It will be better this way. Say the word, Moth—er, lady, and I will consign my body to the murky depths of this tranquil pond, and my spirit to whatever darkness may await it beyond.'

Lady. Such a long time since anyone had called her that, even in jest. Arene looked him over, his broadening smile, teeth strong if a little crooked, jaw firm, a little over-pronounced, and deep blue eyes. His hair was fringed high across the forehead and fell neatly over his ears, as was the current mode. He was tall and straight-backed, the shoulders wide and loose, chest deep, tapering to a narrow waist. His clothing was worn but far from threadbare, and he spoke well. The sword-hilt had a standard, reliable grip, but one feature caught her eye: the tips of the crossbar extended downwards in a pair of blunt metal tines. Arene had little knowledge of weapons but she knew this to be unusual, perhaps a foreign design. The hardened leather of the scabbard, though aged and well-used, revealed good-quality workmanship. This stranger was neither noble nor peasant, if appearances were to be believed. Perhaps the scion of some moderately-sized steader or manorial bailiff. But appearances, here in this land, were frequently deceptive.

Arene was aware, even in the shock and confusion of his sudden appearance, of a deep inward pulse, a warm, poignant, almost forgotten sensation, suffusing low in her belly. It filled her with sad yearning, and chagrin. Ah, she thought, with a longing that echoed back through the years, if I were thirty years younger, the striking beauty I still was then, I would love you, here, in this dappled glade. We would pleasure one another passionately and long, for I see in your bright sapphire eye that you would be of a similar yen. The woods would resound and we would love till we could love no more, then lie together wrapped in sweet, moist exhaustion; ah yes, if things were different.

She smiled a weary, private smile. The irony of it: his eyes beheld only a crone. Flabby, withered flesh and almost more hairs upon her chin than on her crown. Even 'Mother' was a compliment, for Arene was too advanced in years to have pushed from her womb one as youthful and fresh-faced as he.

No fool like an old one.

'That is more like it,' he said. 'Your smile enhances your beauty no end, even if it is a little distant. May I take it then that I am reprieved?'

'No doubt your manner serves you well and has won you into the bedchambers of many a gullible maiden and will do for many more years,' Arene replied, 'but I am long in the tooth. Your charm is worth little here.'

'I will put myself among the tadpoles, then – never again to rise.'

'The tadpoles dropped their tails long ago, boy, and the frogs have fled. You would find it lonely down there among cold trout which have no yen for conversation. Nor are they passionate lovers. No, do not wet yourself on my account. Your crime was not so great. There are beauties yet who must discover pleasure and heartbreak at your hands.'

The young man grinned and Arene caught herself. *Old fool! A hag, charmed despite herself, flirting like a spring nymph!*

She was in danger, aware of the child's warden now standing

a little way behind her, to one side, blinking and disoriented, his hand uncertainly gripping his stout longstaff. He was concerned as to where these two had sprung from. And this youth with whom she bantered: he apparently assumed her to be in company with the warden and child.

Arene glanced down at the child. She was thwarted, for she could not kill it now. Moments ago it had been as though fate had offered her a free hand. She would have set the future at rest; the wars, the bloody intrigues and betrayals, the terrible suffering that was to come – all for so little reason, and all could have been averted here with her single action. But not now. She had hesitated. Was this the price? Now she could only endeavour to extricate herself.

The Foulborn's eyes were on her and she held back a shudder as she recalled once more what she knew. She turned again to the young man, wondering. Was his arrival at such a crucial moment sheer coincidence? Could he be only what he purported to be? A shiver ran down her bowed spine. Here on the borders of Enchantment one could be certain of so little, least of all the true nature of a stranger who stepped unexpectedly out of the wildwood.

The youth was nodding over Arene's shoulder to the warden, and making greeting. Arene interrupted quickly, before things became clear to them both. 'Who are you, boy, and what are you doing here?'

'I am called Shenwolf, and my goal is Enchantment's Edge.'

'Enchantment's Edge?'

'I became lost in the forest. But I see there is a path that leads from here. Is this the right way?'

Arene remained silent for a moment, troubled. His name was unusual, and if he spoke truthfully, what had caused him to leave the forest path? A lone traveller stuck carefully to the marked ways if he had any sense, and this youth seemed no slackwit.

Shenwolf looked beyond her to the warden, who said, 'It is the great castle you mean, not the land, I take it?'

'I do not think I will find my fortune upon a blasted cliff, my friend. Aye, I seek the great city-castle. Is it far from here?'

'On foot? About two days. Maybe three. Aye, that is the way. The path joins a wider track about half a league on. Follow that north-west and it will take you to where you wish to go.'

'I thank you. I will leave you to yourselves, then, and again,

I apologize for having intruded so rudely upon you.' Shenwolf crouched and stroked the child's hair. 'Such a beautiful infant. You are the grandparents?'

The warden looked affronted, and Arene almost cackled through her discomposure. Shenwolf looked at neither. He took from around his neck a narrow leather thong upon which hung a tiny white object. This he placed carefully over the child's head, to hang below the breastbone. 'This is for you, little one. Should we ever meet again, I will know you by it.'

He straightened. 'A humble gift. Now, I will bid you both good-day.'

'May I enquire as to your business at the city-castle?' enquired Arene hurriedly as Shenwolf made off.

He stopped. 'A simple business. I have a yen for adventure, fortune and distinction, nothing more nor less. The Krai move closer, so I believe, and their appetite for conquest grows with every step. King Leth is keen to swell the army's ranks and reassure the populace. It is a soldier's life I seek.'

It is a soldier's *death* you will *find*, if everything I hear is true, thought Arene, but she said nothing. Shenwolf bowed his head and strode away, whistling to himself.

'Wait, young sir!' called the warden. 'We will accompany you a short distance if we may. We are ready to leave.'

'It would be my pleasure.'

The man bent and lifted his ward with one arm, nodded warily to Arene, and set off across the glade. Arene's eyes were on the object around the child's neck. She glimpsed what looked like a tooth or small piece of ivory or perhaps stone, carved into a specific shape, but she could not make out its exact form.

At the edge of the glade Shenwolf turned back to her. 'Are you not coming?'

She shook her head. 'Not yet. I will sit a while longer.'

He nodded and raised his hand. Arene watched their retreating backs. Within moments, almost certainly, each would discover that this old woman in her shabby clothes was unknown to the other. Would they return? She did not intend to wait to find out.

She felt a welter of emotion. So close to achieving her aim, yet the Foulborn still lived. This moment was lost, but an agony hung upon her. The deed had to be done, still. It had taken all her resources to find the strength to do it, and now she must do it again. Hal had revealed the child's dwelling-place to her. She would wait, then, and watch, until another opportunity presented itself. She would find the strength, somehow. She had no other hope.

But what was the gift that Shenwolf had given the Foulborn child? A charm? A protective talisman or amulet? Would her next attempt be fraught with even greater difficulties?

Arene glanced in agitation into the gloom beneath the trees. There was no sign of Hal; she took it that he had fled. She sighed despondently, shaking her head, then stepped from the glade and vanished into the forest's depths.

II

Enchantment's Edge rested upon the very rim of the leagues-long escarpment from which it took its name, its scores of turrets and spires craning and clambering to seemingly impossible heights, like living things, the topmost limbs of colossal petrous trees, straining to taste the sunlight. Massive fortified walls of fused stone encircled it in its entirety, in places spilling over the lip onto the sheer face of the scarp. Over time, within these constantly extending walls, a small city had come into being, burrowing deep into the scarp itself where lack of space denied expansion at ground-level, or alternatively edging upwards like tentative new shoots in the shadows of the hoary, venerable, petrified towers.

Its origins were lost in the intricate meander and blur of fargone history and legend, but written records testified to the great castle's having stood in some form or other throughout the centuries that the gods of Enchantment were known to have warred. The gods, the Highest Ones, to whom even the King was inferior. They battled on, seemingly unaware of or indifferent to the lives of humankind – Enchantment's Edge gazed with wonder, fear, reproach across the deep forest and craggy upthrusts that lay close upon their mysterious domain.

At the hub of Enchantment's Edge was Orbia, the royal palace. It was built almost entirely of semi-translucent marble, pure white in the main, which at times and under certain conditions would glow gently, reflecting the ambient light in its subtle hues. Here and there variations of the stone had been employed to fabulous effect: a tower faced with swirls, whorls and striations of opalescent blues; a minaret shot with deepest lapis; a roseate latticework colouring a dome; soft cerise bands on a balcony; an emerald-specked abutment; coiling veins of variegated greys enlivening the mid-region of a steeple or spire. So extraordinary was this place, so striking to the eye and mind and in places so apparently defiant of physical laws, that many believed it could never have been built by human hands. It was surely the work of the gods themselves, or of one of their number at least.

A minority of these believers took the view further, declaring that the reason Enchantment's Edge knew so many troubles was that the Highest Ones were offended by the presence of humans here, in their domain, and that they wished to reclaim it for themselves. This strand of reasoning had its opponents, who argued simply that if that were so the Highest Ones would simply take it. Men could not stand against gods. If any or all of the warring deities so desired they could expunge the inhabitants of Enchantment's Edge in an instant, down to the last man, woman, waif, workbeast and household pet.

The nature of Orbia was indeed a mystery, these rationalists conceded. But a greater mystery still was the nature of forbidden Enchantment itself. And perhaps the greatest question of all concerned man's existence here. Was the fact that humankind was permitted to remain an indication that the Highest Ones wanted people here, even required a human presence? Was there an unknown purpose that humans had to fulfil? Or were the inhabitants of Enchantment's Edge simply tolerated, or considered unworthy of consideration of any kind by the Highest Ones? Might the gods be genuinely unaware of humans? Or might they simply be wholly indifferent?

These issues and their ramifications created a forum for ongoing debate among the citizens of Enchantment's Edge. Within the great city-castle's Arcane College and the Department of Philosophical Studies uncountable man-hours were devoted to the subject. A whole library existed of texts dedicated solely to the study of the nature of Enchantment, its strange and fearsome inhabitants, and the place of Enchantment's Edge and the palace of Orbia in the overall scheme of things.

Independent groups and factions had also sprung up within the mighty walls. Their members held fixedly to individual codes of beliefs and were uniformly convinced that they alone were custodians of the true facts of their community's existence.

Some of these groups were long-established. They donned the apparel of religio-political faiths – usually with the disapproval of the Crown – and exercised significant influence in the community. Others had been spawned more recently and attracted a smaller and often more youthful following. Several were given to worship of one or more of the warring gods of Enchantment – though tacitly and with circumspect ritual, for a royal edict forbade worship of specific deities – and while the majority preached peacefully in the streets or held regular convocations at allotted places of devotion and instruction, a few tended to extremist views and one or two were prone to unruliness and unorthodox modes of conduct.

Unquestionably all were keen to swell their own numbers, and equally to discredit by fair means or foul the arguments of their rivals. Assassination attempts upon faction heads or senior figures were a regular source of nuisance, and clashes between groups, sometimes bloody, invariably demanded the intervention of the castle militia.

Attempts had even been made to overthrow the monarchy, most recently and infamously the endeavour by Grey Venger, head of the now-outlawed True Sept, to take the life of King Leth. The attempt failed but Venger escaped. Leth arrested Venger's two sons in his stead and announced their deaths should Grey Venger fail to give himself into custody within one week. Venger stayed hidden and the boys died at the appointed time, flung from the beetling walls of the Place of Justice onto the rocks thousands of feet below.

Grey Venger was still believed to be hiding somewhere within Enchantment's Edge, and he remained head of the True Sept, though his popularity had waned following his failure to save his scions. The ban upon his cult posed King Leth's security cadre the problem of locating the shadowy corners where its members still met, along with those other dark nooks that were the secret gathering places of illegal cabals and insurrectionists.

So it went on.

King Leth's family had held the throne by natural succession over nine generations. Leth himself, at thirty-two, was now in his third year as sovereign of Enchantment's Edge and the surrounding lands. His mother, Queen Fallorn, had died soon after relinquishing the throne in his favour at the age of fifty-nine. She passed away peacefully in her sleep following a short bout of influenza. Though she had never spoken of it, Leth had often wondered whether she had somehow known that her worldly time was coming to its end.

On the day following her abdication Leth had been made party to one of the great secrets of Enchantment's Edge. He was summoned to his mother's drawing-room early in the morning. Under the letter of the law the throneless queen no longer had the power of command over her son, but Leth responded without hesitation.

He found Fallorn alone, unusually, seated upon a comfortable winged chair before a blazing hearth.

'Mother.' He took her proffered hand and touched his lips to it, then kissed her cheek and sat opposite her, his torso inclined forward so that he might keep her hand in his.

Fallorn gazed at him tenderly, her eyes shining. 'Leth, my son. I am proud of you. I always have been. I have waited for this day, watching you as you grew into a youth, then a man, then a man equipped and able to rule our difficult land. I saw from the beginning that you would rise with honours to this office, to continue the tradition of benign and just but firm rule that has been our family's hallmark. Now the day is here and I am comforted, privileged and *proud* to be able to gaze upon my son Leth, King of Enchantment's Edge.'

Leth slightly dropped his gaze. He was proud himself, just a little self-conscious under her praise, and aware also that he was perhaps not as wholly-deserving as she believed. He loved his mother dearly and knew the utmost respect for her as a woman and ruler, but he had not always agreed with her decisions. Her advisor and confidant for some years, he had begun to see ways in which his rule, when it came, might differ slightly from hers. He always put forward his view, but if Queen Fallorn overruled him he did not protest. Rather he kept his own counsel more and more, biding his time, for he was young and there had never been any doubt that his day would come.

'King of Enchantment's Edge,' Fallorn repeated, half-whispering and almost in a reverie.

'Not yet, mother,' Leth gently reminded her. 'Not for two more weeks.'

She dismissed this with a short breath and a nonchalant gesture of her hand. 'The coronation is merely protocol and formality, you know that. It is for the people, that they may publicly acknowledge their new monarch, and for the nobility, the knights and grand officiers that they may renew their fealty to the crown. But it is all airs and posture. I am no longer the incumbent sovereign. You are King Leth, I have declared it so, and the world knows and acknowledges it.'

Leth nodded, closing his eyes momentarily to savour the emotion that swept through him. He was realizing his life's ambition. He was popular with the people, courtiers, counsellors, nobles and military alike. He knew his rule would not be trouble-free – there were problems, as always, among the cults and factions; and from the south there had come disturbing rumours of a conflict among the Krai, not so very far beyond the marches of Enchantment's Edge – but Leth believed himself at that time well able to meet any challenge that might confront him.

'It is to this end that I have called you here.' His mother's voice interrupted his thoughts. Opening his eyes he saw that her face had grown sombre. He frowned quizzically.

'There is something I have to reveal to you,' Fallorn went on. 'A confidence, combined with a gift, which will bring you to knowledge of Orbia's most precious secret. This is something that may be imparted only at this time, and only to the assumptive monarch.'

She slid her hand from his and reached down to take a small blue casket, figured with glyphs, which rested on a low ebony table beside her. She held it upon her lap, cupping her hands around it, touching it lightly. She half-smiled to herself and seemed to be in a state of profound inward reflection. Leth watched her curiously.

'This is for you, my son.' Fallorn raised the casket and passed it to him. Seeing that his fingers went immediately to the clasp which held it closed, she quickly covered his hands with hers. 'No. Do not open it. Not now, not here.'

Leth's brow creased again. 'Mother, what is this?'

'It is a wonder, Leth, my son, my king. It is . . .' She stopped herself, pressed his hands as a final admonition, then removed hers and sat back. 'You will understand soon enough. Take this to your chambers and when you are alone, completely alone, preferably today, open it. First be sure to bolt all doors so that you may not be disturbed. Then you will learn.'

Leth's frown deepened. He disliked riddles. A hidden rebelliousness within him spoke sharply, urging defiance of his mother, telling him to break open the box now and see what was within, be done with nonsense. But the mature man, the son and ruler, knew better. Though those aspects of his personality were also irked, they tempered him and bade him to calmness.

'Good.' Fallorn had watched him carefully, and now exhaled a held breath. 'All might have been lost in this moment had you shown yourself less than I believed you to be.'

'Mother, I don't understand—'

'Do just as I have told you. I can say no more. But tell no one. *No one*. Do you understand? Keep this from the eyes of others at all times, and let no person learn of its existence.'

'But Mother—'

'*Is that understood?*'

Leth nodded. 'It is. But—'

'No.' She lifted a hand. 'I can say nothing more. It is not permitted.'

'Not permitted?' Leth was incredulous. 'Mother, you are the Queen!'

'No longer. Hence this mystery is yours. Now, you have much to do. Kiss me and go. And later, when you *know*, do not speak to me of this. In time you will understand why.'

Leth, impatient, opened his mouth as if to ask more. But his mother regally turned her head aside, presenting her cheek, her eyes lowered. He rose and kissed her, and as he did so she briefly clasped his hand in a tight embrace. When he straightened she was looking into the flames of the fire. He bowed and withdrew.

Leth strode directly to his private chambers in the First Tower of Dawn in Orbia's west wing. There he dismissed all attendants, took himself off to his study and, in accordance with his mother's instructions, bolted the door. Wonderingly, he took the little casket, placed it upon his work desk and sat down before it.

He examined the glyphs and symbols upon its surface, but they were of unfamiliar design and meant nothing to him. He ran his fingertips over the beading which curved from the four corners of the casket's base, up over its convex surface, to meet at the exact centre of the lid. The beading was made of small, oval gems, bright, opaque and deep blue. Where they met, in the lid's centre, was set a larger stone. Precious, Leth supposed, though neither the gems nor the larger stone were quite like any he knew.

The emotion that had earlier impelled him to break open the casket without ceremony had now fled him. Instead he found himself almost reluctant to ease open the catch. He sat before the casket for some time, inexplicably overcome with nervousness. It was foolish, he upbraided himself, and he did not know why he should feel this way. But his palms perspired, his mouth was dry and he felt an unaccustomed flush upon his cheeks as though he were succumbing to a sudden fever.

For a moment Leth was tempted to take the casket and fling it from his window to be smashed upon the stones many levels below. That way he would never know, never enter this mystery, this tantalizing secret that had been presented to him, and perhaps that would be better. For he was afraid – he acknowledged this now with anger at himself. His mother's demeanour had unsettled him. He could not recall a time when he had been more impressed by her authority and the gravity of her tone. He was afraid, yes, at what this might signify.

But his curiosity was unappeasable, as Fallorn must have known it would be. He could not resist this; no sane person could. He leaned forward and took the blue casket in his hands. It was light and could hardly contain very much. He eased the little hook that was its catch from its metal eye, freeing the hasp, and raised the lid.

Immediately Leth's chamber was filled with pale blue light. With a startled cry, he threw himself back in his chair, covering his eyes instinctively with an arm. Though pale, the light was bright, and its initial intensity half-blinded him. He squinted, seeking to see through the dazzle, but it pained him to open his eyes more than a fraction, and even then he was forced to clench them shut almost upon the instant.

With his free hand Leth lashed out wildly to knock the casket from the desk, hoping this might diminish or wholly deprive it of its power. But he failed to strike it; in fact he failed to strike the desk in front of him, though the strangeness of this did not immediately become apparent to him. Uppermost in his mind was a sudden, terrible, crippling fear.

'The gods! *I am blind!*'

Leth lurched from his chair with a cry, both hands to his eyes. 'Guards! Guards!'

He staggered towards the door, one hand stretched before him. He had covered several paces before it came to him that he had met no obstacle. Yet there was a divan only a couple of paces from his desk; and beyond that a stone pedestal supporting a bust of his great-grandfather, King Hordicard. And the big chest, the bookshelf, *the wall!* He should have touched the study wall by now, yet there was nothing. Nothing before him, around him; nothing familiar.

'What is happening here?'

He fell to his knees, groping forward for something, *anything*. And slowly he became aware that the intensity of light no longer stabbed through his eyelids. He parted them by degrees, fearfully. The blueness surrounded him but it no longer hurt. It was a gentler luminescence and he could see into it, and what he saw astounded him.

The new king, on hands and knees, stared like a bewildered animal into an endless blue as his mind struggled to make sense of what had happened. He could see walls, blue-toned walls, but they were not the walls of his own apartment, and they appeared to be an infinite distance away, although they surrounded him and towered over him as though close. He could not explain this paradox. The walls were both near and far away. They were everywhere around, forming a vast circular chamber, and they were beneath and above him also. He was in a wide empty space, a uniform misty blueness, and there was nothing else.

He sat, blinking slowly, gazing around in a daze and trying to quell the fear that welled within him and threatened to take his sanity.

'Where am I?'

The silence, he realized, was profound. It was as if there was nothing, nothing at all, anywhere, other than himself. And his heart hammered and he heard the blood roaring through his veins, the air bellowing in his lungs. He had never before been aware of himself like this, and it bore him up to a pitch of panic.

And then a voice spoke. 'Ah, it is the new one.'

King Leth spun. Half-obscured in the strange twilight a figure was approaching. It appeared hunched, crooked, and it limped and slewed as it walked, as though with difficulty, and leaned with two hands upon a stout staff. It walked on two legs, was garbed in long, ill-shapen robes and strips of cloth, and appeared vaguely human. He saw no face, for the light and the angle of the head and the mass of clothing that bulked upon the sloping shoulders concealed it.

The creature, whatever it was, halted a short distance away. Leth saw the head and shoulders incline, as though it nodded to itself, then slowly it began to move around him in that awkward, uneven gait, its feet dragging and slewing upon the blue ground. Leth felt that he was under inspection.

'Yes, yes, quite as I had imagined,' came the voice, dry and cracked. 'Your mother's description was good. She has apprised me of your qualities, too. You are perhaps a little headstrong at times, but we can work on that. Otherwise I think you may do well.'

Leth, endeavouring to re-acquire some semblance of dignity, though he was bewildered beyond imagining, climbed to his feet and stood straight-backed, watching the slowly circling creature.

'Do well? For what? Who, or what, are you? And what is this place? How do I come to be here?'

The hobbling creature emitted a strange, highly-pitched laugh. 'Ah-ha-ha-ha! You are the same, each of you. A flurry of questions! A garble! A gabble! You have it in common, always, without fail.'

'What do you mean? Who?'

'See! See! Again they come! Question after question, allowing no space for an answer. People! People! Who? The new rulers, of course.'

'New rulers?'

'Ha-ha-ha! Yes. You are one, the latest one. You are Leth, are you not?'

Leth brought his thoughts into order. 'I am. But who are you?'

'Ah, good. A single question,' said the creature. 'You are learning already. Who am I? I am, in a manner of speaking, the Orb. Or I am, in another manner of speaking, the voice of the Orb.'

'The Orb? What is that?'

'Ha-ha-ha-ha! Oh, so predictable! The Orb . . .' The strange thing spread wide its lean raggedy arms, gesturing to the blue. 'This is the Orb. And *I* am the Orb. The Orb of Orbia. Yes. But for convenience, and to avoid confusion, you may address me as Orbus whenever we meet.'

Leth's blood came hotly to his cheeks. As heir apparent and now King of Enchantment's Edge, he was accustomed to deference from others, and this creature's manner offended him. But he fought his anger down, for he was dealing here with the utterly unknown. He was powerless until he could be certain of something, anything at all. He glanced quickly beyond Orbus, at the space and the walls around him. There was no door that he could see.

'Ah, good, good, you control yourself with some aptitude,' said Orbus softly. He had ceased circling and leaned on his staff, scrutinizing Leth, still an obscure figure in the filmy blue.

'This is the Orb,' repeated Leth. 'And you too are the Orb. The Orb of Orbia. Nothing of what you have said so far makes sense. Tell me, what is the Orb?'

Orbus seemed to shrug. 'It is this where, which is not truly a 'where' at all. It is, in a manner of speaking, you might say, a prison.'

'Prison?' Leth felt his stomach knot. 'For whom?'

'For what?' Orbus replied, chuckling. 'That is not the question, not yet. Not for you to know. You see, prison is simply one way of perceiving it. It is an existence, also. It is what it is. And it is a nowhere. But it has a role, and that is why you are here, for you too have a role. And that is all you need know for the present.'

Orbus turned and began to walk away.

'Wait!' commanded King Leth, and stepped towards his bent figure. But his movement, strangely, brought him no closer, and Orbus chuckled again, halting.

'Be careful whom you seek to command, King Leth. Are you ruler here?'

'I do not know. Am I a prisoner?'

The bowed head shook slowly from side to side. 'The Orb is not for you, not in that sense. Though it can be, if you make it so. Believe my words, it can.'

'Then . . .'

'Enough! You have learned all you need for now. You will return. Now that you know I am here, you will return. But let me tell you something, King. You have the power, at any time, to take the casket and cast it into the deepest lake or into the bowels of a raging volcano. You may elect to dash it into fragments upon the ground or bury it deep beneath the earth. You can destroy it whenever and howsoever you choose.'

'The casket?' Leth looked about him in confusion, the impossible thought striking him: *am I inside the casket?*

'But you will not,' Orbus continued. 'It is not within you – at least, not yet. Not until you know. But should you be the one, the one who does eventually destroy the Orb, then, for your sake and the sake of your people and all you hold dear, be absolutely certain of one thing: *that you know what it contains!*'

The tone of Orbus's voice as he/it spoke these last words made the hairs on the back of Leth's neck rise. Orbus abruptly turned away again. 'Now, you may return. Say nothing of this to anyone. You will come to me again when you have the crown.'

'How? How do I get out of here?' Leth called.

'Simple.' The figure, almost invisible now, lifted its staff.

Leth was back in his chair, before his desk, staring at the strange blue casket. His hands were still upon it, his thumb at the hasp, and its lid was closed. He blinked, shivered, looked quickly about him. He was in his study, as before. Nothing had changed.

He sat back, wondering for long moments, his mind swimming. Then, on an impulse, he reached again for the casket, slipped the hook and hasp, endeavoured to lift open the lid.

It would not budge.

Leth wrestled with the casket for some moments. He took a knife and tried to wedge it into the seam between lid and base, to lever them apart. But the seam was perfect and not even the narrowest blade could be inserted. Eventually he gave up and thrust the casket from him.

'A curse on you,' he growled. He toyed with the notion of taking a mallet and smashing the casket open, but these thoughts were spurred by frustration, not reason. Leth knew that Orbus had been right: he would not destroy it, even if apparently he could, and it irked him the more for knowing it.

The remainder of that morning was taken up with formal duties and preparations for the forthcoming coronation. Leth applied himself to these moodily and with sparse attention. During luncheon, taken with two of his most senior lords, he hardly spoke a word. As the afternoon passed in similar manner to the morning his impatience grew. He startled aides, servants and advisors alike with his curt manner and sudden bursts of pique. Several remarked upon it, though not within Leth's hearing. But they simply attributed it to the new responsibilities he was assuming. Leth, for his part, was scarcely aware of the effect he was having on those around him.

He could think of nothing but his encounter with Orbus and the opportunity he must contrive to speak privately with his mother, Queen Fallorn.

It was evening before he found himself in his mother's company. The royal family assembled for dinner in the private dining hall: Queen Fallorn, King Leth and his spouse, the beautiful nineteen-year-old Queen-Imminent Issul, and Issul's pregnant sister Mawnie and her husband Hugo, Duke of Giswel, a far-flung province situated to the south-west of Enchantment's Edge. The King's and Queen's two young children, Prince Galry, aged three, and his sister, two-year-old Princess Jace, were brought and allowed to play with the adults. When the servants began bringing in the first platters the children left with their nurses and the meal commenced.

More than once, before they took their places at the table, Leth caught his mother's eye. Her eyes shone knowingly but she declined to hold his gaze, giving her attention to her grandchildren, whom she adored. A small smile hovered at the corners of her mouth, however, and this persisted throughout much of the meal. Several times during the meal Leth found Fallorn watching him, but her eyes slid away the moment he focused upon her. He sensed that she was amused, which did not improve his mood. He ate and drank little, itching to interrogate her but knowing he could say nothing in the company of others.

At length, as the meal drew towards its close, Queen Fallorn professed herself fatigued and announced her intention to retire for the night. Leth at once sprang to his feet, tossing aside his napkin, and moved to her chair, proffering his arm. 'Let me escort you to your rooms, Mother.'

'There is no need, Leth. The way is familiar to me, I have been there countless times before. I am old, I know, and my faculties may not be quite what they were, but you need have no fear that I will lose my way.'

'Even so, Mother, it would be my pleasure,' Leth replied, irked by the enjoyment she was deriving from his discomfort and somewhat shocked that she could make light of such a momentous issue.

As they made their way arm-in-arm along the cresseted corridors of Orbia, Leth said in a low voice, striving to contain his emotion, 'Mother, who is this creature, this Orbus whom you have brought to me?'

'My son, I told you this morning I cannot speak any more of this. To learn of Orbus you must consult Orbus.'

'But you know! Plainly you know far more than I. There is magic here, and a secret I have known nothing of. How long have you known of him? How did you come upon the casket? What does he want?'

'The casket entered my possession when I took the throne, as it has yours. And that is the first I knew of it. So has it been for more generations than I know. What does Orbus want? You must ask Orbus.'

'I have. He answers only in riddles, if he answers at all.'

'He is testing you, Leth, as he tested me, and my father before me, and my grandfather, and his mother, Queen Alsur, before him. So it goes on.'

'For what?'

'To determine suitability.'

'Mother, I am becoming exasperated. Suitability for what?'

'For what lies ahead. No – stay your questions. Consider from Orbus's point of view. A wise man who holds ten secrets will not reveal them all at once, even to his most trusted confidant, but gradually, one at a time. Is that not so?'

'But he has revealed nothing.'

'He has revealed himself, Leth. That is a very substantial nothing, I think.'

Leth pushed out a breath through clenched teeth. 'Mother, his existence, the existence of the casket, threatens us. It undermines our very foundation.'

'I had my fears too, once. And if you truly believe it is so – if you have not the least spectre of doubt – then you must destroy the casket. Has not Orbus told you that you may do that?'

Leth nodded.

'But you will not,' said Fallorn. 'For like I do, you perceive what a tremendous confidence this is that Orbus has given you. And like I do, you entertain spectres.'

They slowly mounted the sweeping stone staircase that led to the first level where Fallorn's apartments were situated. The former Queen leaned her weight more heavily upon her son's right arm. At the top she paused for a moment to regain her breath and coughed slightly into a scented handkerchief.

'Mother, will you tell me nothing more?' pleaded Leth as they moved off again.

'I cannot,' she sighed, the first hint of impatience edging her voice. 'To know more you must speak with Orbus again.'

'But the casket is sealed. It resists my efforts to open it.'

'Did he not tell you to return?'

'After I am crowned.'

'Then that is when it will be open.'

They had arrived before her door. Leth paused, his head bowed, then turned to her in one last endeavour. 'Mother, I cannot *believe* that you have kept this from me all these years.'

She took his hands. To his surprise he saw, in the flamelight, that tears brimmed in her eyes. 'Many times I wanted to tell you. Many, many. And you will wish the same in future days. But I could not, and I knew I could not, and you will do the same. Even in your darkest hours, when your very soul cries to confide in someone, you must not do it, not until the day comes – if it comes – when you will pass the casket on to your heir.'

'And if I have no heir?'

She looked at him in surprise. 'Galry . . .'

Leth swallowed. 'I say only, let us imagine the worst, just for a moment. Let us say there is war, our family is ousted from Enchantment's Edge, a usurper seizes the throne, we suffer a plague. What then?'

Her lips compressed, her eyes burned with sudden ferocity. '*Do not speak so!*'

'I say it only as—'

'Those are not the words of a King! Have I misjudged you? My son?'

'No, you have not! I said it only—'

'Enough! I have said more than I should. The matter is closed. You know your duties, Leth. Be true, that is all.' She took both his hands in hers and squeezed them firmly. 'Now, kiss me, and begone.'

In the ensuing days Leth made no attempt to raise the subject again. In fact, so busy was he that he saw very little of his mother. Twice, in his study, he tried to prise open the blue casket, but to no avail. He stowed it in a secret compartment in the wall and, as best he could, gave his mind over to other matters.

The day of his coronation arrived. The ceremony and subsequent obligations were long and, for Leth, somewhat tedious, conducted with great pomp and majesty. The streets of Enchantment's Edge were bedecked with banners and bunting, the squares lined with stalls, booths and amusements. King Leth, in a golden carriage, his young Queen Issul beside him, toured the main streets, accompanied by an honour guard of one hundred of Orbia's proudest knights, all attired in gleaming ceremonial plate, richly emblazoned silk surcoats and capes, and mounted upon magnificent warhorses clad in barding of equal splendour.

A pleasure fair was set up on the Monarch's Green, outside Orbia's gates, and the citizens of the region flocked to catch a glimpse of their new monarch. The days merged into the nights and the little kingdom rejoiced.

On the third day following his formal accession King Leth was informed that his mother had been taken ill. He went straight away to her bedside and found her weak but conscious, the palace physician in attendance. When he next saw her she was sleeping, and he was assured there was no cause for alarm. A day or so later she appeared to make a brief recovery. She took onion-and-herb broth, and spoke lucidly with her doctor before sinking back into a deep slumber. Leth never spoke to her of Orbus or the casket again, nor of anything else. He sat beside her bed for as long as he was able, holding her frail hand. From time to time her eyelids fluttered and he felt a light pressure upon his fingers, but she did not wake. Before the week was out Queen Fallorn had passed away.

In the three years since her death King Leth had learned many things, not least among them the reason why there were some matters of which he might never speak. It was probably true to say that he had become a different man in many ways. He had been introduced to a mystery more profound than anything he could ever have imagined. He had seen something of the gathering forces that lay so close upon his world. And he knew with a deepening sense of the inevitable that life in Enchantment's Edge was soon to undergo immeasurable change.

TWO

I

Mawnie – Demawndella, Duchess of Giswel – was weeping. Moments earlier her mood had been frivolous and high-spirited. She had discovered something amusing in almost everything she or her sister, Queen Issul, had said. Stepping out onto the verandah on the lower level of Issul's private apartments, a fluted goblet of fruity green Aucos wine in one hand, she had startled into flight a knot of nearby pigeons. A palace cat was painstakingly inching its way along the top of the marble balustrade, intent upon fatally surprising one of the birds. Off-balanced by the unexpected flurry of wings and plump feathered bodies, the cat lunged wildly. It struck out with its front paws but missed its prey and lost its footing. It half-clung for a moment to the edge of the balustrade, then dropped, landing on one of Mawnie's slippered feet.

Mawnie had not seen the cat. She shrieked and dropped her goblet, kicking out. The cat skidded across the polished stone tiles, then turned back and shook itself with a look of feline embarrassment.

Mawnie's laughter – sharp, shrill and sudden – rang out across the wide quadrangle.

Upon hearing the initial shriek and the clatter of the goblet on the tiles, Queen Issul had rushed out onto the verandah. 'Mawnie, what is it?'

Mawnie could barely speak. One hand was pressed to her breast, her cheeks bright pink and streaked with tears of laughter. 'Iss . . . The pigeons . . . the cat. Oh Iss, it startled me! Oh, it was so funny!'

She groped her way to one of three chairs set around a small table on the verandah, and slumped down. She took a blue silk handkerchief from the bosom of her gown and dabbed at her eyes. 'Oh Iss, you should have seen. Look!'

She pointed at the cat which was stalking stiffly away, its head and tail high in a determined show of dignity. Mawnie's mirth found new vent as her sister took a seat beside her.

'Mawnie, you are hanced.'

'Nonsense, sister. I have had but a few sips.' Mawnie wiped her eyes again and tossed back her long pale russet-brown hair, still smiling. 'Most of it went on the floor. It was the cat, that is all.'

Hilarity took her again; Issul shook her head. 'You have been like this all morning. And worse, so lewd! It's always a sign.'

'Lewd? I?' Mawnie feigned shock. 'Iss, I love life and seek to experience it to the full, in all its uncloistered glory. You know that. We differ in this respect. We always have. But I am never lewd.' She pushed herself back in her seat and said loudly, 'Now, do you have a good serving-man handy? I would rather like another goblet.'

She swivelled her eyes coyly to her sister, then giggled behind her hand.

'Do you really want more, Mawnie?'

'I told you, I have hardly had any. Bring me a man, or must I do it myself?'

Issul beckoned forward a servant.

'We are not so different, Mawnie,' she said as her sister's drink was poured. 'We have both changed, it is true, but I do not feel we have grown apart.'

Mawnie appeared not to have heard. Her eyes were on the servant bent beside her. 'Now, this is a sturdy fellow, sister, is he not?' she suddenly blurted out. 'A fine, healthy figure.' To the servant's surprise she slid a hand around the inside of his right thigh. 'Young, robust and surprisingly well-thewed for a mere house-servant. His buttocks are absolutely charming, are they not?'

'Mawnie!'

'Endowed to serve, I don't doubt. His sole aim to attend your pleasure.'

The servant had risen erect, rigid with embarrassment, his gaze fixed dead ahead. Mawnie's hand slipped higher, the tip of her tongue touching her upper front teeth, eyes watching his face. The man half-closed his eyes.

'You may go,' ordered the young Queen.

'Oh, but not too far,' added Mawnie as he withdrew stiffly. 'I may want you again in a moment.' She leaned conspiratorially towards her sister. 'Servants can be such fun sometimes, can't they? Have you never tried one, sister? Shame on you. You should be more ready to explore. Ah, but I see I have gained your disapproval.' She loosely fluttered a hand. 'Let's change the subject, then. What were we talking about before we came out here? Ah yes, that proud new stud of yours. What did you say? 'Sleek and powerful . . . I am so eager to take him for his first ride.' Sister, how can you play so innocent with me?'

'Mawnie, I tire of this.'

Mawnie gazed out across the wide quadrangle at the perimeter of which they sat, a smile still hovering about her lips. She raised her goblet and took a sip, then assumed a more serious expression. 'So . . . it was a gift, you say, from . . . which faction?'

'The Children of Ushcopthe. They seek my favour, and the King's. I expect a petition from them quite soon.'

'But it is a strong and healthy stallion?'

'Yes, but—' she caught her look. 'Mawnie, please.'

Mawnie brought her fingertips to her mouth. 'I am sorry, sister.' After a silence she said, soberly, 'They have grown stronger, haven't they, since the True Sept was outlawed?'

Queen Issul nodded slowly. 'They are trying to consolidate their position while being seen to have the approval of Leth and I. But they have never seriously been troublesome.'

'You know, Iss, dear Leth has been harshly criticized in some quarters for his handling of the True Sept. Many think he was unwise to execute Grey Venger's sons.'

'He did not want to. He agonized over that decision. In the end he was left without a choice.'

'Without a choice? The King?'

'Not all-powerful. Immense pressure from the factions and nobility. Also he has been troubled of late. There is something . . . I do not know . . . I feel there is something he will not confide. He locks himself away at times. It is unlike him. I feel he . . .'

Mawnie was curious. 'He what?'

'I cannot really explain. He is distant sometimes, in a way he never was. The burden of kingship weighs heavily upon him, I think.'

'He neglects you?'

'He loves me still, I am in no doubt of that. And I him. But since ascending to the throne there has been . . . I don't know. *Something.*'

'Be careful, sister. When a man neglects his wife, be he king or peasant, the answer will be found in the bed of another. Believe me, I know.'

'That is not it!' retorted Issul indignantly. 'I would know if it was, Mawnie. Please do not draw such inferences. It is simply not so.'

Mawnie pushed back her long hair and shrugged. 'Very well.'

'And those boys were not innocents, Mawnie. The True Sept had trained them long and hard. They were skilled and highly-ranked, and the Sept has not held sympathy with the Crown for generations, not since King Haruman introduced the Deist Edict. Leth made an example of them. He did not want to, he wanted Venger. Until the last moment he believed Venger would give himself up rather than allow his own children to die. Leth hated what he did, but when it came to it there was no alternative. Blood was demanded, and had he spared them he would have severely weakened his own position and given power to the True Sept.'

'It turned a moderate opponent into a dangerous and invisible enemy.'

'Moderate? A fanatic and highly-trained assassin? He almost succeeded in murdering Leth! That is why there could be no quarter.'

Mawnie traced small circles on the table with the tip of her middle finger. 'Word is that with the Krai moving closer the True Sept are making secret overtures – may already have made contact. So Hugo says.'

'The Krai are still beyond the Bitter Lakes and Uxon's Ridge.'

Mawnie nodded sombrely. Her home, the Duchy of Giswel, was the domain of Enchantment's Edge closest to the lands now occupied by the Krai. Their advance had been remorseless and, though the threat to Enchantment's Edge was not immediate, King Leth had dispatched extra troops to Giswel as a show of strength. Now Duke Hugo had come to Orbia with Mawnie, bringing word of his latest discovery: the Krai appeared to be in league with one of the gods of Enchantment. The Krai, who were not wholly human themselves, had things in their ranks that had never been seen before.

This was daunting news which had sent King Leth and all his advisors and officers into urgent conference.

Mawnie said, 'It is a short distance if they decide to move against us.'

Then she stood, abruptly. 'Iss, I don't want to talk of these things now. I don't want to be fearful or sad. The world is in turmoil, everyone speaks as though we are at our final days, as though doom waits poised to swallow us at any moment. I don't want this. I want to be happy. I won't think of the Krai or their alliances. I want to laugh and sing and dance, the way we used to. Remember, Iss, when we were children? When Ressa was alive. It wasn't so long ago. We were happy then. It was so different. Oh yes, it was.'

She had taken up her goblet and held it to her with both hands. Now she moved to the balustrade and stood looking out again across the quadrangle. A few figures could be seen on the far side: a maid scrubbing the stoop outside the Lord Constable's offices; a lad in the long sepia gown of the Library clerks, hurrying with a stack of fat books in his arms; two officers of the militia striding purposefully towards a side-port in the Guardian's Wall. Beyond the quadrangle Orbia's myriad towers rose into a clear azure sky, marvellous and bright in the warm golden light of early autumn. The sun was high and the world revealed in clear, sharp relief, bar the few dark shadows where its rays could not penetrate. Mawnie lifted her slim shoulders and let out a long sigh. 'How I wish that Ressa could be here again.'

Now it was that Mawnie, falling silent, bowed her head and wept.

'Mawnie . . .' Queen Issul rose and went to her sister, took the goblet from her and held her in her arms as Mawnie's shoulders were racked with sobs. 'Mawnie, Mawnie. I knew there was something. It isn't the Krai, is it, though there is enough there to fear. That's not what troubles you now.'

'It is *everything!*' cried Mawnie. 'Oh Iss, I am so unhappy!'

Issul waited, stroking her sister's pale hair and rocking her slowly from side to side, watching the pigeons that were gathering again along the verandah, and gradually Mawnie's sobs began to abate.

'Let's walk a little,' Issul suggested softly when Mawnie was sufficiently calm. She linked arms with her sister and guided her back indoors. They passed through her rooms and out to the passage from which stairs descended to the door that led outside. In the sunlight they began to walk slowly along the straight stone path that traversed the quad.

Queen Issul walked straight-backed, her head high, her pale green gaze inward and reflective. She stood an inch or so taller than her sister. Her hair was notably fairer and, when freed of thc chignon and plaits which now held it close to her skull, was looser, more naturally wavy and slightly longer. She was a beauty, if at times a little solemn. Her oval face was pale, the skin fresh, the cheeks lightly freckled. Aged just twenty-two, she was two years older than Mawnie.

The death some four years earlier of Issul's other sister, Mawnie's twin, Ressa, had caused Issul to become fiercely protective of Mawnie. She perceived in Mawnie's behaviour worrisome signs of dissipation. Issul was torn. Mawnie and Ressa had been inseparable and Mawnie had never really recovered from the loss. Moreover, there were elements to the tragedy which Issul was bound to keep secret, even from Mawnie.

Mawnie, in contrast to her older sister, walked with drooping shoulders and a heavy gait. Her feet struck the floor as though falling rather than placed. She too could be striking to the eye. Light and slender of build like her sister, she lacked Issul's natural poise, and her gaze, now upon the ground before her, tended often to flit here and there, as though she was constantly searching for something undefined. She laughed as readily as she cried, and was given to temper just as easily. Her expression in its unguarded state was open-eyed and vulnerable, her look seeming to hold a sad acknowledgement that the thing she sought would never be found.

'Is it Hugo?' Issul enquired after they had gone a dozen paces or so. She had purposely avoided talking of Ressa. It would elicit further tears and little else. Issul suspected that matters of the present had brought on Mawnie's current mood.

'He is a pig,' said Mawnie heatedly. 'I hate him.'

'Truly? You loved him once.'

'I admired him, I was infatuated by him. I lusted after him. All this is true, but it is not the same thing.' Mawnie pressed her handkerchief to her reddened nose, and halted. 'He doesn't love me. He never has. He loved Ressa, you know that, Iss.'

Issul remained silent, pensive.

'He turned to me when she died, trying to rediscover her in me, because we were so alike,' Mawnie went on. 'But I was always second choice and I could never live up to his expectations, though I tried. I could only be me, not Ressa, and that is not what Hugo wanted.'

'Has he said as much?' Issul pressed her arm and encouraged her to walk again.

'He doesn't need to. No, he says nothing. I hardly see him. He prefers the company of scullery-maids or countesses – he makes no distinction. They satisfy his needs. But his lawful spouse and mother of his child fails to interest him in any way. And he makes no secret of what he does. It is as if I don't exist, I don't matter.'

'It might have been the same if Ressa had lived, Mawnie. His love for her might have dwindled. Hugo is a handsome man, and powerful. He is restless, ambitious, an idealist. For him there are no ordinary comforts. I believe the world cannot satisfy him. He is good at heart, I think, and does not mean to hurt you—'

'Then why does he do it?'

'Perhaps he cannot help himself.'

'You are defending him, Iss! How can you?'

Issul shook her head. 'Not defending, nor condoning. But I am trying to understand. Simply to hate and condemn is to be blind to the whole picture.'

'Yes, you have studied with mages and perhaps see things with wiser eyes than mine. But you are free of the pain. I know only how I feel.'

'You are wrong, Mawnie. I am Queen, and it is an exalted position, but I am not free of pain, as many would believe. You know that. I am pained when I see the problems that beset our people and our land, and I am pained when I see how you hurt. Do you really think I feel nothing? I love you and am unhappy for you when I see what this is doing to you. And I fear for what I see you doing to yourself.'

'It is what *he* is doing to me!' Mawnie cried.

'You are letting yourself be his victim, then. I don't think even Hugo wants that.'

'But what can I do? If I take a lover I am condemned, not only by Hugo but by everyone, including you. If I don't I am his victim.'

'You are letting yourself be his victim whether you take lovers or not. I think you are trying to spite him.'

Mawnie snorted. 'Nothing I do spites him in any way. He has the sensitivity of a granite hillock. I just want to be happy, Iss. I want to enjoy my life again.'

They had arrived at the far side of the quadrangle and passed now through a small portal into a heavily lime-pleached alley which ran along the side of a walled knot garden. Roses still bloomed beside the lawn to one end, and Issul breathed in the air deeply as they passed. 'It is good, Mawnie. The sunlight, the flowers. These things make recompense for the toils we bear. I wonder sometimes whether our hopes and expectations are simply misdirected.'

'I just want to be happy,' reiterated Mawnie miserably. 'I want it to be like it was.'

'You have to accept that the past is gone,' Issul replied.

'Oh no, it is not!' Mawnie declared vehemently. 'If only it were. The past never leaves us, Iss. We are its prisoners and it will not let us go.'

A short arcade now took them back indoors and eventually to an intersection of corridors. One way led deeper into the palace precincts, the other towards the military parade grounds, barracks and stables. Mawnie chose the latter and soon they found themselves, still arm-in-arm, at the edge of the vast dusty square that was Orbia's main parade and training ground. Formations of troops, mounted and foot, drilled in the sun, and the air was cut with the bellowed commands of drill-sergeants and training officers. A squad of élite Palace Guards, alert to the arrival of the royal sisters, moved discreetly into protective positions close by.

After a few moments quietly observing the soldiers Mawnie quite suddenly bobbed onto her tip-toes and pointed. 'Oh look, Iss! I think that is the one I told you about! There! Do you see?'

Queen Issul followed the direction of her sister's pointing finger. A cavalry squad, a dozen strong, trotted towards them from the right, about thirty paces distant. 'What am I looking at, Mawnie?'

'That soldier, closest to us in the fourth rank. I told you earlier, yesterday afternoon he came to my assistance when I slipped on a loose flag in the Cutter's Alley. He was walking by with another and caught my arm and saved me from falling. I think that is he. Wait till they come closer.'

The soldiers were now within twenty paces of the two young women, passing by almost directly in front of them.

'Yes, it is him!' said Mawnie, and clapped her hands. 'Oh, what a surprise he will get when he sees me now. He took me for a governess or lady's maid or something. Watch!'

At an order from their drill-sergeant the troopers' heads turned as one and they raised their hands in salute as they passed before the young Queen and Duchess.

'Coo-ee!' said Mawnie, far too softly for anyone but her sister to hear. But she slightly lifted one hand and waved with her fingers.

The men's features were set in concentration, but as Queen Issul watched, sure enough the gaze of the soldier Mawnie had indicated had focused more directly upon them. His eyes passed from Mawnie to herself, then back again, lingering an instant longer than his fellow-soldiers', as if questioning something. Then their heads swivelled smartly to the front and they rode on past.

'Did you see?' said Mawnie. 'He's quite handsome, isn't he? And young.'

'Mawnie, I hope—' Issul began.

'No, nothing like that, sister. I merely observed, that is all. But he was gallant, and very agreeable. He held my hand, so gently, until I assured him I needed no further assistance. He is newly-recruited to the King's Cavalry, he told me, coming from beyond the forest in answer to Leth's call. His name is Shenwolf.'

'You appear to have discovered a lot about him, for such a brief encounter.'

'That is the sum total of my knowledge. We were together for mere moments, and he was in company, as I said, though I confess I do not recall much about his companion.' Mawnie rolled her tongue inside her cheek. 'He does have rather charming buttocks, though, too. Don't you think?'

The Queen half-smiled. 'I cannot say that I noticed. Perhaps I should summon him over for inspection.'

'Perhaps you should.' Mawnie laughed, and as the soldiers rode away the two sisters moved on and left the parade-ground.

II

Later in the day Queen Issul was in her office, ostensibly inspecting proposals submitted by one of the factions, the Far Flame, for an extension to their Grand Lodge. In point of fact her mind was far away.

She was recalling her conversation with Mawnie, thinking of Ressa, thinking of Leth. Issul felt a great weight upon her. She wondered, not by any means for the first time, whether she had been wise to encourage the marriage between Mawnie and Duke Hugo. At the time it had seemed the right thing. It had given Mawnie something to live for after the terrible loss of her twin, and politically and socially the marriage had been advantageous to both sides. But Issul had been aware in her heart that Mawnie, and Hugo too, might be entering into a fragile pact.

After a year had come the birth of a daughter, Lir. Issul had hoped that motherhood, too, would help Mawnie rediscover the focus she had lost. But Lir was two and a half now and spent almost all her time with nannies, seeing her mother irregularly and only for moments at a time, and her father even less.

'Mawnie, Mawnie,' Issul whispered. 'Don't do this to yourself.'

With a pang of guilt she thought of her own children, Prince Galry and Princess Jace. She, too, saw far less of them than she would wish. In her case it was the exigencies of duty that claimed her time, rather than any wild and desperate search for bygone happinesses. She rejoiced in the hours they did spend together, but when she kissed them goodbye and left them with their nanny or governess Issul felt wretched.

And there was Leth. Something preyed upon his mind. He spent so much time locked in his study. Passing by one evening, Issul had noticed seeping beneath his study door a strange blue lucency which pulsed dimly as she watched. She thought she had heard the murmur of voices within.

When she had spoken of it to Leth later that night he replied curtly that he had merely been engaged in his researches. He was alone, he said. The voices must have been servants talking in the passage outside, or in a chamber above. Or perhaps it had been the wind shifting the heavy drapes beside the window, or the fallen leaves outside. Or perhaps it had been nothing at all.

Issul wondered about Leth's researches and the source of the blue light. Might he be investigating magic? Why so secretively? There were magicians aplenty in and about Enchantment's Edge. Some held advisory positions in court, and any of them could have been summoned to personally instruct the King. Indeed, the land itself was magical, imbued with the strange and indiscernible energies that seeped out of Enchantment. Magic remained a mystery, but not a secret. But Leth had professed no special interest before, and Issul's subsequent enquiries in the accredited schools and amongst the greater and lesser mages known to her had failed to identify a teacher.

Issul gazed through her high window at the lands beyond. Far below, the vast forest stretched to the horizon, an ocean, near-still, of ruffled greens and blues, overlaid in places with deep pools and lengthening strands of soft grey mist. In the furthest distance clumps of purplish-hued cloud hung motionless in a yellowing sky, pierced by the visible peaks of Enchantment. *This land*, she thought, her eyes stung by tears, *this world. This existence. We find ourselves here, not knowing how or why. It is all so strange*. Her eyes strained to see the far mountains more clearly. *What lies there?*

There came a soft knock at Issul's door, rousing her from her musings. At Issul's call her secretary, Hullie, entered. 'The Lord High Invigilate requests an immediate audience, ma'am.'

'Fectur?' Issul frowned to herself. Lord Fectur was Master of Security for all of Enchantment's Edge, and an infrequent visitor. For a bare moment Issul wondered what his business with her could be, then felt the blood draw back from her face. She closed her eyes. There was surely only one reason for the High Invigilate's call!

She rose, moved to the window, composing herself, then said, 'Send him in.'

A moment later Lord Fectur strode into her office, a stout man of average height, clad in a blue, ermine-trimmed robe and ankle-boots of softest doeskin. He bowed curtly, and said in a voice bereft of warmth, 'I am in possession of something of importance to you.'

Issul moved back to her desk and sat down, determined not to be intimidated. This man was, after all, her servant. She met his eyes – they were grey and lustreless, somewhat protruding, the pupils minute, emotionless as a carp's. He was in his forties, broad in the chest, short in the leg and just a touch paunchy. His silver-grey hair was swept severely back from a high wide brow and tucked behind his ears. The face, set with a small fleshy nose, was rather flat and firm-set.

At first glance he was an unimposing figure, but one had only to spend a short time in Lord Fectur's company to discover a chill and ruthless personality, an unsettling intelligence at work behind the veiled eyes. His charm, when he chose to employ it, was seductive, but anyone who knew him, or knew of him, was aware that it was simply a tool.

Fectur was immensely powerful, a man not given to questioning himself. He controlled a great network of agents spread throughout the kingdom. Fectur the Spectre was his sobriquet – though never spoken within his hearing – for it could seem that he lurked invisibly, ever listening, ever watching, and knowing more than he should know. To underestimate him was to invite severe regret.

Issul held his cold gaze for a moment. She was almost certain of what was to come. 'My lord, do you intend telling me what it is, or are we playing guessing games?'

The Lord High Invigilate leaned towards her and extended one arm, the fingers bunched. He rotated the hand and slowly unfurled the fingers, his eyes never leaving her face. Issul stared at the object he held, her worst fears confirmed.

'Where did you get this?'

'I recall that you requested that I deliver it to you, should it ever come into my possession. A cool morning on the third melday of Nont, a little over three years ago. You summoned me to you, here in this very office, and showed me a duplicate of the object I hold. "My lord Fectur," you said, "should the twin of this piece ever come, by any means, into your possession, you are to detain its bearer and bring it without an instant's pause to me." Am I not correct, my lady?'

Queen Issul took the object from him. It had originally been an ear-pendant, though the clasp had been removed. What Fectur held was a small carving in black onyx representing the figure of a robed woman, kneeling. Once it had been Issul's. 'Who has brought it?'

'A woman, a peasant who calls herself Ohirbe. She says she is from the village of Lastmeadow.'

Issul sat stiffly, striving to conceal the tumult in her breast. Now there was no possible doubt. Was there no end to this? What was it Mawnie had said, just hours ago? *The past never leaves us. It will not let us go.*

She looked up again to meet Fectur's gaze. 'I will see her. Where is she now?'

'In my official chambers.' He straightened. 'I will bring her immediately.'

'No! Take me to her.'

'Take you?' One of Fectur's thin eyebrows arched slightly in surprise. 'My lady, I—'

'Lord Fectur, this woman does not know who I am. She believes me to be a woman of respectable station, but nothing more. It is vital that it remains this way. I will go to her, not vice versa. Do not say or do anything in her presence that might give me away. Do you understand?'

'Perfectly, my lady.'

'Good. Now, give me a moment. Wait outside.'

Lord Fectur withdrew, his curiosity almost tangible. Issul departed via a door in the west wall and went hastily to her apartments. There she changed from the robe she wore into a simpler dress of heavy grey cotton. She rouged her cheeks, applied make up about her eyes and freed her hair so that it tumbled about her shoulders. Lastly she donned a long damask hooded cloak, then returned to the lobby outside her office where Fectur waited.

She noted his look as she approached. The eyes settled on her now with single-minded intent. The look held a certainty and a promise; it could make a man's blood run cold. 'I know you have something to tell me', it said, and its promise was of the pain to come if that information was not given freely.

How dare he! Issul fought back her indignation. *As if I am some common criminal or suspected subversive; as if he cannot wait to have me before him in his dungeon!*

She fought down her fear, too. Fectur was not a man to be on the wrong side of. She recalled how she had first instructed the woman, Ohirbe, that it was to Lord Fectur that the onyx pendant should be brought. The poor woman had blanched and quaked, the tears had started to her eyes and she had become almost hysterical with terror. And Issul had reassured her: Fectur was not the monster he was reputed to be. It was only to lawbreakers and those disloyal to the Crown that he directed his attentions. He did not harm the innocent. As long as Ohirbe followed her instructions precisely she would be safe. Indeed, the Lord High Invigilate would look favourably upon her actions.

Issul had felt no pride then. She had known that the very mention of Fectur's name, the fear that he too was involved in this queer affair, would doubly ensure Ohirbe's compliance and, equally importantly, her silence.

It had been necessary, that was all. Ohirbe could have delivered the pendant to Issul by other channels, still not knowing that it was the Queen with whom she dealt. But Issul had been considering her own safety, too. She had hoped never to see the pendant again, for fear of what it could mean. But if it was ever returned, then it was advisable that the Lord High Invigilate be made aware.

Fectur did not have to know everything – at least, not yet. But he had to be satisfied that, whatever Issul's business was, it was not being undertaken without his knowledge. That way he might be less inclined to initiate covert investigations of his own. And any case he might attempt to construct against Issul would be undermined by the fact that she had openly sought his involvement.

'I am ready,' said Issul. 'Take me to her now. And remember, show no undue deference.'

Fectur's gaze had become almost placid as he rose from his seat, but Issul felt herself bristling. *No undue deference* – what irony! She had only to look at his complacent blandness to be left in no doubt as to whom he believed to be superior. She felt naked, vulnerable and angry. To Fectur's way of thinking no one, *no one*, was totally beyond his grasp. Not even the Queen. Not even the King.

The terrible thing was, he was right.

'My lady, is there something I should know?' asked Fectur silkily.

Queen Issul briskly gathered her cloak about her. 'Perhaps. In due course.'

She strode off down the corridor, leaving Fectur to bring himself abreast of her.

The woman Ohirbe, Queen Issul was gratified to note, had been left in a windowed waiting room rather than a cell. She had been given water, fruit and honeycakes, none of which she had touched, and the door to the adjoining chamber, where a clerk worked at his desk, had been left ajar. Fectur knew his business.

As Lord Fectur ushered Issul in, Ohirbe threw herself from the bench upon which she sat, onto hands and knees at her feet.

'Oh, Mistress, I 'aven't done nuthin'. I just done what you said. I came straight to—' – she lacked the courage even to speak Fectur's name – '—straight 'ere, just like you said I must. I only done what you said.'

'I know, Ohirbe. I know. Thank you. You have done the right thing and I am pleased. Plainly I made the right choice in you, and I never doubted that.' She bent and took Ohirbe's arm. 'Please, get up now. I want you to sit with me and tell me what has happened.'

With nervous glances Ohirbe began to clamber to her feet. Issul straightened and faced Lord Fectur. 'Thank you, my lord. You may leave us now.'

She saw his hesitation, just a fraction of an instant, and the flicker of irritation at the corners of his eyes. He radiated resentment, almost knocking her back, but she stood unflinchingly and somehow held his gaze.

Disobey me, I dare you!

With a curt nod Fectur swivelled on his heel and departed.

Issul closed the door behind him, her heart beating fast, afraid, yes, but also suddenly borne high on the sense of victory, tiny though it might have been. She turned quickly back to Ohirbe, who stood before the bench, head bowed, fiddling nervously with the hem of her tattered shawl. 'Be seated, please. Would you like something to eat or drink? I can have other things brought. Perhaps a little watered wine?'

'Oh no. No, Mistress. I'm fine. Don't you be thinkin' of me. I'm quite all right, thankin' you.' She was a plain woman, ruddy-cheeked and raw-boned, aged around thirty, with lank dark brown hair, streaked with grey. She wore a blue-grey linen skirt, a blouse of similar material and leather slippers.

Ohirbe sat, and Issul lowered herself beside her. She kept the hood of her cloak up. This was the same cloak she had worn when she first met Ohirbe three years ago, and then, too, she had endeavoured to keep her features at least partially obscured. The hood was perhaps almost unnecessary, for now, as then, Ohirbe was too timid to lift her eyes to Issul's face.

'Then tell me why you have come,' said Issul softly.

'Because you told me to, Mistress. That's what you said, if ever there was anythin' at all uncommon, if ever anyone seemed to be showin' an unusual interest, I should come immediate to the Palace and give the little figure to the Lordship.'

'That's right.' Issul held onto her patience as the nervousness rose within her. 'So, has something happened?'

Ohirbe clutched harder at her shawl. 'Oh Mistress, I've a strange tale to tell. Somethin' is 'appenin' now, I'm sure of it. We've been so 'appy, Arrin and me and the little one. There's been no trouble at all. We named the baby Moscul, which is what I would've called my own baby if it'd lived. Little Moscul's been just like our own, the joy of our lives.'

'Nobody ever suspected that Moscul was not yours?' Issul enquired.

'Why should they, Mistress? My baby came early, and was dead, as you know, but I was 'ere at my sister's at the time, in Enchantment's Edge, so no one from the village knew. And then, just days later you came along with the little one. Why should anyone think anythin'? We get a bit of joshin' from time to time, 'cos Moscul's so fair-headed and we're both dark – 'specially Arrin – but we don't take no notice, and it's just a bit of banter, nothin' more. And we counts ourselves so lucky. Not only 'ave we got the most beautiful child, but the money you sends us from time to time, it makes all the difference. We're so grateful, Mistress.'

'And Moscul has kept well?'

'Oh yes. Just like any other child, 'cept . . .'

'Except what?'

'Well, there's a fierce intelligence there for one so young. Sometimes you think . . . there's an understandin', a knowin'. You see the little one watchin' and listenin' and you think: "Nothin's passin' that one by!" Not like the other children in the village. Much brighter, but quiet too. Moscul doesn't say much, never 'as. But in the mind, oh, there's a rare one there, I reckon. Even Arrin said once – only jokin', mind – 'e said that Moscul might be a child on the outside, but inside there's somethin' else. You cold, Mistress?'

'No, no. Well, yes, a little.' Issul stood quickly, agitated. Not cold, no. But Ohirbe's words had sent a shiver down her spine. 'Please go on, Ohirbe. Tell me what has happened now.'

'It was a couple of weeks ago, Mistress. I was took ill for a spell, and Arrin had been doin' most of the carin' for Moscul. But then 'e twisted 'is ankle and couldn't get about much. So one day we asked Arrin's cousin, Julion, to mind the little one. 'E's done it before once or twice. 'E took Moscul off to the Old Pond in the woods, where 'e likes to do a bit of fishin'. But it seems that 'e dozed off and didn't do any fishin'. And when 'e woke up there were two people by the pond, right next to little Moscul. An old woman and a strappin' young man, by Julion's account. They were just standin' there talkin'.'

'What did they want?' asked Issul anxiously.

'Well, it seems like they didn't want anythin'. At least, not just then, as they left straight away. I mean, the young man left. Julion took Moscul and went with 'im a short ways. But the old woman stayed behind, and Julion got talkin' a bit to the young man and found that 'e didn't know 'er. 'E'd just come by and saw 'er there with Moscul.'

Issul froze. 'With Moscul?'

'Oh Mistress,' Ohirbe frantically twisted the ends of her shawl. ''Ave I done wrong?'

'No, no. Not at all. But this happened two weeks ago, you say? Why have you only come to me now, Ohirbe?'

'I didn't know nothin' about it till a few nights ago, Mistress. See, I 'appened to mention at supper one night that I'd seen an old woman. Once when I was pickin' apples, and another time early in the mornin' when I went out to milk the cow. The first time I 'ad Moscul with me. She came to the orchard, and she was watchin' Moscul, from the edge. I'm sure of it. I tried to speak to 'er, but she walked away. The second time gave me a bit of a turn. She was outside the cottage, standin' in the mist aside the path, just watchin'. It'd 'ardly even got light. Moment she saw me she left. So I brought this up at supper and Julion – 'e'd 'appened to call round – told me 'bout what 'appened at the pond. 'E isn't the cleverest of men, Julion, but I've no doubt from what 'e said that it was the same woman.'

Issul pressed her hand to her forehead, thinking furiously. 'You've never seen this woman before?'

'No, Mistress.'

'What about the young man? Julion walked with him, you say? Did he find out anything about him?'

'I didn't think to ask, Mistress.'

'Where's Moscul now?'

''Ome, Mistress. With Arrin and Julion. Julion stayed over.' Ohirbe sniffed, her face crumpling, and a thin quaver came into her voice. 'Mistress, nothin' bad's goin' to 'appen to Moscul, is it? We do love that little one so.'

Issul released a pent-up breath. She sat beside Ohirbe again and took her hand. 'I'm going to do everything I can to make sure nothing bad happens, Ohirbe. But we may have to make some changes. For now, I want you to go home. I will arrange an escort for you. These men will stay with you for the time being, to watch over you and your family. Is that all right?'

Ohirbe nodded.

'Good. Good-bye for now, and thank you for coming to me. I will be in touch with you quite soon, I think.'

Outside, Issul spoke quietly to Lord Fectur. 'Have three armed men escort Ohirbe back to Lastmeadow. They should wear no uniform or distinctive garb, and will remain with her and her child until further notice.'

'Very good, my lady. There are one or two questions I would like to ask her first. I assume you have no objections?'

'Ohirbe is not to be touched!' hissed Issul, with sudden anger. 'Nor interrogated. She can tell you nothing, for she knows nothing. Do you understand'

Fectur nodded slowly to himself. 'In that case, I think perhaps now there is something I should be told, is there not?'

Issul hesitated. Sooner or later his personal involvement would be unavoidable, but for now, until she had discovered more, she preferred to keep him at bay. 'This is a personal matter, Lord Fectur.'

He took the snub in silence, but she knew he had absorbed it, added it to other petty resentments he was storing for a possible reckoning later. His memory was near-perfect, it was said. He saw almost all and forgot nothing. Issul suspected that he had a greater knowledge of her than she would wish. It was common knowledge, though unprovable, that his spy network extended into the royal household.

'I will escort you back,' said Fectur.

She shook her head. 'I am not going back. Not yet. I am going into the town, to Overlip.'

Fectur hooked his thumbs into the ermine lapel of his robe. 'Where in Overlip?'

'The Tavern of the Veiled Light.'

She sensed his tension. 'I will assign soldiers.'

'No. I go as I am, anonymously, as you see me now, not as the Queen.'

'It is dangerous. I cannot permit you to go there alone.'

'One man may walk at my side to discourage pests. But inside the tavern he will leave me. Others may be assigned at your discretion, but I do not want to be aware of their presence – unless their intervention is demanded. Is that understood?'

'Quite, my lady.'

'And they will intervene only in the most grievous of circumstances. Remember, my lord, I am capable of looking after myself. I was trained by yourself, after all.'

Dusk was descending as the carriage drew up at an intersection of ways just a short walk from where the area known as Overlip began. Issul stepped down and issued an instruction to the driver to wait. Her hand slid beneath her cloak and felt the reassuring bulk of the peen-hilted, bladed bodkin she carried. She cast her gaze quickly around, scanning nearby buildings, trees and streets, and walked away.

From the shadows of a building a figure emerged and took step beside her. Issul glanced aside, seeking the face and seeing that it was no one known to her. But he raised a hand as if to scratch his cheek and she saw the fingers form a sign. He was the Spectre's man.

She found herself glad of his company. She was relieved, too, to see that it was not Fectur himself who walked beside her. She had half-suspected that the Lord High Invigilate, unbearably curious as well as fearing for her safety, might have taken it upon himself to escort her in person. It would have been unwise. In Overlip, and most particularly in the Tavern of the Veiled Light, Fectur would himself have been at great risk, even disguised. He had more enemies there than he could count.

Issul envisaged Lord Fectur now, pacing his chamber in agitation. At moments of high stress red welts appeared upon his face and hands, betraying him. And this would be a time of inordinately high stress: as Master of Security the Queen's welfare, as much as the

King's, was his responsibility. He would know almost certain ruin should harm befall her. Issul almost smiled to herself. The image pleased her.

There were numerous folk on the street any of them might have been Fectur's. He would have placed a team perhaps eight or nine strong, watching her every movement. Others would be standing-by in force, primed for immediate response should the circumstances warrant.

The street, inclining gently downhill, came to an abrupt end at a low stone wall with a narrow gate. Beyond lay emptiness, wide dusky space over the dark rugged sea of forest so far below. This was the lip of Enchantment's Edge, and the quarter that lay beyond it, on the other side of the wall, clinging to the face of the plunging scarp, was Overlip. Here people lived and worked in burrows bored into the rock, or houses hollowed out of it or built against its very face. For the unwary it was a dangerous place, literally the overspill from the city above, literally its underworld. Lack of living-space had forced the dwellers of Overlip back on their resources; a subculture of sorts thrived here, complete with its own unique laws and customs.

Issul passed through the gate to the head of a flight of steep stone stairs which vanished into an opening in the rock. Her companion moved ahead of her. 'Give me your hand.'

She did so, smiling to herself. How would he have responded had he known it was the Queen whose hand now slipped into his?

They descended carefully, the steps weakly illuminated by oil lamps set upon the rock wall, and came out onto a small rock platform. From this position – the roof of somebody's home, Issul knew – they could look again over the darkening, mist-laden forest. It was a soaring, giddying sensation, to stand there upon the very edge of nothing, witnessing the dimming light, the vanishing of the lands that surrounded them.

The sky was turning to the deepest tones of blue, and a sprinkling of bright stars could be seen, the first of numberless specks of white fire that would soon grace the night. All around them, above and below, tiny lamps glowed in the rock. And far to the south, above the waning horizon about Enchantment's peaks, could be seen the first hazy glow of the weird-lights. Strange and wonderful, shifting, changing colours that were discernible in some measure most nights.

Issul stood for a moment and watched, wondering, as she often did. Many attempts had been made to explain the strange phenomenon. Most popular was the theory that the lights were the glows of immense conflagrations, the effects of unleashed magic of the gods. But no one really knew, for no one had ever been there. Or more precisely – for from time to time dashing heroes or foolhardy adventurers *had* ridden forth to investigate Enchantment's mysteries – no one had ever returned.

Issul moved on, clinging both to a handrail set into the rock and to her guard's strong arm as she negotiated her way down uneven steps which twisted almost sheer down the cliff-face. She grew warm from the exertion and was grateful for the cool caress of a breeze upon her cheeks. Eventually they passed through a narrow gap hewn out of the rock, deep windows on either side revealing dimly-lit interiors and shadowy figures, and emerged onto a narrow, winding, bustling street.

Issul paused to regain her breath, then resumed. An opening led into the cliff. Oil-lamps revealed a network of passages. Bodies pushed past her; peddlers called to her or tugged at her sleeve, trying to interest her in their wares. Issul ignored them as best she could.

Sure of her way she moved off leftwards. Past a butcher's hovel and a dim alcove where an old charm-seller sang and shook sprigs of sweet-smelling herbs and clusters of tiny balls at passers-by. The air was thick with innumerable smells. Issul turned a corner, passed along a narrow way, climbed a flight of steps. A little distance further on she veered into a short, dark cul-de-sac. Before her was a door set into the rock beneath the sign of the Veiled Light, the entrance to the tavern mooted to be the meeting-place of the outlawed sect of the True Sept.

As she drew closer she heard muted sounds of revelry from within.

'You enter first,' she instructed her guard. 'Once inside make no attempt to communicate with me.'

She stood alone, glancing quickly about her, feeling her nervousness grow, then pushed upon the door and entered.

A good business was being done in the tavern. Through a murk of smoke Issul saw that most of the tables were occupied. The hot air against her face was heavy with the mixed stench of ale and crude wine, food, sweat, cheap perfume and the pungent reek of burning shar, a narcotic leaf enjoyed by many. She pushed between the bodies towards the counter, not bothering to look for her guard. There would be others of the Spectre's agents here, she had no doubt.

A man barred her way, big and loutish and drunk enough to believe himself interesting. He threw an arm about her waist and drew her to him. 'Ah, sweet, a kiss, eh? A kiss?'

Issul pulled back, freeing herself, gagging on the stink and coarseness of him. 'Leave me, oaf, I have business here, and it is not with you.'

'Oh, now you speak like a thoroughbred, but you're no sweet cherry, I'll wager. Come, give me . . .' He reached for her again, and his cheeks bulged suddenly in pained surprise. A rush of air burst free of his lips and he staggered back, not yet knowing that it was the peen-hilt of Issul's bodkin that had rammed so forcefully into his solar-plexus.

Somebody laughed raucously. Issul moved on, grateful for that. She reached the counter where a pot-bellied landlord wiped slops into a pail.

'Iklar, is he here?'

'Who asks?'

'Someone who seeks the light. I have a word for him.'

He threw her a sceptical look, hardly pausing in his task, then nodded over his shoulder. 'The third cubicle.'

Issul moved around. The men and women here were generally well-hanced, or at least wholly occupied, and none gave her more than a passing or admiring glance. A row of cubicles occupied one end of the room, hewn into sweating rock, offering privacy of a kind. Each was set with a table and barrel seats or benches. In the third two men were seated, heads close over the table, a clay pitcher and twin tankards of dark ale before them. Both looked up as she moved into their nook. One beamed. 'Well, look at this! The evening shows sudden promise!'

Issul ignored him. She spoke to the second man, a dark-haired, bearded individual whose grimy open shirt displayed a broad chest, matted with hair and sweat. A faint purplish latticework upon the irises of his eyes revealed the presence of otherling blood in his, veins. 'Iklar, we must speak of sacred things.'

The man called Iklar leaned back, a finger poised before his mouth, surveying her. Then he nodded to the other man, who rose without another word, taking his tankard, and left. Issul slipped into his seat.

'Sacred things?' queried Iklar, lazily stroking his beard. 'Sacred things have a sacred word, so I am told.'

'The word is of the gods.'

'Then perhaps I am listening.'

Issul leaned towards him. 'Listen well, I will not repeat it: Go to your master—'

'I acknowledge no master save the King.'

'Go to Grey Venger—'

'I do not consort with outlaws.'

'Your play grows tiresome, Iklar. Let us say that if you know someone, who might know someone, who might have a contact with another person, say, who is able to pass a word to Grey Venger or someone close to him, then take this word now, for he will want to know it and will be ill-pleased to learn that the messenger has been tardy. Tell him this: the Child is known. Venger must show himself now. *It has begun!*'

Without waiting for his response Issul pushed herself out from the table, rose, and left the cubicle. Iklar would not follow her. She pushed quickly back through the loud throng towards the door. The oaf she had winded was waiting for her. His eyes burned. There was no way around him.

Move! she pleaded silently. She gripped her weapon beneath her cloak. This time it would be the blade. No choice. Across the face or into the groin – *if* he gave her the opportunity.

An ugly sneer spread across his face. He lurched forward, sure of her this time.

Someone stood abruptly at a table close by, thrust backwards as if by hazard, knocked the big man off-balance. A second fellow came from the other side, taking the oaf's arm and using his own motion to swing him around, bring him low and push him hard into a group seated at another table.

Issul slipped quickly past.

Thank you, Fectur! You have your uses!

She was outside, breathing hard, though the air within the tunnels was hardly more breathable than that of the Veiled Light. Fectur's man materialized at her side.

'Where now?'

'Back. It is done.'

Done, yes. But she felt only nervous premonition as the perspiration began to dry upon her skin. Venger would have to come now; it was all he could do. And what else? Today the world had slewed out of kilter. An unknown had stirred.

This much was done. But something far greater had only just begun.

THREE

I

Back at the palace of Orbia Queen Issul made haste, not to her apartments but beyond. Past the First and Second Towers of Dawn, exiting the Royal Wing, her hurry noticeable to those she passed, until she came at length to the entrance to the slender White Eaglet's Tower, situated in the older, Eastern sector of the great marble palace.

She pushed open the door at the foot of the tower and mounted the spiralling staircase within, not slowing her pace. Up she climbed, passing doors, alcoves, window-slits, high, high, until she arrived at last, breathless, at the head of the stairway. A studded, arched door of stained dark carmine oak set with black iron straps faced her across the bare stone of the landing. A black iron ring hung from the jaw of a red ram's head. Issul paused momentarily to regain her breath, grateful for the chill breeze that wafted from below, then grasped the ring and hammered loudly three times. There was a silence, then from somewhere behind the door a muffled voice called: 'Enter.'

Issul pushed against the door and stepped into a murky space, a short dim corridor, cobwebby and musty, lined with stone columns. It opened into a larger, slightly lighter room. There a figure was bent over a wide wooden desk, an elderly man, small of build and framed in purplish light. He was half-obscured behind several leaning piles of leather-bound books, rows of flasks and retorts, and strange items and paraphernalia for which Issul had no names. He wore a voluminous dark green robe, patched in places and ragged at the hems, and had long, curling, thin grey hair descending from the sides of a near-bald pate. At first he barely glanced Issul's way as she approached, so engrossed was he in the tome he was studying. But then, as if unsure of something, he looked up directly at her, raising a pair of circular glass discs to his eyes, peered and suddenly straightened.

'Why . . . Yes . . . in the name of . . . It is! Majesty! My Queen! I hardly recognized you.'

The little man seemed taken aback, flustered, wiping his hands hurriedly and distractedly upon his robe. 'I was not told you were coming. Please forgive me. I would not have been . . . It would have . . .'

Issul smiled. 'Relax, Pader Luminis. You do not have to stand on ceremony with me, you know that. I am sorry for intruding like this without warning, but I had to come.'

'It has been so long.' The little man gazed at her as if in a daze. Burnished brown skin and prominent ridges of bone beneath his eyes accentuating the high cheekbones exposed his otherling origins: Pader Luminis was of the Murinean, a race of small-boned, nimble woodland-folk who had populated the land around Enchantment's Edge long before humans came.

Issul gazed fondly at him, nodding. 'Yes, it has. The privileges of my station now deprive me of time I would rather spend in the company of friends like yourself.'

He beamed. 'Child. My kind, sweet Issul. My Queen. Please, take a seat. I shall make you special tea.' He darted away towards one end of the large chamber, calling back over his shoulder, 'Tell me, to what do I owe this immeasurable honour and pleasure?'

Issul located an old chair, upholstered in faded and worn crimson velvet, which stood at one side of the large room close beside the hearth where a few sorry flames sputtered beneath the charred remains of logs. Pader Luminis pottered about a great stove, gathering mugs and an earthenware pot, then returned quickly to revive the neglected fire, poking and prodding with an iron as he added more wood.

'I wish I could say I had come purely to sit and hear you talk, as when I was younger, or to receive new lessons in mage lore and the endless arcane secrets you hold,' said Issul. 'But it is not so. I come seeking the advice and wisdom of a venerated Murinean, a Master Arcanist, who is without peer in his knowledge of the mysteries.'

'Issul, my child, it is not so, and you know it. But I am glad that you are here, whatever the reason. So glad. But . . .' he straightened, surveying her with a reproving eye, '. . . I have to say that my joy at beholding you once more, though boundless as the cosmos itself, is yet tempered just a little, for I perceive that you are troubled, though you endeavour to hide it. Tell me, if I am not too impertinent, what brings such a cloud to your brow and droop to your lips? Why such a careworn cast upon your sweet young face?'

'Grave matters, Pader. But sit, please. I cannot talk while you are fidgeting and dancing before the fire.'

'Of course, my fair Majesty. But the tea first, yes?' Pader Luminis made off across the chamber with nimble steps, clattered a little in a darkened corner, then came back carrying a pair of matching mugs and the lidded pot. He set them down before Issul on a low table, then seated himself cross-legged on a low chair opposite her. 'It is hot, as you can see. Would you like to pour, my lady Issul, or shall I? Or do you prefer that I call my boy?'

'I shall pour,' said Issul. 'It will be like it used to be, in happier days when I was your eager student, largely ignorant of the turmoil and pain that beset the world.'

'Ah, you are truly troubled.' Pader Luminis shook his head. 'But it was not so. Even when you first came to me, though an innocent, it is true, you were yet a troubled child in many ways. You sensed the pain that permeates our world, without knowing that that was what you felt. It was one of the things that singled you out, one of the reasons I chose you.'

'Was it so?'

'You were older than your years, dear Issul. As in some ways you are still. You saw, or endeavoured to see, beyond the obscuring veil, the illusory, the transitory and superficial. You wished to know and to understand all things – a mighty endeavour! But you showed yourself many times to be diligent and hard-working. I, and the others of the Arcane College active in your selection, saw then what you might be. So we gave you a little knowledge, and you absorbed it and grew from it, and we saw how you valued it for what it was, and possibly even more importantly we saw that you did not abuse it or deploy it as a means to make others feel subordinate to you. And in the years that have passed since then, you have not disappointed us.'

'But I know nothing,' said Issul.

Pader Luminis grinned, unwrapped his legs and re-crossed them. 'Ah no, nor I. It is a lamentable state, this ignorance, is it not?

Perhaps we should sit together and grow old talking of the myriad things of which we have no knowledge.'

Issul sat pensively for a moment, then said, 'Pader, your boy, is he here?'

'Somewhere . . .' Pader Luminis raised his voice, 'the lazy, good-for-nothing, shirking, drag-footed, slackslothing, insolent, wretched little twenty-fingered, logheaded numpty.'

Issul suppressed a smile. 'I would prefer that we were alone, Pader. The matters of which I wish to speak should be heard by none but yourself.'

Pader Luminis raised himself in his seat, craning his neck forward to peer into dense shadows at the furthest end of the room. 'Radius!'

There was a stirring somewhere in the depths of the shadow. Issul, turning her head, perceived a movement on a shelf above a desk. A small figure unfolded itself, shunted to one side and hopped down, to stand sleepily rubbing its eyes before them. 'Yes, Master?'

'Abscond.'

'To where, Master?'

'Wherever you like. I have no further need of you this evening. Begone, but keep out of trouble and annoy no one, or you will know my wrath.'

'When will I be needed again, Master?'

'You may bring my breakfast at the usual hour. Can you manage that?'

'Master. Mistress.' Radius, feigning ignorance of Issul's identity, gave a small tilt of the head and scampered away. The door swung shut with a boom.

'Understand,' said Pader Luminis confidingly, 'as I have told you many times before, that for we who live here, on the Edge, life is always a struggle between extremes. We are upon the borders, between worlds. On the one hand is Enchantment, the Unknown and Unknowable; we may taste it, be witness to its strange nature, but we cannot enter. On the other are the Kingdoms of the Mondane, whose folk shun and fear us, perhaps wisely. Some think it would be simpler to live like them, free of our conflict and uncertainty. Yet we are privileged, for though we may at times be afraid and may not understand all that we experience here, we do at least experience it. That is a prize we should never take for granted. Now, child, proceed.'

Issul leaned forward and took up the pot of tea. She began to pour into the two mugs, the greenish-gold liquid tumbling in a rippling column from the spout. And something strange happened. As the tea touched the base of the first mug the fluid column suddenly turned sinuously upon itself, as though it had gained a life of its own. Like an eyeless viridescent snake it twisted, flew from the mug and sped towards the rafters above.

Issul cried out in astonishment. The steaming liquid looped itself into knots above her head, then untwined and spread into a thin hovering pool, suspended in the air. Without warning it rushed at Issul's head.

She threw herself back in her chair to avoid being scalded, but too slowly. The tea splashed into her face, but as it did so it transformed into a cloud of tiny emerald-and-blue butterflies, their wings shimmering and bright, which fluttered about her head and away.

'Oh!' Enchanted, Issul reached out to touch one. The butterfly and all its companions became sparkling dust which fell in a shower to the floor and vanished.

Issul laughed and clapped her hands in delight. 'Oh, marvellous! Pader! Marvellous!'

Pader Luminis beamed at her, his cheeks flushed, and slapped his knee. 'You see!' he pointed at her. 'You laugh. You are gay again. You come from yourself and this dark mood that oppresses you. Now is the time to talk. You know, sweet Issul, I have always said that one should meet grave matters with a light spirit if one does not wish to be dragged further down. Remember that.'

'But how did you do that, Pader?' asked Issul wonderingly.

'It is nothing.'

'To a Murinean, perhaps.'

'One does not have to be Murinean to create fripperies such as these. It was a simple illusion, that is all, without real value. Had you been able to remain my student you would have mastered such fancies long ago. Now, the tea, my dear, if you please.'

Issul poured again, and this time the tea remained tea. She smiled at Pader Luminis, who sipped from his mug, gave a sigh of satisfaction, then said, 'Now, it is time to speak, I think.'

Issul's smile diminished as she remembered again her reasons for coming here, and one hand went to her brow. 'Something has happened today which I believe may darken the future for us all.

Pader, I wish you to tell me all that you know of Enchantment and its strange denizens, of the Krai and the war that threatens and, most particularly, of the True Sept and the creed its members follow.'

'You have several days to spare, I take it?'

Issul shook her head. 'I have so little time. Even now I should be with my children, readying them for their beds, and with Leth. But . . . Tell me what you can in whatever time we have now, and be aware that I shall be returning to you as and when I can for further discussion. Most particularly, I want to know about the Legendary Child.'

Now it was Pader Luminis who frowned. 'The Legendary Child? As described in the teachings of the True Sept?'

'And anywhere else. I need to know everything possible.'

Pader Luminis put down his mug. He nodded thoughtfully to himself, settling himself back in his chair and steepling his fingers beneath his chin. 'Very well.'

When Issul emerged later from Pader Luminis's apartment high in the White Eaglet's Tower, her head was ringing with all that she had heard. She would have stayed longer, so avid was she to hear all that Pader knew, but old Pader had been growing tired and she could see that the task of remembering and recounting so much was taking its toll. He had advised her, too, that to continue would require his researching in some depth the histories of the land, the various factions and their beliefs, and more. He did not wish to present her with unreliable information, preferring to refresh his own memory before continuing. Pader had promised to commence his researches first thing on the morrow but he had warned her that certain details she had requested were inaccessible even to him. They had agreed that Issul might return at any time, without notice, should she require further guidance.

Issul did not know whether she would need to return. With what she had so far learned she felt as though the ground had begun to crumble beneath her feet. She walked like a hollow creature, pale and drawn, trying to persuade herself that what she had done almost four years earlier could not possibly have the consequences she now feared. She had acted for the good, in innocence, not knowing what other choice she had – apart from the unthinkable. It was only afterwards that the real possibilities had become known to her, and she had endeavoured to put them from her mind. She did not want to contemplate what they might mean, and persuaded herself that her fears were hysterical and unfounded. For it all seemed so far-fetched.

But no longer. Now her worst fears had virtually been confirmed.

Could she tell anyone? Leth? Issul felt suddenly terrifyingly alone. *Dear Leth, what will this do to us? Will it drive us apart? And more? Am I guilty of bringing about the ruin of us and all we love and hold dear? Am I, ultimately, the destroyer of Enchantment's Edge?*

Issul wept silently as she made her way back. She could not tell. King Leth, her husband whom she loved so dearly, could not know. At least, not yet. Not until Issul had wholly ascertained the truth and worked out whether there was any way of undoing what had already been done. She would have to go in the first instance to the village of Lastmeadow and the home of Ohirbe and her husband, Arrin. She would question everybody, take whatever steps necessary to locate the old woman whom Ohirbe reported to be showing such an unnatural interest in her young ward, Moscul. And her companion too, if it was at all possible: the young man who had been with her at the poolside. Issul would spare no effort. It was imperative that she discover what these two knew, and what they intended.

And she had to talk to the child, Moscul. It was possible that Moscul might be able to provide her with some of the answers she sought.

Into Issul's mind sprang an image of her dead sister, Ressa, Mawnie's twin. *Oh Ressa, I did this for you, just as you asked. For you and for Mawnie. We could not have known. That is my only excuse. We could not have known!*

II

Arriving back at her apartment Issul cleaned her face of the make-up she had applied earlier and donned garments more appropriate for the Queen of Enchantment's Edge. She sat for a few moments in silence, endeavouring to calm her thoughts and rid her mind of the turmoil that beset it, employing techniques taught her over years. Presently, a little less fraught, she rose and left her rooms.

She had seen no sign of Lord Fectur since her return from Overlip. This vaguely surprised her. She had anticipated a visit. He would have certainly received a detailed report of her activities from his men and would be thirsting to know what she was up to.

Unless he already knew! For a moment the thought chilled her, then she put it aside as improbable. She trusted that Fectur would have made no attempt to apprehend Iklar, with whom she had spoken at the Tavern of the Veiled Light. To do so would have been reckless without a small army at his disposal within Overlip, inviting almost certain failure and bloodshed. Fectur was neither reckless nor a fool. Even had he been able he would have known that to arrest Iklar would serve him nothing. Iklar was little more than a messenger, with no direct access to Grey Venger. Fectur would wait and watch, biding his time, gathering intelligence, setting up his targets, anticipating the right moment to strike, as was his habit. But Issul, though relieved at his absence now, could not help but wonder whether it boded ill.

She entered the nursery where her children, Prince Galry and Princess Jace, slept soundly. In a cot in the same chamber young Lir, the daughter of Mawnie and Duke Hugo, also slept. Issul had hoped in her heart to find her children awake so that she might spend a few precious minutes with them, but had known that it was hardly likely to be so. She enquired softly of the night-nanny as to how they had spent their day, then sat beside them, holding their hands and gazing lovingly and regretfully at their sleeping faces. The nanny told her that King Leth had been in only a few moments before and had left word for Issul that he was going to dine. To Issul's further enquiry she replied that Lir had not seen her mother, Duchess Demawndella, all day.

Presently Issul rose, tenderly kissed her children and niece goodnight, and made her way to join her husband.

Seeing Leth, smiling as he took her hands and embraced and kissed her, Issul felt her tensions slip away for a few short moments. She had not seen him since early morning, and then it had been but briefly as they rose from their bed and made themselves ready for another day of duty and formality. As she relaxed now in his strong arms, her head upon his shoulder, she thought of past days. Leth had been a dutiful and passionate suitor. Dashing, considerate, gallant, ambitious even then, and a man much absorbed in work and state duty, he had yet pursued her as though his life depended upon it. Those had been carefree, intoxicating days compared to now; they had laughed and played and loved and dreamed and loved some more. Issul's love for him had not diminished over the years – nor, she believed, had his for her – but the time in which to express it grew less and less, and close though they were they no longer shared exclusively the same world.

Issul watched her husband as they sat together to eat, noting the dreamy look of his eyes. It had been one of the qualities that attracted her to him, a sense of entering a warm and inviting inner world. It kept him slightly detached – only proper for a future monarch – but fascinating, and helped bestow upon him a quiet confidence and resoluteness.

But more recently, that dreaminess had taken on a different quality. His eyes were glassier, more inwardly penetrating, darkened around their rims. Leth seemed haunted, more fragile than she had ever known him. Issul wondered what had changed in his inner world, for it seemed it was no longer a place where he might always find sanctuary and certainty.

Questioning a house-servant on her way here Issul had learned that Leth had spent some hours locked in his study earlier in the evening. It was at these times that Leth became most inwardly-inclined, and she recalled again the strange blue lucency seeping beneath his door she had seen on that single occasion. She said nothing, for she knew he would evade her questioning and might grow impatient should she persist. But with his accession to the throne it had become plain that Leth had taken on burdens he could not discuss, even with her, and this concerned Issul.

Secrets. There had been a time when they had kept nothing from each other. Nothing at all. Now . . . with a sharp inward pang she thought of her own inner darkness, which she dared not allow Leth to enter. It had once been so different.

'How went your conference?' she asked.

Leth waited as a servant filled his goblet with dark ruby wine. He had spent much of the day with Hugo and others of his most senior advisors, debating the Krai crisis. 'Inconclusive,' he said. 'The Krai are encamped barely seven leagues from Giswel. If they keep to their previous pattern, they have every intention of moving against us.'

'But you are not sure.'

'It would be madness to assume otherwise.'

'Can we meet them, man for man?'

'You know we cannot. Not without help. Even then . . . The reports Hugo has received he considers reliable without question: the Krai have troll-things and winged demons in their ranks. These creatures must have come from Enchantment. We can only infer that they have elicited the help of one of the gods of Enchantment. It is unheard of.'

'And is there still no offer of assistance from the Mondane Kingdoms?'

Leth dolefully shook his head. 'They will not help us. I received a missive today from the last of the northern kings, Galomard. He, like the others, declines to involve his nation in a dispute he sees as having nothing to do with him. He states that his decision is unequivocal and irrevocable, and plainly wishes no further communication.'

'They are mad!' Issul declared. 'All of them! Can they not see what will happen if Enchantment's Edge should fall to the Krai? They will surely be next, each of them, one by one.'

'They fear us, my love. You know that. Our proximity to Enchantment marks us as tainted, otherlings, contaminated by powers and mysteries Mondane knows nothing of. They fear curses, possessions, demonization should they venture here. There has been nothing but the most elementary contact between Enchantment's Edge and the Mondane Kingdoms for more generations than I know.'

'But I have heard talk of the arrival of foreign soldiers,' Issul said.

'A few brave or penniless mercenaries, odd stragglers and would-be heroes. They trickle in in answer to my call, but they are not enough to make a difference.'

'Winter's approach may be our most reliable ally, then.'

Leth shrugged, chewing his food without great conviction, then dabbed his mouth with a napkin. 'We do not know the minds of the Krai. And winter is not so close. If they struck quickly they could make serious inroads, certainly into Giswel.'

Issul weighed this, then said, 'The Krai prince, Anzejarl – has there been any communication with him?'

'None. I have proposed sending a delegation to speak with Anzejarl, with the hope of arriving at a peaceful resolution. The idea was met with unanimous disapproval.'

'On what grounds?'

'On the grounds that Anzejarl is not known to be a man – or a Krai – given to discussion. He would likely take me hostage, or return my head in a bag.'

'You? Leth, you would go?'

'The Krai are a proud people. Anzejarl would deem it a gross insult were I to send someone of inferior rank. If it was to be done, it could be no one but myself.'

'You must not go.' Issul reached out and grasped his hand. 'Leth, I will not allow you.'

Leth gave a disconsolate smile. 'As I say, my proposal met with disapproval. And indeed, it was considered premature. As yet the Krai have committed no offence against Enchantment's Edge. It is their proximity and infamy which lead us to act almost as though war had already been declared.'

'There will be no declaration,' Issul said with certainty. 'We will be attacked, if that is Prince Anzejarl's design. He has never declared war, simply struck with little warning. Are there no other options open to us?'

'There is the Orb's Soul,' said Leth. His voice was low and tinged with a cynical edge.

'What is that?'

'A lost artefact; a powerful effectuary. Or a figment of an overactive imagination.'

'I have never heard of it.'

'Nor I, until very recently.' He gave a mirthless smile. 'My love, do not take me seriously. I spoke half in jest. This object probably does not exist, and even if it does it cannot help us. It is an example of the kind of thing fearful minds reach for in times such as this.'

'But if it exists . . . how can it help Enchantment's Edge?'

'I do not know. Issul, put it from your mind. Forget it. The Orb's Soul is a product of hearsay. The story I was told is that it was lost eons ago, within Enchantment.'

'Enchantment?' Issul's face fell.

'You see? Even were its location known, it would remain unreachable. We are not able to enter Enchantment.'

'Who told you of this?' asked Issul after a moment's thought.

King Leth hesitated, lowering his gaze. 'It is just wild talk passing around. As I said, such notions are the common refuge of desperate, frightened minds at times like these.'

'But who precisely did you hear speak of this object, Leth? I would like to talk to them.'

'No one!' Leth's irritation was plain. 'I have told you, it is just wild rumour. One among many. There are airy saviours in abundance queueing up to bring us salvation – for a price. You do not know how my time is taken up just now with farseers, miracle-workers, nod-heads with channels to the gods and who knows what else. I spoke lightly. Please let us speak no more of it.'

Issul fell silent, deeply concerned, wildly speculating. Ordinarily she would, like Leth, have taken little note of notions such as this. There was nothing new in ideas of magical artefacts, powerful relicts and rare and fabulous treasures lying within Enchantment. But in her talk earlier with Pader Luminis, Pader had made lengthy reference to Enchantment and what was known of its history. He had referred to artefacts of the gods, among many other things. He had not been specific, and certainly had made no mention of anything called the Orb's Soul. More, Pader had stressed that the stories he was relating were fables, legends, ancient tales with little or no foundation in historical fact. But his words had greatly excited Issul's imagination, taking her back to her childhood and later years as a student, when she had sat enrapt by stories such as these.

Why had Leth mentioned this now? Specifically, this one object out of so many? Could there be something? She made a mental note to speak to Pader.

Ah, but Enchantment . . . It was impossible, she knew it. No one could go there.

She fell back, forlorn and annoyed at her own credulity, for having permitted herself to be led by imagination and desperate hope.

Presently, breaking the silence between them, she said, 'Mawnie believes the True Sept may be making overtures to the Krai.'

'Mawnie,' said Leth, almost derisorily, then changed his tone. 'Yes, it may well be so. Hugo has said as much. But it is nothing I am not aware of, and ultimately it can make little difference.' He looked searchingly into her face. 'I understand you were in Overlip earlier.'

Issul felt a slight prickling warmth in her cheeks. Fectur had not been remiss, then. She nodded.

'At the Veiled Light.'

She nodded again, thinking furiously.

'Why?'

'I wanted to try to contact Grey Venger.'

'Why?'

How she wanted to tell him all – but she couldn't. Not yet. Not until she knew more. But she would not lie, either. 'I will tell you precisely at a more appropriate time, my love. Suffice to say that I believe we must establish relations with Venger now. We cannot eradicate the True Sept, and it serves us no good to force it underground.'

'Is that not for the King to decide?'

'Yes, but the King has always consulted wisely before making important decisions.' She saw how this pricked him. 'Leth, I have reason to believe that the creed of the True Sept, and particularly the prophecy of the Legendary Child, may be of significance at this time.' Her heart beat fast as she said these words and she felt her throat constrict.

'In what way?' enquired Leth.

'Until I have learned more I would prefer not to say.'

'There are proper diplomatic channels for these things.'

'And they are lined with many ears. The other ways, if technically illegal, are more direct and private, and often offer more effective results.'

'But you went without proper escort, in disguise!'

'Would you have me go as the Queen with a retinue of fifty

knights? There would have been pandemonium in Overlip, and the Veiled Light would have been empty when I got there. This was the better way, my love. Fectur was fully informed, and he provided more than adequate cover.'

'Even so, it was dangerous.'

'These are dangerous times, calling for sometimes unorthodox and perhaps risky ventures. But I do not feel that I placed myself at great peril. Leth, if a communication is received from a representative of the True Sept, or anything that in any way may relate to the True Sept, will you inform me immediately? Please?'

King Leth eyed her, then gave a single nod. 'Will you not tell me what it is about?'

Issul moved closer to him, taking one of his hands in both of hers. She kissed his forehead. 'When I know more.'

They said little else but, their meal over, they sat together, lost in their individual thoughts. Issul gently stroked her husband's hair, her other hand holding his in her lap, his head resting upon her shoulder. After a while she placed a kiss upon his neck. 'Tired?'

He nodded slowly, then lifted his head and met her gaze. A twinkle lit his eye. 'Well, perhaps not so.'

Issul smiled. She kissed him, rising, taking both his hands. 'Well, noble sir, will you not then escort this fair maiden to her bed?'

They stood together in their bedchamber beside the bed, slowly disrobing each other, warmed and illuminated by the orange flames of the great fire that burned in the hearth. When he was naked before her, Issul's hands slid down to take his manhood gently, caressing, slowly, responding to the mounting pulse of him, her own ardour growing as the sound of his breathing deepened and his own hands played over her breasts. His sighs became moans as her motions grew more rapid and his hips began to thrust involuntarily towards her in a growing rhythm.

Smiling, she knelt before him, planted soft kisses upon his stomach, his thighs, the soft mass of his hair, gently plying his hardness against her cheek, breathing in the familiar smell of him. Then she eased her head back and took him into the warm cavern of her mouth, heard him moan as her lips closed about him and her fingers slid between his thighs to stroke and caress his balls tenderly. Leth's hands went to her head, urging her, throbbing in her mouth as her tongue played, drawing him to greater pleasures.

Expertly she brought him closer to his peak, and when she felt and heard him reach it and knew that he could go no higher, she grasped the base of his shaft and squeezed firmly, holding him back. Releasing him from her mouth she stood slowly, kissing her way up his strong body until their mouths met. They fell together upon the bed. Issul straddled him, taking him into her, sliding fully, drawing him deep inside, crying out. A few short strokes and Leth could hold back no longer. With long ecstatic shouts, his hips bucking he poured himself into her, and as the liquid gush of his seed filled her she felt the waves of her own climax, thrusting down, arching her spine and throwing back her head in delirious abandon, transported and beyond herself, until she fell limply, joyful and exhausted, and his powerful arms slipped around her and held her to him, their bodies slick and spent.

III

Leth slept, deeply, his breathing even, somehow able to free himself of the trials that beset him. But Issul, though she slumbered after their lovemaking, became restless, fitful, troubled by strange dreams. Eventually she found herself awake in the near-dark and unable to return to sleep.

She lay for some time, watching Leth's sleeping face in the coppery light cast by the dying fire. His eyelids flickered from time to time, the eyeballs rolling beneath, and occasionally he would half-mumble something. Once he cried out as if in protest or anger, but he did not wake and the words were incomprehensible, giving Issul no clue as to the content of his dreams.

She stroked his forehead and he sank back into deep sleep. Though she tried, Issul, still in his embrace, remained wakeful. She lay for some time upon her back, then eventually unwound Leth's arms carefully from about her and rose from the bed. She slipped on a quilted night-robe and went to stand beside the window.

Enchantment's Edge was silent and cloaked in utter black, relieved only here and there by the dim glow of a lantern. Overhead the firmament was a starry mass, filling her with painful wonder as she gazed. Cold beauty. A vastness beyond comprehension, and she its dazzled, uncomprehending witness. *Are there others out there?* she asked silently as she had asked so many times before. Did they gaze towards her from their own lonely stars, their hearts and minds filled with the same profound wonder, the same unanswerable questions?

Issul lowered her gaze, her eyes drawn to another mystery, far-off, yet, compared to the stars, no more than a hand's reach away: the weird lights of Enchantment. They were a bright shifting blur in the distance, vermilions, golds, greens and blues, hovering about an unseen horizon.

Now here was a mystery that might be solved, she thought. For what are you? Enigmatic glows upon a strange and forbidden land, yet so close. The impulse was upon her to leave upon the instant, ride forth from Enchantment's Edge, through the forest to Enchantment itself. Surely, surely, there must be a way?

But Issul knew that of those who had done just that, none had returned to tell their story. The remains of some had been found in the forest, though not in her lifetime. Their bones had been picked clean by unknown carnivores, their belongings scattered amongst the roots and bushes. But more had simply disappeared, never to be heard of again. And nothing had been learned of the mystery they had set out to explore.

No, it was impossible. For all its apparent proximity, for all the tantalizing, eerie glow of its beautiful lights, Enchantment might as well have lain beyond the most distant star.

The last champion known to have ventured there was named Greth the Bold. Pader Luminis had spoken of him only hours earlier as he recounted to Issul tales of their age. He had been a knight of Enchantment's Edge, a mighty warrior and, so it was rumoured, a lover of Queen Fallorn. With a dozen men-at-arms and two adepts of the Arcane College, Greth the Bold had ridden forth, pledged to return with accounts of the gods and their land. That had been more than thirty years ago. Greth and all his followers had vanished like so many before them, and nothing was known of their fate.

And yet, out there, is it possible that there may lie the answer to our troubles? Issul pressed her head back against the wall, fighting back tears of frustration, her heart welling within her breast.

The Orb's Soul.

No, it was a dream. As Leth had said, a refuge of frightened minds in desperate times. Nothing more.

And even if it was more substantial than a dream, neither she nor any other could ever go in search of it to Enchantment.

Issul's mind ran over other elements of the conversation she had had with Pader Luminis, most notably his references to the Legendary Child of the True Sept. Details were scant, known only to the hereditary leaders of the Sept, who were bound to absolute secrecy. Pader had been able to fill in little more than Issul already knew: the Legendary Child was said to be the spawn of one of Enchantment's gods, let loose upon the world to wreak havoc and destruction. Its very presence, it was said, would be the cause of ruination and war. Why, was unclear. The True Sept held knowledge of its coming, the conditions that would pertain, and the reasons for its arrival among men. The True Sept prepared the way. At Issul's entreaty Pader Luminis had promised to scour the library, delve into every corner in an effort to find out more, but he did not hold out great hope.

'The creed of the True Sept is held within its heart. Nothing more than these most basic details have ever been revealed, and the leaders of the Sept decline to affirm or deny even this, so we can be sure of nothing. The ranks of the Sept have never been infiltrated – at least not to bring out that knowledge.' He had scratched his pate, pursing his lips in concentration. 'Still, I will try, my dear. For you, I will try.'

He had not enquired into the reasons for Issul's sudden interest.

Issul squeezed shut her eyes. *Am I really the cause of all this? Have I brought about our destruction?*

Again Ressa's smiling face rose before her. So like Mawnie. Almost indistinguishable.

Ressa, I did it for you! Ressa, oh Ressa, if only it had been different! I loved you so. We all did. You should have lived. It was unfair, so unfair!

She turned away, forcing the demons from her mind. Tomorrow. Tomorrow she would ride to Lastmeadow.

Issul turned back towards the bed. Her husband still slept, one bare arm lying upon the cover. She moved back to join him, though she still felt she would not sleep. As she cast off her robe something caught her eye. She stared for a moment at Leth. Nothing seemed amiss, and yet . . .

She peered more closely. There was nothing. It must have been her tiredness. She bent to draw back the cover and climb in beside him, and glimpsed it again. A faint glow, so faint, barely discernible. It seemed to come from his skin.

But again, as she stared at him, she could see nothing.

Issul glanced away, beyond Leth, but keeping him within the edge of her vision. There! Now she could see it, when her gaze was slightly averted. It was definite, the dimmest luminescence, bluish in colour, clinging to him.

She looked directly at him once more: it was indiscernible. But it was no visual fallacy nor the product of her overwrought brain. She focused beyond him and saw it again.

Her heart thumping, Issul pulled the cover back, exposing Leth's entire naked body. She let her eyes pass beyond him. There it was, the dimmest aura, clinging to him from head to toe.

Issul recalled the strange lucency she had descried that night beneath his study door.

Leth! Leth!

She was afraid to wake him. She lay beside him, pulling the cover over them both, her thoughts spinning once more. And when the first grey light of dawn seeped into the chamber she lay there still, wakeful and wondering.

IV

Far away, though far too close in the minds of many, the same grey dawn broke upon another scene. A blue command pavilion had been pitched in a grassy meadow which let onto the shore of a long misted lake. Around this, beyond the edges of the meadow, spreading along the shore, over nearby heathland, up the slopes of nearby hillsides, were pitched hundreds upon hundreds of other, smaller tents. Campfires smouldered in the chill morning, a thousand smoke plumes lazily curling to merge with the mist. Huddled figures moved between the tents and fires, lugging pots and cauldrons, bundles of kindling and logs, sacks of meal, tack, dried meat and other basic foodstuffs, and barrels of ale, spirits and, more commonly, water. The air carried the odours of cooking food as, in the tents, sleepy figures began gradually to stir. The Krai army was waking.

From the blue pavilion came Anzejarl, Prince of the Krai peoples, to stand upon the dewy grass and gaze out upon the misted terrain. Around the meadow sharp-pointed stakes rose from the ground, some three score or so in number. Impaled upon these were the tormented bodies of men and women, mostly corpses by now, though one or two of the least fortunate still somehow clung to the unremitting agony that was all life had been reduced to.

Living or dead, Anzejarl paid them no heed. He stared instead out across the lake to where, above the densest layers of mist, the topmost bulk of a high, rugged, saddle-backed ridge loomed darkly in the half-lit morning.

Anzejarl was tall, unusually so for a Krai, and his face, long and deeply-seamed in the character of his people, wore a cast both mournful and coldly proud. He was garbed in stuffed and studded black leather armour and boots, a black cloak slung about his shoulders. His eyes, like the eyes of all Krai, were a total searing blue, scored by the narrowest slit-pupils of weltering jade. In one fist he grasped a bunch of bruised *ghinz* leaves, raising one from time to time to his lips. Chewing, his gaze growing glassier and more intense as the narcotic worked to quell his senses, he stared into the distance for some time. Eventually he lowered his eyes, slowly shaking his head, and breathed a long harsh sigh. 'Enough of this. Now. Enough.'

Behind him a woman had emerged from the pavilion. She was startlingly beautiful, her hair long and lustrous red. She wore a long deep green dress which hugged her figure, voluptuously accentuating the curves and swells of her body. She moved up beside Prince Anzejarl and rested her hands upon his arm, gazed for a moment at the far ridge, then looked up into his eyes.

'I sense your anger. It is not necessary.'

'It is not necessary. Pah!' Anzejarl's jaw tightened. 'It should end, now.'

'It cannot.'

'The price is far too high.'

'But you are rewarded.'

Anzejarl spat mashed *ghinz* onto the grass, inserted another leaf between his teeth. 'I am enslaved.'

'You have your desire.'

'Perhaps that is what I mean.'

The woman took his free hand and raised it to place it upon one of her breasts. She held it there, squeezing, feeling her nipple harden. 'Are you saying this is not enough?'

Anzejarl breathed deeply and looked into her eyes. With satisfaction she saw his features slacken, saw the burning in his eyes and felt his great hand move at his own volition upon her breast. She pressed against it, reached up and curled her arm around the back of his head, drawing his lips down to hers and kissing him fiercely.

Anzejarl let the *ghinz* leaves fall. He pulled her hard against him, one hand sliding to her buttocks. 'Olmana, Olmana.'

She broke free of the kiss, gasping, 'Now, do you still say it should end?'

His mouth travelled over her neck, her shoulder. He bent to kiss the swell of her breast.

'Remember, I can take it all away. And more.'

'No. No.' He gripped her shoulders, stared into her face.

'You are pledged, Anzejarl. At any price. There is no turning back. Remember that.'

'I can never forget,' he growled, sullen and aroused.

'The Child will be found, will it not?'

'It will. If the entire world must burn in the process, it will.'

'Good. Then . . .' Olmana arched her neck, rolling her eyes towards the high ridge.

'We will move today,' muttered Anzejarl. 'Soon we will see how the good soldiers of the Edge have prepared for us.'

'They are aware that you are coming?'

'Of course. More than two years of conquests will hardly have passed unnoticed, even to the dim eyes of Enchantment's Edge. And their scouts have been spotted shadowing us on more than one occasion.'

'And your contact in the capital? Is there no indication there?'

'Of the Child?'

'Or anything other.'

Anzejarl shook his head. 'I have received no word. But good King Leth is bound for a surprise.'

Olmana smiled to herself. She slid a hand to his groin and caressed him through the leather, coaxing, 'I wonder whether they might appreciate a small taste of what is to come.'

Anzejarl's eyes closed and he grunted in pleasure. 'I dispatched special advance units some time ago. They will be in place now and will begin providing a few distractions.'

'Good. But I thought . . .' her eyes went to a small grove of trees on the edge of the meadow. Dark, bulky forms could be seen roosting on their lower limbs. Beneath were strewn bones and mauled tatters of human meat.

'Do you wish me to send slooths, Olmana?'

'Why not? They could be there in, what, two days? Three?'

Prince Anzejarl nodded.

'Good. Send them, then. Not in force. Just enough to put fear into the populace and more pressure upon Leth. Kill a few. Make it plain to them all that the towering walls and high cliffs of Enchantment's Edge are of little count against a superior enemy who can strike from the air. I think, between the slooths and your special units, we should achieve an encouraging level of demoralization.'

Prince Anzejarl looked into her eyes and smiled. 'As it happens, it is already done. A small detachment of slooths departed in the wake of the special units. I would imagine they will be making their presence known very soon.'

Olmana smiled. 'Good. It seems you deserve your reward, Anzejarl.'

She brought his head down and he sought her mouth hungrily again, gathering her to him and carrying her back into his pavilion.

FOUR

I

It was Orbus, the ragged-garbed tenant of the strange blue casket, who had told King Leth about the Orb's Soul. He had done so only hours before Leth mentioned it to Issul. But he had spoken of it imprecisely, and in terms of loss and inaccessibility. Leth came away without a clear description, knowing the Orb's Soul only as something that probably did not exist and certainly could never be found.

In the three years since becoming King, Leth had been summoned several times to Orbus's enclosed blue world. Always it was Orbus who commanded him, establishing the times and conditions; never did Leth enter unnannounced.

Over this time he had been granted brief glimpses of an extraordinary knowledge. He came away at times with his mind reeling. But the unusual master/student relationship he had with Orbus had a somewhat oppressive quality. Orbus often spoke in a way that seemed calculated to confuse. Leth always sensed that he was holding something back, that there were things he was not willing to reveal, and yet that he was building up to something. That which he did reveal, though it might make good sense, was largely unverifiable from Leth's position. Leth proceeded largely on trust, never quite sure whether everything was to be wholly believed. He had to fight sometimes to contain his frustration and impatience.

Orbus's personality was one of extremes, a conglomeration of quirks and idiosyncrasies, overlaid with an arrogance and an air of superiority which Leth found grating. Orbus made no deference to him as King. He would happily humiliate or make fun of Leth, though at other times he might show sympathy or humour, and on occasion was even downcast and apathetic.

Over time, though, Leth began to understand why Orbus might be the way he was. Leth became less inclined to criticism; Orbus confided more. While Orbus's attitude was still irksome, Leth resolved to bear it largely in silence.

Indeed, he had little choice. He was obliged to be ever-alert to Orbus's beck or call, something he found barely tolerable, and for all the knowledge he gained he never became entirely comfortable in the strange creature's presence. The very fact of Orbus's existence was something which in many ways threatened Leth's own.

The things Orbus told him ultimately laid a further weight upon his soul. The history of Orbia was related to him in a way he had never heard before. The nature of Enchantment and its god-beings was unfolded, piece by piece. Leth marvelled, but was filled too with foreboding. The more he learned, the more he came to feel his place and the place of his people to be insignificant in the shattering light of a callous and unforgiving universe.

And he could counsel no other, being bound to silence. To reveal anything would have been to invite suspicion and investigation. Leth was coming to an understanding of what Orbus really represented. Were the blue casket, and consequently Orbus himself, to fall into the hands of others, or somehow be destroyed, Enchantment's Edge would surely suffer a disaster too terrible to contemplate. Orbus made King Leth realize that he was invaluable, and he played upon this. Leth felt that his own power was waning under the influence of this enigmatic ally. Haunted by the fear that Orbus might yet have hidden designs beyond and above his declared aims, Leth grew gradually more sombre with every passing day.

Orbus held a hook ever baited just beyond Leth's reach. Thus Leth left his bizarre presence always on the brink of discovering some new secret, avid to return for more. Initially it had been the mere baffling fact of Orbus's existence that drew the King of Enchantment's Edge. After his coronation he had gone at the first opportunity to his study and taken the blue casket from hiding and attempted to open it. But to his dismay the casket was firmly sealed.

Had there been a mistake? Had he somehow misheard or misinterpreted Orbus's first instruction? Leth returned to the casket later the same night, stealing from his bed while Issul slept. But to no avail.

He had pounded the floor of his study till the early hours, gripped in near frenzy. Fearing that what he had so newly gained had now been lost, he had taken up the casket again and again. But it continued to resist all his efforts. Eventually he had returned it to its hidden compartment and departed.

The following evening had told a similar tale, as had the next. Leth, defying earlier instructions, had then attempted to speak to his mother, Queen Fallorn. But she had been sharp, refusing to respond to any mention of the casket. She had professed herself weary and retired early to her bed. The next day Leth had learned of her illness.

Two further efforts to open the casket met with failure. King Leth felt that he was living in a nightmare. Could he have imagined what had happened? Surely he was not capable of conjuring anything so weird? Fallorn had given him the casket; he had spoken with her about Orbus. Or might that have been imagination, too? Was his mind diseased?

On the morning following Queen Fallorn's death Leth, bowed down with grief and confusion, had shut himself away again in his study. He sat alone at his desk for some while, barely mindful of the casket, his thoughts on his life past and the way it must change now with the loss of the mother he had loved so dearly. He had little time, for his day was filled with meetings, petty adjudications and other duties of state. He raised himself heavily from his chair, went once more to the hidden compartment in the wall and brought forth the blue casket. Returning with it to the desk he had found to his surprise that the hook slipped easily from its catch.

Leth's heart had skipped a beat. He raised the casket's lid.

As before, there was a blinding flash, a dazzle of blue. Leth quickly closed his eyes, taken less by surprise this time. When he opened them again, blinking, he had found himself once more in the vast walled blueness that was Orbus's indefinable domain.

It was as before. The watery blue seemed to extend forever, yet simultaneously its towering walls were all about him. Leth could not explain this paradox. It was enough that he perceived it, as though his senses worked on another, wholly alien plane. All he could do was accept.

The blueness was empty and terrifyingly silent. Again Leth had been aware of nothing but the roar of his breathing, the blood surging through his veins, the creak of sinew and joint as he shifted stance. Into his mind had leapt the notion of the casket, the Orb, being a prison. An unnerving sensation had gripped him, and he spoke out 'Are you here?'

There was no reply. Leth turned, slowly scanning the empty distance.

At last, a sound. A faint, uneven shuffling, the thump of a staff upon the ground, far off, barely audible. Leth strained his eyes, peering into the unrelenting blue. The sound became slightly louder and then he saw the bent, hobbling figure, far off, approaching slowly out of the blue obscurity, his staff tapping upon the ground.

It took an age for Orbus to reach him. When he did he stood a short distance away, leaning upon his staff. His face and much of his form were obscured as before by the bulk of rags wound about his head and shoulders.

'I have the Crown,' Leth had said, and held forth the bejewelled golden Monarch's Crown of State which had been set upon his head for the first time only days earlier.

Orbus was silent. He seemed to be scrutinizing the Crown, though he had come no closer and made no attempt to touch it or take it from Leth. Then, at last, his bundled head began to nod slowly.

'Good,' he said, then turned and began to move away.

'Wait!' Leth cried in complete dismay.

Orbus did not pause. Leth stepped towards his retreating back, but strangely, as before, he found himself no closer to the ragged creature.

'Orbus, wait! Is that all?'

'What else? You came, as I asked.' The crooked figure had shuffled on.

'My mother is dead.' Leth did not know why he said this, except that the pain of it was dominant in his mind. But it had an effect. Orbus hesitated in his step, just for a moment, though he did not turn around.

'It proceeds,' he had said in a low voice, and resumed walking.

Leth stood alone. 'Is there nothing more?'

'We will talk again. Be alert for my summons.'

Orbus raised his staff. Leth, blinking, had found himself at his desk, staring at the closed blue casket.

II

'*Be alert for my summons.*'

In fact many weeks were to pass before Orbus again summoned the King. During that time the first reliable reports concerning the Krai conflict had begun to filter through to Enchantment's Edge.

Information to date had consisted of little more than rumours or second- or third-hand accounts of some kind of uprising in the Krai capital, Zhang. Now a more detailed picture had begun to emerge, of conflict and bloodshed involving the Krai royal family, and events escalating into a bloody civil war. Domestic issues of this kind were generally of interest but not necessarily major concern or alarm to other nations of the Mondane or Enchantment's Edge, but when it was among the Krai it was a different tale. They had always been thought immune to civil conflict, by virtue of an unusual social structure and fierce national pride. The idea of bitter, bloody rivalry among members of their royal family would previously have been deemed implausible.

Then later, more disturbingly, there came news of a vast Krai army on the march just beyond the borders of its homeland.

The origins of the Krai were somewhat obscure. Pale-skinned and inscrutable, they had once had a reputation as a proudly independent sea-faring folk who had settled in what was now their accepted homeland several centuries earlier, driving out the indigenous tribal communities with much blood though the Krai had faced comparatively little meaningful resistance. They had then adopted a policy of virtual isolationism which had largely persisted to the present day.

Their strange and rather forbidding physical features and love of fighting caused the Krai to be regarded with wary suspicion by their Mondane neighbours. Merchants and traders, permitted entry into their lands, brought back stories of a proud, aloof race, with an almost fanatical devotion to both family and monarchy. All Krai were held to have descended from one original pairing and, theoretically at least, every individual member of the Krai nation could trace his or her lineage directly to the incumbent monarch, and thence to the founding parents of the Krai people.

From where they had come before settling in their new homeland was not known.

No matter the fears of their neighbours, in the centuries since their arrival on the southern shores close upon mysterious Enchantment the Krai had remained within their borders, keeping to themselves and troubling no one.

The latest reports, then, had caused urgent speculation. Violent confrontations between Krai royalty and ensuing civil war went against their most sanctified traditions, the very core of their social structure and constitution. What could have brought about such upheaval? The reports of the marching Krai army sent nervous tremors across the continent. King Leth had immediately charged his Lord High Invigilate, Fectur, with the task of gathering intelligence as a matter of utmost priority.

It had been spring when Leth was crowned. The days passed, drawing into a hot, sultry summer. Leth thought often about Orbus, wondering in what manner his summons might come. He examined the blue casket frequently, hoping to find it unsealed, thinking he might somehow have missed its strange inhabitant's call. But always it was the same: the casket was sealed fast. Little by little, with so many other concerns to occupy him, Leth had found Orbus less frequently occupying his thoughts.

The Far Flame, one of Enchantment's Edge's dominant factions, introduced a motion for the reversal of King Haruman's Deist Edict. Leth was aware that, to a great extent, this was a means of putting his new kingship to the test. The leaders of the Far Flame were not so naive as to imagine they could gain a full reversal – the Deist Edict had become fundamental to social order throughout Enchantment's Edge. Nonetheless, they might be expecting concessions or backsteps on certain clauses, none of which Leth would have been happy to give.

It was an important issue which required delicate and precise handling. Inter-factional disputes had been largely put aside during its debate, so that the Far Flame came to the table with the active support of many of the other sects and factions. It was, in effect, a majority assault upon Leth's government.

After consideration and counsel King Leth had resolved to deal decisively and summarily with the issue. In consideration of this he passed instructions to senior officers of the militia and security cadre to put city troops on high alert, ready to quell instantly any unrest that might follow as a consequence.

King Haruman had instigated the Deist Edict almost two centuries earlier. At that time the throne had come under unprecedented threat from internal forces, namely the most powerful of the factions and sects. Worship of the various gods of Enchantment had reached an alarming level. The factions, vigorously promoting the supposed desires and objectives of their individual deities, exerted an ever greater influence over the populace. Intolerance and fanaticism were growing, widening divisions fragmenting the greater community, and civil unrest reached dangerous levels. King Haruman faced a growing instability which, if not curbed, threatened the Crown itself.

Haruman therefore decreed an absolute ban upon the worship of specific deities, namely those believed to dwell within Enchantment. Construction of temples and shrines and other places of worship was prohibited; those already in place were torn down. Lodges were permitted, but no sect or faction might conduct ceremonies or publish notices or pamphlets which encouraged worship of one or more of the gods.

This was not achieved without serious dissent. The government was gravely split and for a while Haruman had faced rebellion within the army. There were riots in the streets and bloody clashes with the sects. But the King held fast, addressing massed crowds in person, sending out dozens of official emissaries and posting notices around the great city-castle and in outlying towns and villages ever exhorting the people to understand what damage such worship had caused and threatened to cause in the future. And he established the Arcane College, a sacred centre for study in matters both spiritual and mundane, devoted to the unbiased search for knowledge, truth, understanding and wisdom.

The Arcane College existed in mutual exclusion to the sects and factions. No member of the College might be simultaneously a member of any sect. The most brilliant minds from Enchantment's Edge and beyond were encouraged to take up lodging in the capital and take advantage of the unique research and teaching facilities the Arcane College offered.

Haruman won the day eventually, though not without the imprisonment and execution of several militant faction heads. He had halved the power of the factions, and the gods of Enchantment – or their self-styled ambassadors, at least – lost their stranglehold upon Enchantment's Edge.

Haruman received dire warnings that his insult would surely bring down the wrath of the gods. His successors received similar predictions and every monarch since his time had had to contend with his legacy. Every ill that beset Enchantment's Edge, large or small, was ascribed to godly vengeance. But the Deist Edict remained in force despite many attempts to have it repealed. Now, at a time when faction-based influence over the populace was greater than at any time since Haruman's day, it was King Leth's turn to defend it.

Fittingly, Leth had chosen to meet with the leaders of the Far Flame in Haruman's Hall of Wise Counsel. He was accompanied by his closest advisors, Lord Fectur and Pader Luminis among them. With the Far Flame were high-ranking representatives of other factions: Astress, Vestal Guardian of the Children of Ushcopthe; Chandiston, the obstreperous High-Secretary of the Mark of the Golden Thought; Grey Venger of the True Sept, and others. It was an ominous development.

Edric, Deacon of the Far Flame, put forward his case in an accusing tone, stressing that he spoke for all gathered before the King. His line followed more or less the expected pattern: the Deist Edict was an example of unlawful legislation by the Crown against the populace; a ban on religious worship was a ban on individual freedom, a sure mark of repression; the people should have the right to worship whensoever and howsoever they chose; to deny the gods their due obeisances was to invite their retaliation; the illustrious King Haruman, for all his many virtues, had yet been short-sighted when instituting the Edict, failing to take into account the possible long-term consequences. And so on.

When all had been said, King Leth had waited thoughtfully for a short while. Then he stood and delivered his reply evenly. 'When my great ancestor King Haruman instituted the Deist Edict it was not to oppress or restrict the citizens of Enchantment's Edge. It was to free them. It was not to bring down the wrath of the Higher Ones upon us. It was to free us of them also. Haruman perceived that the forms the many religions had taken were based almost purely on fallacies, misplaced ideas, unfounded notions of what the unknown gods of Enchantment might be. He saw that religion had become, not a genuine source of succour and hope, but a means of manipulating and enslaving minds. A power base from which unscrupulous persons might grow wealthy and powerful while disrupting society to their own ends and undermining the power of the throne. You, my honourable, loyal subjects, are, I know, sincere in your aims and would actively revile such practices.'

He paused a moment to let his words sink in. Ecric spoke up. 'Your Majesty, King Haruman denied the gods on the basis that their existence could not be proven. We disagree. The gods are known and must be openly acknowledged.'

King Leth had shaken his head. 'King Haruman denied the practices that had burgeoned in the names of the Higher Ones. He did so on the grounds that it was demonstrably *human* will that was at work, not the will of deities. He did not deny the gods, he denied that we have reliable knowledge of them. Lest you have forgotten, let me quote my illustrious ancestor.' He waited, gathering his thoughts, disregarding the indignation on the faces before him. Then, in sure and fluent tones, he delivered the famous speech given by King Haruman upon the introduction of the Deist Edict: '*"If religion entails the substitution of blind belief in the place of a genuine search for truth and understanding; if religion insists upon attributing to forces of which we know almost nothing the qualities, attributes, desires and predilections that are our own; if religion will knowingly permit peoples to take up arms in the name of a deity of whom it can have no direct knowledge; if religion will give form and voice to a deity or deities, in ignorance of the deity's true nature; if religion will do any or all of these things, then let us have nothing of religion. It can only do us harm, swamping us in a murky sea of ignorance when we would fain travel widely in the clear light skies of Truth, Knowledge and Wisdom*'.

With that King Leth had added pointedly, 'Your request for a revision of the Deist Edict is denied. I thank you for coming here today and making your views known. Lesser petitions may be left with my advisors. They will be given full consideration and my judgement delivered to you in due course.'

He had turned to leave the Hall. A voice, harsh and raised in anger, rang out. 'You are a fool, King Leth!'

Leth swung around, found his accuser. It was Grey Venger, the man who would later attempt to assassinate him. There was stunned silence in the Hall, that anyone should have dared speak so to the King! Venger's face was darkly set. 'The gods are known. They are preparing even now. You will see proof soon enough, when they are ready.'

Leth did not flinch. 'If that is so, Master Venger, then that will perhaps be the time to look again at the Deist Edict. But it will never be said of me that I encouraged my people to embrace ignorance, nor pandered to those who would use it for their own unprincipled ends.'

He had then departed Haruman's Hall of Wise Counsel, allowing the unsettled factional leaders no further response.

Leth had been tired after that. It had taken great effort to face so many and not give way. And throughout a single thought had plagued him, as it had plagued him a thousand times before: *am I right?*

Had Haruman been right to ban the worship of specific gods? Was it possible that the factions, one or more of them, had an answer to the unknown? Everything rebelled against that: the Masters of the Arcane College, dedicated to the search for knowledge, insisted that genuine experience of the gods, their personalities, desires, objectives, had never been achieved. Knowledge had never been brought out of Enchantment – it and its inhabitants remained an awesome mystery.

But could he, Leth, be absolutely sure?

Grey Venger's outburst had nettled him. Venger was so sure of himself. They all were. They always had been. In many ways little had changed. Leth knew that they still adhered to their forms of worship, only since Haruman's time they had done it in darkened corners rather than open plazas or public temples. To survive they had become ever more secretive. In many ways that made them more dangerous.

In a sunlit courtyard Leth had spotted his children, Prince Galry and Princess Jace at play, a nanny in attendance. He had watched from a gallery for some time, taking pleasure in the sight of them, then descended to join them. Issul arrived just moments later and the four had spent the remainder of the afternoon together. It had been a welcome respite, one of the few periods they had passed together as a family for any length of time. And when, much later, Leth had taken Issul to their bed, they had made love with a passion and tenderness that they had hardly known since the earliest days of their marriage.

And that night Leth had woken from a dream. He had seen the blue casket, upon his desk, and a voice had commanded: 'Come now. It is time.'

Leth did not doubt that it was Orbus's promised summons. He had slipped quietly from the bed and gone straightway to his study. There he took the casket from its cavity and found its hasp free.

Orbus was waiting for him when he arrived. He was seated cross-legged upon the floor, his staff laid across his knees. 'Be seated. I have been awaiting you.'

Leth did as he was bidden, lowering himself to the floor opposite the strange figure. He was still unable to make out Orbus's face for the bundled rags that swathed it.

'I am going to impart a message,' said Orbus. 'I wish to tell you something of those whom you call gods.'

'The Higher Ones? The gods of Enchantment?' Leth was deeply intrigued. 'Do you know something of them?'

Orbus rocked slightly as if with dry, silent laughter. 'Ah Leth, King Leth, you are but a child. Know something of them? Ha ha! Of course I do. Of course. But remember, keep this always to yourself. What I am about to say is but a beginning. There will be no more if you speak of it to another. There will be other consequences, too. Others may judge you mad. Even worse, they may take you seriously.'

'That is worse?'

'They would demand proof. How could you convince them? Would you reveal the source of your wisdom? Do so and you would be rendered powerless, for they would seek access to your source by any means. And you would lose me also, of that I can assure you. It would be a loss greater than you can calculate.'

'I will say nothing. But I am confused. You speak of secret knowledge, with the implication that you are possessed of fabulous powers.'

'Believe it.'

'Then why are you here, in this place?'

'Is my being here with you not ample demonstration that I possess such powers?'

'It is, but—'

'In time you may learn more. But not yet.'

'How extensive is your knowledge of us and our world?'

'Far more extensive than your own.' Orbus had given a muffled chuckle. 'Ah, Leth, Leth. Always so many questions. I tell you I am about to impart something of value to you and you do not pause to listen. Instead you demand to know something else. Ah, what should I do with you?'

'Then speak,' said the King, testily.

Orbus settled into silence. They sat warily observing one another, and Leth, sensing that this was deliberate, said nothing. His impatience grew. At length Orbus spoke again.

'Those you call gods are not gods. Not in the true sense.'

'Then what are they?

'Listen! You may consider them gods, for in comparison to you they are mighty beyond calculation. They could wipe you from the face of this world, any one of them, upon a whim. They are truly awesome. But in truth they know little more of the world than do you.'

'We believe that they war with one another constantly, throughout eons.'

'They can do nothing else. They must fight to survive. That is something fundamental to their very being, but even they do not truly understand it. Warfare, as they wage it, creates. That also applies to you almost as much as to them. It is a difficult concept to comprehend, but it is true, nonetheless. And in the case of those you term gods, it is elemental.'

'Are you inciting me to war?'

'Not if it can be avoided, no. Absolutely not.'

'Then . . . what?'

'I have said, the concept is not easily grasped. You should dwell upon it. At a future time we will discuss it further. Consider carefully what I have given you now. Until the next time.'

'*No!*'

Orbus had raised his staff.

'*No!*'

Leth was back at his desk, his head spinning slightly. '*No! No!*' He brought his fist down hard upon the desk, so furious was he at such a peremptory dismissal. '*Orbus!*'

He thrust himself back in his chair, glaring at the casket and muttering futile curses.

A curious thought had stuck him later as, the worst of his anger past, he had made his way back to his bedchamber. He wondered that Orbus had chosen today of all days to speak of the nature of Enchantment's gods, when Leth had only just met with the Far Flame and the other heads.

Did it mean that Orbus was aware of all that went on within Enchantment's Edge?

Time would pass and many changes come about before King Leth learned the full answer to that.

FIVE

I

On that grey, sombre morning when Anzejarl, Prince of the Krai, executed plans for his immediate invasion of Enchantment's Edge, Queen Issul descended to her breakfast room with her children Prince Galry and Princess Jace. Her mind was troubled, though she was careful to maintain a mood of levity before the children. She played with them and told them stories, aware that in a very short time she would be obliged to leave them. This time it would be for days rather than hours. She had made arrangements for an armed escort to accompany her to the village of Lastmeadow.

King Leth had already gone about his duties. They had spent a mere few moments in a lingering embrace before going to the nursery. Leth had amused the children, and himself, for as long as he was able. They rode upon his back with yells of delight, clambered upon his shoulders, begged to be chased and tickled, then cried out for him to cease. But all too soon he had to depart. Issul failed to tell him of her imminent journey. To do so would invite too many awkward questions, and she was afraid that he might well forbid her to go or at least insist upon a larger escort, something she was determined to avoid.

She had watched him carefully that morning. In the early light she had seen no trace of the blue aura of the night before. It had perhaps dispersed, or was simply too faint to be discerned in daylight. Issul had wanted to ask him about it, but she refrained. She could not tell whether he was aware of it but she accepted now that he must be involved in private research of some kind, and would not welcome her enquiries.

Again it struck her that they were keeping secrets from one

another. She pledged to herself that at the earliest opportunity, as soon as she *knew*, she would tell Leth all. With that promise the urgency grew upon her to be away to Lastmeadow.

Little Lir, the infant daughter of Duke Hugo and Duchess Demawndella, had also come to the breakfast room, brought by her nanny. Hugo was now in conference with Leth, but of Mawnie there was no sign. From her enquiries Issul gathered that she had not been seen since the previous day. She, Issul, was one of the last persons to have seen Mawnie, when they had been together in the afternoon.

Issul watched her children, Galry, now aged six, was growing into a tall, well-proportioned lad, robust of build and confident of manner. Bursting with energy, he rarely sat still. This morning he was impatient for the arrival of his arms tutor, Master Meles, with whom he was to have his daily lesson in sword combat. Jace, on the other hand, though energetic, was quieter and showed an inclination towards more scholarly pursuits. Slender, graceful and fair, she resembled her mother in appearance and character.

Their cousin, little Lir, was barely toddling. She was a fey, elfin-faced girl, rather saturnine and given to bursts of temper. She had deep, darkly-lashed green eyes and her small head was crowned with a shock of dense black curls.

Issul held Lir for a short time on her lap, but the child was not inclined to company of any kind. Within moments she had wriggled free of her aunt and taken refuge beneath the table. There she sat, quietly observing all, making not a sound.

Breakfast was done and Issul was regretfully taking leave of her children and niece when a steward entered and approached her. 'Master Briano requests an urgent word, Ma'am. He is outside.'

Briano was Mawnie's head valet. Issul gave word for him to be shown in as the children and nannies left. He entered briskly, a small, neat, worried-faced man with a thin rouged moustache and a puff of dyed orange hair. He performed a low bow, his heels together and spine perfectly straight. 'My Lady, it is the Duchess. I think you should come.'

'Demawndella? What has happened? Is something wrong?' Issul felt herself tense.

Master Briano rolled his eyes nervously. 'My Lady, I think it is better if you allow me to show you.'

Issul followed him through the passages of the royal dwellings to the apartments occupied by the Duke and Duchess of Giswel. Twitching with embarrassment Master Briano stood before an unlocked door. With a pained grimace he placed one hand over his eyes and pushed the door open, showing her into the chamber beyond. There she found Mawnie.

At first Issul thought her sister was soused. She stood for a moment, horrified at the sight. Mawnie lay on her back upon a long table. She was half-naked, draped in loose strips of cloth, apparently the torn remains of a gown she had been wearing earlier. Her breasts and one leg were exposed. Her long pale brown hair was free and utterly dishevelled, her face smudged and stained with kohl and rouge. Her limbs asplay, she writhed upon the table as if with ecstasy or great pain. And she called out in a thin, high voice. 'Oh, it is me! I know now. It is me! In the woods! In the woods!'

'Mawnie!'

Issul rushed forward. Mawnie, vaguely aware of her voice, raised her head shakily. Her glaring eyes settled upon Master Briano who hovered at the door, his fingers a gate before his eyes. With an indignant shriek she reached for a solid gold candlestick which lay toppled on the table beside her. She hurled it at him with all the force she could muster. 'Out! Hound! Low imbecile! Out! Out! Out!'

Master Briano, dancing aside to avoid the missile, threw a terrified glance at Queen Issul. But her back was to him. With a whimper, fluttering his hands in distress, he fled the chamber, pulling the door closed behind him.

'Mawnie, oh Mawnie, what has happened to you?'

Mawnie raised herself sluggishly onto her elbows and stared blearily at her sister, then let her head tip back and laughed out loud. Issul took a cover from a nearby divan and quickly wrapped it around Mawnie's bare shoulders.

'I understand it all now,' Mawnie cried. 'It has all become clear. Now I know everything. It was me. Truly. It was me he wanted. In the woods. In the woods.'

Tears streaked her cheeks. She stared defiantly and imploringly at her sister. Issul held her tight. 'Mawnie, Mawnie. It's all right now. I am here. I will look after you.'

Mawnie cackled. 'Piss upon them all! But I know! I remember now! I know what they wanted. And it was me, all the time. Not Mawnie. Oh no, not Mawnie. It was me!' She suddenly gripped

Issul's arms and squeezed ferociously, her eyes shining. 'Do you see, Iss? It was me, after all. It was me!'

Gradually Issul coaxed her sister from the table and began to steer her from the chamber. In the corridor outside a small knot of servants and palace staff had gathered.

'Away!' Issul fumed. 'To your duties, all of you! Immediately!'

They dispersed hurriedly. Suddenly Mawnie shrank back, covering her head with her hands. 'No! No! Get away!' She lashed out blindly, striking the air, shrieking. 'Get away! Don't! Don't let him!'

'Mawnie!' Issul grasped her wrists. 'Mawnie!'

Her sister continued to struggle. Issul released one wrist and slapped her hard across the cheek. Mawnie ceased her babble and became still. She glared at Issul for a moment then went limp. Her shoulders sagged and she began to sob pathetically.

Issul again took her in her arms and resumed guiding her to her bedchamber. As they entered, the royal physician, Doctor Melropius, arrived, having been summoned by a worried servant. He quickly took charge, manoeuvring poor Mawnie to her bed, then examining her as she lay slackly compliant. She no longer sobbed or babbled, though an occasional spasmodic smile or grimace passed across her pallid face. She seemed largely unaware of her surroundings or company.

'What has happened to her, Doctor?' Asked Issul anxiously when Melropius was done.

'I cannot say with certainty. She is hot – it is perhaps a sudden fever or emotional flux. I smell no spirits on her breath, though she may have ingested something that has affected her mind. I have a potion to help her sleep. With luck she will have recovered by the time she awakens.'

'Do your absolute best.'

'I will station a nurse here in the bedchamber, and will check upon her in person every hour.'

Issul moved to her sister's bedside and took her hand. Mawnie's eyes were open but she seemed unconscious and made no response when Issul spoke to her. A servant brought a chair for Issul and she remained there until Mawnie slept.

II

The sun was well past the midpoint of its ascent and had begun to burn through the heavy morning overcast when Queen Issul eventually departed the palace of Orbia and the great city-castle of Enchantment's Edge. A brisk wind was rising, furthermore, and beginning to dispel the cloud.

Issul had wondered about delaying her departure further, for Mawnie still slept deeply and she was concerned. But it was Doctor Melropius's opinion that Mawnie would not wake for some hours, perhaps even a day. When she did there would be no guarantee she would be lucid. He had promised to maintain a constant watch on her and assured Issul of his very best attention. Issul therefore made the decision to go, fearful that events in Lastmeadow and beyond might overtake her if she did not act quickly.

She had sought out Galry and Jace and explained to them that she would be absent for a few days. She had presented each with a gift – a woollen jerkin for Galry, a lace bonnet for Jace – then hugged them and left, her head bowed to conceal reddened eyes. In her apartment she removed all traces of royal garb and finery and changed into light leather riding gear. Around her waist she strapped a wide leather belt holding smallsword, dagger and several throwing darts, then threw about her shoulders the same damask cape she had worn when interviewing the peasant woman, Ohirbe.

Issul rode upon her favourite mount, a strong grey gelding which she had reared from birth. She was escorted by an eight-strong squad of mounted soldiers, members of Lord Fectur's élite. They were loyal and resourceful fighters all, though Issul had at times wondered whether such men, put to the test, would prove more loyal to Fectur himself than to the Crown. She prayed that test would never come.

Fectur had wanted a significantly larger escort, a minimum of twenty, but Issul flatly refused.

'Eight is quite sufficient to deal with any difficulties we are likely to meet. More will be cumbersome and will invite unwanted attention. Remember I am not the Queen, simply an anonymous lady of some distinction. It must remain so.'

Fectur eventually conceded, though he was inflexible on the matter of uniforms and insignia, which were prominently displayed, identifying the party as both hailing out of Orbia and being under the aegis of the Lord High Invigilate. Issul argued for complete anonymity, but Fectur was not to be budged. 'No brigand band, no matter how ruthless or opportunistic, will willingly harass a party that bears my emblem.'

His tone conveyed the meaning he intended: the sign of the Spectre carried as much weight as, and even more than, that of the royal palace itself.

Fectur was burning with curiosity, seeking insistently to get Issul to divulge the precise purpose of her journey.

'You may know soon enough, my lord,' Issul said. 'But it is a private matter, perhaps too trivial to warrant your attention at all. I thank you for your dutiful concern. Upon my return your men will certainly apprise you of all that transpires.'

'Indeed so, but can it truly be so trivial? My instincts suggest not. Since the unusual events of yesterday I cannot help but think that there is something afoot of which I ought really to be informed.'

'You *are* informed, my lord,' replied Issul sharply. 'You were informed yesterday when the woman Ohirbe brought the pendant to you, in accordance with my instructions. You were informed when I visited Overlip, and were effective in providing protection, for which I thank you. And you are informed now and, in accordance with your position, have taken all correct and proper measures to ensure my safety.'

'But there are details,' persisted Fectur itchingly. 'Yesterday you openly consorted with known criminals, or the associates of known criminals. Why?'

'"*Openly*". You have said it, Lord Fectur. My movements have been within your full purview. They continue to be so.'

'The purpose behind them nevertheless remains a mystery.'

'I am the Queen, sir,' replied Issul firmly.

Lord Fectur lowered his gaze briefly, but there was a sour twist to his mouth.

'I have consulted with the King,' Issul continued. 'You, my lord, are performing your duties admirably, in full accordance with your station. Should I or my husband deem it necessary to inform you more fully on any matter, we will summon you.'

Lord Fectur compressed his lips, absorbing her pointed reminder that, for all his power, he remained her servant. 'My position as Lord High Invigilate and Master of Security empowers me to act at all times in the interest of the Crown and State. Fearing for your safety I would be perfectly within my rights to prevent you leaving until I have better—'

Issul flashed him a fiery glare. 'Try it!'

She saw the satisfaction in his eyes, the barely visible twitch of a smile, and fought back her anger. 'Lord Fectur, any delay in my departure may engender significant and perhaps highly damaging consequences which I am not presently willing to discuss with you, largely because I am unclear myself. But the price could be high for anyone seen to contribute to those consequences, even inadvertently, no matter their station.'

She pushed by him and climbed upon her mount, directly challenging him. Fectur stepped back a small pace: she noted this, an unwitting sign of acquiescence.

'You have consulted the King? I take it he is in favour of your journey?'

'The King trusts my judgement.'

She jerked the rein, directing her horse towards the high arch leading from the court in which they waited. She kept her eyes dead ahead, seething and concerned yet that he might try something. Then she heard the *clop* of hooves at her side and knew that Lord Fectur had signalled his men forward. Warm relief flooded through her; she exhaled a tense breath and allowed herself a small, stiff smile.

As she took her leave of the palace of Orbia, Issul did not look back. She was afraid she might not bear it. The myriad towers soaring over her head, the coloured halls, the spacious apartments, magnificent gardens . . . this was her home. She was leaving it and its security, her family and friends, everything she held dear. For just a short time, yes, but the more she thought about the venture she was embarking upon the more she was aware of her growing uncertainty and fear.

Its outcome was a complete unknown, carrying a threat to the very foundations of her world.

Issul realized, as her horse bore her slowly away, just how much she loved Orbia and all that it represented. She was fortunate, blessed even. She had everything here, had never known poverty or need, had never had to face the privations that were the daily lot of so many. She worked diligently and hard for her people, but she was Queen, remote from the everyday harshnesses and sometimes cruel and unpredictable vagaries of life beyond the walls of Enchantment's Edge. That which dwelt virtually upon the doorsteps of common folk was, to her, barely known.

They passed through the chill streets of the city-castle, exciting little attention. Issul kept her hood up and her gaze low, not wanting to be recognized. They came to the massive barbican and the huge arched gate which let out from the city. Issul felt the wind suddenly stronger against her as they passed beneath the arch and stepped onto the wide causeway which ran for more than a league, almost straight along the ridge of the escarpment. She shivered slightly and gazed out across the far distance. Moving cloud still blanketed much of the great forest below and concealed the remote peaks of Enchantment, so that it seemed she rested upon an island floating in a billowing, endless grey nothing.

Eventually the causeway dipped and they began the long descent via gentle traverses towards the low forest lands. Though the chill cloud remained, visibility was good for fifty paces or more, and the further they descended the more it dispersed. At last they emerged beneath it and found the forest laid before them. Issul looked up and saw blue sky through breaks in the racing cloud.

The commander of her escort, a thickset young knight named Sir Bandullo, brought his horse to trot beside her. 'I anticipate reaching Lastmeadow sometime tomorrow morning, Majesty. I propose resting tonight in the township of Crosswood, which we will reach well before dark.'

Issul nodded. 'Very good. Sir Bandullo, are all your men aware of my identity?'

'Yes, Majesty.'

'Then please instruct them that I am to be addressed as Ma'am. At no time during this journey is my identity to be disclosed by any means. This applies to you, too. Is that understood?'

'Perfectly, Ma'am.'

They rode on, reaching the foot of the scarp and pushing on to the forest road. They passed few travellers: an occasional peasant or labourer; traders or pilgrims making for the city-castle; a solitary wanderer or group of three or four, usually young men, probably bound for enlistment in Leth's army. Later, they would encounter other folk, fleeing the southern towns and villages threatened by the Krai. The forest grew dense around them.

A little further on the leading trooper brought his mount to a halt and pointed skywards. Issul looked up. Far overhead, through a gap in the clouds, huge, ungainly birds could be seen flying north-westwards. They were twenty or so in number and flying too high for any detail to be described. But their shape was unfamiliar to Issul's eyes, and they seemed heavier than any bird she knew.

'What are they?' she asked Sir Bandullo.

The soldier shook his head, one hand shielding his eyes. 'I cannot say. Can they be eagles?'

Issul thought not. The body was too long for any species of eagle she knew. And though it was difficult to see from so far below, the wings seemed of a different shape to eagles'. They looked to be scalloped, resembling more the wings of huge bats than those of birds.

They vanished into a patch of cloud, then reappeared. Sir Bandullo spoke to one of his men. 'Mordon, can you bring one down with a bolt?'

'At this distance?' The man shook his head. 'Impossible. See how they are buffeted by the wind. They climb, they pitch, they roll, all involuntarily. I can assess no path, and my bolt would fly wild once it cleared the treetops.'

The dark flyers laboured on against the unpredictable wind. Issul thought for a moment that she heard a faint harsh cry borne to her through the air. She shivered. The strange birds disappeared again into denser cloud.

'They are going back along the way we came. Towards Enchantment's Edge.'

'Aye.' Sir Bandullo's face was set.

Issul watched the sky a few moments longer, but nothing more was seen.

'On!' Issul urged her mount into a trot. The others moved quickly to take up formation.

At the little market-township of Crosswood, set on an intersection of three ways, Issul and her troop took lodging at an inn called the Green Ram. Issul took a reasonably well-appointed chamber – the best the landlord had to offer – and ate alone. By Sir Bandullo's reckoning Lastmeadow lay barely more than two hours' ride away.

But darkness was closing in and Issul would not risk further travel before morning. She made arrangements for a dawn departure, and retired for the night.

In bed, sinking towards sleep, it came to her for the first time that, now she was so close, she had no clear idea of what she was going to do once she reached the village.

III

Whatever decision she made today would shape the future immutably.

Issul awoke suddenly, drenched in sweat. Morning light was squeezing in through the chinks in the shutters of her chamber window. Her dreams had been haunted: everywhere there was the image of her dead sister, always she was just out of reach.

Oh Ressa, Ressa. Why did this happen to you? To us? Why?

Issul dragged herself from her bed. Her limbs were trembling. She wanted to weep for the sister she had lost and for the weight that now lay upon her. She began to wash. A single thought resounded remorselessly in her head.

Ressa had given birth to the child of a god.

Issul could not doubt that now. But what did it mean? And what was she to do about it?

It is not yet proven, she reminded herself. She had that to clutch at, but it was, truly, only the slenderest of straws.

Grey Venger, speak up now! Tell us what we need to know, if you truly know it! If you fail us we are lost.

But how could she ask favours of her enemy, the man who had tried to murder her husband, whose sons Leth had executed? Venger's heart surely burned with insane rancour now, with a bitter and irreconcilable hatred for her and all she represented. Was the fact that she might be delivering to him the Legendary Child, whose birth the True Sept had predicted for so long, enough to bring him from hiding?

If it did, would it change anything?

Hate us or not, we need you now, Grey Venger. And if we can bring you the Child, surely you must reconsider?

But what did the True Sept really know?

Issul dressed and readied herself for the journey ahead. She had little appetite but she forced down some warm rye bread and posset, keeping to herself again in the bedchamber. And all the time, without mercy, the soul-numbing thought came around and around:

My sister gave birth to the child of a god!

A blustering wind had persisted during the night, sweeping away the remaining cloud so that the day dawned sunny, cool and bright. The dense trees swayed and shivered, then grew still, then whispered, then roared as Issul and the eight members of the Spectre's élite rode out of Crosswood.

The road, hardly more than a rutted grass track laid in places with brash and wood chips, climbed and dipped through the deep forest. The wind whipped and died, whipped and died, flinging leaves from the trees, hammering grass and bushes almost flat. The daylight dimmed as they progressed further, the trees more ancient and vast, overshadowing the way. Presently they came upon a fork in the track, a barely noticeable path leading off to one side. This they took. In due course, rounding the shoulder of a high limestone bluff, Issul found herself looking down into a large clearing in a shallow depression. Rude cottages, farmhouses and outbuildings huddled at its centre, small meadows, orchards and paddocks behind. This was the village of Lastmeadow.

They descended, and in the village came across a peasant girl drawing water from a well. Sir Bandullo asked directions to the home of Ohirbe and Arrin, to which the girl replied in awed tones. They doubled back, following her instructions. A scattering of folk appeared nervously at doors and windows to watch them as they passed. They arrived at a small thatched cottage beside an orchard of apple trees. As they drew up at its little garden gate a man emerged from within, clad in padded leather, a sword at his belt. Seeing Sir Bandullo, he stiffened and saluted. Bandullo acknowledged him with a nod. 'Has there been anything to report?'

'Some talk of an old woman hanging about the village, sir. She was seen a couple of days ago. We've seen nothing.'

Sir Bandullo turned to the Queen. 'Do you wish to enter, Ma'am.'

Issul climbed from her horse and strode up the little path to the front door of the cottage. The soldier pushed open the door for her. She stepped into a dim smoky parlour with an old grey table and chairs at one end. Cedar beams crossed the ceiling. A fire burned in a small hearth and the smell of stew came from an iron pot suspended above the flames. Beside a window stood another of Fectur's men, a crossbow dangling loosely in one hand.

Ohirbe came tentatively from behind a partition formed of faded and threadbare green linen thrown across a piece of cord which was nailed at either end to beams on each side of the room. Seeing Issul, her hands began to dart and dive about her like frightened rabbits.

'Oh Mistress, I didn't know you was comin' so soon. I 'aven't 'ad time to be— Oh, I'm so sorry.' Her cheeks flushed and tears started suddenly to her eyes.

'Relax, Ohirbe. You have nothing to apologize for. I was not expecting any kind of reception. Moscul is here, isn't he?'

'Oh yes, Mistress. He's here all right.' Ohirbe stepped back and gestured nervously behind the linen screen.

Issul's eyes passed around the room. The floor she stood on was straw-strewn dirt; the walls were decaying mortar and stone. Furniture was the simplest imaginable. Everything in sight served a basic function, a basic need; there was no embellishment or ornamentation.

She could have eased the harshness of these people's lives many times over, she realized. She had passed money to Ohirbe from time to time, but the amount had been purposefully minimal. It had been purely to ensure that they did not starve and would be able to attend to the welfare of their young charge.

I should have done more!

But she could not have. Anything more, the least indication, would have singled them out in the village. And from the first day that Ohirbe had taken charge of the baby she named Moscul, it had been imperative to preserve his anonymity. He was to be raised like any other child in the village, giving no one any reason to enquire into his origins.

But Issul was taken aback as she faced the scope of their poverty. She had known they were peasants, but she saw now that she had no true understanding of what that meant. She had not expected this.

Ohirbe nervously twisted her apron in chapped, calloused hands.

'It's not much, Mistress, but we've always done the best we can for the little one. He never went wantin', truly.'

'No, Ohirbe, please, do not misinterpret my look. I merely, I mean, I did not know—' She stopped, deeply ashamed, aware that she was insulting these people.

'We're dignified folk, no matter that we lack finery,' said Ohirbe. 'That's worth more than gold, that is.'

Issul's cheeks burned. She stumbled over her words. 'Ohirbe, you have done a greater service than you know. For that I am very grateful. I always shall be.'

'Did you want to see the little one now, Mistress?'

Issul gave a tense nod. She turned to the two soldiers. 'Wait outside. Is there another of you?'

'Out back, Ma'am,' replied the man who had shown her in.

'Have him remain there until I give further instructions.'

The two bowed their heads and withdrew smartly. Ohirbe, though still too nervous to look Issul in the face, nevertheless could not keep her eyes off her. Clearly she wondered at the status of this young woman who commanded palace troops with such assurance. She took a step back and gestured again to the other side of the screen. ''Ere 'e is, Mistress, 'ere's the little one.'

Issul swallowed, her throat dry. She closed her eyes for a moment and took a long breath, then slowly stepped around the screen.

The child sat alone upon the floor, cross-legged, his spine quite erect, small hands resting limply in his lap. He was garbed in a short grey smock and breeches, in noticeably better repair than anything Ohirbe wore. He was of solid build with fine, intelligent, though not particularly attractive features. His skin was fair and blemish-free, his hair also fair, falling in loose clusters around his face. His eyes were an unusual dark violet in hue. His gaze met Issul's as she approached: it was unchildlike and strangely confident, as was his general demeanour.

'Hallo, Moscul,' said Issul, smiling. She lowered herself to her knees before him. 'It is good to see you. How are you? I have brought something for you.'

From within her cloak she produced a small package wrapped in cloth. She handed it to Moscul, who ignored it. His eyes never left her face.

'Take it, sweetie,' urged Ohirbe from behind Issul. 'Moscul, say thank you now. You know 'ow to say thank you.'

Still the child ignored the present, and his gaze was unwavering. Still smiling, Issul unwrapped the little package to reveal a wooden figurine, the image of a soldier, with jointed arms and legs. She held it up, marching it in the air before the child.

'This is for you.'

Still Moscul showed no interest. Issul gently laid the toy soldier upon his lap.

'Moscul!' Ohirbe scolded. 'That's no way to behave!'

'It's all right,' said Issul softly. 'He is bound to be unsure of me. He has never seen me before – at least, not since he was a tiny babe.' She settled back on her haunches. 'Moscul, I am—'

'I know who you are,' the child said quite suddenly. His words were clear and perfectly formed.

'You do?' Issul felt a nervous quiver low in her gut.

'Of course. I knew the moment you entered the room. You are my aunt. Issul. Aunt Issul.'

'That's right,' replied Issul, disquieted. His manner was challenging and more than precocious. His violet gaze still held her, his features remaining set. He spoke unnaturally well for a three-year-old. 'And how did you know that?'

The child gave a mocking shrug. 'I am not stupid, you know.'

'Moscul!' Ohirbe was beside herself with embarrassment. 'Don't you speak so! Oh Mistress, I'm so sorry. I don't know what's come over 'im. 'E's never spoken like that before, not to anyone.'

'Don't worry,' said Issul lifting a hand to calm her. She was in little doubt now; there was something about this child. Moscul returned her gaze. His eyes had never left her face. He had not blinked once.

'What's more, you are the Queen,' he said. 'Queen Issul, fair spouse of Leth, King of Enchantment's Edge.'

There was a great stuttering gasp from Ohirbe.

'It's true, isn't it?' declared Moscul. 'Tell her.'

Issul looked up at Ohirbe. The poor woman was white-faced and trembling, her hands to her mouth and pure terror in her eyes. Issul slowly stood. 'Yes, it is.'

At that Ohirbe gave a loud moan and fell to her knees, sobbing, her head bent almost to the floor. 'Oh Mistress, my lady, your 'ighness! Oh, forgive me, please! I didn't know! I didn't know! Oh, oh, oh!'

The poor woman swayed inconsolably from side to side, her

forehead brushing the floor. One hand clutched her middle, the other groped to touch Issul's feet.

'Ohirbe, please. This is not what I want.' Issul bent and took her arms. 'Get to your feet now. There is no need for this, nothing to apologize for. I am indebted to you, and to Arrin. Please, now, get up. We have to talk.'

There was a strange, high-pitched, staccato sound. Issul turned around to see Moscul, his shoulders hunched, giggling behind his hand. It was the first sign of childlike behaviour he had displayed in her presence. But his amusement at the distress of the woman who had loved him as her own child almost from his birth raised Issul's apprehension further. Moscul had actually engineered this circumstance, when he should not even have been capable of understanding it. Now he took joy at the result.

Ohirbe, shaking like a leaf, stood with her head bowed before the Queen. 'Is – is it true, Mistress? Are you truly the Queen?'

'I am. But—' Issul raised her voice as Ohirbe gave another stricken moan, '—don't be afraid, Ohirbe. I am proud of you. You have done me a great service and I shall see to it that you are well-rewarded.'

'I don't want no reward, Mistr—, High— oh, oh, I don't even know what to call you!'

'Ma'am is all that is necessary, Ohirbe. Now, please, be calm. We have to talk. Arrin too. Is he here?'

'Milkin' the cow.'

'Would you fetch him, please? And what of his cousin, the one who was with Moscul at the poolside, Julion, did you say? Where is he?'

'He lives across the other side of the village.'

'I will send for him. Will you fetch Arrin now?'

Ohirbe nodded and tottered away.

Issul glanced down at little Moscul. He had ceased giggling and was watching her closely again. How could he have known her? Even if he could somehow have gleaned clues which identified her as Queen – and she could not see how that was possible – even if he had done that, there was no person alive who knew that she was his aunt. No one even knew that he had been born to Ressa.

Issul felt chill fingers slip suddenly along her spine. She suppressed a shudder and went outside to order two of Sir Bandullo's troopers to find and bring Julion.

Back indoors she found Ohirbe returning with Arrin. The poor man, like his wife, was reduced to knock-kneed blithering and Issul had to calm him with a mixture of sympathy, support and firmness, while Moscul continued to giggle. Eventually Issul succeeded in getting the two of them seated with her at the table, each with a mug of tea made with crushed flowers of camomile. She proceeded to question them, aware that Moscul, silent now, was hanging on to every word.

She learned little of which she wasn't already aware. The old woman whom Julion had encountered originally at the pond, and whom Ohirbe had also seen later, had indeed been spotted about the village. Since Ohirbe's return with Fectur's three-strong escort late the previous day, there had been no sign of her, and she had not approached Moscul during Ohirbe's absence.

Julion arrived. He was a gangling-fellow, older than Arrin and Ohirbe. He responded to Issul's presence with near-terror, but was eventually able to speak to her.

'I want you to tell me about the day beside the Old Pond, Julion. You saw two people, Ohirbe tells me. An elderly woman and a young man. You then left with the young man.'

'That's so, Ma'am.'

'Can you tell me about them?'

'What's to tell? I thought they were together. Turned out not.'

'You walked with the young man?'

'Just a ways, to the main path.' Julion gave a bashful chuckle. ''E thought she was with me, y'know. Thought we were Moscul's granfolk.'

'When you put him right, did he seem surprised? Did he make any comment?'

'Surprised, aye. So was I. We laughed at it, 'cos 'e'd taken 'er to be with me and I'd taken 'er to be with 'im.'

'It didn't strike you as odd?'

'By that time, Ma'am, it was too late to be doin' anythin' about it. We were close to the path and 'e went on 'is way. I weren't goin' to go back to the Old Pond.'

Issul frowned. 'But if they weren't together, what were they both doing there?'

''E said 'e'd been lost. 'E came out of the forest and found 'er with Moscul.'

'She was actually with Moscul?'

'So 'e said. Right by the waterside.'

Issul put a hand to her forehead. *What had happened there? Or almost happened?*

Julion said, 'If it's any 'elp, Ma'am, 'e did give me 'is name.'

'Really?' Issul turned to Ohirbe. 'You didn't tell me this.'

'I didn't know, Ma'am. Julion, you never told us that before.'

'I forgot.'

'Then what was his name?' asked Issul.

Julion screwed up his face in deepest concentration. 'Sherwal, or Shunwild. Something like that. I don't remember rightly.'

'Think! It's important!' Issul could barely remain seated. 'Please, try to remember.'

'I 'ardly 'eard it, Ma'am. It wasn't a common name, 'n at the time it didn't strike me to take that much notice.'

Issul gave a sigh, 'Well, if it comes to you, be sure to let me know. Is there anything else you can tell me? Anything at all?'

Julion rolled his eyes and shifted nervously on his seat. He had begun almost to relax into the interview, but now seemed suddenly very ill at ease again. He hunched forward; his eyes went half to the window, then nervously back. He shook his head. 'No, Nothin'.'

Issul regarded him for some time. 'Well, again, if anything comes to mind, anything at all, tell me immediately, will you? The tiniest detail may be important.'

A scuffling sound caused Issul to look around. Moscul was striking his heels back and forth across the floor. He smirked at her. She looked back at Julion, who regarded the tabletop.

Issul questioned the three once again, covering everything she had been over before, hoping that some forgotten detail might reveal itself. But she learned nothing.

Leaving the table, she stepped outside for some air, wanting to take a few moments to gather her thoughts. Sir Bandullo's men still waited beside the path, their mounts tethered nearby. The two soldiers who had been inside the cottage upon her arrival were beside the fence. The third, who was with them as she stepped out, turned away to gaze towards the village, scratching his cheek with one hand.

Issul stretched and breathed deeply. She looked back at the men, particularly at the third soldier. Something in his manner struck her as odd. She began to walk slowly down the path towards him. As she drew closer he turned away as though to regard the forest. Issul stood and watched him. He was plainly discomfited.

'You,' she said.

The man began to walk away as though he had not heard her. His hand was to his cheek again.

'I said, "You!" She moved quickly around him. Still he kept his face averted. 'Stand still when you are commanded!'

She strode to him and swept his hand aside, stared into his face. Her fury rose. The man was known to her. His name was Gordallith. He was a senior commander in Fectur's secret intelligence corps.

'Come with me!' she ordered, almost choking on her rage. She strode back into the cottage to where Ohirbe, Arrin and Julion still sat at the table. Swinging around to point at Gordallith she demanded, 'Before I arrived, did this man interrogate you?'

The three sat mute and fearful.

'*Answer me!*' Issul shouted.

Ohirbe clutched her husband's arm, tears streaming down her cheeks. ''E told us not to say anything, Ma'am! 'E said . . . the Lordship . . . 'e said 'e was personally interested an' wouldn't look kindly if we said anythin' to anyone at all.'

Issul's face contorted as her anger boiled. *Fectur! How dare you disobey me! How dare you!*

What had they said to Gordallith? Anything that they had not told her? Fear of the Spectre was such that, as Ohirbe had just made plain, simple mention of his name was sufficient to bend them whichever way he pleased. Even to the extent of resisting their Queen.

She wheeled upon Gordallith. 'Out!'

In the garden she stood before him. 'Did Lord Fectur order you to interrogate these people?'

'In order to secure your safety, Highness.'

'I expressly forbade him!'

'I was not aware of that.' replied Gordallith, unruffled.

'Would it have made a difference?'

'The Lord Invigilate surely acted in the best interests of the Crown. As did I.'

Issul turned to Sir Bandullo, then checked herself, on the point of ordering him to place Gordallith under close arrest. Quite suddenly the precariousness of her position became clear. Would Bandullo obey her? He was Fectur's man also, as were the others.

Gordallith was their superior. As Queen her authority exceeded Fectur's, yet . . .

Did she dare put them to the test?

She felt suddenly vulnerable. All eyes were upon her.

'I merely followed orders, Your Majesty,' said Gordallith softly at her shoulder.

In a way this saved her. It was Fectur who had committed the offence, not Gordallith, though almost certainly Gordallith was more aware of the full circumstances than he was admitting. But in the heat of the moment she had almost failed to see that she had no reasonable grounds for arresting Gordallith.

'Your master exceeded his authority,' she said, clearly, so that all might hear.

Gordallith remained silent.

'We will discuss the matter further upon returning to Orbia. Until then, you are forbidden to speak to these people. Is that understood?'

'Yes, Ma'am.'

'I will speak with you later. I want to know everything they told you. And Commander Gordallith, if they have been subjected to intimidation, you will pay.'

She walked back inside, slamming the door shut behind her.

IV

'Moscul, do you remember much about your life up to now?'

Issul sat with the little boy upon a felled tree-trunk at the back of the cottage. The others remained inside. Fectur's men were still out front.

'Everything,' Moscul replied. 'I remember my birth.'

'Your birth?' Was that possible? She shuddered, remembering.

'Yes, Aunt Issul. You were there. You were the first person I saw. And even before. I recall the warm liquid darkness of my mother's womb. The sounds, the sensations. I recall you from that dark time as well, Aunt Issul. Even before I was born I knew your voice. That is how I recognized you when you arrived, by the sight and sound of you.'

Issul stared at him, her nephew . . . and what else? Her mind went back to the dreadful days prior to his birth, and she shuddered again. *Ressa had been dead three days before he came from her womb.*

Moscul smiled. His smile was proud, he was pleased with himself for revealing this to her. But there was quiet menace in his eyes and she realized she feared him greatly.

'Aunt Issul,' he said, and laid his head against her shoulder.

Issul almost recoiled. He was playing with her. He was *performing* as a child, displaying affection in a measured, calculated, deliberate way. Nothing was spontaneous.

'Will you tell me?' she asked.

'Tell you what?'

'Well, let us begin with your memories of your mother. She was my sister, you know.'

'Yes, I do know. You grieved sorely at her death, and you miss her still.'

'That is true. I loved her very much.'

'I don't want to talk about her,' Moscul said. He scrambled to the ground, squatted down and began poking at the soil with a stick.

'Very well. What would you like to talk about?'

'Why have you come?'

Issul hesitated. 'Because I believe you may be in danger.'

He looked back at her, puzzlement creasing his fair brow.

How much does he know? she wondered. *Does he yet know what he truly is?*

'Who from?'

'That I have yet to determine.' She couldn't hold his gaze. *The greatest danger may come from you!*

'The old woman who came to me at the Old Pond – did she want to harm me?'

'It is possible. I don't yet know.' She felt uncomfortable, talking with him as she would with an adult, when physically he was simply a three-year-old.

'She wasn't with the other one.'

'The young man? Are you sure of that, Moscul?'

'Oh yes. They came separately and did not know one another.'

'Julion said the young man told him his name. Did you catch it?'

Moscul nodded.

'Can you tell me?'

'No.'

'I think you can.'

'Think what you like, Aunt Issul, Queen of Enchantment's Edge.'

Issul sat quietly for a moment, then said, 'You drew my attention when I was talking to Julion. Why?'

'He was lying.'

'What about?'

'That's for you to find out.'

'This is important, Moscul!' Issul said sharply.

The child's violet eyes gleamed impudently. 'Then it's important that you find out, isn't it, Aunt?'

Issul held her feelings in check. 'Did Julion, or Ohirbe, or Arrin tell the soldier anything different to what they told me?'

'I don't know. The soldier did not interview them in my hearing.'

Issul slipped down from the trunk and held out her hand. 'Come. We will go back inside.'

Like a true innocent, Moscul slipped his warm little hand into hers and trotted beside her back into the cottage. Ohirbe, Arrin and Julion sat as Issul had left them. Moscul made off to his area behind the screen. Issul joined the three adults. After a moment's consideration she said, 'I must return to the palace. I will be taking Moscul with me.'

Ohirbe gave a whimper. 'Takin' 'im? The little one?'

Issul reached out and took her hand. 'I have to, Ohirbe. It's for the best.'

'Oh, Mistress. Oh, Ma'am. No, you mustn't take 'im from me. Please.'

Issul looked into her face and saw the shock and misery there. For the first time it came to her, what she had done to these poor people. She had given them the baby. They had reared him as their own almost from the day of his birth. To their minds he *was* their child. They had no notion that he might be anything other than the innocent he appeared.

What right had I to do this to them?

Yes, she had warned Ohirbe at the beginning that, one day, she might return, that the child might not spend his entire life with them.

But Ohirbe had just lost her own baby. To her this child had been a miracle sent – Issul felt the irony – sent by the gods in answer to her prayers and sorrow. At the time she had been in no state to take in fully what she was being told. She had heard only what she so desperately wanted to hear.

Even so, Ohirbe had been obedient to Issul's instructions, had come to her the moment she had felt anything amiss. And now Issul was repaying her by snatching away her only child.

She thought quickly. 'Ohirbe, I want you to come too. And Arrin. Julion also, if he so wishes. You will be employed in my staff. You will continue to raise Moscul, but at Orbia, not here. How does that sound?

She only had to glimpse the woman's face to know the answer. Ohirbe and Arrin clutched each other, not quite able to take it in. To live and work in the royal palace! They spluttered their gratitude while Julion sat bemused. Issul hid her doubts. Knowing what she knew about Moscul, suspecting what she did, she feared that what she was now offering them was not quite the kindness that they perceived.

She turned to Julion. 'There is something you have not told me, Julion. I would like you to tell me now.'

Julion blanched. He sat stiff as a dry twig, his eyes glued to the table. Ohirbe and Arrin were suddenly silent, staring at their cousin.

'Julion,' Issul repeated softly. 'There will be no repercussions, not if you tell me now.' Her voice hardened. 'Now, Julion.'

'There was somethin'. I remember now.' Julion mumbled. His eyes flicked nervously at Ohirbe, then back to the table. He tried to look at Issul, but was defeated.

Issul nodded. 'Yes?'

'Yes, that's right now. The young man . . . at the Old Pond . . . 'e— 'e gave Moscul somethin'. A gift.'

'Julion! You never told us this!' blurted Ohirbe incredulously.

Issul silenced her. 'What sort of gift, Julion?'

'It was a little carving in white tusk. On a thong.'

'What sort of carving?'

'I don't know. It was an odd shape, not anythin' I could say.'

'Julion, what're you sayin'? Mistress, 'e's never mentioned this before, 'as 'e, Arrin? Not ever. We would've said. Julion, I'll never forgive you for this!'

'So, the stranger gave Moscul an ivory carving on a thong,' said Issul. 'He actually gave it to Moscul?'

''E put it 'round the little one's neck.'

'And what happened to it?'

Julion swallowed, shamefaced. He tried to speak. Something caught in his throat. He bowed his head. 'I took it, Ma'am.'

'*Julion!* You—'

'Be quiet, Ohirbe!'

'I didn't mean no 'arm,' Julion pleaded. 'I thought it might be worth somethin'.'

Issul closed her eyes.

'I thought I'd take it when I go to market, next week. Someone in town ought to be able to give me a price.'

'So you have not yet sold it?' said Issul.

'No, Ma'am.'

'Where is it? Will you show it to me?'

'Can't, Ma'am. The soldier took it. When 'e questioned me last night. 'E really frightened me. I 'ad to tell 'im.'

Issul leapt up from her seat. 'Stay here!'

She stormed outside. Sir Bandullo's men were lounging on the grass before the cottage. They leapt to their feet as she came out.

'Where is Commander Gordallith?'

'Gone, Ma'am,' replied Sir Bandullo.

'Where?'

'To Orbia.'

Issul swore, barely able to contain her emotion, then, 'How long?'

'Good half-hour, Ma'am.'

He must have set off virtually the moment she left him to speak with Moscul, she realized. 'The other two went with him?'

'Yes.'

'Saddle up, we are leaving.'

V

Issul knew there was no hope of catching Gordallith. She was hampered by the presence of Ohirbe, Arrin and Moscul. They rode behind her now in an ancient cart drawn by a single old drayhorse, their sole workbeast.

She estimated they could be at Orbia within a few hours of Gordallith. She would order him, or more probably Fectur, to hand over the ivory carving.

She fumed silently, cursing Fectur again and again.

The wind had almost died and the sun shone warmly upon the vast green forest. With the cart determining their pace Sir Bandullo calculated that they would reach Crosswood sometime before dusk.

Issul began to sink into gloom. She felt assailed on all sides. It seemed there were forces ranged against her that she could not even begin to comprehend, let alone combat. Moscul – what *was* he? What was his future? To find the answer to that would entail drawing out the secrets of the True Sept. She did not know how to go about doing this. She relied upon Grey Venger's full co-operation, or that of his deputies. Even were she successful, could she be sure that the True Sept had the answers? Could the Sept be little more than a repository of superstition and baseless, fabricated beliefs?

She felt uncertain of everything.

An abrupt yell roused her suddenly from her reverie. Ahead of her one of Sir Bandullo's men fell back from his horse. There was a rushing, whistling sound in the air. Another man slumped, clutching at the shaft of an arrow which stuck from his flank.

Instinctively Issul yanked her horse's head about, urging it to drop. Grabbing her crossbow, she leapt from the saddle as the mount obediently sank to the ground. She took shelter behind its bulk.

She was aware of movement in the trees on both sides of the track. Another flight of arrows hissed. There was a shriek. Issul saw Sir Bandullo and three others leaping to the ground, scrambling for cover. She loosed a bolt at a shadowy figure crouched in the undergrowth. The man screamed and fell back, thrashing. But there were more of them, many more.

She was covered by her horse on only one side. She rolled, then ran for a tree beside which Sir Bandullo lay. She threw herself down beside him. 'How many are there?'

'Too many!'

Issul heard a woman's shout. She glanced around to the cart. Moscul had leapt to the ground and was running back along the track. Ohirbe was clambering down to take off in pursuit. Arrin, who had the reins, stood as though to jump down, then reeled, clutching at his throat, an arrow jutting bloodily there.

'Moscul!'

Discarding her crossbow and drawing her smallsword Issul raced after the little boy. Sir Bandullo and two others followed. The air sang with arrows. Moscul had disappeared into the dense undergrowth about twenty paces away. Ohirbe followed, crying for him. Issul, conscious that she was in the open, threw herself from the track into the trees.

A man's figure loomed before her, a sword raised. She ducked, slashed, her blade biting into his ribs. Another came at her but was met by Sir Bandullo.

'Moscul!'

She drew her sword free and raced on, darting and dodging, estimating the place where she thought the boy must be. Shadowed figures moved beneath the trees. She heard the drum of hooves back on the track. Louder shouts, many more of them. How many ambushers were there?

Abruptly the sound of fighting was behind her. A dense wall of hazel blocked her way. She slipped around, seeking a way through. There was a harsh scream ahead of her, on the other side of the hazel. A woman's scream.

Issul thrust through, fighting against the hazel branches. She tumbled to her knees and emerged into a small clearing. On the other side, a few paces away, a woman was on hands and knees, climbing to her feet. At first Issul took it to be Ohirbe, then realized the clothing was wrong. And this woman was older and of greater bulk.

Issul stood, breathless. The woman turned towards her. Blood streamed down one cheek. She was quite old, her hair grey and wild.

This must be her! The one at the Old Pond!

Issul advanced towards her. 'Where is the boy?'

The old woman, stricken-faced, raised a hand and pointed at Issul, shaking her head.

'It has begun!' she cried.

'What? What do you mean? Has he come this way?'

'It's too late now! I tried, but it's too late!'

The woman's eyes blazed, then flickered suddenly away, focusing on something behind Issul. Issul was still moving forward, aware of a rustling at her back. She felt a blinding, deafening pain, was knocked forward, glimpsed a gloved hand before it clamped across her mouth and dragged her back.

Her senses rang. She was sinking, her legs no longer hers. A dreadful moan as the world retreated. No pain now. Dragged across the grass, sky brilliant and spinning overhead. The voices, just one roar, trees so strangely high, also spinning, spiralling away from her, nauseous as it all vanished into darkness.

SIX

I

The gods were not gods.

So the mysterious Orbus had informed King Leth. In a later meeting within the blue casket-chamber he had begun to enlarge upon this. He put forward an explanation of the evolution of the gods and of Enchantment itself, unlike anything Leth had heard before.

'I feel you have reached a position where you may be ready to listen,' he had said. 'In our last few meetings you have shown yourself less inclined to ignore what I say in favour of posing other questions. This is an encouraging sign.'

They sat, as had become their custom, cross-legged upon the ground, facing one another. Orbus had his staff laid across his thighs.

These meetings were always tense for Leth, not least because he never knew when they might end. Without warning, perhaps on a whim or out of irritation, perhaps not needing a reason at all, Orbus could raise his staff. Leth would find himself cast from the blue world, back to his own study. He was then obliged to await his next summons which, usually manifesting in the form of a dream, might be days, weeks, or on occasion even months away.

'Listen well,' said Orbus without further preamble. 'Enchantment is formed of the raw stuff of unconsciousness, of pre-consciousness, of unthought thought and undreamed dream. It is the manifestation of potential, of immateriality metamorphosing into materiality, chaos churning into form, of Cosmic pre-mind. It is unstable, even though Cosmic laws govern its creation. They are not the laws that govern the formed world, nor are they laws that you might hope to gain any understanding of.'

He paused a moment, apparently studying Leth's face from within his bundled rags. 'Imagine this world as a single unconscious thought or impulse made manifest. Where did the impulse originate? Surely it had to come out of a far greater pre-thought state, a Cosmic Potential from which all things come. But now, imagine that between that condition of pre-thought and the finished world, or manifest thought, there is a process, an uncertainty, which is the forming itself. That process is Enchantment.'

'But who or what is doing the thinking?' mused Leth.

'Hah! You must dwell upon that. But I will say this: Who or what thinks your thoughts? Truly. From what source do they originate? And when they have become conscious in your mind, what then do they become?'

Leth sat in puzzled silence before asking, 'Are you saying, then, that the world we know was once like Enchantment?'

'Once *was* Enchantment!' corrected Orbus. 'And before that it was Cosmic Chaos, and before that, awesome Potentia, awaiting the process. But to talk of "before" and "after", of things linear and sequential, is itself inaccurate. Time is non-existent, except as a rationale of the mind. Everything simply is; but not necessarily as you perceive it.'

'I am lost,' said Leth.

Orbus chuckled. 'What I am telling you is beyond simple intellectual grasp. It has to be assimilated over weeks, months, *eons!* It is but a beginning. Dwell on it, mull over it, dream it. In time I will no longer be required for the telling. It will become a part of you. It *is* a part of you, so far unrealized. But it must be gradual or you will be overwhelmed. You cannot treat it as you would a lesson in elementary mathematics or geography.'

'If the world once was Enchantment and is now formed reality, but Enchantment, or a part of it, still exists, does that mean that Enchantment is diminishing?' enquired Leth.

'Excellent! Except that that is no longer the case, and this I will explain presently. First let me tell you that Enchantment is a misnomer, as are all the other appellations by which it is known.'

'In what way?'

'If a thing has more than one name, which name is correct?'

'Each name will have a different meaning or interpretation to different individuals.'

'But does that mean it is correct, or even partially correct? Names are labels, tags, attached to things as a way of trying to identify and explain them. But the human mind accepts the tag as though it is the thing itself. It prefers the tag, the outer manifestation, and makes little or no endeavour to understand the actuality that the tag conceals.'

'Again, I am lost.'

'You are Leth, are you not?'

'I am.'

'But what is Leth? Does Leth explain the extraordinary phenomena that comprise you? Does Leth tell me anything of your inner world, of your deepest, most private thoughts? Does Leth tell me what you are, in all your aspects? Does it explain your birth, your existence, your eventual passing? Does it tell me anything, other than how to recognize your physical manifestation in its simplest aspect, or communicate knowledge of that manifestation to other minds?'

Leth gave a slow shake of the head.

'It is a tag, but it is far from being the actuality. So it is with Enchantment. Your kind call it that, for to you it consists of things magical and awesomely powerful, things you cannot know or understand. Enchantment is known by many other names in other cultures: Mystery, Otherworld, Eidolos, Selph, Land of Gods, Ylem, Fear, Faerie, Mobania, Phor, Tol . . . there are many, many others. All are correct inasmuch as they represent endeavours to explain the inexplicable. And all are incorrect, for at best they explain but a single aspect of that multi-faceted phenomenon, or a simple belief attached to it. We require names, labels and tags simply to differentiate and recognize. But we should be aware that they can so easily become forms of concealment. This applies to all things, from cats and apples to worlds and numina. Language informs no more than it obscures. Consider that, *King Leth*.'

Orbus had ended the meeting at that point. A week later he summoned Leth once more:

'The gods, who are not gods, make war upon one another. That process, the very conflict itself, the conscious manipulation of the very stuff of which Enchantment is formed, is what sustains Enchantment.'

'You said before that it is diminishing,' said Leth.

'No, you did. I said it is no longer the case. And that is why.

The conflict creates, even as it destroys. It maintains the flux.' Orbus paused. 'The gods, if you like, are aberrations. They formed unnaturally out of the process that is Enchantment. They are conscious beings of immense power. That power enables them to manipulate the forces and energies of the creation of which they are a part.'

'Are you saying they should not exist?' asked Leth.

'Oh, should not, shmud not! There is no should about it. What is is, what is not is not.'

'But you said "unnatural".'

'They are nodes, uncommon concentrations of energy, even within the strange process of Enchantment. We are also lesser nodes, as are all living things.'

'But do they exist as recognizable beings?'

'Oh, they do. They are. But they can change themselves at will. And, dependent upon the power – the magic, as you would term it – that they command at any given time, they can alter the environment in many different ways.'

'Is there a limit to their power?'

'Yes. As I said, Enchantment can be seen as the process between the formed and the unformed world. In many ways it is therefore almost as your world is, but not quite. And in even its small differences it is profound. In the same way, the so-called gods are akin to denizens of your world. But they are different and, of course, far more powerful than anything you have ever known. In fact,' Orbus chuckled, 'from your point of view they may as well be gods!'

'But they are threatened!' exclaimed Leth with sudden insight. 'Enchantment diminishes – why? Because it is the process of creation, not the creation itself! It cannot sustain, it must become! And the formed world which we inhabit is what it should become. But the very consciousnesses that have developed within it – the gods – prevent it doing so. They war – they engender chaos – in order to prevent their world becoming ours!'

'You are learning fast,' said Orbus with satisfaction.

'But then surely the fact that they war must also ultimately ensure their end?'

'Yes, if they were to succeed in destroying one another to the last individual. Then the natural diminishment could continue. Enchantment would, in time, become as the world that you know.'

'How long would that process take?'

'Oh, a thousand eons. Perhaps two. It is difficult to be precise.'

'Are the gods aware of this? Do they know that they must endeavour to destroy one another to prevent Enchantment dying, while simultaneously they must also ensure that they live – some of them, at least – in order to maintain the process?'

'Some are aware of that paradox, to some degree at least. Others are not. Some of them are really quite stupid.'

'How many are there?'

'Twenty-four in total. How many still survive in their full potency I do not know.'

'Do they threaten us? Are they interested in us in any way, or even aware of us?'

'They know that a world exists beyond their borders. Except in quite exceptional circumstances they are unable to enter that world. They would lose their powers, you see. They are generally only powerful within their own flux, their own environment. Of course, they are jealous of your world.'

'Jealous?'

'It threatens them. You threaten them. The gods would expand Enchantment if they could, for if they could spread its flux across the entire world it would stabilize, if that is not a contradiction of terms. The world would stabilize into the instability that is Enchantment.' Orbus placed his hands upon his knees and rocked slightly from the waist. 'They direct their researches towards that end. Now, we have spoken enough for today.'

Leth, while his mind spun with the information it had been presented with, was nonetheless pleased to note that Orbus had announced the end of their meeting rather than simply terminating it with a sudden, brusque shift of his staff, as before. A hundred questions hummed in Leth's head, but he kept silence rather than irritate the strange mage.

'Before you leave I have a favour to ask of you,' Orbus had then said. 'Next time you come, could you possibly bring some cheese?'

'Cheese?'

'Yes. The pale, soft, tangy kind, made from goat's milk, if you can.'

'Of course. May I ask why?'

'I have a liking for it. And it is rather difficult to get hold of in here.'

'I would be pleased to bring you cheese,' said Leth. Orbus nodded his thanks. He raised his staff.

II

On the morning that Queen Issul departed Orbia for the village of Lastmeadow, King Leth was for several hours locked in tense debate with his cousin, Duke Hugo, and other military and political advisors. Hugo was planning on leaving for his castle of Giswel Holt the following day. He urged Leth to permit him to take more troops to reinforce those already in Giswel.

'If the Krai strike it will be there first. They cannot avoid Giswel if they plan to move into our heartland, unless they take to the forest, which would take weeks.'

Leth was less keen. 'You have as many men as I can safely spare. I dare not deplete Enchantment's Edge further. Prince Anzejarl may not move directly against Giswel. He could leave a substantial force in the area to keep you tied up, and swing to the east to bring his main army directly here.'

'Via The Plain of Sighs?' Hugo shook his head. 'It would add too much time to his journey.'

'Time is hardly a factor. His army is well-supplied and winter is not close enough to be a reliable ally.'

Hugo sat back in his seat. He was tall, striking, of powerful athletic build. He was aged twenty-eight, in his prime, a gifted and popular leader of men, if at times temperamental and vulnerable to passion. His hair was long and almost jet black, swept back from his face and held with a silver clasp at the neck. A neatly-trimmed black beard adorned his chin; he moved easily, confidently, and his blue eyes held a glimmer that could shift from merriment to anger in an instant.

'I would send a strong force south, while Anzejarl is on the march, to harry him and cut his supply lines. He would be slowed significantly. But I can do that only if a substantial garrison remains to secure Giswel.'

Leth gravely shook his head. 'It would be too easy to become trapped between Anzejarl and the Krai homelands. No, I can send no more men south, at least until I have more accurate intelligence.'

'If we allow him to force us into a head-on confrontation we will be crushed,' Hugo protested.

Leth turned to one of his generals. 'Sir Cathbo, you have said little so far, What is your opinion?'

Sir Cathbo shrugged. 'A messenger pigeon arrived yesterday bringing the news that Anzejarl is still beyond the Bitter Lakes. He has made no direct move against us—'

'But he surely will!' stormed Hugo. 'It makes better sense to pre-empt him. Strikes now against his supply lines and the army on the move could make all the difference.'

'Or so he may wish us to think,' said Leth. 'I know Anzejarl to be a clever and resourceful strategist. No, we need better intelligence. We still do not know the reason for this Krai war. It is almost impossible to gain information from Krai itself, with every foreigner being conspicuous by virtue of physical differences, and automatically subject to suspicion. Yet plainly the Krai nation has suffered tremendous upheaval. Anzejarl has usurped his father's place; he has murdered his own brother. Why? The very fabric of Krai society has been rent and sundered by his actions, yet he still leads his people. How? He almost certainly has the support of a god. Again, how? If we had answers to these questions we might be better equipped to deal with him.'

In regard to the latter question, Leth had put it to Orbus only the night before. It was not the first time he had posed it, but previously Orbus had given no comprehensible reply. This time he said only that he could conceive of ways by which such a union might be feasible. Leth had pressed him for more, but Orbus had seemed evasive. Leth had the impression this was something that worried Orbus.

It was last night, also, that Orbus had mentioned the Orb's Soul for the first time. He had spoken half lightly, half wistfully. 'Your problems might be solved were you to bring me the Orb's Soul.'

At Leth's enquiry he had then become dismissive. 'Who knows if it exists, or in what form? If it does it is lost or hidden within Enchantment, where neither you nor your people nor I may go.'

'But what is it?' Leth pressed him. 'You say our problems might be solved if it were found?'

Orbus's ragged head shook heavily upon his bowed shoulders. 'Leth, Leth, think no more of the Orb's Soul. I mentioned it as one might mention a god to whom one addresses prayers that are never answered. It is a chimera; it is perhaps nothing. Whatever it is, it cannot be reached.'

And then something extraordinary had happened. Orbus stood, as did Leth, and as they were about to part Orbus had approached Leth and embraced him. It was the first time they had made physical contact. It had been brief and Orbus, upon releasing him, had raised his staff without another word.

A little dazed, back in his study, Leth had felt his skin tingling warmly. In the subdued light he saw a faint bluish blur seemingly clinging to him. It had faded quickly and he had come away believing it to have dispersed entirely.

'Does Anzejarl need reasons?' demanded Hugo. 'He has done what he has done. He was successful and launched his army upon a campaign of conquest, again successfully. Perhaps the Krai have spent centuries awaiting this moment. It matters little in the face of events. What relevance the reasons when their army sits just beyond our border, poised to attack us?'

So the argument went back and forth for much of the morning. Leth remained adamant: he would send no more troops to Giswel, at least until he had a more reliable assessment of Krai intentions. He scarcely doubted that Anzejarl would now move against Enchantment's Edge, but much depended upon the manner and time, and Leth was loath to concentrate all his forces until he could better determine the Krai strategy.

The meeting broke up with little resolved. Leth and Hugo departed together. In a corridor they were approached by Master Briano, Duchess Mawnie's head valet. In paroxysms of anguish Briano brought the sad news of Mawnie's breakdown. Tearfully he followed as the two, Duke and King, made straightway for Mawnie's bedchamber.

Mawnie slept, almost deathlike, for she was perfectly still and ghastly pale. A nurse waited beside her bed and by chance Doctor Melropius arrived to make his hourly check. He told Hugo and Leth what he had told Issul: that Mawnie would be unlikely to wake for several hours.

'And what will be her state of mind?' asked Hugo.

Melropius could only guess. 'She may be calm, with no recollection of what happened. She may be melancholic. She may be unnaturally gay, or she could remain in the grip of the phantoms that have possessed her. In short, I have no useful answer to your question.'

Duke Hugo took Leth aside. 'I cannot delay my departure tomorrow. As it happens, I had already made the decision that Mawnie will remain here. Lir, too. They will be safer.'

Leth nodded. 'Mawnie will have the very best attention, cousin. Be assured of that.'

'I know it.' He glanced back at his wife, whose still face rested in shadow upon her pillow, then strode from the chamber.

A short time later, working at his desk, Leth was visited by Lord Fectur.

'I wished to speak with you on the subject of the Queen's journey, Sire,' he said, settling himself upon a comfortable padded chair before the King.

'What journey is this?'

'To the village, Lastmeadow. I must confess I harbour misgivings about the security arrangements. I am also concerned about the reasons for the journey, which the Queen declines to reveal to me.'

'Fectur, I do not know what you are talking about,' said Leth, mildly irritated. 'I know nothing of any journey, to Lastmeadow or anywhere. When does the Queen plan to undertake it?'

Fectur's thin eyebrows arched as if in surprise. 'When? Sire, she has already departed, some time ago this morning.'

'Already departed?' Leth recalled their conversation last night. Had Issul made any mention of a journey? He was sure not.

'Sire, she impressed upon me that she had your confidence,' said Fectur. 'I believed you knew. Can I have been misled? I can think of no reason why.'

Leth thought rapidly. 'You say she did not disclose the reason for this journey?'

'No matter my endeavours, she would say nothing. I am inclined, however, to infer a link with her visit to Overlip yesterday, of which I informed you.'

'Why?'

'She received a visitor yesterday, under my auspices. A peasant woman named Ohirbe, who hails from Lastmeadow. It was immediately after interviewing this Ohirbe that the Queen went to Overlip.'

'What did they speak of, the Queen and Ohirbe?'

'I was not permitted to attend the interview.'

Leth was dumbfounded. Issul had spoken last night of the Legendary Child of the True Sept – this in connection with her visit to Overlip. There must be a link, then, with her sudden departure for Lastmeadow. He admonished her silently for not having been more explicit.

He glanced at Fectur, who sat with his hands raised before him, stubby fingers loosely interlaced. Fectur was smug, and far more was going on behind that calculatedly bland brow than his expression would suggest. Leth felt an urge to be free of him.

'You are concerned about the Queen's security, you say. Why?'

'I recommended that she take an escort of, at minimum, a full platoon of the King's Cavalry. She would have none of it, disregarding my protestations. She took a mere eight, though they are among my best.'

'Eight!' Leth rose suddenly. 'By the gods! And you let her go?'

'Sire, the Queen made it plain that I had no choice. She stressed the importance of relative anonymity – I should add that she is disguised, though my men are in full livery. She made it plain that her wrath would know no bounds were I to interfere. I would have prevented her, truly, but again I was led to believe that your permission had been granted.'

Leth thought furiously. *Issul, what are you doing? You place yourself at great risk!*

Should he trust her judgement, allow her to go her own way? No, he loved her too dearly. No matter her cause, he feared for her. If someone should learn her identity . . . Eight men, no matter their skill, would be of little help against a determined enemy. At this, of all times!

Issul, what has got into you?

'I want a mounted platoon sent after her immediately. They will escort her to Lastmeadow and back.'

Fectur rose. 'Very good, sire. I regret, they will almost certainly not now reach her before she arrives at the village.'

'Then they will simply bring her back to Orbia when her business is done. Send them now, Fectur.'

Fectur gave a curt bow and departed.

King Leth paced the room, deeply troubled. What was Issul playing at? He regretted that he had not questioned her more throughly last night. This business must be linked to her reference to the Legendary Child and Grey Venger. She had spoken as if anticipating a communication from Venger. Leth had received nothing, but his mind seethed now with questions.

Quite suddenly he was desolate as the realization slammed home that Issul was no longer at his side. He was overcome with the fear that he might never see her again. Never had he doubted how much he loved her; now he realized that without her he would have no desire to live.

You should have told me, Iss!

He left his chambers, unable to concentrate on work.

When fatigued or troubled, Leth often took to the parapets of Orbia's great walls. From there he could gaze either upon the palace or out over the clambering, bustling city of Enchantment's Edge and the wildness beyond. This he did now.

The wind was strong, whipping and moaning about the myriad marble towers. Cloud scudded rapidly south-westward. Above it wide blue spaces spread about a dazzling sun.

Leth strode, his hands locked behind his back, telling himself that his fears were unfounded. Issul would soon be back, safe in his arms. It was unlikely that any unit bearing full Orbia livery would come under attack from brigands. Had she believed herself at risk she would never have gone.

Moderately calmed, Leth stood and savoured the wind upon his cheeks, the sunlight warming his skin. A little further on, passing above a quadrangle, he spotted Pader Luminis coming from a library. Leth cupped hands to mouth and hailed him. Pader, halting, took a moment to locate his summoner. Leth waved. Pader waved back and made haste to join him.

'It is a while since we have spoken, Pader,' said Leth as the little man came up, somewhat breathless, beside him. 'Let us walk. I have a yen to pick your brain.'

'Yours for the picking, my lord,' replied Pader Luminis. 'Though I fear you will find it to be but humble and disappointing grey matter. It rarely fails to disappoint me.'

Leth thought it might be interesting to compare the opinions of Pader Luminis – arguably Enchantment's Edge's wisest, most learned mage – with what he had learned from Orbus. He took care in couching his questions, though, for Pader must not suspect that he was in possession of extraordinary knowledge. 'Tell me of the gods, Pader. Do you believe they exist, as actual personalities?'

'There can be little doubt that they exist in some form,' replied Pader after a moment's thought. 'But their personalities, as Haruman's Edict so rightly asserts, cannot be known.'

'Cannot? Absolutely?'

'Were we able to enter Enchantment, or were they to apply themselves directly to us, then the story might be different. But as yet, I say firmly, we cannot know them.'

Leth nodded. Recently Orbus had begun revealing to him something of the personalities of the so-called gods. 'How do you think they came into being?'

'That is a difficult one, my lord. How do we come into being? We are the product of our parents. If the gods exist as physical beings, then the same must surely hold for them. But if they are truly gods, then they will have come from a divine source. Perhaps Enchantment itself is that source.'

'Do you know anything of the Legendary Child, Pader?' said Leth, shifting abruptly.

'Why, that is the very topic I have just come from researching, at the behest of the Queen.'

'Issul?'

'We had a long talk last night. She is keen to know all that is known of the subject. Regrettably, I am able to furnish her, or you, with very little. It is to the True Sept that we must turn to learn the full story.'

'Do you believe the Sept has the answers?'

'They know more than we,' asserted Pader.

They stepped onto the battlements of the main parade ground. Leth saw horses being saddled and readied for a journey. Soldiers nearby wore the livery of the King's Cavalry.

'Bring her home safely,' he whispered.

He and Pader reached Orbia's outer wall, the wind whipping about their heads. Leth paused, resting one foot within a crenellation. He leaned forward, his elbow upon his thigh, and let his eyes travel over the myriad towers and cluttered roofs of the city-castle, and far off the faintest shimmer that betrayed the brooding presence of the mountains of Enchantment above the low broken cloud.

Closer by, on the other side of the wide moat at the foot of the wall and a short way off the main boulevard that led from the palace, a small plaza played regular host to a market. The plaza was lively now. Brightly-hued awnings flapped in the wind; traders and craftsmen were at their stalls beneath, and entertainers of varying types and talents sought to amuse the citizens present and separate them from a modest portion of their wealth.

'Did Issul give her reasons for seeking information about the True Sept, Pader?' asked Leth.

The Murinean shook his head. 'She was deeply troubled. She said something had happened which she believed darkened the future for us all. She did not elucidate and gave no hint that I should enquire further. But she wished to know whatever I might be able to tell her, not just about the Legendary Child, but about Enchantment, and the Krai also.'

'Surely these topics were covered in her years of schooling?'

'I think she wished to be fully reminded, as much as anything. And of course, she sought to pick my brain, as you do, wrongly imagining that it is superior to her own.'

'Is it not? Are you here on false pretences, Pader?'

'It is older, that is all. There are many times I would trade it for another if I could. One less prone to forgetfulness and distraction.'

Leth grinned. 'Your brain is a national asset, Pader. We would be lost without it.'

'Then I bequeath it to you, my lord, gladly. When I am gone from this world, take this brain of mine and pick it as you have picked it all these years. It will pine otherwise, for it has grown accustomed to the practice.'

'Ha!' Leth slapped his shoulder. 'Let us hope that day is far away.'

He cast his gaze absently over the rooftops and back to the little plaza. Something half-noticed caused him to look again. He squinnied his eyes.

'Pader, do you see that?' He pointed.

'See what, my lord?'

'On the lip of the roof of that house, there, on the far side of the square. Do you see?'

'Alas, my eyesight has gone the way of my brain.'

Leth turned back. A sentry stood a way along the parapet. Leth beckoned him.

He came running and stiffened to attention. 'Sire!'

'Do you see that rooftop? Is there someone atop it?'

The sentry peered hard, then drew forth a spyglass from his belt and put it to one eye. He tensed. 'By the—'

'What is it, man?' Leth snatched the glass, which the sentry now held for him. He found the roof he had pinpointed, and gave a gasp. 'What is that?'

In the circle of the glass he could see a figure, hunched and dark, large, possibly the size of a small man, but birdlike in form. It rested in perfect stillness, like a gargoyle, but its eyes slowly blinked as it observed the crowded plaza below.

'There is another, Sire!' blurted the sentry.

Leth followed the direction of his finger. The spyglass found a parapet surrounding a slender pink tower. There squatted another of the creatures, its attitude like that of the first. And further along was a third.

Leth quickly scanned the area around the plaza. With quickening alarm he identified as many as a dozen more, resting in the high places all about the plaza. Motionless, silent, menacing and, as far as those below were concerned, quite invisible.

'By the gods,' Leth breathed with sudden alarm, knowing what this must mean. 'We are attacked! Sentry, sound the tocsin!'

Even as he spoke one of the bird-things stretched and spread its broad wings. In helpless horror Leth watched as it launched itself from its roost, circled, then swooped upon the crowd below. Others now followed, gliding with sinister grace, circling once, then diving.

The first of them rose again. In its talons it held a woman. Leth marvelled at its strength as it back-flapped into the air, pecking savagely at its victim's head. High over the plaza it released her, and as she fell it dived again.

The tocsin rang out. The folk in the plaza milled in sudden panic. Their screams were borne to Leth's ears intermittently, at the caprice of the wind. Again and again the dark death from above descended upon them.

Soldiers came running along the parapet to join their King, but they, like Leth, could do nothing. Though they bore crossbows, at this distance they were as likely to strike innocents as the creatures they were intended for.

The cavalry platoon assigned to intercept Queen Issul now cantered into sight through the great outer gate of Orbia's barbican.

Alerted by the tocsin the commander quickly identified the source of the disturbance and ordered his men instantly into the fray. At full gallop they made for the plaza, some with swords drawn, others loading crossbows in the saddle.

A little girl in a bright blue frock and grey shawl, aged perhaps seven or eight, had broken out of the plaza and was running across an area of open ground towards the moat. Horrified, Leth saw a shadow cross her path. A winged-thing wheeled, gliding fast, low above the ground, heading straight for her.

Leth cried out, helpless. The creature stretched out its lower limbs, cruel talons extended, preparing for the strike. A single horseman had veered away from his platoon. Half-erect in the stirrups he brought his crossbow to his shoulder and loosed a bolt at the speeding monster.

The bolt struck home, bringing a harsh shriek from the bird-thing. The monster slewed in its path, but only momentarily. The bolt had not been enough to kill or incapacitate it. It adjusted its path and flew again for the child.

The soldier leapt from his saddle, drawing his sword, and ran, placing himself between the little girl and her winged assailant. The creature threw back its head. The soldier ducked as it swooped at him. He stabbed, dived to the side, slashed and slashed again, then threw himself down and rolled. The bird-thing struck the ground and wheeled around, hopping and flapping. The soldier darted forward and hacked into its neck, nimbly dodging talons and beak. He struck a second time, a third, and the head rolled from its body. Without pausing the soldier gathered the child in his arms and ran for his horse.

A mass of people were streaming out of the plaza now, falling over one another in their efforts to get away. The cavalry platoon were loosing crossbow bolts at the creatures in the air, but Leth saw no more of the bird-things brought down. A soldier was plucked from the saddle and borne high, then dropped. Another was struck from behind and sent flying to the ground, the bird-thing settling upon him and pecking viciously at his head.

At that moment the soldier who had rescued the little girl sped past. He still held the child in his embrace, but he leaned from his saddle and swung his sword cleanly at the bird-thing's neck. The creature arched and shrieked, blood gushing from the wound. It lifted off, abandoning the soldier it was attacking, and took flight.

Quite suddenly all the bird-creatures were in the air. They rose as one, and made off at an almost leisurely pace, across the city and away.

Leth turned and raced along the parapet, down the stairway four steps at a time, to the parade-ground below. A squad of élite guardsmen fell in behind him, striving to keep pace. A cavalry mount stood tethered nearby. Leth vaulted into the saddle and galloped for the gate. In dismay his guardsmen pounded in his wake.

Without pause he raced through the barbican and out onto the thoroughfare, then veered towards the plaza.

The scene that met him was one of carnage. People wandered dazed and weeping. Many were bloodied; a considerable number, from his initial assessment, were dead. The cavalrymen had taken charge, establishing order as best they could and endeavouring to attend to the wounded. Squads of city militia were arriving at the double to take over.

Leth passed among the wounded and distressed, giving words of comfort. He came upon a young mother clutching a little girl to her bosom. Leth recognized the child who had so nearly come to grief beside the moat. He knelt beside them.

'Your daughter is safe.'

The woman nodded, not knowing the king. Her eyes were filled with tears and she was too overcome to speak. Leth tenderly stroked the child's head, then rose and walked across to inspect the corpse of the winged creature. It was, he saw, birdlike only in its large, horny curved bill and prehensile toes with their cruel long talons. It was unfeathered. Its bulky body, packed with muscle, was clothed in short, dark, densely packed, mottled-brown hair. The skin was tough, calloused and leathery. The stub of the crossbow bolt, which would surely have stopped and probably killed a man, even armoured, protruded from its breast. The wings were of broad span, formed of a webby, fleshy membrane, small, horribly clawed hands at the midpoint of their upper side. The head, which lay close by, was flat and broad, emerging from the shoulders with little in the way of a neck. Narrow yellow eyes were set beneath a wrinkled pate.

'It is a slooth,' said a voice at Leth's shoulder. It was Pader Luminis, who had arrived behind the squad of guards.

'A slooth?'

'Fabled creatures said to haunt the mountains of Enchantment. Before today I had seen them only in paintings. They are more horrible in the flesh.'

'A fearsome foe,' muttered Leth, mindful that only the one had been brought down. He had little doubt that this was the first word from the Krai.

The platoon commander came alongside him. Leth said, 'Can you locate the man who slew this thing?'

Moments later a young soldier stood before him, tall, lean and fair-headed. 'I commend you for your bravery,' said Leth. 'Your actions were exemplary, saving both the life of a child and one of your comrades. Was he badly wounded?'

'He has lost an eye, Sire, and is severely mauled, but his life is not in danger.'

'You came close to bringing down a second of these creatures.'

'Regrettably, not close enough.'

Leth spoke to his commander. 'What of casualties?'

'Two of my men dead, at least four others injured. Of the citizens I have no final count, but the dead number at least seven, with several others harmed.'

Leth looked at the faces around him, which were uniformly pale and grim. 'You all acquitted yourselves well. I am proud of you,' he said, then turned again to the young soldier. 'I note no insignia upon your arm. Are you newly-recruited?'

'Aye, Sire.'

'What is your name?'

'Shenwolf.'

'Well, Shenwolf, let it be known that I have commended your actions today. Continue to show the spirit, courage and initiative that you have displayed here, and you can expect to go far. Now,' he nodded towards the plaza, where the young woman now stood holding her daughter's hand, nervously watching them. 'There are two others whom I believe may wish to speak to you.'

Shenwolf bowed and withdrew. Leth spoke once more to his commander. 'You were bound for Lastmeadow, were you not?'

'Aye, Sire. But though my orders were urgent, I felt I had no choice but to intervene here.'

'Quite so. I would have expected nothing else. Your actions, and those of these good men whom you command, have averted what might have been a massacre. Are you able to continue now?'

'I will have to return to the barracks for replacements.'

'Do so, and depart as soon as you can. Your mission is of the highest priority.'

The commander saluted and made off with his men. Leth cast his eye wearily about him once more, then looked at Pader Luminis.

'We can doubt no longer, Pader. War has begun.'

III

'How am I expected to respond to this? I do not even know what is going on!'

In exasperation King Leth cast his eyes again over the sealed letter that had just been brought to him. It was addressed to *The Godless and Intolerant Monarch, Leth*. Its message, written in blood-red ink, had brought a jolt to Leth, being perhaps the last thing he had expected at this time. It read:

This word is written on behalf of one whom you wrongly term outcast, outlaw and criminal, whom sane and considerate men and women know truly as a man of courage, righteousness, wisdom and conviction. This man, known to you as Grey Venger, acknowledges a word and a request believed to come from your authority. The word is that the sacred Child is known. The request is that Grey Venger, Enlightened Master of the One True Sept, should show himself.

To you, Leth, we say: bring forth the proof, Deliver your evidence of the Child forthwith.

Bring also your proclamation absolving the Grey Venger of all blame for crimes you have accused him of. Make it known that by your authority the Grey Venger is declared immune to prosecution or punishment in any form for said crimes, from the Crown or any other authority or individual. In short, restore Grey Venger his due status as a free citizen of Enchantment's Edge, accorded the rights and privileges of all who enjoy that status. Furthermore, make it known that the True Sept is restored to full legitimacy, that all charges and restrictions pertaining to it are rescinded and that it is free to practise in accordance with the rights and privileges granted to any other legitimate body.

Publish this proclamation so that all may be aware of it. Then shall you know more.

The letter was unsigned, though it bore the insignia of the outlawed True Sept. Leth passed it to Lord Fectur and waited while he scanned it.

'Is this true, Sire, that you have knowledge of the Legendary Child?' enquired Fectur when he had done.

'Not I,' muttered Leth.

'The Queen, then?' Fectur placed the letter upon Leth's desk and hooked his thumbs into the lapels of his gown. 'This would explain her visit to Overlip yesterday. But can it be true, that she knows something of the Legendary Child?'

Leth was reluctant to comment. He could almost hear the thoughts burrowing through the labyrinthine passages of Fectur's mind. He felt, uneasily, that anything he might say would be a betrayal of the woman he loved. But he could not dismiss Fectur now, much as he would have liked to.

'And her journey to Lastmeadow, the visit from the peasant woman Ohirbe . . .' mused the Lord High Invigilate. 'It is surely the same business. Yet she kept you in ignorance, Sire?'

'No,' replied Leth firmly. 'She made mention of the Legendary Child. She told me also to be alert for a communication such as this. Issul herself was uncertain, and unwilling to speak further until she had learned more.'

'Perhaps, had you informed me of this earlier, Sire, I might have been able to make more appropriate arrangements in regard to the Queen's journey to Lastmeadow. I might have been better placed to deal with the situation as a whole.' Fectur rocked slowly on the balls of his feet. 'You recall, of course, that the True Sept has endeavoured to establish contact with the Krai?'

Leth grew warm with anger. 'What do you insinuate?'

'No insinuation, Sire. I am, rather, thinking aloud, trying to fit the pieces of this intriguing puzzle together.'

Leth stared down at the letter. 'Who brought this?'

'A boy. I questioned him. He knows nothing.'

'Questioned?' Leth well knew the implications of that word when used by Fectur.

'An informal chat, Sire. The boy understood perfectly. He had been given the letter to deliver by a man he did not know. He was paid quite handsomely. It is probably almost true. I let him go.'

Leth moved to the window and gazed out. To him it seemed that too much was happening at once. *Issul, you should have told me more!*

'Do you have instructions for me, Sire, in regard to this matter?' enquired Fectur softly.

'I will wait, for the nonce. I can do little else. Barring hazard, the Queen will be back the morning after tomorrow. I will consult with her then, and make a decision based upon her words.'

Barring hazard! He shut the thought from his mind. She would be safe. She had to be.

'I could bring in the individual with whom the Queen spoke yesterday evening, in the Tavern of the Veiled Light,' said Fectur. 'My men have him marked.'

'Do nothing of the kind!' Leth turned back. 'You would send Grey Venger scurrying far beyond anyone's reach.'

'Not if he believes we have access to the Legendary Child.'

'He does not believe it. Not yet.'

'But the thought that we might surely tantalizes him. I do not think he will willingly sever communications without being certain, one way or the other.'

'All the same, you will do nothing for the present.'

'Then . . . there remains this absurd and grotesque demand, Sire, that you pardon Grey Venger and restore the True Sept to legitimate status. It is beneath contempt, truly.'

'If Issul is able to furnish evidence of the existence of the Legendary Child we will have a point of negotiation.'

'Such negotiations will not be viewed favourably among the other sects and factions.'

Leth compressed his lips mirthlessly. It was not so long ago that the factions had shown a united front in opposition to him and his stance on the Deist Edict. Later, after Venger's failed assassination attempt, the others had turned upon the True Sept, unanimous in their call for the head of its leader. The influential Sept's fall allowed each of them to jostle for a more favourable position. They would not welcome any move to have the Sept reinstated.

'It is complex,' said Leth, unable to escape the feeling that Fectur was himself manoeuvring into a position of personal advantage.

'But Venger will hardly reveal himself in the knowledge that it is only to part company with his head, no matter the inducement. The situation may call for unusual measures. To this end I am prepared to call a special assembly of all faction heads and advisors. All depends upon Issul's news.'

IV

Issul's news.

What would she bring? What obscure business could she be involved in that would compel her to hold vital secrets from him, her husband? Secrets which were, moreover, of value to her country?

Leth was hurt and angry. This was not like her; they were confidantes. They had always trusted one another implicitly. There had never been secrets between them. Until now.

Except . . . Leth denied the uncomfortable thought that nagged at him. But another leapt forward in its place: surely whatever it was that Issul was engaged upon had not sprung suddenly upon her, out of nowhere. There was a new development in something that was longstanding, this was plain. For it to have propelled her into such swift and impetuous a response implied foreknowledge or familiarity of some kind.

Ah, but what of your own omissions, Leth? The voice taunted him again from within. *Are you so blameless?*

He knew he was not. He recalled the look on Issul's face the night she had enquired about the blue light she had seen beneath his study door. He had shamed himself with his peevish evasion. She had tried to hide it, but he knew he had hurt her.

But it was different, Leth protested. *Orbus had to remain a secret, even from Issul. So much was at stake. He had no choice.*

Leth thought about it. Issul might face similar pressures, a similar lack of choice. He was being unfair on her, then. But even so, if Issul had information about the Legendary Child, what influence could have been so strong as to discourage her from discussing it with him?

Leth was not thinking clearly. He was tired. He was dazed by the manner in which events had escalated, so suddenly, on so many fronts. Talk was spreading throughout Enchantment's Edge like a breeze through a field of corn. Certain parties had been quick to seize upon the slooths' attack as yet one more indication that the gods were angry. Reports were coming through of unofficial gatherings in streets and squares. The word had been put about that Crown policy in regard to the Deist Edict was the cause of this latest misfortune, as it was all others. These were warnings, stated the doomsayers and political manipulators. The gods were jealous. They would strike again, and again, each blow being more powerful, more terrifying, more destructive. They would punish Enchantment's Edge without remorse until they were once more granted their due recognition in the form of obeisances and worship.

So the talk went. Of course, people were in shock. The slooths' attack had struck terror into the very heart of Enchantment's Edge, and such reactions were to be expected. So Leth passed no orders for the gatherings to be dispersed. Things would quickly settle down once more, providing the attacks were not repeated.

But they would be repeated.

This he could virtually guarantee. Despite his hopes and efforts to the contrary he was now at war with the Krai, for he did not doubt that it was from Prince Anzejarl that the slooths had come. How Anzejarl had tamed them to his will remained a mystery, but the brutal fact remained that terror could rain from the skies at any time.

Leth had doubled crossbow troops all across the city-castle and palace. He had ordered ropes, nets and sheets of steel mesh to be slung between towers, over streets and, where possible, over more open areas. These would provide a hindrance to the slooths when they next came. But these articles were in relatively short supply, and Enchantment's Edge was vast. He could not hope to cover more than a small area.

Leth knew himself to be occupying a more and more precarious position. His people were afraid and were looking to him for decisive actions and a swift resolution of the crisis. And the factions were losing no opportunity to exploit his dilemma and propose their own remedies.

Despite all his efforts to keep private the news that the Krai were in league with a god, word had leaked out some days ago. This reinforced the factions' position, giving fuel to the notion that the gods sought revenge. Leth could feel the growing tension in the air now, not so far short of hysteria. A spindrift of violence, still rarefied and without form, but requiring little to transform it into a wave capable of immense and perhaps irreparable damage.

Is this how you work, Anzejarl?

If so, Leth could but admire his enemy. But could Anzejarl be so cunning, so resourceful, so knowledgeable as to have precipitated all this? He was more than a man if it were so. More than a Krai. He was virtually a god himself, and for this reason Leth doubted. It had to be that the matter of the Legendary Child, if not entirely coincidental, was at least not directly related to Anzejarl's campaign.

Leth considered what he knew of the tale of the Legendary Child. Said to be the spawn of a god, a demon, a source of destruction beyond imagining. Beyond that only the leaders of the True Sept knew, or so they claimed.

But this news – the mere rumour that the Legendary Child existed – could be enough to swell the great wave that Leth feared. He had commanded Fectur to absolute silence, but he knew he could not delay in dealing with the issue for long. Grey Venger would demand acknowledgement in some form. Everything depended upon the news that Issul brought.

But the night passed, and the following day and another night. And in the morning Issul did not return.

Another night, sleepless for the tormented King. Lord Fectur brought the news that three of his men, sent in advance of Issul with the peasant woman Ohirbe, had returned. They had left the Queen in Lastmeadow, expecting her to follow almost in their wake. Upon the road they had passed the platoon of King's Cavalry sent by Leth to guard her.

Still Issul did not return. Leth's fears mounted and by the next morning an abyss of gloom had begun to open beneath him. He fought against the thoughts that rose to taunt and enfeeble him, but with growing conviction found himself contemplating what he had never before had to contemplate. Something terrible had happened. He had not been there when she needed him most. Now . . .

Alone in their bedchamber he buried his face in his hands. He could keep it at bay no longer.

She was lost.

SEVEN

I

An eternity, it seemed, of pain. Sickening, lurching motion. The world was topsy-turvy, tossed and hurled, a pounding blur of grass and earth and leaves, impossibly above her. A mouldering woody smell, mingled with leather and the warm fleshy odour of a horse.

She could not move, nor bear to keep her eyes open. The agony in her head was blinding and fierce. She was jogged and rocked nauseatingly. Her whole body cried out, but she could do nothing. The darkness came and drew her back.

When she next came to nothing had changed. The muscles of her gut and back ached abominably; she was stretched and restricted unnaturally, and afflicted by a raging thirst. The pain in her head remained, though its ferocity had abated slightly and the light no longer forced her to close her eyes. Wisps of her own fair hair hung within her vision and the ground still passed over her head in a horrible rolling blur.

Still she could not move. But now she saw the horse's hooves and understood at last that the earth was not passing above her. She was slung over the animal's back, her ankles and wrists bound and linked by a taut thong passed beneath its belly.

Twisting her head Issul saw the booted feet of her abductor, or one of her abductors, plodding just ahead, leading the horse. Straining the other way she saw others marching behind. She could not tell how many. Because of her awkward position and an excruciating stiffness at the back of her neck she could barely lift her head, and thus could see no faces or even identifying uniforms or emblems.

They marched in silence, and the world slewed and jolted and swayed. Nausea swelled dangerously on the back of her pain. She clamped shut her jaw and her eyes, fighting it back. She tried to make herself think clearly, for everything was a red haze of pain.

She was a captive, that was plain. But of whom – or of what?

They were taking her somewhere. Where?

Anyone's guess. But she lived, and that in itself suggested her captors had some purpose in mind for her.

Did they know who she was?

She had no way of telling.

She wondered about the wisdom of letting them know that she was conscious. Nothing could be worse than the agony she was currently suffering. Her thirst had become unbearable, her wrists and ankles chafed by the rope that bound them. Her back, gut, neck and head felt as though they were being wrenched asunder.

Issul called out, but her voice emerged as a dry rasp, barely audible. She tried again, this time making no effort to form words, simply letting out a long, arid moan as loudly as she could.

The horse upon which she was slung came abruptly to a halt. The world rotated slowly, dizzyingly, disorientating her further. Through the throbbing, swirling fog of her pain she made out the booted feet, moving close into her line of vision. A hand grasped her hair and swept it aside, twisting her head around. Issul rolled her eyes to try to see, but her captor remained beyond her view.

'She is awake,' said a voice.

Another replied: 'Release her.'

Big, pale, wrinkled hands reached down to release the thong that linked her wrists to her ankles. Then the boots passed around the rear of the horse and Issul felt the bindings at her ankles being untied. Not cut. She noted this: whoever they were, her captors were not wasteful. The bindings were valuable to them.

She was grasped by her belt and hauled from the horse. Sharp spasms of pain lanced through her entire body, and she cried out again, this time involuntarily. Her feet, numb and bloodless, gave way and she fell. Strong hands saved her from harm and allowed her to sink onto her buttocks on the ground.

'Water,' Issul rasped. A leather bottle was placed in her hands, which were still bound together at the wrists. Gratefully she raised the bottle and drank with long, greedy draughts.

'Can you stand?'

'Give me a moment.'

She stretched and rotated her feet, crooked and extended her legs to ease the stiffness, and massaged the muscles with her bound hands, then nodded. A hand beneath her armpit helped her upright. She took quick note of her surroundings: deep forest, the dull light above, then she was propelled forward. She staggered limply around the horse, and came face to face with a man the like of whom she had never seen before.

Issul had read and heard descriptions and seen likenesses in books and paintings, of course, but this was the first time she had found herself locking eyes with a living Krai. And what she saw shocked her.

It was not that the Krai were so different from humans. Rather it was that they were so similar, but those differences they possessed were striking and made them appear utterly alien. The man – the Krai warrior – she faced was no taller than she. His face was pale and long and deeply lined and seamed. The pallid flesh brought to mind that of an etiolated raisin. The mouth was a small, tight gash, the lips almost colourless. But it was the eyes that drew. The globes themselves were almost pure turquoise in hue. A fine latticework of vessels of a darker tone could just he made out, tracing a filigree pattern across their surfaces. There appeared to be no iris, but the pupil was a gleaming horizontal slit of darkest malachite.

Gem-eyes. Issul had heard the Krai referred to that way many times, and the term was fully justified. Stories were told of Krai being murdered, or at least mutilated, for their eyes. The globes, however, quickly faded and decayed once deprived of a blood supply, so the practice never gained great popularity. Krai ornamental slaves were spoken of, though: individuals abducted or purchased by ruthless nabobs and condemned to a life of absolute immobility confined in imaginatively-fashioned cages, their vocal organs removed and only their marvellous eyes visible for any who passed to admire.

But what startled Issul as much as the visual impact of the eyes was the fact that she could read nothing in them. No hint of the thoughts or emotions that resided behind them. In that sense they were even more like gems: fascinating and beautiful, bright and utterly strange, but without sensitivity or soul.

As she gathered her thoughts she realized something else, perhaps even more startling. It was the fact that this *was* a Krai. They were here, deep within the wildlands of Enchantment's Edge. So close!

She glanced aside. From what she could see, at least fifteen Krai warriors made up her party. There could have been more, though, concealed by the deep, close forest. She noted that some wore bloody bandages.

The Krai who faced her, apparently in command, spoke. 'You are a lady.'

'Your intelligence is astonishing. Are all of your race so perceptive?' Issul stood proud and scornful, determined to conceal the fact that she was, in truth, deeply afraid.

The Krai captain remained impassive, as though the taunt had no meaning to him. 'I mean, you ride with an escort. You have rank. You come from Orbia palace.'

Issul thought swiftly. Obviously he did not know who she was. She must keep it that way. What would the knowledge that their enemy Queen was in their hands be worth to them? 'I am a lady-in-waiting, to the family of the Lord Treasurer.'

'You will be missed?'

She shrugged. 'Yes, but quickly replaced.'

Immediately she regretted it. It was possible the Krai was assessing her ransom value, and she had just declared herself virtually worthless. *A ransom demand for the lady-in-waiting to the family of the Lord Treasurer? They would guess that it was me. Leth would know it immediately!*

'However,' she quickly added, 'they will do all in their power to get me back.'

The Krai captain weighed this emotionlessly. His continuing lack of expression, fully implied by the eyes, disconcerted her. It was impossible to gain any inkling of his thoughts.

'Why were you on the road? Where were you going?'

Suddenly it was all flooding back to her. Her pain and confusion had been blocking it. Ohirbe and Arrin. The ambush. The old woman in the woods. Moscul!

Issul turned to the side to see if any other captives were among the party. The Krai captain reached out quickly and took her jaw between fingers and thumb, brought her head around to face him again. His grip was strong but not excessively forceful, and he did not maintain it longer than was required to make his point and achieve his aim.

But Issul went rigid, her hackles rising. *That he should touch her like this!* She fought down her emotion, the urge to strike him on the shin or in the groin. *He must have no clue as to who I am!*

'Why were you on the road? Where were you going?' the Krai repeated with perfect precision.

'I was returning to Orbia after visiting my family.'

Again no response.

She held up her wrists. 'Can this be untied, please?'

'No.'

'Where am I being taken?'

He ignored her. 'Can you walk?'

'I – I think so.' She flexed the muscles of her legs again and arched her back, stretching the spine. Gradually the blood had flowed back into her limbs; she was fairly sure that, though stiff, bruised and grazed, she had suffered no serious injury. Her neck was painful to turn, however, and the pain in her head still raged.

'Good.' The Krai captain nodded towards the waiting men. Issul saw that, in the midst of the Krai soldiers, there were a pair of prisoners. They were both men, neither known to her, one grey-haired and elderly and one youthful, quite slim but robust. Their wrists were bound like hers, and a length of slender rope was stretched between the two, linking them.

The Krai who had taken her from the horse now guided her to where the two stood. She was placed behind them and another line attached between her and the younger prisoner. The horse that she had ridden, the only animal in the party, was now loaded with baggage, which had previously been lugged by the two prisoners and a couple of soldiers. There was a short wait as the Krai captain conferred with one of his men. The man then turned and made off down the pathway, back the way they had come. Ten or so Krai warriors went with him, armed with bows and swords.

Issul wondered how much time had passed since she had been ambushed and captured. She thought it unlikely that she had been unconscious for more than a day. The ambush had taken place some time after midday. It was now, by her estimate, late afternoon. The same day? Short of asking the Krai, who presumably would not reply, she had no way of knowing.

She thought about Sir Bandullo and the others of her escort. All dead? Ohirbe? *Moscul?*

Perhaps she would never know. She felt confused and suddenly deeply despondent.

The Krai captain motioned with his arm and they moved on.

II

They walked for as long as the light held. The trees obscured much of the sky, but Issul saw that the brightest of the dying light was concentrated obliquely towards her rear. Her direction of travel, then, was generally south. Towards Enchantment.

She tried speaking to the two prisoners in front of her, hoping to gain some basic information, most particularly about her missing companions. But though she put her words in an undertone, she had barely opened her mouth before a Krai guard stepped in and prodded her roughly in the back, ordering her to silence.

When the light became too dim for further travel the Krai captain brought them to a halt. Issul was grateful. Though she had walked for no more than a couple of hours, she was weak and her limbs ached. She longed for rest. The older of the two prisoners had also been stumbling and dragging his feet, as though the effort pained him.

A couple of Krai herded her and the other two to one side. They were ordered to sit, their ankles tied and food was then brought: a chunk of hardtack, cold rice and water. The Krai warriors formed a wide circle around them. No one lit a fire; no one spoke, other than to issue the occasional curt, hushed command.

Issul ate, finding the food barely palatable, but too hungry to leave even a single grain of rice. She observed the Krai warriors as they sat hunched in the twilight, and noted that they ate the same rations as she. In due course the captain came and stood before the three of them, his wrinkled face a pale blotch in the near-dark. He carried blankets, and dropped one at the feet of each. 'Sleep now. Do not talk. Tomorrow we leave early.'

As he walked away Issul pulled the blanket around her and lay back upon the hard earth. She was weary and miserable, and she lay with her eyes open staring at the great mist of stars in the blackness overhead.

Are you there, now? Do you look and wonder from afar, ask yourself what is happening here, on this distant world? Do you suffer as we do? Or are we truly as alone as we feel?

The older man beside her had begun to snore. She heard an owl screech in the woods nearby. It came to her that she might have fared worse. She was the only woman in the party, young and beautiful, even with scuffs and bruises. But no one had so much as looked at her with the kind of interest she might have expected. The prisoners were frightened and subdued. They had barely raised their eyes when she joined them. And the Krai . . . Well, the Krai were the Krai.

It was small comfort, for who knew what awaited her tomorrow? Where were they taking her?

With these questions uppermost in her mind she fell eventually into sleep.

Dawn brought a light, cool breeze snaking through the forest. Issul awoke shivering; her single blanket had been less than adequate protection against the night's chill. The cold hardness of the earth beneath her seemed to have seeped through her flesh to penetrate her very bones. A Krai stomped past, slapping her buttocks with a switch to rouse her. She sat up with abrupt anger, but forced herself to keep it inside. The soldier paid her no heed, but moved on to rouse the other two prisoners in the same manner.

The Krai were up, stamping and shaking themselves into wakefulness. Food was brought: the same basic rations of the night before. Then the blankets and other accoutrements were swiftly and efficiently packed away by ever-silent Krai, and they resumed their march.

They had walked for perhaps an hour, following no discernible path, twisting and looping deeper into the forest, when Issul heard a strange, soft, sound overhead. Arhythmically pulsing, breathy and indefinable. She looked up, in time to see passing above the trees a group of those same huge birdlike creatures that she had seen previously from the road beyond Enchantment's Edge. They were lower than before, travelling in roughly the same direction as she. Broad wings patiently beat the air with a sound somewhere between a sigh and a slap. It seemed to Issul now that they were not birds at all, though what they were she could not say. She shuddered, counting thirteen of the dark creatures before the dense canopy of trees obscured them from her sight. The other two prisoners also gaped at them and exchanged fearful glances, but the Krai appeared indifferent to their passage.

A little later she grew aware that the company had swelled. More warriors had joined them. Issul took them to be the ones who had left them the previous afternoon. From time to time she twisted her head and tried to count them. She had the impression that they had not all returned.

Further and further they advanced into the deep primordial wood. The gargantuan trees crowded ever closer, their shade ever denser. From time to time they had to scramble up steep banks or rocky spurs, or descend into gulleys and ravines. Issul lost track of their direction, but the Krai appeared to know where they were bound. The pace, though not particularly fast, was nonetheless gruelling. Issul saw that the older man ahead of her was finding it heavy going. When she could she assisted him, as did his young companion.

At midday they paused. All three flopped down upon the dark earth, hot, sweating and weary. They wolfed their ration of food, the cool water sweet and merciful in their parched throats. But the respite was brief, and soon they were stumbling forward again.

Sometime in the mid-afternoon they broke suddenly from the trees into a wide grassy clearing. A camp of sorts had been established here, a palisade of sharpened stakes forming its perimeter. Wooden guardtowers had been erected within, and a Krai sentry was stationed in each.

They made their way to the gate, which drew open to admit them. Several large tents and a few wooden huts had been erected inside. There were more Krai, and here a fire burned, a slaughtered buck's carcass roasting on a spit above the flames, tended by a plump Krai soldier. Issul and the other two captives were conducted to one of the larger huts. The door was barred behind them and an armed sentry posted outside.

There were no windows within the hut; the only light came via chinks in the rough timberwork of the walls and roof. As her eyes adjusted to the dimness Issul made out three rows of makeshift beds upon the floor. They were made of dry grass and leaves, with a blanket or old sacking on each. There were a couple of dozen in all, laid almost side to side, with narrow aisles between.

Issul moved to one and sank down, as did the others. She lay in silence for some time, absorbed in her thoughts and fears. No matter her weariness, her immediate concern was escape.

But escape to where?

She had no notion of where she was. Enchantment's Edge lay away to the north . . . somewhere. Were she somehow to succeed in breaking free of the Krai, she had little hope of surviving alone in the forest. The wildwood was haunted by creatures which, though they might have avoided a party of armed Krai, would have no hesitation in stalking and preying upon a solitary wanderer.

Still, she would not abandon the thought of freeing herself from her captors; to do so was to abandon hope. Issul spoke to the other two. 'Where are you from? How long have you been prisoners?'

The voice that replied was that of the elder man. 'The hamlet of Glux. We are charcoal burners. I am Miseon, this is my son, Herbin. We were at work in the woods, not far from Glux, when six of these warriors came upon us. They killed my other son, Demsolt, when he tried to resist, then tied us and led us away. We joined the larger party just a short way into the forest. You were already strapped across the horse.'

'Then you know nothing of a skirmish that took place upon the road to Crosswood?'

Miseon shook his head, then asked, 'What is your name, child?'

Issul hesitated. 'Jace.'

It was the first name that came to mind, after her own. No one was likely to make a connection, whereas her name might just cause men to look twice. But as she said it the sweet face of her little fair-haired daughter formed before her, gazing up at her, her brother Galry at her side. Issul squeezed back tears and stifled the sob that rose suddenly in her breast. *My babies, I will find my way back to you! Believe me, I will. This I swear!*

'Well, Jace, I suggest we rest and conserve our strength. I for one am bone-weary after the long march, and though we seem to have arrived at our destination I do not anticipate tomorrow being a much easier day.'

'Are we to be used for slave-labour, do you think, Miseon?'

'Who knows? It is in the hands of the gods.'

Later, when the day had faded outside so that barely any light was visible through the chinks in the wood, the door to the hut was thrown open suddenly. Issul, who was seated at the far end of the hut with her back against the wall, saw several dark figures outside. One brought in an oil-lamp which he hung upon a peg just inside the door. They filed into the hut one by one, eight or nine in number, and collapsed onto the litters.

Issul grew wary. From what she could see they were all men. They were roughly clothed and unarmed. Prisoners, she gathered, like herself. But a common plight did not make them less dangerous.

The hut had filled with the odours of the mens' sweat. The lamp cast minimal light, but it was enough to reveal her and her two companions to the newcomers. By and large they seemed indifferent at first. Issul wondered whether indeed she and the others had been noticed. But presently a loud coarse voice spoke out from one side. 'What's this, then? More recruits to our merry gang?'

A bulky figure stirred and leaned towards the three, then rose and approached. He peered down at them, a huge man with a mass of shaggy black hair, then looked more closely at Issul.

'By the devils and demons, we've got a woman 'ere! And a perfect pretty one, too! Maybe the Gem-eyes are not so heartless after all.'

He stooped, resting hands upon knees, and pushed his face towards her. His features gleamed with sweat. Issul felt herself pressing back involuntarily against the timber wall. Behind the big man others were rousing and making moves to investigate. Their eyes glittered as they crowded around, peering curiously as though she were a freak or some kind of strange and desirable exhibit put on display. Her fear mounted, but anger came through on top of it.

The big man reached towards her with one hand, as though to touch her face. Issul brushed his wrist aside with a swift sweep of her arm. 'Don't touch me!'

'Oh, a polecat!' He straightened, putting his hands on his hips, and turned to the others. 'She has spirit, this beauty! As though she cannot resist Ombo's charms!'

One or two laughed. The big man, Ombo, turned back. 'Now, sweet one, be a bit more friendly, won't you? There's no harm in showing a little friendship, now, is there?'

'None whatsoever, but I have not invited you to touch me.'

'Aww, now that's not the way,' said Ombo. 'Come now . . .'

He reached forward again.

'Stop!'

It was Herbin, Miseon's son, who spoke. He came from the side, a slight figure beside Ombo. 'Leave her. Do not treat her so. She has suffered greatly, as have we all.'

Ombo, still bent over towards Issul, turned his head to stare at him mockingly. 'Oh, and is that so, now? And who are you?'

'My name is Herbin. I am a captive of the Krai, as are you all, are you not? I have been brought here today with my father, Miseon, and Jace. When I saw you men enter, my heart was gladdened. Here, I thought, here are others with whom we share common misfortune. Here are men who will share with us our hatred of these jewel-eyed barbarians who have taken us from our homes and families. Here are men who will join with us to resist them. Yet now, what do I see? That no sooner are you through the door than you turn like beasts upon the most vulnerable among us.'

Ombo, for a moment, seemed lost for words. Issul began to scramble to her feet, but he extended a beefy arm and pushed her roughly back. He rose erect to face the young man.

'Well, Herbin, I hear your words, and it's a fine speech you have given. But I disagree. You see, the way I view it is that the Gem-eyes have decided to reward us for our labours. They've given us this little . . . Jace is her name? . . . they've given her to us as a little bit of consolation, as a way of saying thank you for all the hard work we've been doing for them these past weeks. Now, if you disagree, then as I see it, the way to settle the disagreement is for you and I to meet like men and fight it out. Winner takes all. What do you say to that?'

'I do not feel that fighting will get us anywhere, unless it is against our abductors,' replied Herbin falteringly, his nerves betraying him.

'Oh, but I do,' said Ombo, and launched himself forward, striking hard with his forearm. The blow caught Herbin by surprise, on the chin. It lifted him off his feet and pitched him backwards into the wall behind. Ombo went after him, took him beneath the arms and lifted him, swinging him around.

'No!' Issul yelled. She was on her feet, facing Ombo, her teeth bared in anger. 'It is you and I who will fight, Ombo. If that is your way.'

Ombo's big head jerked back on his shoulders. 'Ombo? Fight a woman?'

He thrust the dazed Herbin aside.

'That is what I said.' Issul adjusted her balance, felt the ground with her feet, securing her stance, and sensed the space around her. 'Or are you afraid?'

Ombo gave a laugh. 'I do not know how to be afraid.'

'I can believe that.'

Somebody chuckled, which gave her heart. They were not all against her; not entirely.

She sized the big man up, not at all sure of herself. She had learned tricks of combat over the years – Lord Fectur in particular had been a master of the art of fighting beneath rules, and had passed some of his wisdom on to her – but her experience was limited purely to training. Never had she had to fight for real.

Ombo dwarfed her. He was plainly immensely strong, strong enough to snap her neck with one hand. Her only hope was her agility.

'D'you hear this, lads? Little Jace wants to fight me,' Ombo roared. Was there unease behind his bluster? He had probably rarely, if ever, been challenged before. Certainly never by a woman.

'There is one condition,' said Issul. 'If I win, I and my two friends here are to be left alone. Is that agreed?'

'If you win?' Ombo was incredulous. 'There is no chance of that, little Jace. We are about to have us some sport!'

He threw himself forward, arms extended. Issul dropped and rolled. A sharp pain hammered at the back of her skull, reminding her that only recently she had been injured by a blow there. She came up against the wall and sprang to her feet, wincing as a strained muscle in her back rebelled at the sudden movement.

Ombo's momentum had taken him beyond her. He spun lumberingly around. Issul took two steps, leapt high and kicked out. The tensed edge of her foot slammed into his face.

Ombo shook his head as she landed lightly upon her feet. A little blood trickled from his nose. Now Issul knew she had trouble. The blow, impacting with as much force as she could muster, had barely shaken him.

'Well, little Jace, that's fancy, that is. Very fancy. Now this time I'd like you to wrap those slender little thews around my head. Can you do that for Ombo? I'll reward you, you'll see.'

He made an obscene gesture with his tongue. Some of the men sniggered. Until now they had been almost silent, which Issul took to be a positive sign. She had confused them, and the fact that they were not vociferously egging Ombo on suggested they might not be unanimously behind him.

Ombo advanced again, more warily this time. He guarded his head with his arms, and weaved and bobbed. He might have been fighting another man. This respect gratified Issul, though it made her task more difficult, for he was no longer taking her quite for granted.

She backed a step. Ombo came forward. His stance was wide, the knees bent. He reached for her, a cuffing blow that would have sent her reeling had it connected. But she slid back, waiting, cautious with her movements lest the pain of her head and limbs distract her. But she had seen his weakness. He came in once more. Issul dropped to the floor, slid into him and quickly snapped one foot, then the other, hard into his groin.

There was an empathic gasp from the others. Ombo doubled over and sank to the floor in agony, clutching himself and groaning. Issul was on her feet, ready to move in and slam his head against the floor. But at that moment the door of the hut opened. All the men melted back to their litters. Issul instinctively did likewise.

Two men shuffled in. Between them swung a large, heavy metal pot, which they bore on a stout pole supported on their shoulders. Each also carried a sack bound across his back. A Krai guard entered behind them.

They set the pot down inside and unslung their sacks. Steam rose from the pot and Issul caught the appetizing aroma of some kind of soup or stew. The guard's eyes settled upon Ombo, who had tried to roll to his litter but who was still doubled up in pain.

'Touch of wind!' came a voice from one of the litters. ''E'll be all right.'

The guard showed no expression. 'Line up.'

Obediently the prisoners formed a line before the pot. Issul, Herbin and Miseon took their places behind them. Ombo got to his feet and hobbled over to join them, glowering murderously at Issul as he passed. The two who had brought in the pot opened their sacks: one was filled with battered tin bowls and crude wooden spoons, the other bulged with thick slices of hard grey bread. Each prisoner took a spoon and bowl as he passed. One of the men ladled soup into each bowl, the other handed out a single piece of bread to each.

The prisoners grumbled as they passed, accusing the ladler of not dipping deeply enough into the pot to catch the pieces of food that resided at the bottom, or complaining that their chunk of bread was smaller than their neighbour's. When it came to Issul's turn she took her bowl and spoon and held them forward. The man with the ladle, a sinewy fellow with wispy pale hair, stopped and gaped at her.

'What's the matter? Have you never seen a woman before?' She pushed her tin towards him and assumed a tone of authority. 'Dig deep, please. I am hungry.'

He obeyed, she took her bread and made off to the end of the hut. She tested the soup tentatively. It was fatty and salty, but otherwise of not bad quality. Several vegetables and small pieces of meat floated in it and she judged it quite nourishing.

The men slurped noisily under the watchful eye of the guard. Though some soup remained in the pot, second helpings were not permitted. Bowls and spoons were collected and the pot taken away by the same two prisoners who had brought it. They returned a short time later, one of them carrying a large bucket with a heavy lid, which he placed in a corner. Issul noted that the litters closest to that corner were unclaimed.

As the guard was about to leave, Issul stood. 'Do you intend leaving me here with these men?'

'I have been given no other orders.'

'Then give me a knife that I may kill myself now.'

The Krai walked slowly down the centre of the hut towards her. 'They will not touch you.'

'You know little about men,' retorted Issul.

Like the Krai captain the previous day, the guard was unaffected. He looked at her with detached certainty, shook his head, and said, in a strong, clear voice, 'Not one of these men will lay a finger on you tonight. Not one. Now, there will be silence until morning.'

He swivelled upon his heel and strode from the hut, taking the lamp with him and bolting the door.

Issul stood alone in the darkness, aware that her limbs were trembling. She could hear the loud breathing of the men in the hut, feel their body heat, smell their sweat. She waited, sure that they would come.

She realized suddenly that more than one was snoring. Someone else moved, groped about in the dark. Issul tensed, but his sounds told her he was moving away from her, towards the corner where the bucket was set. More sounds made plain the bucket's purpose. Issul's anger and revulsion rose. Was she expected to share such a basic facility, to make use of it in the presence of these men?

She sat down, furious and disgusted. A voice a little way off whispered, 'Sleep, woman. You will not be harmed, and tomorrow you will need your strength.'

She did not know who had spoken. 'What happens here?' she whispered back. 'What do the Krai have you do?'

'Just sleep. You will know soon enough.'

III

Issul did sleep, eventually, though it was fitful and broken frequently by the sounds of men stirring and using the bucket. And no one troubled her, though occasional groans made her wonder about the content of their dreams. She wondered too at the implicit threat in the Krai guard's short speech, that it could so suppress the appetites of men like these.

And when she slept, she dreamed. One dream, which itself was a memory she had never wholly buried. It repeated itself again and again. A dream of her younger sister, Ressa, on that day of darkness when the terrible and unthinkable had happened, of which no one had been fully aware.

It had been Springtime. The day was warm and bright, a carefree, cloudless day that gave no hint of the shadows that hovered at its edge. The three sisters were walking in the meadows close to their parents' summer villa, Saroon. Issul had sat down to dangle her toes in the cool water of a pool which lay close upon the fringe of the woodlands behind Saroon. The twins, tarrying a short while, had then gone on, arm in arm, taking a well-worn path into the woods which led to Sentinel's Peak, a high promontory which commanded a view of the countryside for some leagues, and the distant, mysterious Enchantment peaks beyond.

Issul had dozed in the sunlight. Now, as she dreamed, the idyll was obliterated, and she was forced to relive only the horror that followed.

She dreamed that she dreamed, and that in that dream an animal was crying in distress. She wanted to help it, but could not determine the source of the plaintive sounds. And then she woke and was beside the tranquil pool in the warm sunlight, and the cries had not ceased. But they were a maiden's cries, not those of any animal. Issul leapt to her feet and ran, along the pathway, into the woods from where her sister called out her pain.

The first thing she saw, a little way along the path, was Mawnie. Staggering towards her, her clothing torn and her long hair in disarray. Mawnie was not crying, but the screams had not ceased.

'Mawnie! Mawnie! What has happened to you? Where's Ressa? Where's Ressa?'

Mawnie's eyes were wide, her lips stretched in a rictus. She pushed past her sister, pointing distractedly back the way she had come, gasping but unable to speak. To Issul's eyes she was not seriously hurt, and after a moment's indecision she let her go in order to run on deeper into the wood in search of Ressa.

The screams had stopped, which terrified Issul more deeply than when they had sounded. She scrambled up the rocky way that led to the promontory, and there saw something that froze her in her tracks. Ressa lay upon the grass thirty paces away, in a small grassy hollow well-known to the sisters, for they had come there often to sit and talk and play and while away the hours. Ressa was apparently unconscious, perhaps even dead. She was spreadeagled upon the ground, her face turned towards Issul, bloody and naked but for a few remaining tatters of her frock.

But it was not the sight of Ressa that held Issul rooted to the spot so much as that of the creature that had mounted her. With harsh grunts it completed its frenzied motions, its back arched, shoulders high and head thrown back. Then it climbed to its feet, a mannish thing, but more powerful in its physique than any man Issul had seen. A double row of knobbly spines extended down the length of its back and along the lashing tail. A bony crest stood erect from its crown. It was naked, its skin pale blue-grey from head to toe. It turned and glared for a moment at Issul. She saw the fiery redness of its eyes and believed herself doomed. It took a step towards her, then sprang, away, onto a rock, then leapt out over the lip of the promontory and was lost from sight.

Issul ran shaking to the edge and peered over. There was no sign of the thing. She rushed down to her sister.

She woke.

Her horror at the recurrent dream was turned to despair as she recognized her surroundings, which somehow, in an earlier state of half-sleep, she had half-persuaded herself were themselves the product of a ghastly dream. But the interior of the hut was dimly illumined by splinters of weak grey light piercing the gaps in the timber. She saw the hunched shapeless masses of her fellow prisoners huddled beneath their blankets, smelt the rimy stench and heard the noise of their breathing. Outside birds were singing.

Birdsong. In the past it had never failed to lift her spirit, now it mocked her. It was the sound of freedom and made her more brutally aware of her anguish.

She had little time to contemplate her wretchedness. There was a heavy footstep outside, the bolt on the door was released and the door flew open, a dazzling rectangle of light. The Krai guard framed there stepped back, one hand to his nose. The two men who had last night brought the soup leapt from their litters and ran outside.

'You! Woman!' called the guard.

Issul rose. He pointed to the right-bucket. 'Take it.'

Issul recoiled. 'I will not!'

'Take it!'

Somebody spoke up behind her. 'I'll help her. She doesn't know where.'

A hand grasped one of Issul's and a man's voice whispered in her ear, 'If you want to live another minute, don't resist.'

The hand pulled her towards the bucket. She looked at the prisoner who held her. He was dark-haired, bearded. His eyes met hers for a moment and she saw the warning there. He took the night bucket, its lid already on, and lifted the handle, dragging Issul so that her own hand was also clasped around the handle.

'I will show her,' he said to the guard, who nodded once in acquiescence.

Together they took the bucket out and, accompanied by another Krai, made their way across the camp compound.

'Jace, listen to me,' said her companion. 'The Krai like to run an efficient camp here. If they order you to do something, do it, no matter how distasteful. They don't tolerate anything but absolute obedience. Do you understand?'

'Yes, but—'

'No buts. That is the first law of survival here. Not that it's worth much, for we grow fewer every day.'

'Why? What do you do here?'

'It isn't what we do, though that's hard enough.'

'Then what?'

He clenched his jaw, and looked away. 'You'll know soon enough. Now, my name's Kol and remember, you almost lost your life back there.'

'Thank you, Kol.'

'Don't thank me. I'm not seeking favours. Just be mindful of what it takes to survive, even if it's only for one more day.'

They reached the far side of the camp. A wooden screen had been erected, behind which a system of planks set above holes in the ground formed a latrine. Kol emptied the bucket into one of the holes and made to return.

'Wait,' said Issul. She spoke to the guard and gained permission to use the latrine, for she had spent the night in some discomfort rather than suffer the humiliation of using the bucket.

As they walked back she cast her eyes about the compound. To one side Krai fighters silently engaged one another in combat drill. Others stood guard beside huts, tents and in the towers. There were no women as far as she could see. She estimated at least forty Krai. She took the camp to be some kind of forward base. From here lightning raids could be launched, designed to terrorize and disrupt. Small towns, villages and farms would be the probable targets, as well as lightly- or un-armed travellers upon the roads near Enchantment's Edge. What she was not clear about was why they kept prisoners.

A man came from another hut carrying a bucket similar to that which she and Kol had. Two others transported a large pot and sacks inside. So there were other prisoners. She quickly scanned the compound again. As far as she could make out, they were housed in only the two huts.

'We must escape,' she whispered to Kol, taking care that the guard was out of earshot. But Kol looked at her as if she were a child.

The Krai favoured cleanliness as well as orderliness, and she and Kol were permitted to wash quickly in cold water before re-entering the hut. Inside the prisoners queued for breakfast, a thick, grainy gruel and the staple grey bread and water. As soon as they had eaten they were summoned outside where they lined up in a double row. Strong, light chains were shackled to their ankles, but before Issul's were applied a short, thickset Krai approached and drew her aside. 'You will stay here.'

The men, guards at their side, shuffled across the compound and passed from sight behind the tents. The thickset Krai issued Issul with instructions for the day. She was to begin by washing the pots, bowls, spoons and mugs from the two prisoners' huts, then similar utensils of the Krai themselves. When she had completed that she was taken to a wide, fast-flowing stream at the edge of the camp and there made to wash the Krai soldiers' clothing with a brush, stone and a hard sandy ball of soap. Later in the day she was taken to another hut where a mound of similar clothing awaited repair. Issul was given needles and thick thread and left to get on with it.

In short, she had been appointed scullion, washerwoman and seamstress to the Krai. A guard was assigned to her at all times; others were always close at hand. No one spoke to her, except to give orders. She was not permitted to cease working, other than for a short break at midday when she was given soup and water.

The work was exhausting. Issul had never done anything of its kind. The art of sewing, particularly, she had to learn from scratch. But midway through the morning she learned the cost of protesting when, after a short time scrubbing tunics in the cold stream, she stopped. Her fingers were numb with cold and her back ached from constantly bending.

'I can't do this,' she said, standing stiffly.

'You do it,' said her guard. Two others a short way off took a keen interest.

'I can't. I don't know how.'

'You learn, then.'

Issul shook her head, exasperated rather than bloody-minded. The guard stepped forward and punched her in the stomach. Before she could respond she was picked up and pushed into the stream, her head held under. Gasping from the pain of the blow, Issul took in water. She struggled frantically, feeling her consciousness ebb as a booted foot pressed her head down. Kol's words echoed somewhere in her dying mind: the Krai don't tolerate anything but absolute obedience. Her lungs were bursting, convulsing – then she was hauled up by the hair and dragged to the shore where she lay coughing and gasping in the mud.

'Now, you do the work. Understand?'

IV

At the day's end, as dusk began to shroud the forest, Issul was escorted back to her hut. The prisoners were brought in at more or less the same time, tired and dirty. Issul, exhausted, slumped down upon her litter. Young Herbin came and sat beside her, but his father, Miseon, was absent. Issul enquired about him.

'They came and took him away when they were removing our chains,' said Herbin.

Issul looked at him. Herbin was weary and forlorn, and clearly worried. She recalled how he had stood up for her against the brutish Ombo last night. It had taken immense courage to do that. He had been no match for Ombo, and she admired him for it. She spoke to the others. 'Does anyone know where they have taken Miseon?'

No one replied, none of them would meet her eye, except for Ombo who watched her with a surly smirk.

'Kol?' said Issul. 'Can you tell us?'

But Kol also was reluctant to speak.

'What of your labour today?' Issul asked Herbin softly.

'Heavy construction and excavation. I cannot grasp what for.'

'Miseon is not a young man. How did he bear up?'

'He made every effort to keep up, but it is gruelling work, even for the strongest among us. Late in the day Miseon collapsed and had to rest for some time.'

'Perhaps they have taken him for medical treatment, then,' said Issul.

Across the room Ombo guffawed loudly. Issul felt the blood colour her cheeks. Somehow she sensed that they would not see Miseon again.

The next day Issul was taken off latrine-duty, on the purely practical grounds that she lacked the physical strength to carry the full bucket without risk of spillage. The other prisoners were marched away and the remainder of her day passed in similar manner to the first.

As she worked she kept herself alert for possible routes of escape. The camp was well-guarded and regularly patrolled, the Krai apparently tireless in their surveillance. Always there were eyes upon her, not only those of the guard assigned to her, but of others, in a watchtower, beside a tent, across the compound. The only feasible escape route was via the stream where she washed the clothes. The stream lay outside the main compound and was reached via a secondary gate. But it was deep and fast-flowing. In the time it would take her to cross it and make for the wood beyond she could guarantee she would be spotted and, almost certainly, fired upon.

And she reminded herself once more that, even were she successful in getting free of the camp, the forest and all its denizens still remained.

The prisoners were having their chains removed as she returned to the hut that evening. She watched them line up for inspection before the Krai commander, who conferred briefly with one of the guards who had accompanied them on their work detail. The men were gaunt and hollow-eyed; she sensed their fear.

The commander nodded towards one, a lean man in his fifties whom Issul had not spoken to. The guard separated him from the group. Two men then made off with another guard to collect the evening's soup pot. The main group shuffled into the hut and the solitary prisoner was led away towards the far side of the camp.

Issul glanced across towards the other prison hut. A similar ritual seemed to have taken place there; a prisoner, young but with a pronounced limp, was being steered towards the far side of the compound.

EIGHT

I

On her third day as a prisoner of the Krai, Issul witnessed something unusual that she was not to understand for some time. It took place in the late morning. The male prisoners were away at their work and Issul was returning with her guard from the stream where she had been scrubbing. She was being escorted to the sewing hut.

Earlier in the morning, soon after the prisoners were led away, a detachment of armed Krai had left the camp through the main gate. They were about fifteen strong, and took with them the single horse laden with equipment. Issul took them to be another raiding party, off to cause havoc and disruption within the kingdom.

As she approached the door of the sewing hut, Issul cast her eyes across the compound, seeking, as always, some possible clue to a way of breaking free from the Krai. Across the camp she saw a man, a Krai, drop suddenly to the ground and lie motionless. Almost immediately two others ran towards him. An instant later another fell, this one a sentry posted at the entrance of a tent towards one side of the camp. She saw nothing more, for she had reached the sewing-hut and her guard had opened the door and pushed her inside.

Issul moved instantly to the window (unlike the dormitory, light was required in the sewing-hut to allow her to work). Wooden bars prevented her putting her head out, and the wall blocked her line of view. But she heard shouts and an armed squad crossed her field of view, running at the double towards the spot where the first soldier had fallen. Then all shouting ceased and the accustomed Krai silence resumed. Issul knelt down in the centre of the room and began her work, wondering what could have happened.

The remainder of the day passed without notable incident. During her short midday meal break, Issul stood beside the window but detected nothing to suggest that anything was amiss.

In the hut that evening Issul spoke quietly to Kol and Herbin. 'We have to organize an escape. I cannot do it alone. Who among us can be trusted?'

But Kol was pessimistic. 'It was tried before, Jace. The Krai are too alert. Apart from the troops here in the camp, they have set traps in the surrounding woods. It is deadly. On the day I arrived here they were bringing back three prisoners who had tried to escape. The Krai put them on display as an example to us. One was still alive, poor bastard.'

'But they are taking us and destroying us as they will. They use our labour for just as long as it suits them.'

Earlier Issul had noticed that the same number of prisoners who had left that morning had returned in the evening. On the previous two days the weakest individual from each hut had been led away and had not returned. The prisoners seemed to accept that as the norm. She wondered what had changed today.

'Where are they taken?' she asked.

Kol shook his head. 'We know only that they do not come back, and tomorrow it could be any one of us. Most especially if our work is not up to standard.'

'What is the work you do?'

Kol more or less echoed Herbin's words of the night before. 'We are building something at the back of the camp. A large construction, partly underground. I do not know its purpose.'

'But tonight no one was taken. Why?'

Kol shrugged. 'Sometimes it is like that. For a day, even two. We begin to hope, and then one of us is taken again.'

'We have to do something,' reiterated Issul. 'And the best time to do it would be, as today, when a significant part of the Krai force is elsewhere.'

'Do you have a plan?' asked Herbin.

She shook her head. 'Just a will, at present. But I need to know who is with me. Herbin?'

The young man nodded. 'Aye. I will not rot or die here if I have a choice. But I will not go until I know what has happened to my father.'

Issul nodded. 'Kol?'

'I support you, Jace. But I say again, I do not believe it is possible.'

'Then *I* say again, who else can we trust?'

Another voice interrupted out of the dark. 'Be silent over there or we will all suffer!'

It was Ombo. Issul stared hotly at his bulk, outlined in the dimness, but she held her tongue. He was right; the Krai inflicted harsh punishments for speaking without permission, and not always on the perpetrators alone.

'I will find out what I can,' whispered Kol. 'Say nothing to the others.'

He rolled away, as did Herbin. Issul sank down on her litter. She was bone-weary. The unaccustomed work had raised huge blisters and painful calluses on her fingers and thumbs. She was afraid that her work output would suffer as a result, for it was difficult to hold a needle or to apply sufficient pressure when scrubbing or squeezing wet clothing. She understood now how the Krai achieved their aims with their captives. Each prisoner had a vested interest in demonstrating to his slave-masters his ability to work hard and efficiently, if possible outstripping his companions. Anything less invited the nameless fate of the evening selection.

The next day passed without excitement or distraction. Issul worked, though her whole body rebelled. Each morning there was more clothing to be washed, and in the sewing hut the pile of garments awaiting repair was forever being renewed. She forced herself to ignore her pains, glancing nervously at her guard, fearing he would see that her work-rate had slipped. Before now she had wondered about secreting about her person a needle or the cutters she was given to work with. Such items might prove of value in any escape attempt. But she had abandoned the idea, for all equipment was thoroughly checked and accounted for by the Krai before she was permitted to leave.

At dusk she returned to her hut a little behind the others. Inside she counted her fellow prisoners, and by the light of the oil lamp scanned their faces. They numbered seven, plus herself. One less than yesterday. At first she could not place the man who was missing, but a little later, as she was lining up for soup, she noticed that the ladler was not the usual man. Issul was faintly surprised. The ladler, Eklen by name, had been a robust fellow.

She would not have thought him an obvious candidate for the selection, though it was true that there were no elderly or visibly weak members among the prisoners now.

She snatched brief words with Kol, who confirmed that Eklen had been led away upon their return to the camp.

Was there any particular reason? she enquired, and Kol nodded and whispered hurriedly, 'Bringing the lunchtime soup he stumbled and let the pot drop. His legs and feet were severely scalded. By this evening he was barely able to walk.'

And so our numbers dwindle almost by the day, thought Issul. *And no doubt fresh blood is being brought even now to replenish us. Can I doubt that it will be my turn soon?*

Almost certainly the Krai party that had left the camp the previous day would bring back new prisoners. Stronger, better fed, perhaps better able to withstand the harsh rigours of camp life, at least initially.

Issul had learned that none of her companions had been in the camp for more than a month. The camp itself could not have existed for much longer than that. Now they all showed signs of fatigue, were all growing thinner. Minor illnesses, lesions, sores, strains were commonplace. Even Ombo complained of a wrenched shoulder. By the natural order of things in this cruel microcosm of life, all their days were indelibly numbered.

Issul grew aware that Ombo was watching her, as he often did. He had made no attempt to approach or speak to her since the first evening, but his look smouldered. She had humiliated him. His status among the others had suffered since her arrival. She had the impression that, before, he had been the dominant character, by reason of brute force more than anything. But now . . . his power had waned. He was sullen and brooding. He had been bested by a mere slip of a woman.

Among the prisoners Issul's own status had risen. Nothing had been said but it was evident that her conflict with Ombo had earned their respect. She hated having to sleep in their company each night, but she no longer felt threatened by them. In the mornings and evenings she found that the others lined up behind her in the food queue. The ladle always dipped deeply and brought forth choice pieces of meat and vegetable, and her chunk of bread was unfailingly among the largest.

But she regretted that she had achieved their respect by humbling

Ombo. His size and strength would have been a great asset in any endeavour against their captors.

II

The following day Issul witnessed a recurrence of the strange disturbance that she had seen two days earlier. This time she was closer. She had just finished cleaning the Krai bowls, spoons and mugs, and was being escorted across the camp towards the stream where she washed the clothing. As she and her guard approached the watchtower beside the secondary gate that led to the streamside, she heard a dull groan from the sentry in the tower. She glanced up and saw him stumble back, collide with an upright post and topple headlong down the steps of the tower. He lay upon his back on the dirt of the compound, unmoving. A bright wet stain of blood gathered on his chest, and protruding from its centre was the short stub of a crossbow-bolt.

Immediately Issul was grabbed by her guard and bundled quickly away. There were yells, and a ten-strong squad of Krai, bearing shields and clad in armour of ringed-leather and thick felt padding, came from one of the tents and rushed for the gate. Others with bows took up positions in the tower and behind the palisade. Issul was thrust into the empty dormitory hut and the door bolted behind her.

All quickly grew quiet. Issul knelt and peered through a narrow gap in the wall but saw nothing. An hour passed. Then brief shouts again. Through the gap Issul glimpsed only running Krai feet. The usual silence descended again.

In due course the door was unbolted and her guard ordered her outside. In the brightness of the compound the Krai were on alert, crouched in the watchtowers and beside huts. No one walked openly in the compound; all carried shields. Issul was conducted quickly to the sewing-hut and shut inside. She did no work at the stream that day.

At dusk she was taken back to the dormitory hut as usual. In the middle of the compound a pair of perpendicular wooden frames had been erected, from which two men were suspended by their wrists. Their unkempt appearance and rough garb identified them as prisoners, though they were not from Issul's hut.

Inside, her enquiries brought the information that the two were from the second work-gang housed in the other hut. They had been selected by the guards during the afternoon, seemingly at random, and marched away.

'What is their crime?' Issul asked.

'As far as is known they have committed none,' Kol replied. 'Word has it that someone is hidden in the woods and has been taking potshots at the Krai with a bow. These two are being displayed as a warning. I suspect they will be tortured to death if another shaft is fired, and others of us strung up in their place. Jace, we've heard there've been Krai killed. Do you know anything?'

Issul recounted what she had seen. 'At least three Krai were struck. I do not know if they died.'

There was an air of contained excitement and tension in the hut that night, tempered by the infrequent cries of the men on the frames. The night was cold and the two had been give neither food nor drink. The guards emphasized absolute silence among the prisoners, but Issul did not doubt that each man's mind, like her own, was filled with thoughts of the bowman in the woods.

Issul woke abruptly late in the night to feel a hand on her shoulder.

'Ssh, it's me. Kol. I think we've got three men we can trust to work with us on an escape. Alippo, Mondam and Phisusandra. Plus Herbin. I would have said maybe Jerum too, but he was taken away tonight.'

Issul weighed this. She had still formulated no plan. 'Is it possible to break away from your work gang?'

'Never. Too many guards, and we're chained so we can't run.'

The only possibilities were across the stream or through the main gate, then. Both were immensely dangerous, and certainly could only be attempted after dark. But she was certain the Krai would be no less vigilant at night, most especially now, with the threat from the mysterious bowman. Moreover, Krai were believed to possess superior night-vision to humans.

Issul felt helpless. How were they to break free of the hut without rousing the guards? She had already inspected the hut walls, seeking a weakness, a fault, a loose beam. But the hut was solidly built and revealed nothing that could be prised or forced without tools. She had considered tunneling out underneath one of the walls, but her investigations had revealed that less than a finger's depth into the soil was a bed of solid rock. Kol and Herbin had later confirmed that their own explorations had brought the same result. Parts of the hut's foundations, it appeared, had been sunk into the rock itself.

And then there was the forest, a mass of lethal traps and who knew what else? Despondency began to settle upon Issul again. 'We have an ally out there, at least.'

'A single fighter can hardly hope to kill over thirty Krai,' whispered Kol. 'More, if the others return. And the Krai will surely kill us all if his actions continue.'

'We must let him know, somehow, that he can trust us to work with him,' said Issul. But she was not to be given that opportunity.

As dusk came and she ended her work the following day, she was brought from the sewing-hut and marched away. Not towards her dormitory but across the compound, past the frames where the two prisoners still hung, and away towards the far side of the camp in the direction she had seen so many others led before her.

Her heart was in her mouth as she walked. No explanation was given or required. She knew this was her time. From the corner of her eye she saw her companions grouped outside the hut, watching her as the chains were unfastened from their ankles. She wanted to call to them, illogically some word of reassurance, but her throat had suddenly constricted. Two guards now gripped her arms to ensure she did not run away. Ahead of her a young prisoner from the other hut was being similarly guided. She saw his legs going rubbery beneath him and from time to time heard his terrified sobs.

Does he know more than I?

They passed behind the Krai tents and huts into an area of the camp she had not seen before. Close beside a watchtower a small gate led into a narrow passage flanked on each side by a wall of sharpened stakes. The passage turned at a right angle, led away towards the trees which rose beyond. At the end was another guardtower, larger than the others and manned by several Krai. At its base was a sturdy gate. Three more guards fell in with the little party. A wooden portcullis was winched high and the gate opened.

They passed through onto a grassy causeway which twisted between the trees and opened into another large clearing. A sickly, putrid odour reached Issul's nostrils. In the middle of the clearing two heavy wooden posts, set about fifteen paces apart, were sunk into the ground, standing free by about the height of a tall man. All around the clearing sentinel trees rose tall and dark.

Issul was led to one of the posts, the young prisoner to the other. As she approached she saw bones, tatters of dry flesh and scraps of clothing strewn across the ground. She was ordered to sit, her back to the post, as was the other captive. Five of the guards had drawn their swords as if to caution against resisting. Issul's arms were pulled behind the posts and bound tightly at the wrists. Then her ankles were also tied. The Krai guards stood back. One of them spoke words in a language Issul did not understand. To her ears it sounded like an invocation or prayer of some kind.

'Be brave,' he then said. 'You serve a higher cause.'

All seven Krai bowed their heads, first towards Issul, then to the other prisoner. They turned upon their heels and marched back across the clearing to the camp.

Issul sat in bewildered silence. The other prisoner was weeping, his eyes tight shut, limbs trembling violently. At first Issul felt pity for him through her own fear, then gradually impatience. She gazed edgily about her, at the trees, silent and sombre in the dying light. She flexed her muscles against the bonds that held her, but they were tight and did not give. The charnel evidence scattered about the clearing, and the sickly-sweet stink that it exuded heightened her fear and made her nauseous. She found the sweat, cold and clammy, pouring down her back, gluing her hair to her skin.

And then she saw the face.

She almost screamed. The head was turned towards her, resting at a slight tilt just a few paces away upon a clump of grass. The flesh was spoiled, half torn from the skull; the eyes were gone, just black sockets staring emptily at her. Strands of grey hair lifted and fell in the light breeze that played across the grass. Issul, having first closed her eyes, now stared, unable to take her eyes off it. Despite its terrible mutilation she believed she recognized the face. It was Miseon, Herbin's father, with whom she had been brought to the camp. It was what was left of him.

Her breath came hard, in shallow, racing gasps as she fought to control her shock and terror. Now she saw, nearer to her, a finger, part of a foot, white bones sticking from what remained of the flesh. Her mouth was dry; she strained against her bonds.

The young prisoner was bawling loudly now. 'Mama, help me! Mama, Mama, please! Oh help me! Don't let me die!'

'Shut up!' Issul yelled. His screams were driving her mad. 'Shut up and do something! Test your ropes. You may be able to free yourself.'

She suspected it was hopeless, but anything to stop his maddening noise. He stopped yelling and stared at her for a moment through his tears.

'Test the ropes!' she shouted again.

He tried, struggling, straining. 'It's no good!'

He began to blubber again. Issul stared about her, waiting for whatever horror might come.

But nothing happened.

Above the high wall of the trees, which were now softly merging into the deepening dusk, the sky showed stains of fiery red and vibrant orange, deepest purple and myriad shades of violet. It was becoming chill. The camp was invisible behind the narrow belt of forest that separated it from the dying ground. The young prisoner's crying began to ebb. A terrible silence fell across the clearing.

Issul rested her head against the post behind her and felt tears start to her own eyes. *Leth, my babies, will I never see you again?*

So afraid, and not knowing what it was that she was to be afraid of.

She turned her head from one side to the other, strained to see behind her. But still there was nothing. It was the waiting, the terrible suspense, that drained her and threatened to pummel her into submission.

Then she heard a sound.

It was in the trees, off to her left. Issul strained her eyes, all her senses pared, penetrating the crepuscular gloom. The leaves upon a heavy branch of an oak were shaking. The branch gave a shudder. She thought she saw, for an instant, the glimmer of yellow eyes. But it was a distance away, hard to make out. Maybe there were no eyes. Maybe the movement had been a gust of breeze.

But she dared not take her eyes away. And the other prisoner had heard it too. His gaze was fixed rigid upon the same spot. He was wheezing and jabbering with terror again.

The branch shifted again, as though borne down by a great

weight. Now! A movement! Something of bulk, dark in the shadow, swaying. A monk-like form, hunched and shrouded.

Issul's heart hammered. She struggled desperately against her ropes. And the thing she was watching seemed abruptly to expand, its form stretching impossibly to either side. The limb of the oak shook again, rose suddenly as with the release of some unknown pressure. And the creature grew yet larger.

Suddenly Issul realized what it was she was seeing. The thing had stretched and spread its broad wings, launched itself from the tree. It was gliding rapidly across the glade towards her now, talons stretched, beak wide, just a cubit above the grass. She had seen its like twice before: in the sky above the road outside Enchantment's Edge, and again, returning, just above the treetops as she was brought to the Krai camp.

They are creatures of the Krai! This is their feeding pen!

She wrenched herself back against her bindings, closing her eyes in sheer horror as the thing rammed through the air towards her. A harsh grating cry reverberated through her skull. She braced herself against the strike. A wind rushed about her and a stale, fleshy odour assaulted her nostrils. But the expected strike, the claws and hooked bill tearing into her flesh, did not come.

Issul opened her eyes. The thing had flown past her to alight upon the ground close to the other prisoner. The leathery membranes of its great wings were folding. The broad flat head was held high. It seemed to be inspecting its prey, who sat rigid, eyes squeezed shut.

'No!' screamed Issul. 'No! No! No!'

The thing strutted forward and struck suddenly, hammering down with its beak and plucking out an eye.

As the prisoner's screams rang across the wood the creature tipped back its head, swallowed, then went for the second eye. Then there was rustling in the trees. Issul glanced around. Another bulking shape upon a limb. And another. As if they had been roosting, sleeping, and were waking one by one.

The young prisoner's agony rent the air, the winged thing tearing and gulping. Issul raged hopelessly against her bonds. Then, quite suddenly, she was aware of something breaking from the undergrowth across the clearing. A human figure, a man, bent and running, a sword in his hands.

Almost at the same moment another of the flying creatures had launched itself from the trees and was bearing straight towards Issul. Surprised by the appearance of the swordsman it swerved, then veered towards him. He maintained his pace; the creature extended its claws to pluck him from the earth. At the last instant he dived, rolled, came up and swung hard with his sword. The blade sheared into a wing. The flying beast emitted an ear-splitting shriek and careered to the ground. The swordsman sped on towards Issul.

The thing, flightless, bounded after him with long flapping leaps. But its movements were unco-ordinated, the wing bloody and virtually useless. He arrived at Issul's side, breathing hard, drew a knife from his belt and sawed at the ropes that bound her wrists. As her hands came free he thrust the knife at her. 'Free your legs!'

'Look out!' she cried, for the flapping creature was almost upon him. He span around, rolling onto his back and stabbed upwards with his sword into the creature's breast. A spray of warm blood showered the side of Issul's face as she cut at the rope around her ankles. Her rescuer was on his feet, hacking at the beast. He glanced around, saw that she had freed herself. The wounded creature screamed its agony and rage. The fighter struck once more and it slumped, not quite dead, to the ground.

The first creature had turned from the meal it was making of the other prisoner. Issul's rescuer took her hand. 'Come, this way. They cannot fly under the trees.'

'What about him?' She pointed at the tormented figure slumped before the other post, but even as she spoke she could see that there was nothing to be done for him. She began to run, following her rescuer. Another dark shape came from the high branches across the clearing. Her rescuer had hold of her arm, was propelling her forward. They reached the edge of the glade and he pushed her into the brush, then dived after her. Issul heard the heavy beat of wings, glimpsed a dark shadow shoot past. She scrambled further beneath the branches, felt a hand grasp her ankle.

'Not too far. There are traps.' He helped her to the trunk of a grand oak, where she sat down, breathless. In the middle of the clearing the first flyer had returned to its meal. Its wounded companion lay upon its side nearby. The third creature glided once around the glade then came to land and began pecking at the ravaged cadaver of the prisoner.

Issul rested herself against the tree-trunk, recovering her breath.

Her rescuer, sheathing his word, stood looking up into the dense branches. He was a young man, tall and rangily built. He had stained his face with soil or dark juice, and wore leathers with a lightly-padded jupon and a steel helmet. A short tabard, torn and dirty, bore the emblem of Orbia. He glanced at Issul and pointed upwards. Perched upon a high limb she saw one of the flying creatures, its yellow eyes blinking minatorily down at her.

'Don't worry,' said the stranger. 'It cannot attack unless we are in the open.'

Despite his assurance Issul was loath to let her eyes wander from the thing for more than a moment.

'Your appearance was timely,' she said. 'Though a few instants earlier would have saved two lives rather than the one.'

The young man looked ruefully towards the clearing. 'I take it that is your way of saying thank you, Majesty.'

Majesty! He knows me. But, of course, he would if he wears the uniform of Orbia.

'I do thank you. You have certainly saved me from a fate too horrible to contemplate. Yet that same fate has befallen my companion, and too many before him.'

The young man nodded. 'I did not know of this place until yesterday. The woods are lethally trapped, and movement within them is difficult. But when I saw you being led here I could only act at my greatest speed, even a little recklessly. Regretfully my greatest speed was insufficient to save any other.'

'How are you here? Are you alone?'

'Presently, yes. I am one of a platoon of the King's Cavalry, 1st Light Battalion. My name is Shenwolf.'

Shenwolf. The name seemed distantly familiar, but she could not think why.

'Where are the others of your platoon?'

'Lost, or killed, or returned to Orbia. I do not know. We were sent by King Leth to find you. You were reported to have gone to the village of Lastmeadow. Our task was to escort you back. We came across your party some way west of Crosswood. You were under attack, several of your men had already been killed. We arrived too late to do anything more than force the Krai to retreat.'

The moments of her frantic dash into the forest to locate Moscul came back to Issul now. She recalled becoming aware, momentarily, of the noise of a greater clash at her back, as though the fighting had suddenly escalated. Then she had come upon the old woman with the bleeding face; then all was darkness.

'You came after me alone?' she enquired.

'Not at first. I had glimpsed you disappearing into the woods, and several of us took chase. But the Krai came at us out of the trees, then vanished again leaving two more dead and three wounded. Still we came on. We were attacked again, and again – a few flights of arrows, then they melted away before we could fully respond. My group was down to five. An arrow struck my helmet and I stumbled, fell into a low ravine. When I came around I was alone. I knew by the light that several hours had passed. Was I to try to pursue you or to return in the hope of finding survivors of my platoon? Some, surely, must have survived.'

'But you chose to come for me?'

'That was the mission I had been assigned by the King.'

Issul nodded to herself. 'It is you, then, who has been killing Krai from the fringes of the forest these past days.'

'It is. I hoped to impel them into some rash action by my slow attrition of their numbers. But my resources were limited. I had but nine bolts, and five I have now used up.'

'Five? I witnessed but three strikes, and heard one more.'

'One missed. I am not perfect.'

'But you are very brave. I shall commend your actions upon our return, Shenwolf. It took extraordinary courage to do what you have done, most especially this.' She nodded towards the clearing.

'No, Majesty. It took only devotion to my country, my King and his young Queen.'

'How difficult was it to follow me here?'

'Not easy. I have followed tracks before, generally those of animals that have strayed or been stolen. Following fifteen Krai and their captives should have been simpler, but they took pains to cover their tracks. I also had to avoid the squads they sent back to deter pursuers.'

'But you made it, so others of the King's troops can follow, may already be doing so.'

Shenwolf shook his head. 'We are deep in the forest, and there has been heavy rain. It did not reach this area, but I watched dark sheets swamping the region at my back. I think there will be no tracks now. What is more, a strong Krai squad has gone north again from the camp. I do not doubt that King Leth will send forth a small army to find you, but the chances of his discovering this camp, so remote and well-hidden, are almost nil.'

Issul absorbed this solemnly. 'Then we must find our way back.'

Two more of the dark flyers had alighted in the centre of the clearing and were squabbling over the flesh of the young prisoner whose fate she had so nearly shared. 'These foul creatures. They are truly the stuff of nightmares. I have seen their like only in books. How is it they are with the Krai?'

'They are called slooths,' said Shenwolf. 'So I heard when we fought them in Enchantment's Edge. As to their association with the Krai, I have no answer.'

'They were at Enchantment's Edge?' demanded Issul with sudden alarm.

'A flight struck into the heart of the city, caused panic and disruption and took several lives.'

'Leth? My children?'

'The slooths did not enter Orbia or its environs. I can tell you little more, for my platoon was on its way to find you when they struck. It must be from here that they were dispatched. Some days ago I saw them fly north again for an unknown destination, and return a day later.'

Issul nodded. Three evenings ago the Krai had not led any prisoners away towards this terrible glade.

'I will destroy this place before I leave,' she swore to herself.

'That may not be possible, Majesty,' said Shenwolf. 'Not until we can return with a strong force.'

'I am known here as Jace,' Issul cautioned him. 'It is safer to keep it that way. Dispense, then, with all references and formalities that might in any way indicate my true status. Until I state otherwise.'

'Jace. That is your daughter's name, Princess Jace, is it not?'

She nodded, the thought of her daughter raising a torrent of emotions in her breast. Then she frowned. 'What are you doing?'

Shenwolf had shrugged off his shirt and jupon and was stepping out of his trousers. 'Majesty – Jace – will you give me your clothes?'

'What?'

'Take mine for now, please. It is important that the Krai believe you have perished here. Your torn clothing will be evidence. Just the outer garments will suffice, I think.'

'What about you?' she asked.

He dropped his garments upon the ground at her feet and stood before her in loincloth and boots, his swordbelt still buckled at his waist. 'There is plenty of discarded clothing in the clearing. I shall make use of that.'

He was well-formed, she noted quickly, the body young, lithe and adequately muscled, softly pale in the closing dark. He was smiling, the mouth broad, eyes shining. She shifted her gaze. 'You are audacious, Shenwolf.'

'I am acting only in your interests, Jace. I will avert my eyes.'

He turned away and Issul moved behind the trunk of the oak and removed her outer garments, which were drenched with the sweat of her terror. She slipped into his. They swamped her, but she was able to secure the trousers with her belt, and roll up the hems so that they did not drag around her feet.

'We will find something more suitable in due course,' said Shenwolf, grinning.

'Just give me a needle, strong thread and cutters. The Krai have made me an expert in the art of patching, darning and adjusting.'

He took her clothes and began to tear them.

'You are going back out there, now?'

'It is as good a time as any. Wait here.'

Before she could say anything more he had dashed from the cover of the trees and was making for the centre of the clearing. Seven slooths fed there now, unaware of him. He ran directly at them, brandishing his sword, and as he closed on them began to shout loudly. The slooths scattered, shrieking their annoyance. To Issul's shock, Shenwolf ran straight into their midst and threw himself onto the ground beside what remained of the other prisoner. Issul saw that he was draping her clothing across the corpse, pressing it against the flesh and bones. Then he stood, whirling his blade as the slooths closed in. They drew back again with harsh cries. Shenwolf took the garments and threw them at the nearest slooth.

Above Issul's head there was a sudden shaking and shuddering.

'Shenwolf!' she screamed as the great dark body of the roosting slooth slid free and glided rapidly across the glade towards him. Shenwolf glanced around, saw the new threat, and ran, weaving nimbly between the winged beasts, two of which were now rising into the air. He stood, legs apart, facing the slooth that soared towards him. At the last instant he dropped flat once again. The slooth glided over him, its talons missing him by a breath. He leapt to his feet, glancing behind him to gauge the positions of the others, and charged towards Issul.

He threw himself down panting beside her and held up a tatter of green cloth stained with dry blood. 'Hmm. I think it was once a shirt, but now it is perhaps not as useful as I had hoped.'

'You were foolish,' said Issul. 'You were very nearly killed.'

He nodded. 'I had the advantage, for they were distracted while they fed. Of course they are angered by being obliged to make do with half-rations, but even so they are only at their most dangerous when in flight. On the ground they are ungainly and not difficult to avoid.'

'You seem to know much about them.'

He shook his head. 'Only what I noted when they attacked Enchantment's Edge. Note, should you ever have to fight them, their hide is very tough. If you can, strike at the wings to cripple them. Then run.'

'What were you doing with my clothing?'

'Bloodying it for the Krai. They do not expect to find it crisp and clean. Now, I will have to think again in regard to garbing myself. I have a den in the woods on the other side of the camp. Let us go there quickly while some light remains. Follow precisely in my footsteps, Jace' – he grinned, giving particular inflection to the name: he seemed distinctly to be enjoying himself – 'and do not waver by a single step. I have disabled a number of traps and established a safe path, but to wander from it may bring a nasty surprise. One thing I will say for the Krai; they are ingenious.'

NINE

I

The den turned out to be a hollow formed naturally beneath a fallen tree and a formation of moss-blanketed boulders. It lay a couple of hundred paces into the forest to the north-east of the Krai camp. Shenwolf had burrowed well into the soil, hiding the earth he removed beneath neighbouring rocks and brambles, and had created a comfortable little nest lined with dry grass, bracken and fern. The entrance was well-concealed behind a dense arras of ivy and bindweed.

'I regret there is little space,' he apologized as Issul crawled inside. 'The excavation was done hurriedly and I have had no opportunity to create a guest's suite. But it is adequately ventilated and comparatively safe. As long as we do not thrash I think we will be quite comfortable. Under better circumstances I would of course offer to sleep outside, but I think that would be unwise just now. The Krai regularly search the woods for me. But should you feel . . .'

'It will be fine,' Issul said. She felt claustrophobic in the pitch-black of the den, with earth, rock and roots all around and above her. The ceiling was too low to even sit up; the air was close with the smell of mouldering earth.

'I can offer you only berries, fruit, chanterelles and rabbit meat. The meat is raw, I am afraid, as I dare not risk a fire. My rations are gone, otherwise they would be yours.'

Issul accepted the fruit berries and chanterelles but declined the rabbit. She ate hungrily, not seeing what it was he had given her, then laid her head upon the dry grass litter, thinking. The journey from the slooths' feeding-pens had been laborious and slow in the deepening dark. She was exhausted, and before she knew it she had fallen asleep, dreaming absurdly of hot soup and grey Krai bread.

When she awoke light was filtering in from above through flues in the rocks overhead. She was alone in the den. She crawled to the entrance and peered through the ivy and bindweed. There was nothing to be seen but dense, silent forest, dew-clad and still. Mindful of the risks of emerging Issul slid back down and waited. After a short time there came a footfall outside, the entrance was drawn back and Shenwolf slid nimbly inside.

'Where did you get the clothing?' she asked. He was dressed in a torn grey flannel shirt and rough green trousers.

'I have been back to the feeding-pen. Apart from the clothing, I wanted to check whether the slooth I had wounded was still alive, and if so to kill it and remove the body before the Krai find it. As it happened it was largely unnecessary. Its companions have eaten it. Still, the wings and skeleton remained, and those I have now disposed of. I have brought some more food, all washed in the stream.' He emptied his shirt of white radish, watercress, groundnuts, almonds, wild beans, morels and, lastly and with some pride, a trio of plump black truffles. 'A veritable feast! And raw rabbit is really not so bad once you're used to it.'

Issul again declined the rabbit but satisfied herself with the nuts, radish, beans and fungi.

'I suggest we leave as soon as we have eaten,' said Shenwolf, tearing at the pink rabbit flesh. 'It is a long, slow way to Enchantment's Edge. There is a Krai squad somewhere ahead of us, and in the forest are bears, grullags and worse. We will have to move with extreme caution.'

Issul shook her head. 'I am anxious to return to my husband and children, but I cannot leave the men who have become my companions these last days, knowing they will be dead before I could hope to return.'

Shenwolf ruffled his pale brown hair. 'I had feared as much.'

'If I can I will destroy this place. They are constructing something on the other side of the camp. Do you know what?'

'No. I have observed it with some fascination. Much of it is underground, and very difficult to approach. It is guarded at all times.'

'Take me there. But first we should exchange our clothing again. This that you have brought will be no worse a fit on me than your own. One of us at least should be comfortable.'

When they had done Shenwolf enquired, 'Do you have any weapons training?'

'Sword, knife, bow, crossbow . . .'

'Excellent.' He reached into the back of the den and brought out a shortbow and clutch of arrows. 'I have no spare sword, but you may keep my knife for the time being.'

'Where did you get this?'

'I cut the bow from an ash sapling, the arrows are birch fletched with pheasant feathers. The string is waxed hemp, taken from one of the Krai devices I disabled. I had intended it for when my crossbow-bolts were used up, but I can make another. I regret it lacks professional quality, but it is better than nothing.'

With painstaking slowness they made their way through the woods, Shenwolf with his crossbow across his back, Issul carrying her shortbow. Twice Shenwolf stopped to point at something upon the path close to their feet. On the first occasion Issul could see nothing.

'That branching stick that stands erect,' he whispered, and cast his eyes about the nearest trees and bushes. 'Move back.'

Issul backed away. When he was satisfied she had gone far enough he lay prone upon the ground and, taking his sword, stretched forward to tap the stick he had indicated.

Something moved. There was a snap, a rustle. A powerful branch whipped out across the path they had been following, shooting above Shenwolf's outstretched body and coming to rest. At its tip was fixed a wooden grille from which protruded several slender sharpened sticks, each about a metre long. Had it struck it would have impaled a man in a dozen places.

'They are ingenious,' said Shenwolf, pocketing the twine that had secured the trap. 'And industrious. This device was not here two days ago.'

A little further on he pointed out what looked to Issul like leaf litter upon the ground. Shenwolf brushed it aside and she looked through a hatchwork of fragile, slender branches into a pit filled with sharpened stakes.

'Remember, Jace, never run in these woods unless the path is one we have cleared ourselves during the same day.'

He showed her places for hiding, including a semi-hollow oak. 'This is also an excellent lookout post. From here you have a good view of both the camp and the work area. Climb carefully and take a look.'

Issul climbed up the inside of the the tree, then further into the great boughs towards the light that shone through the mass of slowly yellowing leaves. The camp lay before her, frighteningly close, it seemed. Few Krai were visible; those that were carried shields or knelt behind the parapets of the watchtowers. In the middle of the compound the two prisoners still hung upon the frames.

A little way off, beyond the south-western perimeter of the camp, she saw a secondary compound, itself palisaded. Here the prisoners worked with bent backs, watched by at least a dozen guards. They had constructed a large, flat-roofed stone building with a single entrance, sunk into the ground, which was reached by steps. Issul could make out nothing of its function.

She climbed higher, hoping to gaze across the forest roof and determine the position of Enchantment's Edge. Just to gaze upon her beloved home! But she saw only the billowing sea of greens, yellows and golds stretching away to the horizon beneath a piercingly blue sky. Issul looked all around, and caught her breath. Shining like gigantic distant phantoms were the mountains of Enchantment, touched with blazing snow, extending further than she could see. Were they closer? Yes, for she had never seen such detail on them before. Yet still they seemed so far away.

She descended and sat with Shenwolf at the base of the oak, drinking cool water from his flask.

'What are your thoughts now, Jace?' the young soldier enquired. 'It is a noble endeavour to try to free the prisoners and destroy the camp, but an implausible one. We are but two, after all.'

Issul was thinking to herself: *They believe me dead.*

How could she use this?

She turned to Shenwolf. 'The Krai's methods can be turned against them. It is not such a hopeless task. No, I want to see all of the forest that you have explored around here. I think I know how we can catch two, three, perhaps even four birds with the same stone.'

II

They worked hard that day, and as dusk approached took themselves off to the edge of the slooth feeding-pen and concealed themselves in the undergrowth beneath the trees. They waited and watched, and in due course two bound men were brought from the camp and lashed to the two posts. Issul's heart skipped a beat when she saw that one of the victims was Herbin.

Fate and Fortune give us speed in this endeavour!

She looked up into the branches overhead. Two slooths roosted there, their eyes closed.

She and Shenwolf had arrived here when the light was still strong, hoping to determine the position of each of the flying beasts. Issul remembered counting thirteen passing overhead when she had been brought to the camp. With the one that Shenwolf had killed the night before, that left twelve. And twelve they had now counted roosting in the trees around the clearing.

She watched until the Krai guards had marched from the glade back towards the camp, checked once more above her head, then slapped Shenwolf on the shoulder. 'Go!'

The young soldier, sword and knife drawn and crossbow across his back, rose and sprinted across the glade. Issul notched an arrow to her bow and knelt, eyes keened. She had calculated, as yesterday, that the slooths were sleeping and would not attack immediately, but was taking no unnecessary risks all the same.

Shenwolf arrived beside the nervous Herbin and quickly cut through his bonds. 'Take off your clothes. Do not argue, just do as I say. Quickly!'

When Herbin was down to his undergarments Shenwolf pointed to Issul, who waved him to her.

'Run, fast!' urged Shenwolf, pushing him away, and moved to the second prisoner.

Herbin arrived beside Issul, his face pale and confused. A few moments later came the second prisoner, a swarthy, slightly-built man whose prominent cheekbones suggested Murinean descent and whose name, they would later learn, was Phisusandra. Shenwolf had remained behind, seated against one of the posts. Still no slooth had stirred.

'I will explain everything later,' said Issul. 'For now, can either of you use a bow?'

To her relief both men nodded. She pointed to the base of the tree where a pair of rough ash bows, several arrows and a couple of hastily hewn birch spears lay. 'Arm yourselves and take positions beside me. Whatever you do, do not stray from beneath the trees.'

She watched Shenwolf, her heart thumping. She knew he had to stay there; they had discussed it more than once during the day as they had made their preparations. The slooths had to be lured to their food, as normal. There was no other way.

The waiting was interminable. At last she heard it, a shaking in the branches of a tree some way off to her left. She saw Shenwolf shift his position slightly, and kept her eyes on the glade behind him lest any of the creatures attacked from that direction.

A dark form slid across her vision, gliding straight for Shenwolf. There was a gasp of fear and disbelief from one of the men at her side. Issul levelled her bow.

As the slooth drew close to Shenwolf it raised its wings to land, exposing its breast. Shenwolf lifted his crossbow and fired, then rolled to the side. At almost the same moment Issul loosed her arrow, which sailed straight and true and lodged in the beast's shoulder. Herbin and Phisusandra also fired, but she did not see whose arrows hit.

The slooth shrieked and slewed in sudden agony. Shenwolf leapt to his feet and struck with his sword, hacking, hacking, hacking at the tough hide. At last the slooth fell dead at his feet. He bent, wrenched free the crossbow bolt, took up his crossbow, glanced quickly about the glade, then ran to Issul and the other two.

'Good! They have their dinner!' He lay upon his back for a moment, grinning up at the two slooths roosting overhead, then sat up. 'I shall return in the morning again to remove any telltale remains. The Krai should be none the wiser.' He grinned again. 'Well, now we are four!'

Issul was watching Herbin, whose young face was grey and set, his eyes on the two central posts. 'This is where they have been taking their victims all this time?' he said. 'Here, to become living food for these monsters?'

'I am sorry, Herbin.'

'But you, Jace, you have survived. Are there others?'

'Shenwolf came to my aid yesterday,' she said softly. 'But I am the only one.'

'Then Miseon, my father . . .'

'I am sorry, Herbin.' Silently she offered thanks that he had not spotted the ghastly evidence that she had seen the evening before, though the knowledge of what his father must have suffered could have been little worse.

Herbin's eyes filled with tears, but his mouth was twisted into a grimace of hatred. He stared, trembling, towards the invisible Krai camp. 'They will pay for this, I swear. I swear. I will avenge my father, and my brother also. I will not rest until their murderers are dead.'

III

It was late morning. The Krai guard in one of the watchtowers yelled a warning at the sight of a man creeping between the trees outside the camp. The guard, kneeling, took aim and loosed an arrow. It missed, and the man made off, limping noticeably.

An eight-strong Krai squad came running at the guard's call. They passed through the gate and made for the woods, their quarry just visible. Weapons drawn, they quickened their pace, seeing that their victim seemed unable to outrun them.

Shenwolf glanced back over his shoulder. The Krai were gaining on him, the camp now obscured by trees and undergrowth. He pressed on, gripping his right thigh and twisting between the trees to avoid arrows. He came to a narrow, steep-sided gully, slid carefully down its rocky slope and made his way falteringly along its bed. The Krai appeared behind him at the gully's crest. Their captain issued quick orders, splitting the squad. Two men knelt and drew arrows and bows. Two more descended in Shenwolf's wake. The captain and the remaining three raced along the rim of the gully, around boulders, bushes and tree-trunks, hoping to cut off his escape at the other end.

Shenwolf pushed on, glanced back as an arrow *zinged* off a rock close by. But no more arrows flew. Behind the two archers the figure of Phisusandra appeared wielding a club of solid oak. The first Krai never knew what hit him; the second had time to glimpse and be surprised before Phisusandra's second blow smashed him senseless.

The remaining Krai raced on, unaware of this development. Shenwolf scrambled free of the gully, eschewing all pretence of injury now. He reached the path just yards ahead of the four Krai trying to outflank him. He broke into a run, following a narrow animal track through the bushes. The Krai captain quickened his pace, then halted with his men. Smiling, he watched in anticipation. Shenwolf, just twenty yards ahead, suddenly cried out as the ground gave way beneath him.

'*Ya-ha!*' The Krai's victory shout rang out through the trees. He showed no other emotion but strode to the death-pit into which his quarry had fallen. The other two Krai clambered out of the gully a few paces behind and followed.

The Krai captain peered over the rim of the pit, and his gorgeous eyes widened in surprise. Instead of the bloodied body he had expected to see impaled upon vicious stakes, he found himself staring down the barrel of Shenwolf's crossbow. The bolt passed straight through his wrinkled cheek and out the back of his skull, ruining his Krai good looks. At virtually the same moment a cord snapped and a heavy branch set with spiked poles swept free across the path, striking another Krai instantly dead and knocking the other two from their feet.

The two Krai coming from behind halted short and drew their swords, suddenly uncertain. They saw a young woman leap from the undergrowth, a dagger in her hand, and strike one of their fallen companions. They rushed towards her as Shenwolf sprang grinning from the death-pit, using a rough stairway of boulders he and the others had placed there earlier in the day when they had removed the sharpened stakes that had lined the pit. The two Krai saw his sword flash as he advanced towards them. They did not see Herbin, who came from behind bearing a wooden club similar to that employed so effectively by Phisusandra. And they died without seeing Issul deliver the final knife-blow to their last companion.

'Excellent work!' breathed Issul, sheathing her knife. 'Though the odds are piled immeasurably against us we have proven that spirit, careful planning, resourcefulness and good teamwork can yet win the day.'

Phisusandra arrived, carrying the equipment he had stripped from the two Krai he had killed. Shenwolf made a quick stock-check of Krai possessions. 'Three composite bows of good quality, twenty-seven arrows, eight swords, eight daggers, eight suits of good padded armour, four shields, eight helmets, eight pairs of boots and eight sets of decent clothing.'

'Don't be too sure of the clothing,' warned Issul. 'I happen to know that the seamstress in the camp was half-hearted in her repair work. Indeed, I suspect that some stitching may even have been undone so that trousers may fall down at any time. Undergarments also may be lined with tiny, irritating splinters.'

'Ah well, we will check very carefully when distributing the clothing then. That seamstress did no work on armour or weapons, did she?'

'She did not.'

'I am glad to hear it.'

'We should move quickly now. Those two poor wretches on the frames will be murdered if the Krai suspect anything is amiss. And perhaps others, too.'

They distributed arms and armour, then made their way back through the woods. At least twenty-two Krai still manned the camp, but a dozen of those were supervising the two work gangs. Ten, then, maybe more . . .

From the cover of the forest three guards could be seen in the gate-tower at the main gate. Issul, Shenwolf, Herbin and Phisusandra went swiftly around the camp perimeter to the east side where the stream flowed. There they concealed themselves again and Shenwolf released a single bolt at the guard manning the tower. His shot hummed past the Krai's head and buried itself in a wooden upright behind him. The guard gave a yell. Figures moved behind the palisade. Shenwolf's second bolt took the guard in the neck.

The four waited. Soon the secondary gate opened and five Krai emerged. They were armoured and shielded and moved cautiously towards the stream, eyes upon the forest. But still they believed they were opposed by only one man.

Fifty yards away, high in an oak tree off to their right side, Phisusandra took careful aim with his Krai bow and released an arrow. A Krai fell, pierced through the cheek. The others wheeled reflexively to face the direction of attack. Two more arrows and Shenwolf's last bolt sped from the woods into their now unprotected flank. A Krai died, another took a shaft in the thigh. Quickly they retreated behind their shields back into the camp, dragging the dead and wounded. A few arrows flew from the palisade and tower, but they were aimed wildly into the forest and struck only wood and earth.

'Good, we have them thoroughly at odds,' whispered Issul. 'Now let us exploit that to the full.'

The four melted back into the woods and skirted around to the north-west.

A short time passed and the guards at the main watchtower were alerted by shouts from the forest. Moments later they saw the limping figure of Shenwolf emerging from the forest fringe, pushed roughly and hurriedly forward by three Krai. Two had arrows drawn and were facing guardedly back towards the trees as though fearing attack from that direction. The third, who gripped Shenwolf's arm, had his free hand to his forehead, apparently staunching a bloody wound.

'Quick! Open the gate! We are pursued!'

The gate was drawn open. The prisoner and his three guards passed quickly through. Suddenly, one of the two Krai on the gate gave a shout, only now seeing that the faces beneath the helmets were not Krai.

Issul wheeled on him and ran him through with her sword before he could draw his own. Shenwolf grabbed a sword from Phisusandra and tackled the second Krai. One of the three in the tower had begun to descend, the better to take a look at the captive bowman of the woods who had caused so much trouble. He turned now and tried to scramble back up, and was taken in the back by Herbin's arrow.

Phisusandra loosed a shaft at the two remaining guards in the tower. They ducked back. One reappeared, bowstring taut, and caught Herbin's second arrow in the shoulder. He fell back, crying out, and his shaft went wild.

Shenwolf, disposing of his man, bounded up the steps into the tower. The Krai with the arrow in his shoulder was writhing on the floor. The other was scrambling over the parapet. As Shenwolf stepped forward he pushed himself over, grasping at one of the tower's supporting legs and attempting to slide to the ground. He saw Herbin's bow levelled beneath him and dropped, breaking an ankle as he landed. Issul darted in and finished him.

Shenwolf stood over the wounded Krai, hesitant. Phisusandra's heavy footfall sounded behind him.

'You do not know what we have suffered,' said the Murinean, and plunged his sword into the wounded Krai's chest.

Shenwolf scanned the compound. Five Krai were running towards him across the compound, drawn from the tower on the eastern side.

'Come,' he said to Phisusandra. 'Target practice.'

With two arrows they downed two Krai. The others scattered for cover behind the huts and tents.

'Cover us,' said Shenwolf, and descended.

Issul had run to the frames where the two prisoners hung, and cut their bonds. The men dropped to the earth, too weak to support themselves. She could do no more for the present, and ran on for the cover of the nearest hut, Herbin in close pursuit. She heard a groan behind her, turned and saw that one of the fallen men had been pierced by a Krai arrow.

'No!' She searched the compound furiously, saw a Krai with bow drawn beside the dormitory hut where she had spent so many recent nights. '*No!*'

The Krai staggered back, clutching at his face, dead before he fell as Shenwolf's shaft struck home. Shenwolf ran on, arriving at Issul's side. An arrow slammed into the wall of the hut behind them.

'Quick, inside!'

They dived in together. A surprised Krai rose from a field-desk. Issul pounced, sword flashing, and he fell back dead before he knew it. Shenwolf leapt to the window. 'There is at least one in each of the remaining guard towers. I know of two more hiding behind the tents.'

Issul was at the door. 'The guard in the south-west tower has us pinned.'

'Can you send a couple of arrows his way?'

She nodded. As she loosed her first shaft Shenwolf scrambled through the window. He crept along the wall of the building, located Herbin twenty yards away kneeling beside a tent. Shenwolf pointed towards the tower, indicating that Herbin should do as Issul was doing. The Krai guard there had ducked behind the parapet. Shenwolf sprinted towards the steps. The guard leaned out to fire and was struck by Herbin's arrow.

Issul came from the hut, glanced at Phisusandra in the gate-tower. He pointed to the rear of her hut. Sword drawn, she crept around the other way, surprised a Krai, his back turned, facing Phisusandra's tower, and dispatched him quickly. Now Phisusandra descended and ran to join her.

'One in the eastern tower, one behind the second hut,' he said. 'Perhaps others. Certainly there have been more than we had anticipated.'

As he spoke, Issul saw a figure creeping along the eastern palisade towards the tower. It was Herbin. She marvelled at his courage. Only days ago he had been, by his account, a simple charcoal-burner. Now he was a warrior, without fear, spurred by his hatred of the people who had destroyed his family. Issul notched an arrow to her bow and aimed at the tower, watching for a movement from the hidden guard. Phisusandra did likewise. A moment passed before the guard raised himself from behind the parapet, bow curved to fire at Herbin.

Issul loosed her arrow, as did Phisusandra. At this distance, almost seventy yards, both shots missed but were sufficient to distract the guard. He spun around, seeking. Herbin took the opportunity and sprinted for the steps to the tower. The guard took aim at Issul but, alarmed by the shudder of Herbin's footsteps on the steps, panicked and loosed his shaft too quickly. The arrow buried itself in the earth twenty paces from Issul. She leapt to her feet and ran for the tower to give support to Herbin.

Phisusandra meanwhile had his eyes on the second prison hut. He saw the movement as a Krai tried to slip along the wall. He drew back his notched arrow. The Krai broke free of cover and ran across the compound towards the eastern tower, presumably to aid his comrade there. Phisusandra's bowstring thrummed, but his arrow went wide. He drew his sword and set off to intercept the Krai.

Herbin clashed swords with the Krai in the tower. There was little space for swordplay and they found themselves circling one another at arm's length. But as Issul came up the steps the Krai turned, seeking a better defence. Herbin lunged and took him in the arm.

'Surrender!' cried Issul.

'They cannot,' Herbin said grimly. He lunged again. The Krai fended his blow, stabbed, missed, and died on Issul's sword.

Issul glanced down into the compound where Phisusandra was being forced back by a Krai he had pursued. The guard was a swordsman of some skill, and Phisusandra was hard put to defend himself. Issul leapt down the steps and charged at the Krai, who instantly modified his tactics to take on this new threat.

Between them Issul and Phisusandra gained the upper hand. Issul stared into the Krai's face. There was no emotion there. Grim purpose, yes. Sweat and quiet determination, yes. But anger, fear, joy, despair . . . nothing at all. It was as though she fought a creature who had no knowledge of such things.

Now Herbin was with them, and within moments the Krai was a corpse upon the dirt of the compound.

'Just the south-eastern tower,' said Phisusandra, breathing hard. The tower stood one hundred yards away beside the palisade. A still figure could be seen within. Cautiously they made their way across the compound, keeping to the shelter of the huts and tents, their eyes on the tower. The guard was watching them but, strangely, was taking no action.

'Perhaps at last we have one who is prepared to yield to save his life,' Issul said. But she was wrong. As they drew closer the figure in the tower moved to the steps and began to descend, smiling. It was Shenwolf.

He pointed to the empty west tower. 'One of us should be there. It looks out upon the work area.'

'I will go,' said Phisusandra.

'Before you depart let us take a moment to congratulate ourselves,' said Issul. 'What we have achieved here is remarkable, extraordinary. I believe now, as I think you all do, that we can achieve the impossible. It is almost time for the next phase.'

With Phisusandra in the tower, the three took time to clear the compound of Krai bodies. They took the two prisoners who had been on the frames to one of the huts and gave them water and a small amount of food. Both were in a severe state. Their hands were black, the flesh already putrefying in one case; it was questionable whether either man would ever use them again. The one who had taken the Krai arrow was in the worse condition. Shenwolf removed the arrow from his thigh but expressed concern that he might not survive the shock. Eventually they were obliged to leave the two, for it was midday. Phisusandra signalled from the watch-tower. It was time to free the work-gangs.

'They are coming for their meal,' said Shenwolf. 'Let us take up positions.'

Moments later the gate which led through to the work-compound opened. Two prisoners trotted through, accompanied by a pair of guards. They made for the centre of the camp, where a fire should have burned and soup should have bubbled in its great pot.

'I am sorry,' said Shenwolf, stepping from behind a hut. 'We have had no time to prepare your food. Perhaps this will do instead.'

He tossed swords to the two prisoners. The Krai guards, with expostulations of surprise, drew their blades, but Shenwolf was running at them and Issul and Herbin came from behind and they were slain with little contest. Issul glanced up at the tower where Phisusandra signalled that all was fine.

'Good. Now we are six,' grinned Shenwolf. He spoke to the two former prisoners. 'We will release your shackles, then go to free the others. Perhaps then we can all dine together. There are weapons and armour aplenty, though for now I would advise that you keep your own trousers. Do you join us?'

The two were enthusiastic in their acceptance. They quickly donned armour and chose swords and bows. Phisusandra descended to join them and the six stepped through the gate that led to the work area.

A dirt path, palisaded on both sides, led for fifty paces to a picket gate. Some of the prisoners could be seen labouring beyond, watched by their guards. The closest were within twenty paces of the gate, others were as much as one hundred paces away, for the compound was large. Not all were visible, even when the six had passed through the gate and marched on into the compound. She counted eleven, and almost as many guards. Some, it appeared, were at work underground.

Issul and her companions advanced on towards the workers and their guards, splitting into pairs as they had earlier agreed. Issul was nervous, but the guards so far were paying them no attention. She looked around for faces she recognized and saw Kol hacking at the ground with a pick. A little further off big Ombo levered at a great boulder which was half-buried in the earth. Her heart thumped hard. A guard glanced her way – she could delay no longer. She ran forward, tearing off her helmet and shaking free her long fair hair so that all might see her clearly.

'Friends! We have returned! Free yourselves, now! Now!'

She leapt at the nearest of the Krai, sword whirling, Herbin with her. At the same time she saw from the corner of her eye that Shenwolf and the others were similarly running at the closest guards. They had agreed that, where possible, they would initially take the guards two-to-one. That way they could be sure of killing the first few quickly, leaving them better able to deal with the rest. Her sword plunged into the nearest guard's gut before he had time to react.

The closest of the prisoners, Kol among them, took a moment to understand. Then with a great shout of joy Kol took up his pick and stepped towards the guard standing nearest to him. But he stumbled on his shackles and fell to the dirt. Issul leapt to help him as the guard drew free his sword and moved towards him.

But something terrible was happening in the work-compound. The Krai, the moment they understood what was happening, did not move to defend themselves against their armed attackers. Instead, virtually as one, they threw themselves wordlessly upon the unarmed prisoners. The carnage was terrible. Several prisoners died in the first moments, the guards moving among them quickly and methodically, slashing, stabbing, killing without mercy. The men fought back as best they could, but some were borne down with heavy loads of wood, earth or stone, and stood no chance. Those that did fight with shovels and picks were hampered by their shackles.

Issul blocked the Krai's blow as he swung his blade at Kol on the ground, but the force of the Krai's strike knocked her own sword from her hand. He spun and advanced upon her, lunging. She dodged, reaching for her dagger, and stumbled. The Krai was upon her, blade raised. She heard a great roar, saw something arc through the air and slam into the Krai's head, shattering his skull and knocking him off his feet. Ombo came into view, shuffling awkwardly, but massive and deadly with the bar he wielded.

Two more guards rushed at Ombo. Issul leapt to her feet, grabbed her sword and went to his aid. Behind one of the guards Kol's pick flew high and buried itself between the Krai's shoulder-blades. Herbin came at the other and split his skull with his sword.

'Well, Jace,' Ombo stared down at her. 'You return from the dead and strike terror into the hearts of our enemies! You are a woman like none I have ever known.'

Issul eyed him, unsure of what to make of the expression on his flushed face. 'I saw no terror,' she said. 'But the day is ours, and you are free men again. For that I am glad.'

It was all over in the work-compound, but the cost had been high. Of the eleven workers the Krai had killed four instantly. Three more had died fighting them. Four stood now, looking expectantly at Issul and Shenwolf and the others. She saw with relief that all five of her companions had survived, though Herbin had been stabbed in the shoulder and one of the former soup-carriers was sitting clutching his side, which poured with blood.

Kol approached her. 'Jace, Herbin, I believed you gone forever. Later you must tell me how you survived. First, though, you should know that there are three prisoners down there, with two guards.'

He pointed to the stone steps which led into the underground building.

Issul sat down wearily as Shenwolf came and stood beside her. A welter of thoughts were passing through her mind. The day was won, even if there remained something more to do. But her elation was tempered by other knowledge. She had killed. It was something she had never thought to do. Never wanted. It had begun when she was ambushed on the Crosswood road, but that she had somehow put from her mind. Then it had been blind reaction. But today had been slaughter, planned and achieved. With sword and arrow she had taken lives, and she was changed forever. Her world could never again be the same.

'Do you know the layout down there?' asked Shenwolf.

Kol nodded. 'In part. There is a central chamber where no prisoner is allowed.'

'We must go down,' said Issul, getting to her feet.

'I will come with you,' Kol said. 'Just let me remove these shackles.'

Phisusandra stood beside them. 'I will come too. I sense something . . . something strange.'

Issul turned to him. 'What do you mean?'

'I do not know, but I am Murinean and perhaps more sensitive than you humans to subtle auras or changes in the air.'

'You refer to magic?' Shenwolf asked, his voice low.

Phisusandra shrugged. 'I refer to something I have no words for.'

Issul addressed the remainder of the group. 'Free yourselves of your chains and go to the camp. It is time to celebrate. Get food and drink from the Krai stores, and bandages and medicines for those that need them. Tend to your two companions whom we have freed from the frames. Beware, there may be Krai still hidden in the camp. Take them alive if you can. We will join you presently.'

Kol had found the release key for his shackles on one of the dead Krai.

'Are you ready?' asked Issul as the others shuffled back towards the main compound.

He nodded, taking weapons from the corpse. Swords drawn, they descended the steps. They entered a gloom relieved by a couple of torches set upon the walls, illuminating a short passageway. There was a strange, steely smell in the grim air, mingling with the dank odours of earth and stone.

'The passage turns to the left into another chamber,' whispered Kol.

Around the corner they came upon the body of one of the prisoners, his blood soaking into the dark earth. Issul recognized him as one of the men from her hut.

Kol swore. 'They have no souls.'

Two more bodies lay close upon the threshold of the chamber they now entered. A doorway was set into the wall facing them, and another to the left.

'This one we are not permitted to enter,' Kol said, indicating the door opposite. 'After we had excavated it we were barred.'

'And the other?' asked Issul.

'A long passage set with stalls of some kind.'

Shenwolf turned to Phisusandra. 'What do you feel?'

'I am uneasy. Something is here. I cannot say what.'

They moved towards the door on the left and Shenwolf pushed it cautiously open. The passage beyond was in darkness. They took torches from the walls of the chamber and entered. A central walkway stretched before them, flanked on each side with a row of small compartments, as if for domestic beasts or perhaps for storage of goods of some kind. All the stalls they passed were untenanted.

Further along a wider passage gave off to the right, leading upwards towards a source of light. Shenwolf crept towards the light, vanished for a moment, then returned. 'It leads out directly into the forest.'

'You said there were two Krai down here?' said Issul to Kol, who nodded. 'It looks as though they have escaped through here.'

Further down the long chamber they came upon a strange and eerie sight. Upon the floor of two of the stalls a pile of dry grass, leaves, twigs and mud had been arranged into a rough dish-shape, about two cubits in diameter. In the centre of each of these dishes rested a large mottled grey-brown sphere.

Phisusandra approached the last stall. Something moved, a dark shape rose before him. He leapt back as an ear-splitting shriek rent the air of the long chamber. A slooth hacked at him with its beak, flapping and leaping angrily in the limited space, swiping with its claws. Shenwolf and Issul rushed to the attack. Within moments the thing lay headless at their feet.

'Are you harmed?' asked Issul.

Phisusandra shook his head. 'My bowels are looser.'

'These are brooding pens,' said Shenwolf, gazing around him. 'I believe we disturbed this one as she was laying her egg.'

'Look here!' said Kol. He was at the stall opposite. The single egg in the nest there was broken. Struggling to break through the remaining membrane was a creature the size of a small cat, scrawny, hairless and slime-covered, but otherwise the perfect replica in miniature of the parent-slooth they had just slain.

'By the spirits,' breathed Issul. She turned away, strangely saddened as Phisusandra raised his sword and ended the tiny creature's brief life.

'We should inspect the other chamber,' said Shenwolf when he had assured himself that nothing else lived in the stalls. They quickly destroyed the remaining slooth eggs and made their way back to the ante-chamber. Issul moved to the second door, the one which Kol had said the prisoners had been barred from entering. As she put her hand to it, the door swung slowly back. She looked into a glimmering chamber, lined with earth and shored with stout oak supports. A strange greenish light flickered within, but she could not see its source for much of the chamber was obscured by the door. She stepped cautiously in and peered around the door.

In the centre of the chamber was an object like nothing she had ever seen. An oval, hovering above the ground, not shaped by any frame or definite outline, but rather by a brilliant green mist which fluxed and whorled within it. Issul stepped forward, fascinated. The thing was truly quite beautiful to behold.

As she watched the mist within the oval form became agitated. Its colour changed, to citron, deep orange, pearl, then blue. Quite suddenly a thick plume of vapour gouted forth and enveloped Issul. She felt a strange sensation, nothing dramatic, almost a simple acceptance that things were not as they had been.

She was in another chamber, lined with stone walls. Three figures sat at a table before her. They were children, looking exactly alike except that their ages differed by perhaps a year or two. She would have put them at eight, nine and ten. They were dressed identically in shining blue robes. Their skin was pure white, their hair also, which fell straight and long past their shoulders. Their eyes were the most brilliant piercing blue that Issul had ever seen. She could not tell whether they were male or female.

All three looked up at her, and one – the smallest – said, 'Aha, a visitor. At last.'

All three stood, together, their motion as well as their appearance identical, and they approached her. Issul was aware that the coloured mist still flowed around her, and that though her limbs were free she could not change her position. She seemed in fact to be floating, held in the changing mist like a fish in a bowl of water. The three children inspected her, their eyes passing up and down her body, back and forth, moving around her. Issul strove to look behind her for her companions. She found it impossible to turn right around, but as far as she could make out she was alone.

The younger child spoke again. 'You have come from the Edge.'

The other two smiled.

'She is confused,' said one.

'A visitor from the Edge,' said the other.

'She is beautiful,' said the younger.

'But not ours,' said the elder.

'Not perfectly,' said the middle child. 'Not yet.'

The elder child nodded. 'They are always confused.'

Issul could see through a window in the wall beyond the three children. There were mountains and an impossibly blue sky. There were disturbances in the air. There were colours, changing and shifting. She felt an inexplicable urge to weep. 'Where am I?'

'See,' said the middle child. 'Always so confused. They never understand.'

'Think of this as a dream,' said the younger child. 'For that is what it is. But you are not the dreamer, and the dream is not yours. Do you understand?'

'I am in another's dream?' asked Issul. Her voice sounded distant and detached.

'The dream of many,' said the child. 'And they may not know that they dream. They may not even know that they *are*. And in many instances they *are* not. For nothing here has happened, and perhaps never will. Now, you are even more confused. And I can say nothing more except Welcome. Welcome to the true world, the many-named domain, where all things are possible. Yes, welcome. Welcome to Enchantment.'

PART TWO

TEN

I

King Leth brooded.

What am I to believe? There are gods, but they are not gods. Not as the factions had previously conceived. Yet there are correspondences. They exist; they are powerful; they are vengeful.

King Haruman's Deist Edict denied them.

No! He would not let himself falter on this. The Edict only denied the religions and superstitions that had been purposefully promoted in the gods' names as a means of controlling the will of the people. The factions had become powerful political forces, but for all their preachings they had little to do with spiritual truth or knowledge of the gods. They battled, almost mirroring the endless battles of the gods they worshipped, the gods they did not know. Without the Edict they would have torn Enchantment's Edge apart.

Yet even with the Edict we are being torn apart by those same forces, in ways that I cannot comprehend.

But we have never denied the gods. We have denied only our ability to know them. Haruman established our path. Following him, we have striven to acknowledge and admit to our ignorance in the hope that in that way we might eventually be rid of it. This is what I stand for. The search for true knowledge must be paramount; the gathering of greater clouds of ignorance and superstition can only ultimately harm us. That is the purpose of the Edict. Surely, surely we cannot have been wrong?

But then, what of the Legendary Child? Is its existence – if it does exist – not proof that at least one of the factions may have been right all along? If one, then why not others?

Leth's head rang with unanswered and unanswerable questions.

Issul, Issul, why did you not tell me more?

The import of the knowledge he had been acquiring from Orbus, which he was forbidden to impart, weighed upon him and elated him at the same time.

The gods exist, but not as gods. They number twenty-four. They war in order to create, to extend the borders of their environment which we call Enchantment. They are perhaps only half-aware of the purpose behind their striving. They do not truly know what they are. Generally they have no interest in us, though in pursuing their own aims they would have no qualms in destroying us. One of them at least has aligned itself with the Krai, against we of Enchantment's Edge.

The knowledge that the gods were not as the factions claimed, and that they did not demand worship, was a small comfort. But the very fact that such beings existed strengthened the factions' position.

Leth felt he could be sure of nothing. *All this is brought to me by a magical creature who dwells somehow in an empty blue world contained in a casket no larger than a maid's jewellery box. All this is only true if Orbus can be believed.*

If Orbus can be believed! I take him at his word, with no means to disprove him. Is this the way of a responsible ruler?

II

And now had come definite news. Issul was lost. Perhaps dead. Perhaps a prisoner of the Krai.

Remnants of the platoon Leth had sent to escort her had returned to Orbia with the news of her ambush. Of the eight members of her original escort, led by Sir Bandullo, only two had survived. Sir Bandullo was not one of them. Seven members of the platoon had also been killed, and eight others wounded. One was missing. They had given chase, not aware for some time that it was Krai they pursued, for the attackers had almost vanished into the forest. But some distance into the forest they were attacked again, and then again. Eventually they had lost the trail.

Leth's one consolation was that Issul had not been found among the dead. It gave him some hope that she lived. But what could have become of her? A captive of the Krai?

It was unthinkable. What would they do to her? Or did she yet lie dead in some lonely place still undiscovered by the searchers? Or wander the forest, lost, the eventual prey of those wild creatures which haunted the wood's depths?

King Leth had sent out search parties, had dispatched a force two hundred strong to find her. He had stamped and cursed that he could not accompany them, but the deepening crisis at the capital demanded his presence in Orbia. When the searchers returned some days later it was without sign or news of Issul or the Krai unit that had ambushed her. The trail was cold.

A survivor of the ambush had been the peasant woman, Ohirbe. She was brought to Orbia in a state of near-madness brought on by the events that had overtaken her. She was grief-stricken at the death of her husband, Arrin, and the loss of Moscul, the child she and Arrin had fostered.

What had become of Moscul? Nobody knew. His body had not been recovered. Like Issul he had simply disappeared without trace.

Leth, frantic with worry over Issul, troubled and preoccupied by the issues that hung over him, had ordered that Ohirbe be brought to him. He questioned her about Moscul, and Issul's involvement with the child. But Ohirbe, tearful and dazed, could tell him only that the little boy had been brought to her when he was just a few days old. She had not known it was the Queen who brought him, nor anything of his origins. Nor had she learned anything since.

An unusual child? Yes, she confirmed, little Moscul was not like other children of his age. He was unusually bright, and very precocious, very knowing. And now he was gone. And the Queen was gone. And poor Arrin was dead . . .

Ohirbe believed it must somehow be all her fault. She had done wrong, she knew it. She was a bad person and this was her punishment. She buried her face in her hands and howled her grief, too overcome to feel fear even before the King.

Leth came away from that fruitless meeting with tears staining his own cheeks. *Issul, Issul, my love. Live! Come back. Find your way back to me. I have no will to exist if you are not by my side.*

His days and nights were a torment during this time. He barely slept, but tossed and turned throughout the dark hours, dreaming terrible dreams and lurching into suddenly, dreadfully clear wakefulness, Issul's name upon his lips, the sound of his cry reverberating across the silence of their bedchamber.

Leth spent more time than ever before with their children, Galry and Jace. It was as if his closeness with them might summon Issul, somehow draw her back to complete the unity that her absence prevented. Both children asked about their mother. Leth told them she had gone away on state duties but would be back soon. He instructed their nannies and minders to say likewise.

Leth took immense delight in his childrens' games, but fell into sudden despondency every time he was reminded that their mother was not there, enjoying them. Jace's likeness to her mother struck him more and more, the light on her fair hair, the laughter and sadness in her eyes, the ways she had of unconsciously imitating Issul and her mannerisms and gestures. Whenever chance offered he took the time to put both children to bed, and their cousin Lir also. Lir, too, was deprived of her mother, for Mawnie's recovery was not swift. Lir had become even more silent and withdrawn than usual, and seemed indifferent to Leth.

Leth told them stories of fairies, monsters and gallant knights, and sat by their bedsides until all three slept. When he left them he was cast back into the pit of loneliness and despair which seemed to become more his natural dwelling place with every passing day.

He brooded upon what Ohirbe had said. He considered the accusations of the faction leaders. He wondered: *I have been godless. Has the wrath of divinities fallen upon me? Is this my punishment?*

Somehow – usually – he found the strength within him to fight back: *No! I have never denied the gods. I have sought knowledge and truth, as I do still, in the manner of my predecessors. I will not become the victim of superstition and blind, baseless, fixed belief!*

But in the darkness in which he dwelt more and more it became harder to withstand the taunting voices that echoed in his mind, the recriminations of guilt and irresponsibility.

A few days after Issul's disappearance news arrived at Orbia of a slooth attack on a small market town to the west of Enchantment's

Edge. The assault had been swift and savage. Twenty-one people were killed, randomly and indiscriminately. No slooths had been brought down. Leth despaired. Against attacks of this nature he could offer no defence. He could spare no men to garrison the town: the slooths would almost certainly aim their next attack at some other remote and undefended community. Prince Anzejarl's strategy was apparently to terrorize and demoralize while placing as much pressure upon Leth as he could. In this he was succeeding.

No ransom demand for Issul was received, nor any other indication that Prince Anzejarl had her in his hands. Could he be ignorant, or – more likely – might silence be another element in his overall strategy?

III

On a wet, windy morning Leth met in Special Assembly with the heads of the major factions. Lord Fectur was there, as was Pader Luminis and, representing the military, Sir Cathbo. Palace Guards stood in close attendance, ever wary since Grey Venger's attempt on the King's life. The heads of the Far Flame, the Children of Ushcopthe, the Mark of the Golden Thought, and several others congregated within the hall, all keen to hear what King Leth had to say. They had called for the assembly, though Leth had already come to the decision that such a convocation was the most advisable course.

'I am concerned that word may have leaked out about Issul's petition to Grey Venger and his subsequent reply and declaration of terms,' Leth confided to Pader Luminis on the way to the hall.

'I have heard nothing to that effect,' Pader replied calmly. 'To my knowledge this meeting is to question your methods of dealing with the crisis, to once again make demands, in view of current developments, to rescind the Deist Edict, and to ascertain the status of the Krai prince, Anzejarl, in regard to his alliance with, apparently, a god.'

'Have I done wrong, Pader?' Leth asked. 'Have I handled this badly?'

'I do not think so. From where I stand it appears that you have done what any other in your position would have done under similar circumstances. The problem is that you are beset by potent mysteries and unparalleled menaces the like of which no monarch before you has had to confront. At least, not simultaneously. The factions are using this as a means to their own ends. Unfortunately there is little unity behind you. The crisis to them is most relevant in that they perceive it as an instrument which they may use to bring you down.'

'Am I to be brought down?'

'I for one would hope not. What would be the outcome? Apart from losing a monarch who is perhaps without peer, the realm would succumb to anarchy. The factions have no agreement between themselves. They would fall upon one another, while the Krai moved in almost unopposed. But I say to you now, as your loyal subject and an old friend, that if you falter or glance aside, even for an instant, if you make one wrong decision at this time, your enemies here, within Enchantment's Edge, will seize that moment and use it, if they can, to destroy you. They can see no further than the ends of their noses. Beware, Leth. You are surrounded by wolves.'

'Are you one of them, Pader?' asked Leth, struck with a sudden spasm of doubt.

Pader Luminis halted in his stride. His face showed a hurt but concerned expression. 'Be sure that I am not. I am of the Arcane College, and a lifelong friend and supporter of the Crown. But the fact that you can ask such a question of me is an indication of how serious this matter has become.'

'I feel I may not even lead my people to war against the Krai,' Leth said, 'for so many have been poisoned against me.'

'Then seek diligently for the antidote to the poison. It is the truth that people really seek, though they may not always know it.'

Leth clasped his hand. 'Pader, you are a true friend. This I have never doubted, and I apologize if I have just caused you to question that. Outside of my immediate family there is no other I would trust as I trust you. One day soon, then, I may come to you with a request. A request which at the time may seem unusual. If that happens, I entreat you, do not question me. Do simply as I ask. Much will depend on it.'

Pader Luminis studied him with an intent, questioning, compassionate gaze.

'Ask nothing more, Pader,' said Leth. 'For I can tell you nothing.'

'My lord, you have my word.'

IV

The faction heads were unsympathetic, which came as no surprise. They sought blood, and they smelled it in the air. They had taken their respective places around the great oval table, Gursmaeden, the Table of Debate, and the moment Leth seated himself and declared the assembly open, they were upon him. As Pader Luminis had predicted, their main thrust was against the Deist Edict.

'The evidence which you have so long refused to acknowledge is now laid stark before you, King Leth,' declared Chandiston of the Golden Thought sect. 'Even you can no longer deny what is obvious. The gods are angered by the continuing obstinacy of your family. They have given us signs for so long and you and your predecessors have deliberately ignored them in pursuit of your own repressive aims. Now they bring their wrath down upon us all!'

Opiah Forthruth, imperator of one of the lesser factions, the Hand of Freedom, accused: 'Our people will be destroyed, all bar the true believers who will live on to serve the true gods and spread the knowledge of their ways. And you will bear the blame, King Leth. So will your name be remembered by future generations, the generations of the righteous who will be privileged to survive these dark days.'

'Sire, you would be wise to repeal the Deist Edict now,' opined Astress of the Children of Ushcopthe in less abrasive tones. 'Let us make obeisance and petition our divine rulers for mercy; let them restore order through our efforts, let them turn back the Krai, or Enchantment's Edge is doomed.'

'They have put the Krai upon us!' asserted Madroluardh of the Open Light, gripping his jaw, his face twisted and sour. He suffered from chronic toothache, and spoke in moans. 'They attack us from the skies! Ohhh! We all risk being overwhelmed! And now they have stolen our beloved Queen! Ahhhh-ohhh! What more does it take, King Leth, before you will respond?'

Leth bore the arguments and accusations without interrupting, seated with his elbow resting upon the arm of his chair, a finger crooked beneath his nose, his gaze upon the ancient, gleaming surface of Gursmaeden. In time a tense and indignant silence stole the place of the raised voices. Leth sat back, and said, 'I have heard you, now have the courtesy to hear me. Each of you is quick to find fault in me, so quick that I have cause to wonder whether you have the best interests of the Crown and Enchantment's Edge at heart at all. You storm me with your demands, but let us imagine, for an instant, that I were to heed you. Let us just say that I repealed the Deist Edict here and now. Think of that. What then? What, truly, would be the effect?'

'We have already said, we would petition the gods for mercy and redress.'

'But you do not know the gods.'

This brought a collective gasp from his accusers.

'How can you?' persisted Leth. 'This is the old argument to which none of you, nor your predecessors, have provided a satisfactory answer. You have never been to the gods, they have never come to you. How can you know them?'

'They *have* been to us! It is written in the ancient scriptures! Then there are the sacred relicts, the commandments! What of the visions and visitations of our forefathers!'

'The writings, tales, collections and visions of men long dead!' declared Leth, now impassioned. 'Men who cannot speak for themselves, whose words and experiences may have been misinterpreted or misused by others who came later. Their writings may be valuable as an insight into our past, but let us never forget the power of the written word and the ways it may be used to control as much as to educate and enlighten. Why, I could write a document today filled with falsehoods, and have it published as truth to influence men and women now and in future generations. These examples that you cite are not proof of intimate knowledge of the gods. They are proof of nothing except that they exist in themselves. Those who wrote your scriptures may have been sincere but equally they may not. Who is to say those scriptures have not suffered over the centuries the attentions of others with designs of their own?'

'This is madness!' declared Chandiston. 'Though you are King, you may not trample upon what is sacred. I will hear no more of it!'

'Your sacred scriptures conflict!' cried Leth. 'Yours, Chandiston, do not accord with those of the Far Flame. Theirs contest the veracity of those of the Children of Ushcopthe. You argue, one with the other, throughout time, and thus is your credibility eroded. It is an undeniable fact that you cannot all be right.'

'Sire, you tread upon fragile ground,' said Astress. 'Where we differ is in perception and interpretation. But we all acknowledge the power of the gods and their right to worship.'

'O-ohhh, you will bring doom upon us all!' wailed Madroluardh.

'You speak like a man possessed,' said Edric of the Far Flame, with a voice dark and freighted.

Leth shook his head. 'No. I speak as a man dedicated to truth. I say again, what will happen if I give you what you ask for? You come to me, together, in one voice, seeing me as your common adversary. But dispose of me, allow you your gods once more, and what will you do? Your unity will be instantly a thing of the past. In the name of your individual gods you will fight with one another. The Krai will still advance upon Enchantment's Edge, and you will rattle your relicts and weep and howl your prayers, and nothing will be changed! I say to you now, the gods as you claim to know them do not exist. You, or those who went before you, have created them. Those beings which do exist within Enchantment, though they may as well be gods, yet know nothing of you! Nor would they care if they did!'

Even Lord Fectur's head turned at this, as a shocked silence filled the chamber. He regarded Leth with an expression that was coldly and sternly appraising, while the faction heads sat momentarily stiff in mute outrage.

Leth quickly gathered his thoughts. He had gone further than he had intended. He had hinted at knowledge of the inhabitants of Enchantment! But he would not back down, not now. The kingdom depended upon him. He stood, quickly. 'I say this to you: stand with me now, give me your loyalty, your strength and support. Let us battle our common enemy together, in mutual accord, not fragmented and striving to do one another down. Join me in this hour of need, or begone. Aid me, or put yourselves from my sight and be silent. If you cannot take one of these two courses you will force me into an impossible position, for I have no choice but to view any other action as treason.'

'Treason?' The word flew simultaneously from several mouths.

'If you are not with me you are against me and with my enemies. That is how the Crown must view any action seen to hinder its endeavour to combat this menace. These are dire days, requiring the sternest measures. I am declaring a Condition of Emergency, as of this moment. This Assembly is dissolved.'

Again the silence of disbelief. Leth wheeled before it could break and strode from the hall. Lord Fectur was quickly at his side. 'You may have gone too far, Sire.'

'Not far enough, as far as I am concerned. I will not be opposed now Fectur. Not when so much is at at stake. Understand that. If any of them give me the slightest provocation I will throw them in jail.'

'I would advise against that. I would advise that you reconsider your Declaration of Emergency.'

'Why?'

'It is extreme. It gives you the power of life or death over any person, without recourse to the judiciary.'

'Quite so. I do not intend to invoke that power unless I must, but it is essential that I am not opposed from within. If they will not see sense they must be shown it, or be obliged to keep silence.'

'You will become isolated. Had you consulted me upon this decision I would have recommended strongly against it. The consequences of your action may prove to be more far-reaching than you know. It will not be popular.'

'We are in a state of war, Fectur.'

'Of this I am quite aware.'

'I must have absolute loyalty now. Furthermore, I am faced with the possibility of having to restore the True Sept to legitimacy. I see no other way if I am to meet with Grey Venger and discover what is known of the Legendary Child. At least under Emergency that legitimacy will be limited, and therefore more pleasing to the other factions.'

'As the Sept will perceive. Such conditions may be unacceptable to them.'

'We will see. But the fact is that I had no other choice.'

'Perhaps that is the problem. It may be seen as the tactic of a desperate man.'

Leth strode on, angered. Fectur remained at his shoulder. 'Sire, you implied extraordinary knowledge of Enchantment.'

'I spoke heatedly.'

'Then you do not possess such knowledge?'

'I said only what is obvious to any who are not shackled and blindfolded by their fixed beliefs.'

'You spoke of beings within Enchantment, almost as though you had personal acquaintance. The factions will not let that pass. They will have every justification in calling for an explanation.'

'There is nothing to be explained.'

'Then there is nothing that I should be made aware of?'

'Nothing.'

V

Had he really gone too far? Leth had not planned in advance to invoke the Condition of Emergency. He had considered it in the minutes approaching the meeting, but until a few moments before he had uttered those fateful words he had not really known that he was going to do so.

He had simply wanted to be done with these bawkers and complainers, these bloodsuckers who snagged and snared and sniped. To swipe them aside, at least temporarily, so that he might concentrate to the best of his abilities on the real emergency at hand.

But his action had been impulsive and emotional. Uncharacteristically so. This he acknowledged soberingly as he strode on alone through the corridors of Orbia. Alone, aware more than ever of the gulf that walked beside him now that Issul was no longer here.

How he had relied upon her, even without knowing it!

This is not me! I am not myself!

Orbus, I must speak to you now! I need your advice!

But, as always, the ragged tenant of the blue casket was not answerable to the King's summons. He came when he wanted Leth, but not the other way around.

Leth resolved to consult Pader Luminis at the earliest opportunity and see if he agreed with Fectur's summation. For now, though, Pader remained with the faction leaders in the Hall of Assembly, and Leth had no intention of returning there.

Venger, I must see you. I must! You will tell me your secrets. Somehow I must get you to reveal all that you know of the Legendary Child. How is it that you, my enemy, my would-be assassin, inveigled my darling wife into your ancient labyrinthine schemings? What is your power?

Tears stung Leth's eyes. *Issul, Issul, where are you? Why could you not have told me what you knew? What is this madness that has fallen upon us all?*

Ahead he saw a figure, frail and grey-garbed, passing almost ghostlike along the corridor towards him.

'Mawnie.'

She approached as though drifting, her face almost as grey as her thin gown, her eyes glazed and red from weeping. But a smile flitted ghostlike upon her face as she saw her royal brother-in-law.

'Leth. Oh, Leth.'

She came to him and put her head upon his shoulder. Leth held her gently. 'Mawnie, what are you doing here?'

'Looking for you, Leth. Don't you know?' Mawnie drew back her head, looked smiling into his eyes. She put her hand to his face, then reached up and pressed her lips to his.

Leth pushed her away. 'Mawnie! No! This is wrong. You do not know what you are doing!'

Mawnie gave a harsh laugh. 'Oh I do, Leth. I do. I am looking. It was me, you see. In the woods. They all think Ressa. But truly it was me. But kiss me, Leth. Love me. You do love me, in your most secret heart, don't you?'

She came to him again, but Leth stepped back. 'Mawnie, I will take you back.'

'Back? No. I wish to see Lir. Where is she?'

'In the nursery, I would imagine. Or playing somewhere with her nanny.'

'And where is . . . where is my sister? What has happened to her?'

'Issul? She has gone away for a few days. Come, Mawnie, let us go back to your chamber.'

'Not Issul. I know about Issul,' said Mawnie. 'No. No. It is Ressa. Where is she? Where is Ressa? I want to see her.'

Leth put his arm gently about her shoulder and tried to steer her back the way she had come, towards her chambers.

Mawnie pulled away suddenly, her eyes blazing. '*Bah!* You are just like him. You don't love me. You think me dirty. You think I am *nothing*!' She ripped at her gown, exposing her breasts. 'I am nothing! *Nothing*!'

'Mawnie!'

He took her wrists, for she was striking herself, lacerating her pale flesh with her nails. Mawnie began to scream, fighting against him, then her screams became sobs. 'Oh why, oh why, oh why, oh why? *Oh why, why, why?*'

A servant came running. A little way behind him came Mawnie's nurse, distraught and filled with self-blame. 'I went to get the Duchess water, Sire. She sent me. She had knocked over her pitcher, breaking it and spilling the contents. She said she was parched.'

'Very good. Just help me now.'

Together they got Mawnie back to her bedchamber, but she had to be held down upon the bed. Doctor Melropius came and administered a strong herbal sedative, and eventually Mawnie slept.

'I am in two minds as to whether to recommend restraints,' said Melropius. 'Her condition is not improving and I fear she may be a danger to herself, and also to others. But in the Duke's absence I would require your authority, Sire.'

Leth shook his head. 'Not unless we absolutely must. Assign two nurses to her at all times. If necessary, as now, they must hold her down. But I will not have her strapped. Not yet. I will put a guard upon her apartment door also.'

Melropius nodded. 'And you, Sire? Can I give you something?'

'Me?'

'You are under great strain. You must take care, Sire. A potion to calm your nerves, to help you to sleep, would be of great benefit just now.'

'I have no need of your potions,' Leth flared. 'Save your ministrations for those who need them, Doctor.'

He turned and stormed from the chamber.

Orbus, I have to speak to you!

But only days had passed since he and Orbus had last met. It seemed unlikely that he would be summoned again so soon.

VI

On the occasion that Leth had taken the piece of cheese to Orbus, in line with Orbus's request, something unusual had happened. Orbus asked Leth to place it on the ground between them, then to step back. Then Orbus had shuffled forward and lowered himself to a sitting position before the cheese. He inhaled deeply, seeming to draw the aroma of the cheese into him with some pleasure.

'Aah yes,' he breathed. 'I remember so well.'

A tattered limb had reached out and taken the cheese into his rags. He sat then, quite still, and for a long time was silent. Eventually he had said, 'Good. Good. All is well. Next time, will you bring me water, King Leth? Just a small amount. And a stone, a simple pebble or piece of gravel will suffice. And lastly, for now, something of wood. Small and easy to carry – even a handful of sawdust will do.'

Leth had ventured a question. 'What are these things for?'

He had the impression that Orbus was appraising him, considering the question.

'It is something of an experiment,' Orbus said presently. 'A test. Something that I wish to ascertain after long ages of hope, toil and wonder. But now, Leth, you have begun this session with a question. Previously, in recent meetings, you have listened well. I know there are many questions you would ask if you could. Well, I offer you the opportunity to do so now. Please, ask what you will.'

Leth had hesitated, somewhat surprised. He had grown accustomed to being reprimanded, ignored or even dismissed for introducing questions – at least, those that did not pertain directly to the topic Orbus had chosen to enlighten him on. Now the questions tumbled before his mind's eye, and he hardly knew where to begin.

'This place,' he said, indicating with his arms the vast enclosed blue space that surrounded him. 'What is it? How did it come to be? What is its extent?'

Orbus chuckled to himself. 'It is the Orb, as I am the Orb. No, hold your indignation! I know this is how I answered you when you posed the same question at our first meeting. But I will say more, in so far as I am able. This place is a realm, an otherwhere that exists within, beyond, and dependent upon your own realm. It is, in a sense, a nothing, yet at the same time it exists, and a nothing cannot truly exist, nor can it be described.'

Leth regretted that he had asked. 'You choose to answer me in riddles. Do you make fun of me?'

The great bundled head shook slowly from side to side. 'This place has been created to fulfil a purpose which I cannot yet reveal to you. You ask about its extent. You mean, does it have a beginning and an end? Yes, it does, in a manner of speaking. But only to those who understand its laws. I say to you, does the cosmos in all its fullness have a beginning and an end? Show me its limits. Do consciousness or unconsciousness have a beginning and an end? Show me their limits. Show me the beginning of Creation, then show me where it ends.'

Leth was disquieted by the answer. He looked about him. 'There are walls, in the distance, yet close. But though I move towards them they are never closer.'

'They indicate, perhaps, that no matter how far you go, there will always be something unknown and hidden beyond. Were you to have the means to leave your world and take wing to the stars, how far would you travel, for how long? Would you ever reach the universe's end, or its beginning? If you did, then you would be forced to consider your journey fruitless. For that terminus, that state at which all things begin or end, would reveal to you only that there had to be something beyond, something in which the condition was contained. Another, greater universe. Another, greater realm. An enigma. Perhaps absolutely nothing – yet it would still exist, for if it did not how could you possibly be aware of it? Or is it possible that, in making the awareness, the leap of imagination, you are actually creating the possibility of the existence of the thing itself?

'In fact that journey is not necessary, Leth. Not physically. For you are already blessed with the means to undertake it. Do you see? No matter how far you might travel, the journey, truly, is one that leads inwards.'

'I have contemplated such mysteries before,' said Leth. 'They are unanswerable, futile. The more one considers them the more one is taken through terror to the edge of madness.'

'It is in a kind of madness, a letting-go of all that is known and familiar, that an answer may be found.'

'No!' Leth shook his head emphatically. 'We are going too far.'

'Too far? You, who have lived your entire life on the Edge? Have you not always known, somewhere deep inside you, that one day you might have to step over? You have surely wondered what might lie on the other side? We are entering Mystery, Leth. Do you not wish to travel? Truly, this is only the beginning.'

'Let me get my breath. Let me step back.' Leth had broken into a sweat. His heart pounded, his blood hummed in his ears. 'You are asking me to understand too much that I cannot grasp.'

'It is you who are asking the questions, Leth.'

'But your answers fill me with fear.'

'An important admission from one who is King of his realm.'

'Just let me take my own pace. You said once that this place is a prison. Are you its sole occupant? Can you leave?'

'I said also that it has a role, a purpose.'

'Is its purpose not to contain you?'

'It is, but not for eternity.'

'Then you can leave?'

'When certain conditions are fulfilled.'

'Is it all so empty?'

'It is as you perceive it.'

'Can others exist here? *Do* others exist here?'

'Ah, now that is an interesting point. The laws of this realm are very precise, held on a delicate balance. I have spent many ages trying to understand them and then to effect modifications of them. I have been successful only to a small degree.'

'But you are alone here?'

'The concept has no meaning when you understand that not only am I the tenant of this realm, the Orb, but I am also the Orb itself. *Are you alone, Leth, within yourself?*'

At the time Leth had had no answer. He had not even wanted to answer. The question had, as had the conversation that preceded it, set his mind spinning. He was left seated in numbed silence before the hunched, tattered figure, and then Orbus had said, 'We have spoken enough for today. Think upon these things, Leth. Until the next time.'

And he had raised his staff and cast the King from his blue and empty realm.

Now Leth had an answer. As he came from the bedchamber where Mawnie lay in her madness, sedated and under guard, he knew without question that he was alone. Within and without himself. Issul gone, perhaps dead, perhaps a prisoner of his enemy. His people turning against him, his realm in peril of being overwhelmed and lost. He was anguished and raging, and aware that his judgement was no longer clear.

'*You who have lived your entire life on the Edge. Have you not always known that one day you might have to step over?*'

My duty is to my people. I must protect them. I must bring them back to me.

'*You have surely wondered what might lie on the other side?*'

I have always questioned, thought Leth. Always wished to know. But not like this.

'*We are entering Mystery, Leth. Do you not wish to travel?*'

He shook his head as he walked.

No! Not like this. Absolutely not!

He was overcome with a fear, greater, chiller and more profound than he could explain.

ELEVEN

I

The rain continued to batter Enchantment's Edge that day, borne in sudden violent blasts upon angry winds. In the afternoon Sir Cathbo brought Leth the news that Prince Anzejarl's army had crossed Uxon's Ridge and was now within three leagues of Giswel Holt.

'That is surely his immediate goal. He has taken the march town of Wizard's Lea. It fell without a fight, the majority of its inhabitants having fled. It is an important gain for him, providing him with shelter and an adequate base for supplies.'

'How reliable is the report?' queried Leth.

'It has come by one of Duke Hugo's messenger pigeons. It bears his seal and mark.'

Leth nodded soberly. Wizard's Lea had been an anticipated loss, almost a sacrifice. Its occupation came as no surprise. For weeks its people had been pouring into Giswel Holt and Enchantment's Edge, desperate for shelter, for they had known they would be first in the path of the Krai. Wizard's Lea was indefensible. To have met the Krai in battle there would have resulted in quick and brutal defeat.

Folk were flooding in from other towns and villages, their numbers ever-increasing. They were women, children and old men in the main. The young and able had been drafted into the army. They swelled the population of the great city-castle until its walls groaned and its towers swayed, placing demands upon its storehouses almost beyond its bearable limit. Passions flared in the streets as resident citizens brunted the influx. Order was becoming more difficult to establish or control. Ever more urgent requests came to close the city gates on the growing torrent, but Leth refused to turn his people away.

'Do you ride to meet Anzejarl, Sire?'

Leth remained resolute. 'Hugo can certainly hold out at Giswel Holt for many weeks should the Krai lay siege. Then might come an opportunity to strike Anzejarl in the back. But for now he remains fluid. I do not choose to exhaust our troops by chasing him willy-nilly about the countryside.'

'And if he advances on towards Enchantment's Edge?'

'Then he will be between Hugo and us. Keep me apprised of all reports, Cathbo.'

Sir Cathbo bowed and withdrew. Leth sat in hopeless despair. He had spoken with some bravado but within himself he knew that nothing he could do would be much more than a token gesture against the Krai. Even a strike against the Krai army's rear positions would achieve little. The Krai vastly outnumbered the soldiers and knights of Enchantment's Edge. They were enigmatic, emotionless warriors, skilled in battle, who fought without fear of injury or death. And they did not fight alone. Leth's forces would be thrown into disarray by a simultaneous attack of Anzejarl's terrible slooths from the skies.

How many slooths? Leth could not guess, but fewer than two score, expertly deployed, would be enough to bring havoc and confusion to Leth's ranks which the Krai might exploit to devastating advantage.

And there remained Anzejarl's other forces, the fearsome troll-things, so far unseen within Leth's kingdom. Earlier reports of the Krai campaign had told of the effect these creatures had had as shock troops against the armies of the southern Mondanes Anzejarl had conquered. Bolstered by such redoubtable allies Prince Anzejarl had made himself a virtually invincible foe.

If I could just learn how he has tamed these creatures! Leth slammed his fist down upon the arm of his seat. *If I could discover how he has acquired the patronage of a god, how he has torn his nation's constitution to shreds and yet survived to lead. If, if, if . . .*

His gloomy meditations were interrupted by a servant announcing the Lord High Invigilate. Fectur strode into the chamber, his chest puffed, in his hand a sealed letter which he passed straight to the King.

Leth saw at once the illegal seal of the True Sept.

'They grow audacious,' he said, breaking the seal. The seal on the previous letter had been anonymous, the Sept's insignia contained only on the inside. Leth read the words within:

If the Child is truly known, you are helpless without us.

He handed it to Fectur, who nodded, seemingly gratified. 'They also grow impatient.'

'They burn for contact, for legitimacy. I will exploit this if I can. Yet I have nothing to give them other than the news that the Child may have been found and has now vanished. Hardly enough to persuade Venger to disgorge the Sept's most sacred secrets.'

'But they are keen,' emphasized Fectur. 'Avid. The thought that the Child may be known by us is more than they can bear. The fact that they contact us again proves that.'

'I will send word,' said Leth. 'I will meet with Venger.'

'Restore him? Restore the Sept?'

'Under Emergency.'

Fectur shook his head. 'I think he will remain invisible under Emergency. No matter the temptation, he will know what it means. But I have a better idea. Emergency has not yet been made public. It is not too late for you to rescind it.'

'No!'

'Sire!' Fectur leaned towards him, the muscles of his jaw rippling. 'Listen to me! Rescind it now, bring Venger out, *then* declare Emergency! Thus is he caught!'

'I have thought of that.' Leth's face was rueful and set. 'It is not my way. I would be seen by all to be sly and prevaricating, a King without principle, no matter that it snares Grey Venger. Never again would I have the confidence of my people.'

'But Sire—'

'No! I have declared a Condition of Emergency for a specific, legitimate reason, because the evidence I have convinces me that it is warranted. I will not use such drastic legislation for anything other than its true and proper purpose: to bring order to the realm.'

'Catching an infamous troublemaker, traitor and assassin is surely included under that remit.'

'Not if I must be seen by my people to have stooped to the level of the lowest cheat. That is not the example of a King. No, what is done is done. I have no intention of changing it.'

'Then you must restore Venger and the True Sept. I would have it set on record, Sire, that I do not counsel such a move. It will be another unpopular decision. However, your only alternative, as far as I see it, is to ignore them. One cannot guess the consequences of that.'

'There may be none,' shrugged the King. 'Will the information that the Sept possesses be any more valid than the so-called knowledge of the gods that the other factions claim?'

'Only Venger can answer that.' Fectur grasped his lapels and leaned back. 'Sire, I must state that for you to have legitimate concourse with Venger at this time cannot improve your position. This is the man who almost murdered you, who is known to hate you beyond reason for the deaths of his two sons. He – or the Sept which he represents – is strongly suspected of having contact with the Krai. Acceptance in public will not go down well.'

'Do you have firm evidence that contact was ever made?'

'There was a man brought to my custody. He confessed to being a Sept member, and to having been sent to establish relations with Prince Anzejarl.'

Leth gave a scornful toss of the head. 'In your custody a man will confess to anything, Fectur. Where is he now?'

'He died. Unfortunately.'

'You have channels to the Sept, still? Could you arrange a meeting, in secret?'

'It can be done. But there remain the problems of Venger's proclamation of innocence and the restoration of the Sept.'

'Propose the meeting, Fectur. Let Venger know that I am prepared to *discuss* with him his demands. I leave it to you to establish the conditions, but make it clear that, in this instance at least, Venger will be free of any risk of legal action for the duration of the meeting.'

'Are you sure of this, Sire?'

'I am.'

'I would again impress upon you my reservations.'

'Acknowledged. Now, about your business, man, if there is nothing else you wish to say.'

II

Late that night, sleepless, King Leth stood at the window of his and Issul's bedchamber. The rain still fell, racing cloud concealing the stars, permitting an intermittent, delicate silvered radiance from the moon to bathe the world for brief moments. In the distance the weird lights were a feeble, misted blur, marking the border of Enchantment, definite enough for Leth to discern something of their alternating hues through the low cloud. Between him and the weird lights, beyond the jagged outlines of Enchantment's Edge, lay a dark void, the great forest wilderness, a nothing, cloaked in wet mist, touched here and there with faintest moonlight streaked by rain.

It seemed that he gazed upon a reflection of his misery.

I am King! The people look to me for decisiveness, for resoluteness, for strength. I am not permitted to be a man. More, much more, is demanded of the King. I can show no weakness. I cannot be vulnerable to the pressures and anguishes of ordinary folk.

And I am empty.

His eyes travelled over the great abyss before him. *Issul, Issul. Are you out there somewhere? Do you live? Do you breathe? Do you struggle to return to me, as I yearn to have you return?*

He thrust himself away from the window, unable to contemplate any more. But the candlelit chamber offered no succour, the bed no comfort. He strode the length of the room, then back again. Something caught his eye and he paused, straining to see into one shadowed corner.

A figure seemed to stand there, hardly formed, immaterial. Vaguely the shape of a man, hunched and bowed, bundled in rags, bearing a staff.

'Orbus?'

The figure made no sound, though it moved slightly. It was only half-seen, for an instant became better defined, then faded, faded, and was no more.

Leth blinked, peering hard. Was it hallucination? He was overtired, overwrought. The shadows there were dense and indistinct. Had he conjured only what he wished to see?

He heard a sound, a half-whispered voice: 'Aah, so close . . .'

But no more.

Had he heard it, or imagined it? The wind – it had fooled his ears as the shadows and flickering candlelight had fooled his eyes. There was nothing.

Or was he mad?

Leth advanced cautiously to the corner, his hand before him. But he found only the emptiness of shadows, as he had expected to do.

He turned and flung himself upon the bed, grasped the pillow and gathered it about his head. But nothing could separate him from the torment within.

The night passed slowly. The rain moved on, little by little the wind abated. Leth hovered on the uncertain border between sleep and consciousness, the undefinable edge on either side of which lay the real and palpable, and the hallucinatory and intangible. And at some point, undeterminable in time's sequence, he found himself before the blue casket in a dream, and heard the irresistible summons: 'Come now, Leth.'

Instantly awake, Leth hurled himself from his bed, seized a lamp and rushed to his study. He took the casket from the wall, found it unsealed, and raised its lid. When the familiar dazzle subsided he found himself before Orbus in the great blue chamber.

'You are distraught?'

'I am threatened on all sides. War is upon me. I fear losing all.'

'It is the Krai who advance upon you?' asked Orbus.

'They are within my borders now. I lack the forces to withstand them.'

'They are moving with greater speed than I had anticipated,' Orbus mused. 'Their need is surely urgent.'

'Do you know which god it is that allies itself with the Krai?'

'I could venture guesses as to the most likely, but I would only be furnishing you with a list of as many as ten names to choose from, none of which would mean anything to you. It is therefore pointless to speculate. I presume your spies have witnessed no unusual company in the Krai camp?'

'Anzejarl travels with a consort who is not believed to be Krai.

My agents are unable to get close so it is difficult to be sure. Apart from that there is no one.'

'There is the clue, then. The Krai do not mix with other races.'

'She is the god?' Leth was astounded.

'More likely the servitor, sorcerous fabrication, simulacrum or projection of one. But it is surely through her that Prince Anzejarl commands his unnatural creatures. Still, this does not help me to identify a specific god.'

'What? Why have you not told me this before?' cried Leth.

Orbus stood stock still. 'I did not know before. You have never mentioned her. But what difference does it make?'

'If she, this consort, is the key, then I can direct my actions against her.'

Orbus's great head shook. 'You cannot destroy her. If she is what I say, nothing you can do will affect her. Do you know her name?'

'No. I know nothing about her. But why, Orbus, why has a god allied itself with one race against all others?'

'The issue is complex,' said Orbus. 'But one must assume that they serve mutual ends and that therefore there is something the god seeks and stands to gain through the alliance. I think we will speak of this at another time.'

'You know, don't you!' Leth could not withhold his emotion. 'Do not avoid my questions, Orbus. Do not dismiss me. I believe you know.'

'I know only that this is grave,' Orbus muttered. 'Events are moving too quickly.'

'But not entirely to your surprise! Tell me, Orbus! Tell me what you know! What is happening here?'

The bundled figure hesitated. 'I do not know as much as you wish to believe.'

'But you know far more than I. How? Tell me that? How do you know so much? All that you have told me to date . . . Who – *what* – are you?'

'Surely, Leth, you have guessed the answer to that by now, haven't you?'

Leth stood rigid, quivering. He was eager to press what he perceived had somehow become his advantage. Orbus, for the first time ever, seemed unsure of himself, seemed almost in Leth's palm, as though actually wishing to unburden himself of something. But

Leth was fearful of appearances, knew that his advantage might be brief. He was desperate not to irritate the strange figure and find himself cast peremptorily from the blue realm. 'You are one of them, aren't you? One of the very gods of Enchantment whom you have described to me. That is how you know so much.'

'We are not gods, Leth. Remember that.'

'Please, let us not argue nomenclature now. If you have a soul you will know what pain I bear; you will have no wish to crush me further. To all intents and purposes you are gods. *You*, Orbus. You are one of them!'

To his surprise Orbus laughed. Not a laugh of mockery, but a short musing laugh, coloured with irony.

'Ah Leth, you do not know what you have just said.' Orbus then leaned upon his staff as though weary, his head bowed. 'I was among them, it is true. One of the twenty-four. But no longer. Not for many ages. I was defeated, Leth. Beaten. The first of the twenty-four to suffer such humiliation.'

'But not destroyed.'

'Yes, destroyed. Banished from the world. No longer powerful. I became what I am now. I will not waste time with details of the process, for you would not understand it. But it was destruction, separation from my essence, elimination of the 'god' that I had been. It was death.'

It was not death as Leth understood it, but he was not going to sidetrack or discourage Orbus now with unnecessary questions. Besides, he could never hope for a full intellectual understanding of the concepts he was being introduced to here, in this extraordinary place before this extraordinary being.

'I can tell you little more, Leth,' Orbus said, and his tone was despondent.

'You can tell me what I should do.'

'I do not know. I cannot advise you at this time. I have been striving . . . but if the Krai are truly so close then I have no time. I am as good as powerless.'

'I cannot sit here and simply accept defeat!' protested Leth. 'There must be a way!'

'There are ways, but for your part they are ways of the imagination only. They cannot be followed.'

'Tell me anyway.'

'You could go to Enchantment—'

'I cannot!'

'Precisely.'

Leth clenched his fists before him. 'But if I did?'

'You could attempt to discover the identity of this god who backs the Krai, then appeal to him or her to abandon Anzejarl. Alternatively you could approach another god, an enemy of this one, have him wage war for your cause. As I said, neither course is feasible. Even less so is your final option.'

'Still, I will hear it.'

'You can find and bring to me the Orb's Soul.'

'The Orb's Soul? What is this thing, Orbus? You have mentioned it before but failed to elucidate. Why is it so important?'

'Leth, have you still not understood? You have just said that if I possess a soul I will know what pain you bear. Well, I know your pain. Truly I do. And I know mine also. Yet I am without a soul. It is the Soul of the Orb that was taken from me when I was defeated by my enemies. It is my essence, and without it I am nothing except what you see. It was taken from me and cast away, or buried or hidden – I do not know. But if it could be found and restored to me, I would be again what I once was.'

'It was taken by one of your enemies?'

'Not one; a cabal. Strymnia, who manifests as an Arch-Demonness of immense power; Bartacanes, who favours purple-skinned humanoid appearance and sorcerous talents; and Urch-Malmain, a perverse, normally solitary creature. Perhaps others too!'

'Then they each exist in a single, permanent form?'

'I have told you before, the gods may change their form at will. But each of us adopts a favoured form, and with the passing of the eons that form becomes more the natural state as we succumb to natural laws. Most favour human-like appearance, emulating the dominant species of this world.'

Leth was thoughtful. 'If the Orb's Soul could be found and returned to you, you would become a god again. What then of Enchantment's Edge?'

'I mean you no harm Leth, be assured of that. But if I were empowered again I could confront your enemies and my own on something approaching equal terms. As it is, I can do virtually nothing.'

'It occurs to me that there may be another option open to

me,' said Leth. 'One that you have purposefully failed to mention.'

'What is that?'

'I could take the blue casket, the Orb, and offer it to the god who commands the Krai. Because I think perhaps it is you, Orbus, that this god seeks. I think that may be its reason for joining with the Krai.'

Orbus shook his head. 'Do so, Leth, if you wish. But you would be mistaken. You would lose me forever, and still fall. The god does not seek me. He or she may not know that I am here, but neither would they care particularly. I am not the object of the search. Why would I be? I am without a soul, and helpless.'

'Then there is something else.' Leth said. He fell to thinking.

'It will be better if I leave you now,' said Orbus. 'You have much to dwell upon.'

'No. Not yet. Orbus, too much is at stake and I need you.'

'I, whom you are ready to sacrifice to your enemy and mine?'

'That was not my intention. I was testing you. I sought to know, that is all. The truth is, I do need you. Enchantment's Edge needs you. But with you or without you we seem doomed to fall.'

'Leth, I am here. I can say nothing more under these circumstances. But from this point on the blue casket will be open to you at all times. Learn whatever you can of this god of the Krai. Come to me whenever you need to speak. But be sure no other can find the casket and open it. Now, I think we both have much to think on.'

'I saw you earlier,' said Leth quickly as Orbus stood. 'That is, I thought I did. In my chamber, just for a moment.'

'Ah,' Orbus seemed a little heartened by this. 'That is interesting.'

He began to walk away, his feet and the heavy tatters of his robe dragging across the floor.

'Was it you?' called Leth. 'Were you there, outside the casket?'

Orbus's voice floated back to him through the stillness. 'I do not know.'

As his diminishing figure began to merge into the blue mist, he raised his staff.

III

It was the Child! Leth was as good as convinced of that now. It had to be! Not Orbus that the Krais' god sought, nor necessarily the subjugation of Enchantment's Edge. It was the Legendary Child! Could it be anything else?

His excitement grew. Why would a god seek the Child? He knew too little. It was for Grey Venger to enlighten him. But if the Legendary Child was the spill of a god, then might it be that the parent was for some reason seeking its own offspring? Or was it an enemy, another of the gods, seeking to destroy it?

It was pointless to speculate. Leth knew nothing more of the Legendary Child than that it was said to be somehow the harbinger of tremendous upheaval and destruction in the world. From all indications the predictions were proving true.

He perceived his position modestly strengthened now. Grey Venger, he calculated, must also understand that the Krai god sought the Child. He must surely be desperate to discover what Leth knew.

Again Leth felt his frustration rise. For he knew nothing. It was Issul who had known. And she had vanished at the same time as the Child. Had she survived? Might the Child be with her?

That thought cast him into a renewed welter of nervous speculation. He forced himself to quell his imaginings.

Dawn was creeping from the low east. The rain had swept away and the winds had died. Leth put away the casket, then bathed and changed his clothes. Still tense, he yet felt a vague sense of buoyancy, a glimmer of hope that had been absent earlier in the night. And a feeling of awe. His mind raced, struggling to make best use of the latest information he had gleaned from Orbus. The knowledge that he had, all this time, been conversing with one of the god-beings of Enchantment – albeit one dispossessed and deprived of power – left him both fearful and charged with anticipation. Surely now this must be a key, a means to dealing with the crisis that loomed over his kingdom?

Leth refused to be daunted or cast down by the impossible task that faced him. Finding the Orb's Soul; vanquishing the Krai and their god. He banished these things from his mind, allowing himself to be fired by new hope.

He descended to the breakfast room, wishing to see his children, but it was early and they were still in their beds. In the nursery he sat and watched their tranquil, sleeping faces.

For you, my beautiful babies. For you I will fight to the very end if I must. For you I will overcome all that our enemies may send against us. I will not let your world be destroyed.

Jace woke. Seeing her father, she stretched, yawned, then smiled and climbed from her bed to snuggle upon his lap. A few moments later Galry also woke and joined his sister. Little Lir, oddly, was absent from her cot; Leth did not give this much thought, supposing her to have been moved to her mother's apartment. With his two children sleeping warmly in his arms, Leth's head drooped. His eyes closed and he sank into irresistible sleep.

An hour later the children's nursemaid entered. Leth came blearily to wakefulness. The children were up in an instant, demanding games. Leth played with them, then dressed them and, taking their hands in his, took them to breakfast.

Immediately afterwards he found Lord Fectur waiting for him outside his office. 'Sire, I must speak with you in absolute privacy.'

Leth closed the door on his secretary and bade Fectur sit. 'Have you carried out my instructions?'

'I have. Grey Venger states himself willing to meet with you under the conditions proposed. However, he adds stipulations of his own.'

'And they are?'

'That the meeting takes place in Overlip and that he will choose the precise location. That location will be made known to you after you have entered Overlip. You may be accompanied by a bodyguard twenty strong. For your further reassurance up to forty more troops may be positioned upon the Market Way of Overlip.'

'He instructs the King so? The arrogance of the man!'

'He is powerful in his domain, Sire.'

'What are your feelings on this, Fectur?'

'If Venger wishes you dead, it requires but a single dagger-strike. I am not happy, Sire. I am not happy with this business at all.'

'I take it you will have more of your own men emplaced?'

Fectur nodded.

'What are the chances of capturing Venger?'

'And getting him out of Overlip? With your presence, and under those conditions, almost nil. That is to say, I could not guarantee your safety. Sire, you are not considering—'

'No, I am not. I am trying to view the situation from Venger's position. Has Emergency been made public?'

'To vociferous protest.'

'And Venger is aware of it?'

'Unless he and all his supporters have suddenly been struck deaf, blind and stupid.' Fectur rose in sudden agitation. 'Sire, I say again, I cannot counsel this undertaking. I believe you to be acting unwisely in several respects. You risk coming to grief.'

Leth watched him. There was something in Fectur's manner that suggested he was not being entirely honest, that there were things he had chosen not to say. 'You would prefer that I simply lead an army out to meet the Krai.'

Fectur flushed faintly.

'Solutions, Fectur!' declared Leth irritably, wondering what Fectur could possibly be about. 'Give me solutions, not objections. Then perhaps I might be able to consider your counsel.'

'Then it is your decision to go ahead with this meeting?'

'I have little choice. When does Venger propose it?'

'This evening. After dusk.'

Leth gave himself a moment of sombre reflection, then nodded. 'Make whatever preparations are necessary.'

Fectur stared at him stiffly, then nodded and turned to leave.

'And Fectur . . .'

'Sire?'

'Remember, I have guaranteed Venger's safety. Do nothing to embarrass me. Too much depends upon the outcome of this meeting.'

'Never doubt me, Sire.'

IV

At the setting of the sun the sky low over the mountains of Enchantment showed the most brilliant turquoise light merging nearer the horizon into primrose and deep apricot. The evening was cloudless, as most of the day had been. The rainstorms of the past twenty-four hours were a thing of the past. A gentle breeze blew above the far forest into the city-castle, chill beneath the wide clear sky, speaking persuasively of the cold that the coming weeks and months would bring.

Leth was not afraid. As he descended through the streets towards Overlip – the same streets by which Issul had come, hardly more than a week earlier, to deliver her message to Grey Venger – he felt almost sublime. So much had passed through his mind in recent hours, so much had nagged and hammered, that it was now as though he had somehow, involuntarily, shrugged it all away. His mind no longer dwelt upon his problems. Instead he was able to take pleasure in the lights of the dusky city before him, the great towers, spires, domes, turrets, bartizans spiking the sky all around, the crepuscular forest beyond and so far below, the mysterious mountains and the vast and inexplicable firmament spread above all.

The weirdlights of Enchantment could just be discerned, a shimmering about the peaks, the vaguest sense of visible motion playing upon the air and an almost unseen aura hovering. Leth felt a quickening within him. Issul would have looked upon an almost identical scene when she came this way. For a pulsebeat the thought caused a surge of emotion in his breast. He fought it down, determined that nothing must divert him now.

He rode on horseback, ten of his bravest and most trustworthy knights surrounding him. But he and they were disguised, armoured in light chain and leather with nondescript coverings. Similarly garbed were the ten men of Lord Fectur's security cadre who marched before and behind him. Leth's helmet bore cheekguards and nasal, obscuring most of his face. Doubtless eyes watched from windows, doorways, balconies and street corners. Doubtless much of this quarter of the city would soon be aware that an important entourage had descended to Overlip. But none would know that it was the King himself who had passed. Nor would they know his destination, or the importance of the business he was engaged upon.

Evidence of the time was all around: the streets abnormally crowded, progress slowed and difficult at times, more militia than usual. Beggars had increased tenfold, whole families were camped in the streets and squares; taverns and bordellos were crammed to bursting.

Leth and his men dismounted at the same point at which Issul had passed, where the narrow gate let through the low wall which marked the boundary of the upper city. They passed through the gate and entered the downward-leading rock tunnel on the other side, then descended the giddying, twisting stairway, down and down further, the gulf of the far darkened forest ever before and below them. And at last they stepped out upon the street known as Market Way.

This section of Market Way was empty of its usual bustle and traffic. Palace Guards lined the way, forty strong, liveried as city militia. Sixty more were housed secretly in buildings somewhere nearby. Earlier Leth had questioned the use of so many troops. His preference had been for a minimal guard that would draw no attention to himself. But Fectur had shaken his head adamantly.

'Sire, you admonished me in no uncertain terms for acceding to the Queen's wishes to travel without adequate security. Now the Queen has gone – pray the spirits of Fate and Fortune that she will return safely to us – and I must double my attention to your safety. I cannot prevent you undertaking this mission, but you have properly charged me with security arrangements and I am carrying them out in the way I see most fit.'

'The meeting is supposed to be a secret, dammit!' argued Leth. 'With these many men I may as well go with full panoply and placards advertising my intent.'

'Sire, you have declared Emergency. Under such a ruling no one will be greatly surprised at the sight of large groups of military about the streets. Once within the burrows of Overlip no one will know where you go. Nor will they know who it is that goes. Speculation may be high, and then it will be forgotten. I shall have spread the word that there has been a swoop by the militia upon some criminal den or an illegal temple or lodge. Most importantly, as you will not be seen to have been here, questions regarding the purpose of the exercise will not be directed to you. Rather, they will come to me. And I, as you know, am not expected to offer explanations.'

Leth took note of that. It was a measure of Fectur's power and the fear he instilled that he, unlike the King, could at times operate virtually beyond the law. It could seem, at times, that the Spectre had greater powers than the Crown. Leth could not guess what schemings milled behind Fectur's bland brow, but he had little doubt that the point had been made quite deliberately.

They entered the first of the tunnels of Overlip. Somewhere ahead directions were being issued, conveyed back to the captain of Fectur's guard, so as they passed deeper into the bowels of the great scarp, twisting, winding, climbing and descending, it seemed that they travelled without aim whereas they were in fact being led to some definite but unknown destination. The air was close, thick, smoky, filled with a thousand mingled odours. Natural vents and man-made flues took stale air to the streets of the city above or out to the face of the scarp, so ensuring a flow through the myriad tunnels. Even so, the air of Overlip was difficult to breathe for those unaccustomed to living here. Even among the denizens of this underworld respiratory complaints were common.

It seemed to Leth that they marched for an age. Years had passed since he had last been inside Overlip, and never had he explored it in its entirety. He was staggered now at its extent. Everywhere there were recesses, shelves and tiny chambers hollowed into the rock, serving as homes for Overlip's population. Everywhere new passages led off to gloomy unknowns. The sublime mood of earlier had left him. He began to question the wisdom of entering this place. Would they find their way back? Sweat soaked his skin and clothing. He longed to remove his helmet, his head feeling hot and unnaturally confined.

They were in an unpopulated area now. There were no taverns, no shops, no tiny homes. The passage they occupied widened but came to an abrupt halt in a face of solid rock. Two hooded men, who had guided Leth and his guards here, stood before them with torches.

'Wait here,' said one, and passed his torch to one of Leth's guards.

Both men then pushed past them and disappeared back along the way they had come.

Leth waited uneasily. He could be trapped now. If there was a means of sealing off this passage they could be left to suffocate or starve. Or archers, positioned behind them and on ledges overhead, could pick them off one by one with little effort. But still he held to his conviction that Grey Venger would take no rash action while believing that he, Leth, had information about the Legendary Child.

A harsh voice sounded above Leth's head. 'So, the Godless King has descended into the den of the Righteous and Oppressed.'

Leth looked up. Twenty feet above his head a hooded man stood arms akimbo upon a ledge.

'Say nothing more!' declared Leth. 'We must speak alone!'

'Then send your men back. They can await you in the passage beyond.'

Leth spoke to the captain of his guard of knights. 'Do as he says. I will come to no harm.'

The men marched away. The figure upon the ledge put one hand to his head and drew off his hood. Leth saw again the face he had last seen almost a year earlier. Then it had been a fanatical mask as Venger had charged at him in a crowded street, two daggers raised. Sheer fortune had saved Leth, for Venger had a clear path towards him. A stray dog had run out from the crowd somewhere to the side and had cut straight across Venger's path. Venger had veered and stumbled. The instant was enough for Leth's guards to react. They dragged the King back and formed a protective shield about him. Others fell upon Venger. But Venger himself had been well-protected. Several men in the crowd came to his defence, and in the furious affray that followed Venger had somehow managed to slip away.

Now Leth saw the same face, the same burning eyes. A crazed, mirthless grimace was stretched across Venger's features as he stared down from his ledge.

'Are we to talk like this, on separate levels?' enquired Leth. 'It would seem to imply something of specious symbolic significance, but I would prefer that we stood face to face, if only to prevent a stiffness of the neck.'

Grey Venger made a scornful sound, then kicked at something upon the ledge. A ladder of rope with wooden rungs skittered down the rock face, unravelling itself to terminate close to Leth's feet.

'Ascend, King,' he said with sarcasm.

Hauling himself onto the ledge, Leth was aware that at this moment, more than any other, he was vulnerable. Should the hatred that Venger harboured get the better of him – or should this meeting have been an excuse to exact revenge upon Leth all along – then now was the time to strike. Leth's head was bowed. He was on hands and knees, his bare nape exposed.

But it did not happen. Leth stood, pulled off his helmet and faced his enemy.

Venger was garbed in grey, as was his custom. Grey hose and boots, a padded grey tunic with falchion and dagger at his waist. He was of wiry build, no taller than Leth, aged about forty-five. Long grey hair tumbled about his shoulders, clasped tight to his skull by a slim leather band. A short, unkempt beard sprouted upon his chin. His lips were thin and compressed, given to drooping at the corners, but curled now in contempt. His eyes, above a long hooked nose, were pale blue-grey, the pupils pinpoints of gleaming black, reflecting the torchlight. They were narrowed beneath heavy lids, his gaze hard and unflinching.

'Know that I despise you, Leth. Know that I will not rest until I have avenged the deaths of my children.'

'They did not have to die,' replied Leth with anger. 'They were criminals, like you, fanatics like you, implicated beyond doubt in a plot to kill me. But they should not have died. You had that choice, Venger.'

Grey Venger shook his head, more a reflex than an emotion. His eyes blazed and prominent blue veins pulsed at his temples. He struck his chest with his fist. 'I would have saved them were I other than what I am. But the leader of the True Sept has no such choice. My loyalties lie beyond.'

'Then you deprive yourself of the right to expect justice under the common law. You deprive yourself also of your humanity.'

'Humanity? Pah! You know nothing of the weight that is upon me!'

'I know that your act was that of a traitor to the Crown.' Leth readied himself, for Venger's mouth twitched and his body gave a jerk as though he was about to launch himself upon him. But he stayed rooted to the spot, though the frenzy of emotion that assailed him from within remained like a storm upon his face.

Leth mentally drew back. He had not wanted to goad Venger, only to talk and agree terms in the manner of reasoning men. 'You should have come to me, spoken to me of your convictions.'

'As a man speaks to a beast, or a god to a man, knowing the lower creature cannot comprehend! There was nothing to be told to one such as you, Leth.'

'Preferable to be an outlaw, then. Preferable to face a sentence of death, to allow one's own children to die for no good reason.' Leth hesitated, saw the renewed fury in Venger's eyes. He shook his head. 'This is not what I came to speak of. We must put personal differences to one side if we are to make any progress. The fact that you have agreed to meet me suggests that progress can be made. Let us not, then, stand before one another as antagonists but as men seeking agreement, or a way to agreement, acknowledging a cause to which we are both committed, if perhaps in different ways. Let us meet as men who each have something to give the other.'

'You sent a woman, with word of the Legendary Child.'

Leth nodded, relieved both that Venger had not known that it was Issul and that he was indicating a willingness to talk. 'A child has been found dwelling in the woods. It has come to my attention by roundabout means, but there is no doubt that the child is not like normal children.'

'That is all?'

'There are aspects to the child's background, which I cannot at present divulge, that raise many questions. I and others find ourselves compelled to believe that this may be the Legendary Child. Only you can confirm or deny this.'

He walked on fragile ground, for he knew nothing of the Child's background. Again he wished that Issul had told him more. *Issul, why were you so secretive? It is not like you. What did you know that you couldn't tell even me?*

Venger was appraising him minutely. 'Where is this child now?'

'My men were bringing him into custody. They were attacked by a Krai forward unit. The child escaped.'

Venger gave a harsh hoot of laughter. 'Hah! Do you expect me to believe that? You are a bigger fool than even I had believed, King Leth!'

'It is the truth, Venger. Can you really afford not to believe it? If so, then I will take my leave now, acknowledging that my endeavour has been fruitless. But I believe you more perspicacious than that. I have come to you with open hands, seeking your help, your knowledge and expertise. My troops scour the forest for this child, but I need to know what he is. And if he has fallen into the hands of the Krai, what then?'

The mocking smile vanished. 'Were the Krai seeking him?'

'I do not know. The evidence suggests not. They are here to harass and terrorize. I do not believe they came for the child. But do the Krai know of the Legendary Child, Venger? Is he important to them?'

'He is important to all, *if* he has truly come.'

'How? How is he important?'

But Venger would be drawn no further. He folded his arms upon his chest. 'So, then, Leth, you had the Child and you have lost him. What is it that you seek from Grey Venger?'

'I have already told you that.'

'But if I tell you, you will not believe me! You deny the True Sept its creed!'

'Let me decide what to believe. Answer my questions, Venger, that is all. Tell me the secret of the Legendary Child. Tell me what he is, what his aim is. Should I continue to search for him?'

'The secret? Yes, you are right. I know secrets. Fantastic secrets. Secrets you cannot even imagine. But I cannot pass them to the godless.'

'Not even when the time is right? When the Child is here? We must help each other, Venger. If you cannot see that you will remain an outcast, and the Child will be lost, or will wreak its destruction unopposed.'

'I have told you my conditions. And I know you have invoked Emergency. Did you think I would be fooled by that?'

Leth shook his head. 'If I wanted to entrap you, I would have invoked Emergency when I had you in my grasp, not before Surely you can see that? Emergency is necessary now because circumstances demand. I had no choice. But I could have delayed it. I could have used it to catch you. No, I have played an open hand. That is my way of letting you know that I am sincere.'

Grey Venger scoffed again. 'Sincere! You are the godless; we are the Righteous. You sincerity is meaningless, a poison!'

'Then you will not help?'

'I have said, you know my conditions.'

'I cannot grant you permanent immunity, nor restore the Sept. The law will not permit it, and were I to attempt to change it at this time I would have insurrection on my hands. Your rivals want you dead, or imprisoned or, as you are, outlawed. You became too powerful, Venger. You made an error of judgement when you attempted to kill me. It was your downfall. The other factions will not permit you to rise again, unless . . .'

Venger's eyes were slits. 'Unless what?'

'If your secrets are true, if you have real knowledge of the Legendary Child, knowledge that can be employed to the benefit of the realm, *then* . . . I can make no absolute promises, but if you can help to stem this great tide, this menace that has risen against us, *then* no one could reasonably deny you your place in society. Things might change. Give up your secrets so that they can be used for the greater good, and you will earn my gratitude and support. Consider what this means to you, Venger. You purport to know what it means to have this Child born in our midst. Well, enlighten us and share our endeavour. Or hold on to your secrets, and never know the Child, and never know liberty again. I can say only that together we may have hope.'

'Hope?'

'It is perhaps all that is left to us.'

Grey Venger assumed a haughty expression. 'That is the admission of a weak man.'

'No, it the admission of a man who has been taken to the furthest limit, who has seen that there is still a beyond. A man who knows that without shared knowledge we are doomed. I can say no more, Venger. I will leave you now. But think on what I have said. I believe you will see that there is no other way. Apply to me then. You will be given safe escort.'

Leth turned, bending to climb back down the rope ladder. As he did so he felt a strange impulse. Uncannily he had moved as if to raise his arm, as if his hand clasped a stout staff. For a heartbeat he had felt that he could cast Grey Venger from him.

He stopped. His eyes met Venger's.

'Begone, Leth,' Venger said. Leth could read nothing in his expression. Venger stepped backwards three paces and vanished into a ragged black fissure in the rock at his back.

V

And as the sun had set on that same evening, as King Leth was entering Overlip, Anzejarl, Prince of the Krai, stood upon the crest of a low ridge, gazing across a wide valley at the fires that burned in Giswel Holt. He could see a tower ablaze, perhaps a second, and numerous smaller buildings in the township that clustered about the castle's great walls.

The breeze ruffled Anzejarl's dark hair and his long grey cloak billowed about his ankles. He nodded to himself in brooding acknowledgement of an objective achieved, moodily chewing a mouthful of *ghinz*, drawing free the bitter juice from the mashed leaves and swallowing. From overhead came a sound of a rushing, beating, irregular wind. Anzejarl raised his searing Krai eyes and made out winged shapes, opaque against the darkening sky. As many as fifty slooths were plying their way back towards the woods behind him. He heard distant cries in the air above; pathetic human sounds.

When the slooths had passed Prince Anzejarl turned and marched down the slope to his command pavilion pitched in a hollow beside a twisting brook.

Inside the pavilion Olmana reclined upon pillows. She was robed in a single sheer silken garment of deep damask, open at the front and belted with a fine gold cincture. Anzejarl seated himself upon a stool, his eyes greedy at the sight of her.

'Has it been successful?' Olmana enquired, sipping red wine.

Anzejarl nodded. 'They have experienced their first taste of terror. In the morning my scouts will report the scale of the damage. It will not be massive. Fires are burning but they will be quickly doused. However, the effect will be as desired. Giswel Holt has met slooths for the first time.'

The plan had been simple but innovative. The first rank of slooths gripped in their talons sacks filled with flammable oil. Over the town and castle they released them so that they burst on rooftops and streets. Immediately behind came slooths with long, flaming firebrands in their beaks. Swooping down in the wake of the first wave, they dropped the brands onto the oil, igniting it to cause maximum disruption. Then all had swooped upon townsfolk and soldiers as they rushed to fight the flames.

'Are any slooths lost?' Olmana asked.

'Few, if any. I heard cries – at least some have brought back children.'

Anzejarl closed his eyes.

'Does that trouble you, Anzejarl?'

'Trouble me?' His wrinkled white brow creased further. 'Until recently I would have had no understanding of such a concept. Now . . .' He shook his head and sighed. 'I have no love for this.'

'You tire of your gift, after all it has brought you?'

'Gift? You may call it that, Olmana. I would use a different term.'

'You regret all that you have accomplished?'

'Regret is another term I would not previously have used or understood. I cannot say that I experience regret, but within me there is unease of a kind I have not known until now.'

Olmana smiled, shifting her body. She raised one knee so that her silken garment fell away and exposed her naked thigh. 'Surely it is not all so bad, Anzejarl?'

Anzejarl's eyes travelled lustfully over the pale flesh, then he looked into her face. 'What is your gift, Olmana? You have made me like them, that is all.'

'I have made you a champion of your people, Anzejarl. I have given you the ability to have everything you could ever possibly desire. You are a leader like none before you. A great conqueror beneath whom all the lands of the Mondane and Enchantment's Edge will soon lie. Feel it, Anzejarl. Do not weep for the children who die, for they are insignificant. Feel what is truly there, what you have never felt before.'

'I fear being overwhelmed by it. The gift is a wonder, but it is also almost too much to bear.'

'You have the *ghinz* to blunt its edges. Soon, as you accustom, you will not need that any more. You will need nothing.' She rose and came to him, stood before him and put her hands around his neck, drawing his head towards her breasts. 'Nothing, except for me. Is it so terrible, Anzejarl, to be the supreme conqueror, the greatest champion, the most excellent lover?'

He inhaled the perfumes of her body, delighting in the smooth warm softness of her breast against his cheek. One hand rose to caress it, his fingers seeking the erect red nipple; the other stroked her thigh, then came to rest upon the hot silken soft dampness between her legs.

'Do you truly wish me to take it all away?' Olmana whispered.

His eyes closed, he shook his head, his senses reeling. Olmana placed her legs over his and lowered herself onto his lap. She kissed his eyes, his cheeks, his lips, his neck. 'Is it truly so awful to be like them?'

Anzejarl drew her to him with a soft moan.

She smiled. 'I have awoken you, Anzejarl. That is my gift. Through me you may conquer all. Accept it. Revel in it. Profit from it. Truly, this is only the beginning.'

Later, when Anzejarl slept, Olmana crept from the bed to a small wooden chest at the back of the pavilion. She lifted the lid, delved into her clothing within, and drew forth a small green velvet pouch. Kneeling at the side of the Krai prince she took from the pouch a small crystal, pale rose in hue. This she held cupped in the palms of her two hands and, with her eyes closed, softly began to intone a chant. After a moment the crystal started to glow, softly at first, then with a fiercer light, pulsing red, which radiated within the pavilion.

Had Prince Anzejarl opened his eyes at that moment he would have seen, bathed in the illumination of the pink crystal, not the face of the ravishing beauty with whom he had just spent his passion so pleasurably, but something else. Olmana's features had altered. Her skin had faded and drawn back to reveal grey knobbled flesh. A flat nasal orifice passed inward; a misshapen mouth twisted like a wound of dead tissue, small wet grey teeth within. The eyes were inhuman slits, as red as the glowing crystal in her hands.

But Anzejarl slept soundly and hence was spared from seeing anything but the contents of his dreams.

Taking the burning crystal, Olmana held it carefully against the Krai prince's forehead. 'So my gift is not enough, Anzejarl. Or it is too much. Ah well, soon you will have it no more. Then you will know misery. Then you will know regret. And you will beg for me. But not yet. Not yet. Not until our task is complete.'

Slowly the red radiance diminished, as though it was being drawn into Anzejarl's somnolent flesh. When the crystal glowed no more Olmana returned it to its pouch and concealed the pouch again in the chest. She returned to the bed and stood over the Krai prince, naked, gazing down upon him. Then she lowered herself until her terrible face was over his. With one hand she gently plied open his jaw.

'Not until your task is done.'

She placed her lips above his. A slender, knobbled grey tongue snaked from between her teeth and slid into his mouth.

TWELVE

I

Welcome to the true world, the many-named domain, where all things are possible.

Welcome to Enchantment.

Issul struggled, helpless, her eyes upon the three strange child figures who stood before her. Was it true? How? She had been standing with her comrades in the underground chamber in the Krai camp, standing before the brilliant oval. Now she was . . . where?

Welcome to Enchantment.

The identical white-haired children continued to appraise her, but she focused her gaze beyond, through the window at their backs. She seemed to be in a tower chamber, some distance above the ground. The air was visible, in constant motion, colours forming and altering, fusing, rippling, breaking up. It was beautiful to watch, mesmerizing, but terrifying and bewildering too. Beyond were the mountain peaks, so close, and they seemed to blaze with an extraordinary fire.

'The unstill air,' said one of the children. Issul did not see which.

'Something always becomes,' said another.

'Or strives to become,' said the third.

'This is *Creation*.'

'Energy of Potentia, transforming, seeking to be matter.'

'All is possible here. The formed can be unformed, the unformed formed.'

'Here is raw power. Here is dream. Here is magic.'

'Here is Enchantment.'

Issul swam, supported in her globe of bluish vapour, panic

threatening to overcome her. She strained again to look behind her for her companions, but she still could not turn. Somehow she was sure she was alone but for these three.

'Do not try to understand it,' said the smallest child.

'Who are you?' Issul asked.

'We? We are Triune. Once we were One, then we were made Three but still One. We were broken and scattered, but we were not lost. We returned to become Triune, and soon we shall become One again.'

Simultaneously all three children smiled at her, and in perfect concert blinked their unnaturally blue eyes.

'It may all have been a dream,' said the middle child.

Issul frowned. 'What?'

'Everything you have ever known, everything you recall. It may never have happened, or perhaps it has still to be. Tell us, tell Triune, how can you know?'

Issul began to flail, gasping in sudden terror, struck by the notion that she must somehow have gone utterly mad.

'This is Enchantment,' said the taller child.

The middle child added, 'This is the true world. Many-named, never known. You come here from the realized world, the world made real but not actual or true. This is the only truth.'

'Please, please, stop,' Issul cried, a great sob escaping her. 'It is too much. Please.'

The three children, Triune, observed her with wide clear eyes, their identical gynandrous faces expressionless. All three blinked again.

'She is confused.'

'From the Edge.'

'They always are.'

'Is it better to release her?'

'Perhaps it is best. For now. She is not ready, but she can teach us.'

'Yes.'

The tallest child stepped forward, extending a hand towards Issul. 'This is for you.'

She could not see what the child did, nor did she feel a physical touch. But she felt hope and with it came inquisitiveness. This was not madness, at least not madness as she had previously understood it. This was actually happening, to her, and she was not dreaming. It was too strange for words, but she had to know more.

'You may inform us,' the child was saying. 'Dream and bring Triune forth – we can be with you, but only briefly in the realized realm. Too much will sunder us; but with care it will help us towards reunion. We thank you for this.'

None of it made sense to Issul's mind, and again she felt threatened, as though she was gripped in madness.

'Is this truly Enchantment?' she asked, seeking to seize some hold, however tenuous, on what she was witnessing. 'How is it that I am here?'

'You came here. Through the Farplace Opening.'

'In the chamber? The Krai chamber? Do you aid the Krai?' Another thought struck Issul just then, making her heart pound against her ribcage. 'Triune – are you a god? Do you command the Krai against us?'

The three heads shook as one. 'Triune has acquired the Farplace Opening from the one who aids the Krai. We guard it now, though we do not know for how long.'

'But are you a god?'

'We are Triune. One, then three as one, broken and scattered, and soon One again. Do not try to understand.'

'You say others have been here, before me?'

'Of course. Many have tried to enter Enchantment, by various means.'

'What happened to them?'

'Some remain. All are changed forever.'

'Remain? Where?'

'You must return now.'

'No!' Issul was desperate to learn more, no matter her disorientation and the delirium that threatened to rob her of her mind. 'I want to know!'

'To know? What?'

'So many things . . . Why does a god ally itself with the Krai and make war upon us? How can we fight it? What is—'

'Enough!' Six pale hands were raised, palms towards her, three pairs of bright and luminous lapis eyes shining from the trio of perfectly-formed white faces. 'Triune has no union with these things. Be aware when you dream, for you take something of the true world with you now. Something of Enchantment is yours. In the dream you may not always be the dreamer. The dream may not be yours. Or it may be, and it may become real, now or soon or never. All things may be. Now, return.'

Issul sat upon the dark earth, her head in her hands, sobbing.

'Jace!'

She felt a hand upon her arm, looked around and saw Shenwolf's face beside her, looking at her with concern. She almost fell into his arms, needing the reassurance of a human touch, needing to hide in his strong arms as she poured out her emotion and fear. But she held back.

'Are you all right?'

'I – I think so.' She wiped the tears from her eyes, blinked dazedly, still unsure of what was happening to her. She recognized the underground chamber, saw Phisusandra and Kol watching her from behind Shenwolf. Then her gaze fell upon the oval in the centre of the chamber. The mist within it had dulled, was an almost uniform grey now, billowing slowly in a barely perceptible flux. She drew back.

'Jace, what happened?'

'I am not sure. Did you see something?'

'You vanished. You were approaching the oval. A cloud formed about you and you vanished. I tried to follow but could not get close. Then you reappeared.'

Issul climbed dazedly to her feet, her eyes upon the oval, knowing, or thinking she knew, what it was: a Farplace Opening – a means of transportation to a tower chamber within Enchantment.

'I – I do not know what happened,' she said, but in her mind a single thought resounded: *I have been to Enchantment!*

II

As they returned to the main camp the mammoth bulk of Ombo ambled towards them.

'We found two more,' he said. He nodded to the south-east

corner of the camp. 'Sneaked in from over there. Didn't really seem to know what was going on. They put up one heck of a fight. Krai bastards never know when they're beaten.'

'Are they alive?' asked Issul.

The big man nodded. 'Ilrin isn't, though.'

'They killed him?' Ilrin had been one of the prisoners in Issul's hut.

'I told you, they fought like fury. Got 'em locked in the hut now.'

'They must be the two who were underground,' said Kol.

Issul veered towards the hut that had been her home for the past days. 'Shenwolf, come with me. You others, I smell food cooking. Go, eat and rest yourselves. We will join you presently.'

Inside the prison hut the two Krai were slumped on the litters. They were bruised and bloodied, their wrists bound behind their backs.

'Stand!' ordered Shenwolf as they entered.

With some difficulty both Krai managed to scramble to their feet, though they remained bent and were obviously in pain. The bruises to their faces suggested they had taken a severe beating; probably after having their weapons taken from them. Issul was surprised, in fact, that they were alive. She was heartened, equally, that the former prisoners should have heeded her request not to kill them.

She recognized one of the Krai as a camp officer, and addressed herself to him. 'Listen well. You are our prisoners now. Your companions are dead. I require obedience and answers to my questions. In return you may be permitted to live. Fail to do so and I will pass you into the care of my comrades, who are far less tolerant than I. Is that understood?'

Neither Krai replied.

'Is that understood?' Issul stepped up close to the officer and stared into his gem-eyes. He looked beyond her, through her, the gorgeous expressionless eyes shot with blood, the furrowed pale skin strangely livid with bruising.

'You do not help yourself,' said Issul, becoming irritated. 'I offer you life, perhaps even the chance of freedom.'

The Krai's thin lips moved. 'We are already dead.'

'You look alive enough to me, though a little the worse for wear.'

'We are prisoners, stripped of honour, shamed. The Krai do not become prisoners. They do not know shame. They fight until they are victorious, or they die. Thus you do not look upon the living.'

Issul glanced at his companion, whose expression was equally inscrutable.

'Well, I can revivify you,' she said. 'The process is simple. I ask you questions, you answer. Thus you live again.'

'Only a madwoman would ask questions of the dead. Only a fool would expect answers.'

'I tire of this!' Issul flared.

Shenwolf moved up close behind the Krai and put a hand upon his bruised arm. 'If you wish, I can prove to you that you are alive.'

He squeezed. The Krai flinched and gasped with pain, turned burning, offended eyes to Shenwolf. Shenwolf released him. Issul said, 'Tell me this, how did you construct the oval in the central chamber underground? It is a magical effect. You could not do it alone. Who commands you, above your own Prince Anzejarl?'

The Krai officer turned back to her but remained silent.

Shenwolf moved to one side of the room, indicating to Issul that he wished to speak privately. When she joined him he said, in an undertone, 'I believe I could change his mind if you so order, but in truth it would sicken me to apply such methods.'

'I too. These are a strange people.' She looked again at the Krai. 'Is there nothing you will say for yourselves?'

The Krai officer stared off into the rafters. 'We are the dead.'

As they left the hut Issul mused, 'What am I to make of them? They are an impossible folk. Were they human I would judge them cruel and heartless. We have seen what they have done, the way they use us as slaves without mercy, the way they set upon and murdered unarmed prisoners when they saw themselves beaten. These are inhuman actions. Yet is it possible to judge them by our own terms? They are not human, they are Krai. To deem them cruel has no meaning, for I do not perceive them as deriving pleasure from the harm or suffering they inflict upon us. It is all done with chill efficiency, emotionlessly, unfeelingly. I think they are incapable of knowing how we feel, perhaps even of knowing *that* we feel, just as we are incapable of understanding the concepts they put before us. We differ too radically in our culture, our customs, our very make up. Were they human I would hate them, but they are not, so I find it impossible to feel an appropriate emotion, or to judge them.'

'That is a very magnanimous assessment.'

'No, an impartial one.'

'After what you have suffered and witnessed, you can be impartial?'

'I seek to understand my enemy, that is all. It is possible that at some future time, through the understanding and acceptance of our differences, we may achieve the peace that eludes us now.'

In the middle of the compound a fire blazed, a huge pot suspended above it. The erstwhile prisoners had made a rich venison stew with root vegetables and herbs, accompanied by cheese, fruit and the ubiquitous Krai bread. They gathered eagerly around the fire now as the stew bubbled and seethed. A small amount of ale and spirits had also been discovered in the store hut; the men were anticipating a fine celebration of liberty. Ombo, seated upon an upturned pail, lifted his cup as Issul and Shenwolf joined them.

'Lads, raise your cups! Let us drink to Jace, who has saved us. Jace, a woman of exceptional courage and rare skills. The scourge of our enemies. And to her companion Shenwolf, also; mysterious bowman of the woods, courageous warrior, bedeviller of the bastard Krai!'

The men joined him in the toast, raucously and ebulliently. Issul watched Ombo, wondering what to make of his change of heart. His cheeks were flushed, his movements exaggerated. Plainly much of the ale that had been found already resided in his gut. She stepped into the centre of the circle.

'Men, we have achieved much, but it is not over. Remember, a Krai squad departed this camp just a few days ago. We should anticipate their return at any time. So eat your fill, but drink sparingly lest they march in to find us all soused and sleeping. We are free – let us take care that we remain so.'

Shenwolf took the moment to step up beside her and address the company. 'Much has been achieved, but many tasks lie ahead, and dangers too. If we are to survive we require organization. An organization requires a leader, and I propose that we elect our leader now. We need a person brave, resourceful, inventive, decisive and resolute, someone with a gift for command, and a flare for combat, and lastly someone who has gained the respect and trust of every member of the organization. There is one here who has already proven herself well-qualified in each and all these areas. I nominate Jace to be our leader.'

'I second the nomination!' roared Ombo.

Shenwolf looked about him. 'Are any against? Speak now.'

None spoke.

'Raise your hands, all those who are in favour, then.'

All raised their hands, and Issul was thus enthusiastically elected to leadership of the little band.

'A leader must have a second-in-command,' said Issul. 'My choice is Shenwolf. I ask you to obey him as you would obey me. Now, I need two volunteers immediately upon the gate. You will be replaced within half an hour so that you can eat.'

Kol stood, as did another, a burly fellow named Mondam, and made off for the gate.

'You others eat and drink – but remember, not to your cups. In due course Shenwolf will assign proper guard duties. Do not shirk, and remain alert at all times. Tomorrow we will take our leave of this place forever.'

The food was ladled into bowls and they ate merrily. Issul, seating herself between Shenwolf and Phisusandra, became suddenly aware of how tired and drained she felt. She had no desire to talk, yet some things could not be left alone.

'Phis, what did you sense when we were in that chamber?' she asked the Murinean.

Phisusandra chewed thoughtfully on his food before replying. 'It was as I said, there was something that could not be explained in normal terms. There was magic, if that is an explanation.'

'Was it focused upon the oval?'

'Aye. That "thing" was a focus of strange power. And when it took you the power was amplified – my skin tingled.'

'And upon my return?'

'The same. Do you recall anything of what happened to you?'

Issul glanced to the ground. Part of her seemed not to want to recall. 'I am not sure. It is almost as if I dreamed and only snatches of the dream remain.' She turned to Shenwolf. 'Tomorrow I want that chamber sealed so that none may enter.' She almost added: '*And also so that none may leave!*'

Shenwolf gave a nod. 'We must also dispose as best we can of the slooths that roost around the feeding pen.'

'Of course.' Issul gave a shudder. 'Tonight they will go hungry.'

'Why so?' came Herbin's voice indignantly from the other side of the fire. 'We have their food, trussed up ready in the hut.'

Issul shook her head. 'Herbin, that is not our way.'

'It is what they did to us!'

'Do you harbour a desire to become like them?' asked Shenwolf.

'I wish them to experience what my father experienced,' said Herbin, his voice breaking.

Putting down her bowl, Issul rose and stepped around the fire. She squatted before Herbin and looked into his face. He could not meet her eyes, but she took his hands in hers. 'We are not like the Krai, Herbin, and they are not like us. I know how you must feel—'

'You do not, Jace. How can you?'

Herbin's jaw trembled, his cheeks pale and taut. Tears broke suddenly from his eyes and he turned away, bowing his head. Issul stroked his hair, aware that the others watched and remembering suddenly that they knew nothing of the slooths on the other side of the camp. 'Herbin, we have found freedom today. Rejoice in that. It came too late for Miseon, but you must look to the future now. Do not become bitter and twisted with thoughts of revenge. Do not hate, for it serves no purpose other than to make you less than what you are. More Krai deaths will not assuage your feelings. Your task is to survive, to return to your family as a man who has no crime upon his conscience, a man who can help them to rebuild their lives as you rebuild your own. You understand that, don't you?'

Herbin could not speak, though he nodded his head. Presently Issul left him and returned to her place. 'How do you propose dealing with the slooths?' she asked Shenwolf.

'I have been wondering about that. They are difficult to kill, and we are few in number. I will not knowingly risk any of our lives. But flaming arrows fired at close quarters from beneath the trees where they roost should at least disable some without providing great hazard to ourselves. With your agreement I will take five men before dusk, when the slooths sleep.'

'They should be volunteers, informed of what they are about. But I think Herbin will wish to be among them.'

Finishing her meal Issul felt a desire for solitude. She left the group and took herself off to the Krai command hut. She sat down upon the floor, her back against the wall.

I have been to Enchantment!

The certainty was clear, but her memory was not. It was too dreamlike, just as she had described to Phisusandra. Vivid, disturbing images remained: three identical childlike creatures with unnaturally white hair and eyes like glowing lapis. Triune, broken and scattered, soon to be One again. The changing coloured air outside the high window of the tower, the mountains of unnatural flame. Issul recalled – or thought she recalled – that the tallest child had given her something. She searched her clothing but could find nothing that had not been there before.

What happened to me there? What was the purpose of that place? The three, Triune, had described themselves as guardian of the Farplace Opening, but who or what had been its creator? Had it been created with the intention of allowing something out of Enchantment into the Krai camp and the world of Enchantment's Edge beyond?

Her mind could not cope with it all. Such a tumult of emotion surged within her, and she felt utterly weary. *Leth, I want to come home now. I am tired and I miss you, Galry, Jace, my babies, I miss you so. Mama will come home to you, soon, as soon as I can.*

She was filled with sadness and longing, and the fear that she might never see her children and husband again. Quite suddenly she burst into tears. She slipped to the floor, her head upon the hard wooden boards, and sobbed, more alone than she had ever felt in her life. Within moments she had fallen asleep.

III

When Issul awoke it was dark. She sat up dazedly, gazing about her, at first unsure of where she was. Someone had lit an oil lamp and placed a blanket over her.

As the memory of the past days returned she stood, stiffly, took the lamp and moved to the door and looked out at the compound. All was quiet. The fire burned in the centre and in each of the two watchtowers visible from where she stood Issul could make out the dim silhouette of a guard.

A figure materialized silently at her side. She started, stepping back and reaching for her sword, then recognized the familiar face in the lamplight. 'Shenwolf!'

'I am sorry. I did not mean to startle you.'

'How long have I slept?'

'Six hours, maybe seven.'

'Six hours?' She looked at the stars. 'It must be near midnight, then. You should have woken me.'

'You needed the sleep, and there was no need. I assigned guard duties till morning. Those men not on duty are resting now. If you are hungry, there is food by the fire.'

Issul nodded. 'Will you join me?'

They crossed the compound and Issul slumped upon a stool as Shenwolf prepared to ladle stew from the great pot. Half-consciously she watched his lean figure in the firelight as he bent over the pot, and found for some reason that she was gazing at his buttocks. Quickly she shifted her gaze, but she was struck with a strange, inexplicable notion of having been here before.

'Shenwolf?'

'Jace?' He grinned as he turned to her, as though enjoying the shared pretence of her identity. She studied his young face in the orangey glow, and for the first time she realized that she had seen him before. Somewhere, before he had saved her life in the slooths' feeding pen.

Shenwolf. The name had seemed familiar when he first named himself, but she had not given it another thought since. Now, quite suddenly, she had it. She recalled the afternoon at Orbia, standing with her sister Mawnie on the edge of the sunlit parade-ground. A soldier riding by; one among many.

She smiled to herself as she recalled Mawnie's comments. That was what had drawn Issul's attention to his buttocks.

Shenwolf regarded her with a quizzical smile. 'Jace?'

Issul looked away, her cheeks growing warm. 'I'm sorry, I was in a reverie. It was – I have just recalled seeing you before. I was with my sister—'

'Beside the parade-ground. I remember it well.' Shenwolf passed her a bowl of stew, then filled his own and sat beside her. 'It was a surprise. Though I had encountered your sister briefly before, I did not know she was the Duchess of Giswel. Sister of the Queen, what's more! To then see the two of you . . .'

Issul smiled again, recalling the look upon his face that afternoon.

'You know,' Shenwolf said, 'it was an extraordinary moment for me.'

'How so?'

'I had heard tell of the Queen's beauty many times, but until then I had not witnessed it for myself. But on that day, when I saw you standing there, I saw that the stories had not been exaggerated. And I knew then, without question, that I had found my life's purpose: to be in your service.'

Issul looked away again, a sudden confusion of feelings flaring in her breast. The way he said it, the way he looked at her . . . it had the ring of something more than soldierly devotion.'

'I am sorry, Majesty – Jace. I have spoken out of turn.'

'No. I am honoured, Shenwolf. So many times in the last few days you have demonstrated your complete devotion to the Crown. It will not be forgotten.' She chose her words carefully.

Shenwolf nodded inwardly. 'My greatest reward will be to continue to serve you.'

'My sister was greatly struck by you,' said Issul quickly, her voice a little high. 'She thought you a man of great charm and gallantry.'

'She exaggerates. I was simply on hand when she stumbled.'

'You seem to have a talent for being in the right place at the right time. And thank the spirits that you do. But—' Now into Issul's mind came the memory of the last time she had seen Mawnie. *Oh Mawnie!*

'Jace, is something wrong?'

'No. I am just . . . my sister fell ill just before I left the palace. This talk of her made me . . .' Again she saw her children, and Leth on the night before she had left. Leth, loving her, his kisses and caresses upon her body, Leth inside her, reaching up for her, his hands squeezing her breasts, his ecstatic cries as he emptied his seed into her; his face as he slept. She half-smiled to herself, then the smile faded as she recalled the strange blue aura that had clung all about him.

It was there. I saw it. I know I did. And before, the seeping blue light beneath the door . . .

She turned to the young soldier beside her. 'Shenwolf, I want to go home.'

'I have spoken with the others already. We have three injured, which will slow us. Herbin's shoulder wound is not serious. There remains the problem of what to do with the Krai prisoners.'

'I will decide after I have spoken to them again in the morning. If they prove to be too great a hindrance I may let them go.'

'The big fellow, Ombo, hails from a hamlet called Ghismile, which he calculates to lie no more than three leagues from here through the forest. From there it is an easy march to the Crosswood road. He suggests we rest there and replenish supplies, perhaps even hire horses. The injured can also remain there while we continue on to Enchantment's Edge. We can send help back then. I think it is the best option.'

Issul nodded. 'We will leave tomorrow. But, Shenwolf, watch Ombo. I am not happy with him.'

'He is full of admiration for you.'

'Would that it had been so from the beginning. Now, what of the slooths?'

'We followed the plan I outlined earlier, killing four immediately. They are stupid creatures. Three more returned to pick at the carcasses, and we killed them also. The others flapped away across the forest. Also, we have sealed the chamber with the magical oval device.'

'Is it secure?'

'We boarded it up with stout planks and supports, and piled boulders before it, covered with earth. We also barred and covered other entrances. However, against anyone who knows that the chamber exists and who is determined to enter, I can do little.'

'That will have to suffice.' Issul put aside her bowl, stood and stretched. 'Now, when is my watch duty?'

'Yours? I assigned no duty to you.'

'Then amend that. I will do what I ask others to do. Shenwolf, you look tired. When did you last sleep?'

'I have no need.'

'Sleep. I will take your watch.'

'Truly, I am not tired.'

'Shenwolf, it is an order, not a debating point.'

Shenwolf grinned. 'Very well. My watch is pre-dawn, at the gate-tower.'

He saluted and made off, but Issul called him back. 'There is one other thing. Think back, if you can, to when your platoon intercepted the Krai ambush upon my party, on the road outside Crosswood. At that time did you see any sign of a child?'

'A child?'

'A boy, three years old, with tumbling fair locks.'

Shenwolf shook his head. 'There may have been a child, but I saw none. There was great confusion. I just glimpsed you running into the forest, and went in pursuit.'

'I was chasing the child.'

'I am sorry, I did not see him.'

'What about an old woman, heavily built, poorly dressed, almost in rags.'

'I glimpsed a woman running from the cart.'

'No, another, older and bulkier than she, and with blood upon her cheek.'

Shenwolf's eyes narrowed. 'An old woman in rags and a small fair-haired boy. No, on that day I saw no such pair.'

IV

The hours before dawn were quiet and chill. Issul huddled in a blanket in the gate-tower, walking back and forth in the limited space to keep the blood circulating in her veins and the numbing cold from the tips of her fingers and toes. The forest was beginning to emerge from the enveloping blackness as the first grey light touched the cloudy tree tops. Mist hung still upon the canopy, birds were just beginning to stir and sing, and a faint rose glow was appearing above the trees to the east.

It had been a long watch. She had taken over from Kol some four hours earlier. Now she was looking forward to stepping down and enjoying a mug of hot green tea reinforced with spirit. But thankfully her watch had passed uneventfully. She had been haunted by the thought that the Krai patrol might return this night. Fifteen strong, they could well overcome Issul's group if their senses were pared. She was fearful of the Krai reputation for superior night-vision, though Shenwolf had said he did not believe their vision was significantly better than humans'.

'They do see more than we in darkness, I would say that much, but they are not night creatures. They do not by choice fight or conduct their operations at night, which they would surely do if they could. No, I believe they have only minimal advantage in the dark.'

Still, Issul had not relaxed. Every tiny sound, every rustle in the undergrowth, had seized her attention, had her crouched and peering into the dense black for signs of moving bodies. Now she could look across the camp, see the other three towers and make out her own men in each.

Then she froze. There was a movement, a faint sound, behind her, down in the compound. She watched, thinking she had been mistaken, then saw it again. A shadow, a creeping figure, close to the former dormitory hut in which the two Krai prisoners were held. Issul hesitated. Raise the alarm, or wait? She chose the latter. If the Krai had somehow entered the camp in strength she wanted to establish more of their positions before making any move.

She unslung her bow, notched an arrow, and knelt, waiting. The dark figure moved again, had almost reached the hut now. Then, to her horror, she saw another figure dart from between two of the tents. She took a breath, was about to cry a warning, when the second figure came onto open ground and stole across the compound. To her relief she recognized Shenwolf. He was tailing the intruder by the hut.

Issul put aside her bow and silently descended, intending to give Shenwolf support. Drawing her sword she crept across the cold dirt, arriving beside the dormitory hut. The door was open. Within she could make out a dim figure. Shenwolf appeared on the other side of the door. Issul signalled to draw his attention, and when he had seen her, motioned inwards. Then with a yell she leapt through the door, Shenwolf just behind.

The intruder spun, blade held before him.

'Jace! Shenwolf! Do not strike! It is me!'

'Herbin!'

'What are you doing here?' Shenwolf pushed past Herbin to where the two Krai lay motionless upon the floor.

'I came to deliver justice,' said Herbin. His eyes in the dim light were glassy, his lips tightly compressed. 'But I am too late.'

Shenwolf looked over his shoulder at Issul. 'They are dead.'

'Herbin, you fool!' cried Issul.

Herbin shook his head. 'I have already said, I am too late. The job has been done for me.'

Issul shoved past him, stared down at the two pallid corpses. Neither appeared to bear new wounds, nor was blood to be seen.

'What has happened here?'

Shenwolf was kneeling beside the corpses, examining them. He shook his head. 'I do not know. Herbin, what happened?'

'I did nothing!' declared Herbin vehemently. 'And I feel no pride or pleasure in admitting it. I came here to kill them, to let them taste my steel as my brother tasted theirs. I would give them to the slooths if I could. How my poor father must have suffered! But the sword I took from their comrade was the best I had, and at least I would have been avenged. And, Jace, believe me, I would have made no secret of what I had done. No, you would all have known it was Herbin who had delivered justice and cleansed the world of their vile lives. But I did not do this. I have been cheated.'

'"We are the dead",' said Shenwolf softly. 'I do not know how, but they spoke the truth when they said those words. By some means they have induced their own deaths.'

The Krai officer's eyes were open, fixed sightlessly upon the rafters. Their lustre was gone; no longer did they in any way resemble fabulous gems. The gorgeous blue membrane of the sclera already showed signs of etiolation, the slit of the pupil was dull and turning to grey.

Issul turned away, cursing silently. 'What am I to make of a people like these? Can we ever hope to meet upon common ground?'

THIRTEEN

I

With the morning another death was discovered. One of the two prisoners whom the Krai had hung upon frames, the man who had taken an arrow in the thigh after Issul cut him down, had lacked the strength to survive the shock. The other, whose name was Aurfusk, seemed to be recovering, though he still lacked use of his hands.

With Aurfusk the victorious company was now ten strong. Issul had the able-bodied assemble in the compound. 'All of us are free beings once more. Some of us have homes to return to, loved ones to seek out. Others may not. For my part, I return to Enchantment's Edge where my home lies. Some of you, I know, travel also in that direction, part-way or beyond. Our chances of survival are soundest if we stick together. I occupy good station at the city-castle and can promise remuneration for those who choose to follow me there. But should any choose otherwise, you may go with my blessing and thanks.'

'I was brought here from my farmstead in the south,' said one man, named Carkin. 'That is the way I must go.'

Two others were of similar voice. The rest chose to remain with Issul. Before parting they buried the dead. The Krai were put into a shallow pit in the labour compound. Those who had perished as prisoners were interred at the edge of the forest. Time did not allow the digging of individual graves, so all were laid side by side and covered with earth. Shenwolf and two others also collected the remains of those who had died in the slooths' feeding-pen, and they were laid with the others. The grave was left unmarked, out of concern that it might be desecrated by returning Krai.

The sad task done, the company selected and divided rations

and supplies from the camp. Each man took as much as he could comfortably carry, including a few gold and silver coins. In a storage hut some of the men found items of their own belongings. Issul discovered her own small-sword and dagger, which pleased her for they were lighter and better balanced for her than the more cumbersome Krai weapons. She also found clothing of finer quality than that which she had exchanged with Shenwolf: a thick shirt of pale brown cotton, a loose jerkin, strong trousers and her own damask cape. These, with the padded armour of the Krai, provided her with adequate covering for the journey ahead.

Their final task was to gather fallen branches, leaves and dry grass from the forest's edge. These, with other flammable materials from the Krai huts and tents, they built into pyres at various places about the camp. Then they put torches to the pyres and watched in contemplative silence as the camp burned.

It was time for farewells as the company split into two. Issul felt a twinge of sadness at parting with the three who were travelling south. She, like the others, was aware of the bond that had grown between them all by dint of shared suffering and the successful, if costly, struggle for freedom. Now she wanted to offer assurances of future assistance to those who were departing. But she could not reveal herself. None but Shenwolf knew that she was Queen, and until she was safe within Orbia it had to remain that way.

So they departed that unhappy place and went their separate ways. With bright flames crackling at their backs and thick black smoke pouring into the dull sky, Issul and her small band forded the stream a little way north of where she had been made to scrub Krai clothing, and entered the forest.

Shenwolf took the lead to begin with, for he knew the locations of the traps set by the Krai. These they disarmed as they passed. Later Shenwolf fell back and walked beside Issul.

'I can't help feeling that we should have delayed our departure,' Issul said when they had been walking for half an hour.

'For the Krai squad?'

She nodded. 'They will almost certainly be returning with new prisoners. What will be their fate when the soldiers discover what we have done?'

'We might wait days, or longer. Worse, they might somehow detect something amiss and spring a surprise attack on us. Furthermore, for all we know fresh units could be making their way to the camp from the south-east. No, Jace, we have done the right thing. It would have been rash to have delayed.'

She knew he was right, but the thought of the other prisoners she might have saved haunted her for many days.

They were deep in the forest now, moving slowly and silently. Ombo led, navigating by the sun towards where he believed his home lay. At one point he stopped and pointed. Some distance off a pair of grullags stood beneath the trees, watching them. They were huge creatures with the bodies of hirsute men and heads most closely resembling those of bears. They appeared curious but diffident. Hungry, they would not hesitate to attack a solitary traveller, even a pair. But they were intelligent enough to stay clear of a well-armed group. Even so Shenwolf slipped to the rear as the group moved on, his eyes peeled lest the grullags should decide to stalk them.

Towards the latter part of the afternoon they mounted a low promontory which commanded a view over a wide wooded plain below. Ombo, panting, his face bright with sweat, pointed to where something glittered distantly between the trees.

'I have not led us wrong. There is Ghismile's Tarn. My home, the hamlet of Ghismile, lies close upon its furthest shore.'

Soon they were approaching the outlying buildings of the hamlet. The evening dark was gathering quickly, the curved moon reflected in the still, wide tarn along whose shore they walked. Before an old stone barn Ombo halted. 'The folk of Ghismile are nervous – understandably, considering the proximity of the Krai and the plunder and abductions they have already wreaked upon us. I cannot predict their response to seven armed figures stealing in from the night. I propose going on alone to announce myself to family and friends, and to reassure them in your regard. This way there will be no accidental bloodshed. Wait here in this barn for my return.'

'I am not happy with this,' whispered Issul to Shenwolf after Ombo had departed and they were waiting inside.

Shenwolf nodded in agreement. 'You do not trust Ombo.'

'I have said before, I am unconvinced by his change of heart.'

'Then let's hide outside in the wood and see what transpires.'

The six concealed themselves in the cover of trees and undergrowth beside the path opposite the old barn. Minutes passed, then a swaying light was seen approaching slowly from the hamlet. The mammoth bulk of Ombo came into view, in company with another man, well padded but of shorter stature.

'Ho, comrades!' Ombo thumped upon the door of the barn and pushed it open. 'Come out now. All is safe. Let us to the tavern!'

Issul glanced at Shenwolf, her expression sheepish. Shenwolf grinned. The six stepped out from hiding. 'We are here.'

Ombo's face in the lamplight was bemused.

'We were concerned lest the Krai be here,' Issul said.

'Ah. They have not been seen since my capture, so I am told,' boomed Ombo, though the glint in his eyes said that he doubted her explanation. He indicated the man beside him. 'This is Gramkintle, a farmer of our community.'

'Welcome to our humble hamlet,' said Gramkintle, with a shallow bow. He was short, plump, with extremely wide buttocks, aged about forty. 'I have just heard tell of your heroic exploits against the verminous Krai. Let me say, I am most delighted to welcome you to our little community. Come, join us in our tavern and let us celebrate your freedom.'

They walked on behind Ombo and Gramkintle, passing rude stone cottages and outbuildings, until they came to the centre of the hamlet. Before them stood a rickety tavern which bore no sign. They entered the common room where six or seven men sat at tables, tankards before them.

'Friends, be seated,' said Ombo, gesturing expansively. He turned to the landlord. 'Gassar, the best ale of the house, if you please. This is a night for celebration!'

Issul, Shenwolf and the others seated themselves around an unoccupied table in the centre of the common room. Issul was weary, as she assumed the others to be. By choice she would have gone immediately to the nearest bed or pallet. But she acknowledged that more was expected of her. The community of Ghismile was no doubt excited by the unexpected return of one of their number whom they had considered lost. She prepared herself for a long round of tale-telling and tankard raising.

The landlord, Gassar, came forth, carrying two heavy earthenware pitchers. As he approached the table he lifted the pitchers high and brought them down hard, one then the other, onto the exposed heads of Phisusandra and Herbin. Both men slumped forward, senseless.

With a sharp cry Shenwolf sprang to his feet, drawing his sword, followed by Issul, Kol and Aurfusk. But they found themselves confronted by the tavern's other customers, who had risen as one, swords in hands. At the same moment the door burst open with a crash. Six burly men in helmets and corselets of tarnished mail charged in, swords drawn.

'What is this?' cried Shenwolf. He held his sword before him, but saw that the situation was hopeless. With Phisusandra and Herbin unconscious, and Aurfusk prevented from using his hands, the others were outnumbered by four to one.

Issul turned blazing eyes to Ombo. 'What treachery is this?'

Ombo stood back, grinning, digging between his teeth with a thumb-nail. 'A little unfinished business to attend to, *Jace*. You have not forgotten, have you?'

He turned to the man called Gramkintle. 'Take their weapons and march them to the keep.'

II

They were taken along a narrow dark lane which led uphill to an ancient keep enclosed within mouldering, twenty-foot-high stone walls. Once within the main gate Ombo's thuggish henchmen prodded and pushed them inside, then down a dank flight of stairs into a dungeon area divided into a number of pokey lightless cells. Into one of these Issul was flung. The door closed behind her, keys grating in the lock. In the darkness she heard the dull clang of several other doors closing, and knew that her companions had been dealt similar fare.

The footsteps of Ombo's men receded. She groped her way to her door: a strong frame of stout iron bars, between which she was able to thrust an arm but no more. Enraged and despondent she called out, 'Shenwolf? Herbin? Are any of you there?'

Reassuringly Shenwolf's voice sounded from somewhere along the passage. 'I am here, Jace.'

'And I,' came Kol's voice. Herbin, Phisusandra and Aurfusk also spoke up.

'It seems we are each held in a separate cell,' said Shenwolf.

'Aye, and mine is cold and damp and dark,' added Phisusandra, 'and there are rats scuttling about my feet.'

Shenwolf cursed and Kol cried out, 'This is the most vile treachery. We have fought to win Ombo his freedom. What kind of man is it that treats his comrades so?'

From the darkness at one end of the passage came a deep, booming chuckle. A shriek of metal hinges preceded the opening of a door, which revealed a flickering dull rectangle of yellowish light at the head of a short flight of stone steps. Into this stepped Ombo, ogre-like in silhouette. '*Baron* Ombo, if you don't mind. Lord of Ghismile and the surrounding lands. As long as you are my guests I think I have a right to expect due and proper deference.'

Grasping a torch he descended to the passage and passed before the cells where they waited. 'Still, you are right, this is no way to deal with my comrades-in-arms. And in fact I have no argument with you. Once I have done with sweet Jace here, you others will be free to leave. Although you, Shenwolf, I find rather interesting. I may decide to let you linger a little longer, enjoying my hospitality. At least until I have learned more about you.'

'Ombo, let them go,' demanded Issul. 'You have said your argument is with me. These are men with no connection to me. They wish only to return to their homes.'

'And so they shall in due course. But I need their presence, for a short time at least.' Ombo halted before the bars of Issul's cell and stared at her. 'As insurance, you see. You and I, Jace, we have things to discuss, a little issue to resolve. And I think you will be better behaved knowing that your friends are waiting down here.'

'Ombo, you are making a grave mistake!' cried Shenwolf. 'Leave her be!'

Ombo merely chuckled and jangled the keys to the cells. '*Baron* Ombo, please.'

Inserting a heavy iron key into the lock on Issul's door, he twisted, stepped inside, grasped Issul's arm and hauled her out as though she weighed no more than a child. 'Now come along, *Jace*. Come and see what I have waiting for you upstairs.'

He took her up into the main part of the keep. Despondently Issul became aware of the fine quality and workmanship of the furnishings and hangings, the splendid rugs that adorned the floors. Baron Ombo was plainly a wealthy man.

Ombo led her to his private apartments on the second floor. He thrust her to the centre of the main chamber, then turned and locked the door. Issul looked quickly about the chamber. A great fire burned in the hearth. A pair of deer hounds rested close by upon the floor, their heads upon their paws, indifferent to her arrival. A rack of ceremonial glaives stood to one side; chalices of gold and silver studded with jewels, and urns and precious pots ornamented shelves and ledges. Upon the walls were shields and escutcheons, swords, axes and hunting trophies, as well as rich silk tapestries and paintings in ornate frames. Numbered among the trophies was the head of a male grullag, its lips curled and long teeth ferociously bared.

'Killed 'im myself,' said Ombo proudly, seeing Issul's eyes upon the head. 'And he put up a memorable fight, too!'

She did not care. Ombo strode to a table upon which a firkin of ale rested.

'Ah, it is good to be home!' He grabbed a large metal tankard and thrust it beneath the spigot, watching in anticipation as the turbid brown liquid gushed forth. '*Jace*, let me remind you of something. Your friends languish in the dungeon below. Their sojourn there can be as long or as short as you choose. Do you understand me?'

'Perfectly. You are quite transparent.'

'Now, now.' Ombo straightened, raised the tankard to his lips and emptied it in long, deep draughts, then stuck it beneath the spigot again. 'We have, as I have said, unfinished business to address here. But let us be clear on one thing. You will try no tricks. You will be especially nice to Baron Ombo. If I have cause to complain, one of your friends will die immediately. A second will spend the next two weeks dying. I know you do not want this; neither do I. So let there be no struggle this time, no fight. We will relax and enjoy each other, and your friends will know no discomfort.'

'And afterwards you will let us all go?'

'Mmmm. Afterwards I will think about afterwards.'

Through her teeth Issul said, 'It must smart to have been bested by a woman.'

Ombo froze as the second tankard met his lips, his eyes on her, burning. 'I can start heating a poker for friend Shenwolf *now!*'

Issul stayed silent. He downed the ale, then said, 'I think you are beginning to learn.'

'You seem to have a devoted following here, Ombo.'

'A dozen rogues. They serve me well and enjoy a percentage of my profits.'

'Profits from what?'

'What do you think?'

'You are a brigand, is what I think. You and your band of thugs are fugitives from law. By rights you should now be in the King's army, defending Enchantment's Edge against the Krai menace.'

Ombo stepped forward and cuffed her with a smart backhand across the side of the head. The blow sent Issul sprawling across the chamber. Her head rang, blinding shards of pain hammered through her, but as her senses spun she recognized that she was alive, which was something, for Ombo could easily have killed her with a single blow.

She spat blood from her mouth, then felt herself yanked upwards. Ombo had her by the back of her shirt. He twisted her around and slammed her down upon a table, and leaned over her, his huge leering face thrust before her, his sweat and beer-breath an affront to her nostrils.

'King Leth!' Ombo sneered. 'He is a spineless lizard of a man. Let me tell you something: had the Krai come in here seeking help, I would have joined them. Yes, I would, as would my men, freely and gladly. It is preferable to supporting that weak-willed, godless wretch. He has brought us to this, be sure of that, *Jace*. Leth the Despicable! Leth the Pusillanimous! Leth the Impious!'

'You do not strike me as a pious man, Ombo.'

Ombo drew back. 'You taunt me again, Jace. The poker can be glowing in moments. Have you ever heard how it sizzles in an orifice? Have you ever watched the face or listened to the cries of a man with a glowing poker thrust up his arse? How he feels his innards broil? Let me tell you how it is done. First, while the poker heats, we take a bull's horn and saw off the tip to create a hollow tube. This we thrust deep into the orifice, then the poker follows, melding the horn to the innards as well as penetrating deeper, far deeper than you can imagine. It can be arranged, *Jace*. Very easily.'

Issul clenched her teeth, helpless fury abolishing any fear she felt of the man. The entire side of her face still throbbed with the pain of his blow.

Ombo smirked. 'Yes, I see that you do understand this time. Now, before we partake of our pleasure together, there is one other matter

I wish to address.' He turned and slowly crossed the room, then turned back. 'Jace . . . Jace . . . Why am I so sure that is not your real name?'

He looked at Issul. She said nothing.

'You speak and comport yourself like a woman of status and refinement. You fight like a warrior privileged to have known a rare kind of training. You command like a natural born leader. Men obey you without question. That is interesting, is it not?'

'I do not see it so.'

'Yes, it is. I have wondered about you from the beginning, thinking that you might be more than you endeavoured to seem. You have said that you are from the city-castle. Perhaps somebody there might be willing to pay a substantial reward for your safe return.'

'I would not think so. I am governess to a noble family, that is all. They value me for my work, but I am easily replaced. In fact, I am sure that a replacement will already have been found. As for my family, they are poor folk from the country. Were they to learn that I was the prisoner of a low and heartless brigand, they could offer you little more than a cow or a pig, perhaps a few chickens as well.'

'Is that so?' Ombo ambled back to the barrel of ale to replenish his tankard. 'That is interesting. My assistant, Gramkintle – whom you met earlier – has been to the city-castle in recent days. The streets hum with the news that Leth's wife, the beautiful young Queen, Issul, has vanished. Upon the Crosswood Road, so rumour has it, a matter of less than two weeks ago. It is interesting to speculate on how much the spineless King might be willing to pay in ransom for his Queen, were he to learn that she was alive, is it not?'

'You have a fevered imagination, Ombo. It leads you wildly astray.'

Ombo walked up to her, yanked her from the table so that she stood before him. 'I think not, Queen Issul.'

He walked her backwards, through an arched opening into his bedchamber. Before a wide four-poster bed he grasped the front of her shirt and the vest beneath, tore them effortlessly apart and thrust them back from her shoulders. His eyes bulged as he took in the sight of her naked breasts. 'Remember, my Queen, your good friends below are relying upon you.'

He pushed her back to the bed. 'Disrobe.'

'Ombo—'

He cut her short, lifting her and tossing her back upon the bed. 'Disrobe!'

His great meaty hands were groping at his belt. He thrust his trousers down, his engorged manhood springing forth. Grasping it in one hand he stumbled onto the bed, extending himself above Issul.

'Ombo, this is not the way it should be,' said Issul, somehow bringing a gentle, coaxing tone to her voice. His great weight was suspended above her, his heat and sweat upon her as his free hand struggled to rip away her trousers.

The tone of her voice was unexpected. He glanced down as she forced a nervous smile and lifted her hands to his coarse cheek. She stroked him. He grunted like a troubled beast. She rammed both her thumbs hard and deep into his eyes, twisting, gouging, ripping.

Ombo reeled back with a throttled roar, blood and jelly spurting over his cheeks. Issul twisted from the bed, raced to the main chamber and seized a glaive from the rack. She ran back, lofting it high. Ombo was bawling, his hands to his ruined eyes, trying to sit. As he slid forward from the bed Issul swung downwards and cleaved his head in two.

Now she ran to the door and listened. She had seen Ombo's men about the keep, but none close to his apartments. Nonetheless she stood, shaking, the glaive poised to thrust should anyone enter through the door. The two deer-hounds watched her without interest. She recalled that Ombo had locked the door. There were no sounds from without. She gave herself a moment to take stock.

Through the arch she could see Ombo, slumped in a mound. His bloody, broken head was on the floor, vast white buttocks high, arms awkwardly splayed. A flood of dark blood and soft grey stuff spoiled his valuable rug and bespattered the coverlet upon his bed. Issul approached him and poked him with the tip of the glaive, hardly daring to believe he was dead. He did not stir. She put down the glaive, stooped and wiped the horror from her thumbs, then took Ombo's keys from the trousers bunched about his knees.

She looked about the chamber for a less cumbersome weapon. A slim sword was mounted on one wall. She took it down and tested it, found it double-edged and of decent quality, and light enough for single-handed play. She took Ombo's dagger from his belt, then returned to the door.

No one had investigated Ombo's cries. He had bellowed loudly enough. But the walls were thick and the bedchamber somewhat isolated. It seemed he had not been heard.

Issul unlocked the door carefully and peered into the corridor outside. There was no one in sight. She crept stealthily back the way Ombo had brought her. At the head of a flight of stairs one of Ombo's men stood with his back to her, one shoulder propping the wall, a flask in his hand. Issul hesitated for a pulsebeat, then stepped up behind him as he tipped back his head to drink, and ran her sword through his back. She caught his flask before it could clatter upon the flags, stabbed him once through the heart for certainty, and moved on.

Just beyond the foot of the stairs she heard muffled voices. Two men. No, more. She crept forward. Around the next corner the passage opened into a large chamber. She moved silently to the door and peered in. Four men were playing cards at a table ten paces away. Mugs and a tall pitcher stood between them. Three of them were Ombo's 'soldiers', the fourth was Gramkintle. She flattened herself to the wall, thinking hard. She had to pass through that chamber to reach the dungeons below.

A voice came to her from the past. It was Fectur speaking, and she almost shut it out. But the image it brought to her was strong, and she took note. She slipped back along the passage, around the corner, and removed her clothing, all bar her boots.

She stopped. *Am I insane?* No, it was her best hope. There was no other way. She returned silently to the door of the big chamber, took a deep breath, gripped sword and dagger and stepped inside.

'Gentlemen, there is something we should discuss!'

The four looked around, and gaped. Issul drove straight towards them, not slackening her step. Her blade whirled. The first thug died before he had even risen from his seat, Issul's nakedness the last sight his eyes enjoyed. The second was on the far side of the table, and had a moment more to gather his senses. Even so, his eyes were reluctant to tear themselves from the sight of Issul's lithe body. Only as his comrade died did he seem to gain a clear picture of what was at hand. He snapped from his stupor, half-rose, groping for his sword, but before he had it from his sheath Issul was upon him. He staggered backwards, avoiding her first thrust, but as he regained his balance Issul stepped forward, swinging her sword in a wide arc. He tried to duck, too late. Her blade took off the top of his unprotected head.

She spun around. The other henchman had his sword drawn and was on the other side of the table. Gramkintle was scrambling back from his seat, eyes and mouth agape in terror. He turned and began to run, but he was fat and slow, and though he tried to shout his fear constricted his throat. In four steps Issul had caught him. He staggered on for a few steps more, blood flowering on the back of his jerkin, then slumped dead to the floor.

She turned. The last man seemed frozen in fear. As she advanced upon him he dropped his sword and fell to his knees, begging for his life. She did not look him in the eye, but killed him with a single blow.

Issul cast her eyes quickly about the chamber, breathing hard, then hastened back to the passage to regain her clothes. She felt sick and ebullient, weak and half-crazed, hardly believing what she had done. She thought of Fectur again. Years ago, in combat training, he had told the story of a female bandit he had been assigned to capture.

'Her name was Mirobin,' he had said. 'Mirobin the Cat. She was skilled, wily, and very, very deadly. She led a band of cutthroats, causing havoc across the region. For two years they had avoided capture. Queen Fallorn wanted her imprisoned or dead, and no one but I could accomplish the task. It took a while, but eventually I had her isolated in a cottage in a village. Her men were dead, or prisoners. Seven of my men entered the cottage. We knew she was alone, and there was but one room that she could be in. My men went in by the only two doors, and found it empty. Then, suddenly, Mirobin was among them, dropping from the rafters, utterly naked. These were skilled and disciplined fighters, among my best. But she was a beauty, and no matter the circumstances, a man cannot but gape at the sight of a beautiful woman in all her naked glory. It is instinct, nature, pure and simple. Mirobin needed only a couple of heartbeats in which to act. Three of my seven died before they had taken their eyes from her breasts. The others were dead or wounded when she had done.'

'Did she escape?' Issul had asked, enthralled.

Fectur had smiled his thin, heartless smile. 'She could have done, but she made a single mistake, and of course, she had not calculated on The Spectre.'

'What mistake?'

'She stopped to put her clothes back on. That was when I stepped through the door and killed her. Remember this always. Your beauty can be a weapon to disarm one man, or many. But should you use it so, be brazen, and do not rush to cover your modesty.'

Issul considered this now, glancing up the passage and back. No one crept towards her. Garbed once more, she set off again.

She came across another guard as she approached the dungeon. He was on a chair, his head against the wall, slumbering. She hesitated, wanting no more slaughter. But – a dozen, Ombo had said. And she was alone. She darted forward with resolve and made his slumber permanent. Then, taking a torch, she drew open the portal to the dungeon and descended to the cells.

'Shenwolf?'

'Jace! I am here!'

She hurried to his cell, fumbling with the keys until she found one that fitted.

'How did you—?'

'Ssh!' She thrust the keys into his hand. 'Release the others.'

As he made to obey Issul sank to her knees. Her stomach kicked, chill torrents raced along her spine, and in painful convulsions she retched until she could retch no more.

Shenwolf was beside her, his arms about her, helping her to her feet. She pointed weakly to the door. 'Get weapons. There are still men about.'

She gave her sword and dagger to Phisusandra who, with Kol, raced for the entrance. Kol took the sword from the dead guard outside.

'Jace, do you know how many more there are?'

She was trembling violently. 'Ombo said he had twelve. Five of those are now dead. And the fat man, Gramkintle.'

'What of Ombo?'

Issul straightened, grey-faced, and pushed strands of sweat-damp hair from her face. 'Ombo will trouble no one again.'

Then she let her head tip forward against Shenwolf's shoulder and, uncontrollably, she wept.

III

They moved stealthily through the old keep. Coming upon the corpses of the men Issul had slain, they armed themselves with their weapons, or with weapons taken from the walls. Issul held to the rear of the group, having no taste for more slaying. Shenwolf stayed close, casting her solicitous glances.

In the kitchens they found four more of Ombo's men, quaffing ale and eating cold venison. Better men might have put up a spirited fight, but these were blackguards and bully-boys, slack of habit and discipline and without spirit for combat where the odds were not stacked overwhelmingly in their favour. At the sight of the grim and determined men confronting them with swords drawn they threw down their weapons and called for mercy.

They were quickly trussed up with cord found in a cupboard. Questions about their remaining comrades drew the reply that two were upstairs and another three were at the tavern in the hamlet. Shenwolf led the others to the first floor and in a chamber there they came upon two of Ombo's men making sport with a woman, presumably from the hamlet below. Caught *in flagrante* they were in no position to offer resistance and, like their comrades below, were bound and led off to the cells.

Issul spoke to the woman, who was in some distress and had plainly not been a willing participant. Her name, Issul learned, was Marilene.

'Does this sort of thing happen often?'

'All the time. They come to our homes whenever it suits and take one or more of us off to the keep. Women, young girls, it makes little difference to animals like these. And if we resist they kill us, or kill our menfolk.'

'Well, be assured that is ended now. We think there are but three more, in the tavern. But the landlord, also, seems to be in Ombo's employ.'

'Aye. Gassar. He threw in his lot and makes a pretty penny keeping Ombo and his beasts well-fed and oiled.'

'When Ombo disappeared, was it not any better?'

'The same.'

'How was it that Ombo was taken, do you know?'

Marilene gave a bitter laugh. 'I'll say! My boy, Jorm, was in the forest trying to snare a rabbit. He saw it all. Baron Ombo was out hunting with four others. Jorm had to hide as they passed by, for they would've hung him for poaching. He climbed a tree and saw the Krai appear along the path. There were more than a score. Baron Ombo had his men fight, but he kept himself back, and when the others had been killed he gave himself up. Jorm heard him offering the Krai his services. Even offered them his home as a base to use against the King's forces, and his men as fighters too. But the Krai put a rope around his neck and led him off. We hoped he'd gone forever, but as I say it made no difference, for his pigs remained to oppress us as before.'

Through a window Issul gazed down upon the dark roofs of the hamlet, the canopy of the trees and the glimmering tarn a little way beyond. She consulted briefly with Shenwolf, who made off alone into the hamlet and concealed himself in bushes opposite the tavern. Presently the door opened and Ombo's three remaining men lurched out. Stumbling, slewing, swaying, they made their way back along the lane to the keep, belching and swearing obscenely as they went. As they passed through the gate they were confronted by three armed men and a woman. Shenwolf walked up behind them and relieved them of their swords. Hardly sober enough to grasp what was going on, they were tied and packed off to the cells alongside their mates.

There remained only the landlord, Gassar. Shenwolf and Phisusandra returned to the tavern and hammered on the door until he answered, grumbling and cursing. They dragged him outside. Phisusandra dealt him a couple of hefty blows about the head – 'in payment for the treatment I and my companion received at your hands earlier'. Then he was likewise bound, marched to the keep and thrown into the cells.

'Return now to your home,' Issul told Marilene. 'Alert the other villagers to what has happened here tonight. Tell them their days of oppression are over. They should assemble here tomorrow at midday, in the forecourt of the keep. I will speak to them then.'

Marilene hurried away. Issul turned a pale weary smile to Shenwolf.

'You look haggard,' he observed.

She nodded. 'I mourn.'

'For what?'

'Essentially for the loss of what I was. I have been changed in these past days. I can never be the same again.'

'You are a most remarkable woman, do you know that?'

She shook her head, lowering her eyes. 'I am simply a woman who desires nothing more than to return to her husband and children, and subsequently to live a life free of war and hatred and bitterness and betrayal.'

He gave her a consoling smile. 'I think you will achieve the first very soon now. Sadly, the second may take a little longer.'

IV

Issul slept solidly, not waking until well into the morning. She slept upon a straw mattress in the main chamber. The thought of sleeping in Ombo's comfortable bed had nauseated her; likewise the bed where Marilene and so many others before her had suffered.

She rose, bathed and descended to the kitchen. Shenwolf and Herbin sat at the table. They looked up and grinned as she entered.

Herbin stood. 'Jace, sit down and eat. There is porridge, bacon, sausages, and just about anything else you might fancy.'

'We have found fine clothing and excellent provisions for our journey,' Shenwolf said. 'Also a hoard of gold pieces, plus a stable with a number of sturdy horses.'

Issul ate and changed from her own ripped garments. In due course the villagers arrived in the forecourt, about forty strong, with several small children in tow. Issul and the others stepped out to greet them.

'Baron Ombo is dead,' she announced. 'His men are either dead or imprisoned below. Your days of oppression are behind you.

Soon I and my companions will leave, but one of us is injured and asks if he may remain here until I can send men for him from Enchantment's Edge. He is Aurfusk, with the broken hands. If you are willing to attend to him I will give you the keys to this place. Everything in it is yours to do with as you will. The men I send will also take away the prisoners.'

'Mistress, we are grateful to you, but must we allow those wretches to live?' asked one old man with tearful eyes. He stepped forward and swept a frail arm about. 'They have abused and murdered us. They have treated us as slaves and worse. And we can never be entirely free of them. Look, Look! See what they have left us.'

Issul looked, her eyes passing over the pale, worn, expectant faces before her. At first she did not understand, then it came to her suddenly. So many of the women, tired and drawn and bitter, held babies in their arms, or had scrawny, dead-eyed infants clinging to their skirts.

'They have left their stain upon us for eternity,' declared the old man, his voice cracking. 'They have made certain that we will never be able to forget them. Do you really ask us to let these devils live?'

Issul felt a weight of sorrow upon her. She struggled with herself for a moment, then said in subdued tones. 'I can say only that there is wealth enough here to improve your lives. When the soldiers come they will have instructions to collect any prisoners that might be found. If none can be found, well, they will simply depart with Aurfusk.'

Marilene spoke up from the front of the crowd. 'We will gladly take care of your friend.'

Issul was aware of Shenwolf's gaze upon her. She tossed the keys to the ground before the old man. 'You should elect a leader,' she said, then turned and walked back indoors.

'What else could I say?' she asked as Shenwolf came alongside her.

'I was not passing judgement.'

'I know. But I was.'

'They are undeserving of consideration. They have ensured that the memories of the evil they have committed will be long in passing from this place.'

'Still, you were surprised that I was prepared to sanction their deaths, for that is surely what they can expect when we have gone.' She turned and looked at him, her face sorrowful. 'Did you see the children? Innocents, every one. But what must they now live with?' She was silent for a few paces, then said, 'It was as I told you last night, I have changed. But last night I mourned for myself and what I have lost. Now I see that my own suffering is mild compared to that of these poor people and what they all must bear, always, even in freedom.'

An hour later Issul and her four companions said farewell to Aurfusk and the villagers who remained at the keep. The villagers had elected a leader from among themselves, the old man who had addressed Issul earlier. He pledged to oversee the fair distribution of the wealth left inside the keep, and once again the villagers gave their thanks. The five passed down the lane and departed the hamlet of Ghismile. Their path took them for a league or so through the forest, before they broke out upon the road south of Crosswood. A ways further on Herbin announced his departure.

'My home lies a short way yonder,' he said, nodding to a track which led off into the forest. 'I am sad to be leaving you. A while ago, before my capture, I had made the decision to leave my home to join the King's army and fight the Krai while my brother stayed at home to help my parents. Now, with both my father and brother dead, I am obliged to return to look after my mother. Still—' he held up the modest bag of coins that Issul had permitted him, and the others, to remove from Ombo's keep '—at least our lives, though filled with loss, will not be as harsh.'

'Go well, Herbin,' said Issul, and smiled. 'We will meet again, and when we do I think you will be surprised. In the meantime, be sure that I will not forget you. I shall send word to you, soon.'

With that Issul turned away and began the final stage of her journey back to the great city-castle of Enchantment's Edge.

FOURTEEN

I

On the day after his meeting with Grey Venger in the burrows of Overlip, King Leth received Venger's reply. Venger agreed. He would come. He would come to Orbia and speak to Leth of the Legendary Child. How much he was likely to reveal Leth could not begin to guess. But the fact that he was willing to place himself in the King's custody and say anything at all indicated just how much value he and the True Sept laid on the matter.

Leth allowed himself a few moments of satisfaction. He had gambled, placing more than he could afford to lose upon the table, and his gambit had paid off. But it was a gambit only. There was still an immeasurable distance to go.

Almost immediately Leth's satisfaction gave way to misgivings. He had allowed Venger to believe that he was in possession of information relating to the suspected Child's background, when in fact he wasn't. Venger would now demand that information. How would he respond when he learned the truth? Leth knew that he had acted with a certain impetuousness, for he had had nothing more to go on than Issul's suspicions, later backed up by the report from Fectur's men who had escorted Ohirbe to Lastmeadow. It was still not much. Issul had been so certain, yet even she, by her own account, had still been awaiting confirmation of the Child's existence.

He knew her so well. Her word, the look upon her face when she had spoken of the Legendary Child, had been enough to convince him that she knew what she was doing. But that would not be enough for Grey Venger.

What was it that had made her so sure? What had she known

that she could not divulge to her own husband? And now, her disappearance at the same time as that of the Child . . . a connection was strongly implied. Yet still it was hardly sufficient evidence to coax Venger into yielding his ancient secrets.

'He must come to no harm,' Leth instructed Lord Fectur. 'He has my guarantee. Is that understood?'

'Quite.' Fectur faced him with his hands linked behind his back, his eyes steely.

'You will bring him here and then leave us. Venger is bringing information of vital importance which he will not give up casually. I will not have him compromised, nor made to feel menaced in any way. He is a guest, Fectur. A dignitary, to be accorded the respect and attention reserved for personages of high station.'

'I understand perfectly, Sire. But I would reiterate my view, if I may, that you have embarked upon an extremely dangerous course. If word leaks out that you entertain Grey Venger—'

'Word will not leak out, unless you wish it, Fectur.'

'Sire, it is not so simple. The factions have spies in cracks in the walls. No matter his own efforts to maintain secrecy, Venger cannot be so naive as to believe that none will be aware that he has entered Orbia and confers with the King.'

'None knew that I entered Overlip, and Venger is accustomed to hiding his movements. Why should it be any different for him?'

'I say only that nothing is guaranteed.'

'*Make* it guaranteed, Fectur. Your position depends upon it. Do you understand?'

'I can guarantee his safety, Sire,' said Fectur testily. 'Beyond that I am not prepared to go. However, I wish to make plain my personal opposition to this venture.'

'Yes, yes. You have done that.' Again Leth wondered about Fectur's anxiousness to distance himself. He displayed solicitude, but something in his attitude made Leth apprehensive. 'Now, Cathbo waits without. If you are done . . .'

'I am done, Sire. For now.' Fectur bowed, stony-faced, and took his leave.

Sir Cathbo entered, bringing news of the slooths' fire-attack upon Giswel Holt.

'What is the damage?' enquired Leth.

'Several deaths, a few buildings gutted. The fires were extinguished before they could spread. But the bulk of the Krai army now sits afore Giswel Holt. Sire, what are your instructions?'

'They are as before. We wait.'

Sir Cathbo puffed his cheeks, cleared his throat, shuffled his feet.

'Sit down, Cathbo, and tell me what it is that prickles you.'

Sir Cathbo took a seat, contemplated his fingernails for a moment, then spoke out. 'I am a soldier, Sire. I am unaccustomed to inaction in the face of adversity. When an enemy advances upon me, my instinct is to move against him while there remains space to move in.'

'Even when he is immensely stronger and battle-hardened? Even when he has supernatural allies?'

'I do not deny his advantage, yet he must be met at some point.'

'Do you consider me overly meek or cowardly, Cathbo?'

Sir Cathbo reddened. 'No, Sire. I know that you are not. I intended no slur.'

'Do not think that I make this decision easily, Cathbo. I understand your impatience and frustration, and am not immune to such feelings myself. I would love nothing more than to ride forth and take the Krai by the throat. But tell me, what will happen if I do?'

'If we attack their rear positions while they sit before Giswel Holt – if Duke Hugo strikes simultaneously – we can do them serious harm. We have a chance!'

Leth shook his head.

'My troops are truly chafing at the bit.'

'Then they must chafe some more. I will not send good men to fight knowing that I am sending them to their deaths. It is a trap, pure and simple.'

'A trap?'

'Anzejarl goads us, Cathbo. He antagonizes us with acts of audacious violence, and beckons us to him by placing his army where we may strike on two flanks. But he is not a fool.'

'I do not suggest that we charge in blindly,' the knight protested. 'But we could position our forces within striking distance, seek moments of opportunity.'

Again Leth shook his head. 'I will rather wait if I can, in the hope of finding a sure alternative. He wants a clean kill, and I will not give it to him. Enchantment's Edge is his goal and his greatest obstacle. If he wants it he must come to me, and then blood will flow, but much of it will be Krai blood.'

Sir Cathbo sat stiffly, his mouth atwitch.

'There is something more you wish to say, Cathbo. Come on, out with it.'

'You asked if I think you meek, Sire. I reiterate, I do not. But the people talk, morale is low, speculation flies and certain persons in positions of influence take advantage.'

'I am accused of cowardice, publicly?'

Sir Cathbo drew in his chin. 'The Krai are here, yet you do nothing. That is how the people perceive it.'

'And the army?'

'Many of the men are unhappy, Sire.'

'So for the sake of temporarily appeasing the people, and those villains who stir them, you would have me lead the army of Enchantment's Edge into a battle that we cannot win? Would you? Really?'

'Passions are high, Sire. That is all I am saying.'

Leth rose and went pensively to his window. 'Do you still have scouting units observing Krai movements?'

'Of course.'

'But you have learned nothing more of Prince Anzejarl's consort?'

'It is impossible to get near her, Sire. Only a Krai could infiltrate the camp.'

'Even at night? A skilled group?'

'It would be inadvisable.'

'But if there was a diversion?'

'Of what kind?'

Leth gave a short ironic laugh, then said, 'Cathbo, send a force: three hundred élite fighters. Place them close to the Krai, but not so close that they will be detected. I do not want Anzejarl aware of their presence. Have them depart over today and tomorrow, in companies of fifty, with hours between each company's departure. You will go with the last company. Perhaps we can test the Krai a little, and even appease our citizens. Also, send word to Duke Hugo: he is to sit tight inside Giswel Holt until receiving specific instructions to the contrary.'

'What is your plan, Sire?'

'I will discuss that with you immediately prior to your departure. But inform all scout units to seek out the troll-creatures that Anzejarl commands, as a matter of priority.'

II

Did he dare? Had he time? A ghost of a plan was forming in Leth's mind, prompted both by Sir Cathbo's assertions of the sentiments of the people and army, and by Prince Anzejarl's irksome attacks. If it worked he might deliver Anzejarl a damaging blow; if it failed Leth might still escape with minimal losses.

Leth sat in fevered thought. Four days of travel would put his troops within striking distance of the Krai. He itched to be with them, but with so much else to occupy him he knew that was impossible. He would have to be precise in his instructions to Sir Cathbo.

Leth left his office in the base of First Tower of Dawn and went to his private study. He locked the door and brought forth the blue casket from its compartment.

'Orbus, are you here?' he called when he had entered the blue world. For some time there was silence. The absolute silence that had so frightened Leth when he had first entered this strange place, the silence that made him so utterly aware of himself. His breath roared, his heart pounded, the flow of his blood raged in his ears.

'Orbus, are you here?'

At last a sound that was not his own broke through the cacophony of silence. A familiar dragging, shuffling, thumping, coming from an indiscernible distance. Leth gave a relieved sigh. Moments later the stooped figure of Orbus hove into view, forming out of the mist, hauling itself forward with a laboured gait.

'My apologies. I had to arrange myself,' said the ancient god-thing. 'Have you learned something more?'

Leth shook his head. 'I seek more answers.'

'Ah. Well, ask away, though I am not sure I can provide you with anything more that will help you at the current time.'

'The Legendary Child. Does this mean anything to you?'

Orbus was still for a moment, then his great head shifted ponderously from side to side. 'What is this thing?'

'An obscure tale around which a powerful system of belief has formed among a certain section of my people. I know little other than that it purports to tell of a god spawning a human-ish child who will unleash destruction upon the world.'

'Hmm. I know nothing of it, but then, if it is a tale composed by humans it is unlikely that I would. It may be more or less than it appears. Without knowing more it is impossible to say.'

'Could such a child exist?'

'Ah, now that is interesting. But I require clarification. Do you mean a child who is literally born of a god, or one expelled from the womb of a human mother?'

Leth had never considered this. It seemed suddenly that he had been given a clue. 'I – I do not know.'

'Let me think . . . For a child of Enchantment to exist as a human outside of Enchantment for any appreciable span, it would require human attributes. Before my death I would have said it could not happen. My adversaries, and myself also, could not have impregnated a human being.'

'Why not?'

'Well, in the first instance the world originally lacked humans.' There was a hint of a smile in his voice as he said this. 'As Enchantment diminished creatures evolved in the formed world. Humans were among them. But we of Enchantment, no matter our talents, could not survive beyond Enchantment's borders – not with our powers intact. And you of course could not exist within it. That is to say, we could not ordinarily meet. Even had one of us consorted with one of you, no child could have been conceived. But, eons have passed. The world has changed. Those 'gods' who remain in Enchantment are cunning and resourceful. They will have pursued many forms of research. Who knows what they will have come up with? Certainly it is not inconceivable – *ahem*! Forgive the pun – it is not inconceivable that such a thing could have been achieved.'

'For what purpose?'

'If a god could produce spawn which carried something of its essence into the formed world, they would be mighty among men.'

'Do you think it has happened?'

'How can I say? From your attitude I read a likelihood. Certainly you believe it. But why do you ask about it now?'

'I am half-persuaded that the Child exists and that it is he whom the god of the Krai seeks. In a short while I am due to interview a man who claims to know far more than I about the subject. He is my sworn enemy. Beyond that I am not clear as to where his loyalties lie. I had hoped you might have information by which I could compare his tale and yours and thus measure the veracity of his words.'

'I am sorry I do not. But it would interest me to know what this man tells you.'

'When I have done I will return here and tell you. But let me be clear on something. You and your kind are unable to exist outside of Enchantment, if you wish to retain your powers. How is it then that you survive, and more importantly, how does the woman who travels with the Krai prince survive?'

'For my part, I am deprived of my powers, and I exist only inasmuch as I am here, within my own world. I *am* my own world also – a vital point to consider – and am endeavouring to develop, but that is another issue. Orbus could not survive without the Orb, that is, the blue casket as you perceive it, for the Orb is what he is. As for the woman, I have already told you that she must be a sorcerous projection or fabrication. Even so, her powers will wane the further she travels outside Enchantment and the longer she remains. Your land, Enchantment's Edge, is not as enfeebling to us as the Mondane kingdoms and the further lands. It is imbued with a residual magic of Enchantment and hence allows us a semblance of life. So here is something you may find useful: almost certainly Anzejarl's consort will have with her, close upon her person, a magical artefact of some kind which renews her essence, enabling her to persist without enfeeblement. I think she must carry something else, too, something which gives her control of Anzejarl and allows him to command the Enchantment-creatures he sets against you.'

'You should have told me of this before!'

'Had you told me of her before, I would have done so.'

Leth swallowed the rebuke. 'These artefacts – how would I know them?'

'Ah, that I cannot say. They might take any form. But they would probably be exotic or fabulous, even alien, to your eyes. The only sure way to know them is to see them used.'

'What of the Orb's Soul? How might that be known?'

'The Orb's Soul?' Orbus's voice took on a timbre of distance. 'Again, it might be in any form, or have no perceivable form. Bring it to me and I would know it. *It* would know me.'

'It is a living thing?'

'Of course. It is my soul.'

'But were I to seek it, how would I find it?'

'Leth, you cannot find it. I have told you, it is within Enchantment.'

'But if I could send someone?'

'Who could you send?'

'I do not know, but please answer my question.'

'I could teach you how to recognize it, but you would still have to search all of Enchantment unless you were able to persuade my enemies to reveal its whereabouts.'

'Perhaps that is not so far-fetched.'

'Leth, is there something you have not apprised me of?'

'No. My imagination plays me like a marionette. I am keeping nothing from you except fantastic dreams, absurd hopes and desperate aspirations.'

'The stuff of which universes are made.'

'And for that reason I cannot abandon them. But I must go now and prepare myself for my meeting.'

'I wish you success. Before you leave, I have a favour to ask. Would you take the knife that hangs at your belt and cut for me a small section from your trousers? A few threads will suffice.'

Leth had grown used to Orbus's odd requests. Even so he could not resist commenting as he cut the threads from his trousers, 'I am intrigued. Over many months I have brought you a variety of articles: cheese, wood, metal, water, stone . . . Many times I have wondered what these things are for.'

'There is little I can tell you. I seek to slowly introduce new elements to this world that is the Orb, that is also me. The laws here are precisely and delicately balanced, and I must take care. But over time I find that I am able to introduce tiny but significant changes. Do return and let me know what you discover of the Legendary Child.'

III

Leth quickly left his study and, on the way to his office, was met by Master Briano, Mawnie's head valet.

'Sire, the Duchess has asked for you,' said Briano in excruciation, wringing his hands and writhing heels against ankles.

Leth heaved a sigh. Mawnie's condition had not improved. On those occasions when, looking in upon her, Leth had found her awake, she had been either raving or in ecstatic transport. Doctor Melropius reported infrequent periods of relative lucidity, during which she was generally subdued and melancholic.

'Is she conscious?' Leth demanded.

Master Briano lifted his eyes to the fan-vault ceiling, puckering his lips, and nodded. 'She has been asking for you repeatedly, Majesty.'

Leth changed his direction and made rapidly for Mawnie's chambers, Master Briano a respectful distance behind, scurrying on tip-toes to keep up.

Mawnie was seated in a chair beside the window when Leth arrived, a small china cup of green tea held lightly in the fingers of both hands. She wore a simple green robe, her light brown hair loose and somewhat lank about her shoulders. She was pale and thin and there was a haunted look in her eyes.

'Leth,' she gave a flickering smile and put aside her cup.

'How are you, Mawnie?'

'There is something I must tell you.' Her look was penetrating, hopeful, diffident. Then it was disconsolate. 'Oh.'

'What is it, Mawnie?'

'Where is my sister?'

'Issul? She has had to go away for a while.'

'Iss. Yes. I felt, I thought, something bad had happened to her. I would like to see her.'

'The moment she returns I will send her to you.'

'Not *the moment* she returns, dear Leth. You will want to take her to your bed and love her first, won't you?'

'Well, I suppose, yes, that is a likelihood. Immediately after, then.'

'Do you miss her?'

'Very much.'

Mawnie turned to the window. 'How fortunate dear Iss is, having someone who misses her.'

'Mawnie, you said you had something to tell me.'

'Hmm? Oh. Yes. Now, what was it? Yes, Leth, something terrible has happened. To me.' She turned, her eyes strained and brimming, and took his hands. 'Leth, I do not think I should live any longer.'

'What? Mawnie, that is absurd. Why do you say such a thing?'

'Because of what happened, Leth, dear Leth. In the woods. In the woods.'

Leth concealed his impatience. He knew of the attack upon Ressa and Mawnie on Sentinel's Peak, the wooded promontory behind the three sisters' family home, Saroon. He knew that Mawnie's twin, Ressa, had died as a result. But neither he nor anyone else save Issul knew of the child that had been born to Ressa after her death. 'Mawnie, you are not to blame for what happened in the woods. It was a long time ago. You must put it from your mind.'

'But I have to tell you. I wanted to tell Issul, but she is not here, so I must tell you. You see, it spoke.'

Leth frowned. 'Who? What?'

Mawnie suddenly froze, her eyes wide with fear. 'The – the thing. It told me. It told Ressa.'

'What did it tell you, Mawnie?' Leth held her cold hands. She was beginning to shake. Beginning to whimper.

'Oh, it told us it was going to destroy us all. Destroy us all. It said it had come from Enchantment and that the world would soon know why. Oh Leth, I was so *frightened!* It killed Ressa. It killed sweet Ressa. It should have been me. Oh, why, why wasn't it me?'

She was distraught, drained, limp with sorrow, then suddenly rigid, trying to turn away from something only she saw, her body making spasmodic jerks, her mouth wide in a rictus of terror.

An anguished, gasping scream was squeezed from the back of her throat. She drew back, then tore her hands free and began to fight.

Leth held her. She fought against him, but he held her so that she could not move. She bit his neck. He cried out in pain. A nurse came to his assistance and they wrestled Mawnie to the bed as she struggled and howled.

Doctor Melropius applied a salve to the wound on Leth's neck and the King departed. Mawnie's words had made no sense to him. Her assailant on Sentinel's Peak, whatever it was that had caused Ressa's subsequent death, had never been found, and the incident had faded from most people's minds. Leth could conceive of no reason why it should resurface now, other than that it had plainly left a painful and indelible scar upon Mawnie's memory. Except . . . Mawnie's statement that it claimed to have come from Enchantment made him uneasy. But he put the matter from his mind, the better that he might concentrate upon his meeting with Grey Venger.

In the middle of the evening, a couple of hours after darkness had descended upon Enchantment's Edge, Lord Fectur announced that Grey Venger was safely within his custody.

'Did it go smoothly?' asked Leth.

'Perfectly, Sire. We established that we would await him outside the inn of the Tinted Domes, close upon the edge of Overlip. A password was agreed and passed to him via an intermediary, calling himself Iklar, who is also the man with whom the Queen made contact in the Tavern of the Veiled Light. By this means we were identified by Venger's followers. Venger emerged from a nearby house and gave himself over. The house is now under surveillance.'

'Hardly necessary at this juncture, I would have thought.'

Fectur shrugged.

'Were you present when Venger gave himself over?'

'On an issue so important I deemed my attendance as your official representative imperative,' replied Fectur coldly.

Leth wondered at that, wondered whether words had passed between the two. There was no point in asking. Neither Fectur or Grey Venger could be relied upon to give him an honest reply.

'Where is he now?'

'Under guard in my guest's quarters.'

'But not under restraint.'

'None. Of course, he is confined to his chamber. He has dined – with some relish – and now reclines in comfort, awaiting your summons.'

'Did he drink?'

'He did. Good Aucos red, in some quantity. He seemed to lack concern for the effect it might have upon his tongue.'

Leth breathed deeply. Venger wanted to talk! 'Bring him here, then, Fectur.'

'Here? Do you intend to interrogate him in your private apartments?'

'It is a meeting of minds, not an interrogation.'

'But would a more formal environment not be more appropriate?'

'Informality will be more conducive.'

'But Sire, there are no guards here.'

'Quite.'

'I will substitute my own men for your house-servants.'

'You will not, Fectur. I am dismissing the servants.'

'You cannot intend to seclude yourself here alone with Grey Venger!'

'That is precisely what I do intend. Venger will do me no harm.'

'No! No! Sire, if you will permit no guards I must insist upon being present myself.'

'Certainly not!'

'My lord, I have the right to insist. Your welfare is my concern.'

Leth stared him in the eye. Fectur was unflinching. 'Fectur, you jeopardize everything!'

'Your life is in my hands,' said Fectur, with weight.

'Do not overstep yourself. The future of Enchantment's Edge quite possibly rests upon the outcome of this meeting.'

'The Lord High Invigilate is charged with the well-being of the sovereign in order to protect the welfare of the kingdom. To leave you alone with this man would be an indefensible dereliction of my duties.'

Leth fumed silently to himself. 'Bring him here.'

IV

'We were to speak alone, *Leth*. That was my understanding,' declared Grey Venger, turning daggered eyes to Fectur.

'The Lord High Invigilate insists, against my wishes, that he must be present,' Leth replied.

'I have nothing to say in his presence.'

'Master Venger—' Fectur began.

Grey Venger, garbed in his customary grey, turned away, his arms folded. 'You have broken the terms of our agreement, King Leth. I will say nothing if we are not alone.'

'It is not I, Venger,' said Leth.

'You are King and sovereign.'

'Even so . . . You are aware of the circumstances that press upon me.'

Venger addressed Fectur. 'You may escort me back.'

'Master Venger, I—'

'*You may escort me back!*'

Fectur stiffened in inexpressible fury, faint red welts appearing about his temples and jaw.

Leth looked at him, concealing his satisfaction. 'Well, there you have it, Lord Fectur. It has all been for nothing.'

'My lord, this man has tried to murder you.'

'Aye. But an understanding has been reached between Grey Venger and myself. Grey Venger has declared his willingness to impart, in the first instance only to me, information that may prove vital to the state. He deems me capable of judging its relevance and validity, and declares his unwillingness for any other person to be present. The circumstances are unusual, but I have agreed to his terms. Later you may be made party to all relevant details of what passes between us. For now, I ask once more that you reconsider your position, bearing in mind that your refusal could represent a threat to our nation.'

Fectur gripped the arms of his seat, his knuckles white, contrasting with his bulging face. Then he stood, almost quivering. He gave a barely perceptible nod, and turned to walk with stiff-backed formality from the chamber.

Leth basked for a moment. He looked at Venger, hoping to see perhaps a hint of a mutuality of feeling, of shared endeavour, but Venger's eyes were as hard as glass.

The leader of the True Sept sat before Leth and regarded him coldly. 'Does it not strike you as odd, *Leth,* that I should come here on such a flimsy pretext as that put forward by you, and offer you secrets that have not been revealed in centuries?'

'I simply assume that you have seen the sense, indeed the necessity, of my argument.'

Venger gave a harsh laugh. 'Not so. At least, not as you perceive it. No. Firstly I will say, I am irrelevant. Should you betray me, all that I know has been passed to another. My imprisonment or death will not harm the True Sept. We would in fact become stronger. But there is another reason. The simple fact is: *it has begun.* The Legendary Child *is* here, as was foretold. History will now unfold in the manner foreseen by our wise and holy forefathers. Nothing you or anyone else can do will change that now. For my part it is enough that I observe your face as I reveal the One Truth to you. And I will take great pleasure in hearing you admit publicly that you have been wrong.'

'You are so sure?' queried Leth, his nerves stretched. 'What is your evidence?'

'The signs. Everything accords with the prophecies of the founding fathers of the True Sept. Everything.'

'Give me examples'

'No. Not yet. First, Leth, I will hear you.'

Leth hesitated. 'I have little to offer you, Venger. As I indicated to you in Overlip, we found the Child – one whom we are informed must be the Child – but we have lost him.'

'The Child in whom you do not believe,' taunted Venger. 'But you spoke of his background.'

'I hope I have not implied a greater knowledge than I actually possess. The truth is that the matter is shrouded in mystery.' Leth paused, aware that he was about to venture into territory only suggested to him during his meeting with Orbus earlier. He was keen to observe the minutest response in Venger. 'I have learned that the Child is almost certainly born of a human mother—'

It hit him then like a cudgel blow. Mawnie! *Ressa!* Was that what Mawnie had been talking about?

Ressa had been raped by a monster unknown!

His mind spun. This explained Issul's certainty. She had known! Issul had known! The child had survived, she had suspected something, had hidden it away with the peasant family!

He considered this for a moment, then tried to reject the idea. How could it be so? Ressa had died of her injuries weeks after that event. She had never been pregnant.

He thought back, desperately trying to recall the details surrounding that tragic day. He had not seen Ressa after the attack. She was confined to her chambers in Saroon. She had few visitors other than immediate family. Leth could have visited her, of course, but formal duties had occupied him and he had not made the journey. He had preferred to await her recovery, for at the time she had been expected to recover. It was a month after the rape that her health had quite suddenly deteriorated, and soon afterwards she had died.

But there had been no pregnancy.

Or had Issul kept something from him all this time?

Where else could the newborn babe which Issul had placed in the care of the peasant woman, Ohirbe, have come from? Logically, he reasoned, almost anywhere – but why? What other cause would have possessed Issul to act so secretively?

No, no. It was too far-fetched. He was over-imaginative. There had been no time for gestation before Ressa died.

But would godspawn gestate in the normal human span?

Leth shook his head, stunned and prevented from thinking clearly.

'You were saying?'

Grey Venger's voice jolted him back to awareness of himself. He thought again, rapidly, again committing himself to uncertain ground. 'And . . . we may have a description of the god who is its father.'

Venger tried to show indifference, but Leth detected a new degree of tension in his posture. 'The god appeared?'

Leth nodded. 'It may be worth little, of course, for who knows how many forms a god may adopt?'

Leth recalled the description of Ressa's assailant. Both Mawnie and Issul had described it. For a moment he wondered about the wisdom of revealing the description to Grey Venger, then did so anyway. 'It was man-like but far more powerful than a man. Its skin was bluish-silver-grey, its eyes crimson. It had a tail, and knobbled spines extending the length of its spine.'

'That is little to go on,' said Grey Venger, but his attitude had undergone another subtle change and he was plainly more intrigued than he wished to convey.

Leth gave a nod. 'As I say, much is mystery and I rely upon you to fill in the gaps.'

His thoughts were racing insanely, trying to piece together a picture that did not want to fall into place. *It could not have been a god. According to Orbus the gods cannot survive outside Enchantment.*

That is, not for long . . .

What other explanation was there? And not for the first time the thought hit him: *I have always taken Orbus at his word. But how do I know he is to be believed?*

'Did it speak?'

'It told of destruction, that it had come out of Enchantment, that the world would soon know why.'

Venger absorbed this, leaning back in his seat, seeming to weigh him up. Leth said, 'You spoke of signs.'

Venger was silent for a while longer, then, 'I will tell you this: when your messenger sent word into Overlip that the Child had been found, we were not surprised. I had been waiting for this moment, seeing that everything was in place.'

'You have still not said what things.'

Venger suddenly rose, threw his head back and his arms wide, and began to intone, almost as though gripped in a trance. 'The time will be drawn by the sins of the Godless. It will be known by the Righteous Powers which will range themselves against the Unbelievers. All will be aligned to fight the Great Battle so that the King Without A Soul may be ousted. He will struggle in his terror and his oppression of the Righteous will be great and cruel. There will be times when it will seem that he has succeeded, but it will not be so. The Righteous will achieve ultimate victory over the Godless.

'So watch. A Child will come, the Child of Legend, born when the King without a Soul rises. Born of Righteousness, the vengeful spawn of the Highest of the High Ones. The Child of Legend will restore the True Faith, through blood and turmoil, through destruction never known before. The gods themselves will war outside their domain, for such is the insult of the King without a Soul, whose soul has been cast away. They will join with those of the outlands and all will march against him. The Unbelievers will be wiped from the world so that Righteous peace may be restored. And the Legendary Child, the Child of the True Faith, will be supreme over all. All will know his name, and the land will become the domain of the One True God once again.' Venger stopped, his face sheened with perspiration, and glared at Leth with a venom that was almost palpable. 'There is more, much more, but you will not hear it.'

'From where do these words come?' asked Leth, apprehensively.

'From the Screed of the One and True Sept, Ancient and Revered.'

'I have many questions.'

'I know. I will hear them, and judge.'

'Do you have power over the Child, if it is found?'

'Ha! The Child empowers the True Sept. It will know its own followers.'

'Who, by your account, is the One True God?'

'You will all know soon enough.'

'Had you succeeded in assassinating me, would the Child still have come?'

'There is no question of that. My failure to kill you was a prerequisite.'

'A pre—' Leth was astonished. 'Do you mean my death was never intended?'

'It is written that when the Child is already in the world, the King without a Soul will be seen to escape death at the hands of a Servant of the Truth. That act, combined with the other signs, will tell the faithful that the final days of the godless are close.'

'You—I cannot take this in—you deliberately faked the attempt upon my life, and then allowed your sons to die!'

Venger's lip curled. 'I told you before, Leth, you can know nothing of the weight that is upon me. The Grey Venger puts himself aside in order to do what must be done for the Greater Truth.'

Leth stared in mute disbelief, deep into that tortured, terrible face. This was fanaticism more extreme than he could fathom, and within himself he reeled, repelled by it.

'Do you understand my hatred for you, Leth? Your existence has been the force that has shaped mine. Your godlessness infests the world, bringing misery and decay, killing the Faithful whose only crime has been to be born into the wrong time.'

'And if I died, now? What then would be achieved?'

'No. You cannot die now, not by my hand or the hand of any other mortal. You are without a soul, it has been cast away. Thus the world can only be purged of your presence and your taint by one qualified to perform that act. But first you must live to see the destruction you have wrought, to witness the extirpation of your people and your kind. All of them will be punished. And when they have gone, to the last man and woman, only then can the True Faith be restored, the Faithful dwell again and the Highest Ones rule once more.'

Leth struggled to make connections that just eluded his grasp. Something was ringing clamorously in his mind. The King without a Soul, whose soul has been cast away. Venger applied it to him, Leth, but Venger knew nothing of Orbus, a god whose soul had been taken from him.

Somewhere in the True Sept's credo, amongst the babble, the hyperbole, the dogma, the rhetoric, were there genuine references to what was happening now?

Not for the first time in recent days Leth felt that the world had spun askew. Unseen forces moved to shape events, and he had been pushed into the position of a mere witness, a victim, even an unwitting instrument. Could he, now, change anything?

V

Leth felt half mad when he left his chamber and made for Pader Luminis's apartment high in the White Eaglet's Tower. Grey Venger had been escorted to his guest apartment, expressing tiredness. Leth wished to speak with him again very soon, but first he needed to talk to a sane man, someone he trusted.

'It does not undermine the Deist Edict, if that is what you fear,' said Pader when he had heard all. 'At the heart of the Edict is the self-evident truth that we do not know the gods or their wishes. I have heard nothing so far to convince me that the True Sept knows otherwise.'

'But their prophecies are coming true.'

'Prophecies? They have always claimed oracular knowledge, secrets ancient and profound, but apart from the rumour of the Child they have revealed nothing until now, when the facts are assembled for all to see.'

'But they know of the coming of the Child, and that the Child is born of a god. That is prophetic.'

'But we need not necessarily infer contact with or knowledge of the gods,' said Pader. 'Let us say that, a millenium ago, a man or woman attempting to study the mysteries of Enchantment dreamed a dream. That person might have been entranced, drugged, soused, half-mad, or simply foolish. He dreamed that a god spoke directly to him and imparted a message for humanity. Transported, the dreamer woke, did not know he had slumbered, believed the dream was real and rushed to tell his fellows the wondrous news. Most disbelieved him, laughed in his face, called him mad. But a few wondered otherwise. The few told their friends. Before he knew it the dreamer, perhaps now outcast from his own society, had followers in some number. One or two among these wrote down the dreamer's words and broadcast them as far afield as they might. Years passed, the dreamer became famous, and eventually died. But his words remained, as did his followers and the children of his followers. More words were added to the dreamer's original words; perhaps a few unscrupulous men inserted phrases of their own, seeking in them a way to personal fame, influence and wealth. Perhaps phrases were added in a genuine attempt to clarify or better understand the original, or to include knowledge or beliefs drawn from other sources. It matters little in essence. The words were powerful, the descendants of the dreamer determined to spread them and gather more followers. The generations succeeded one another . . . a religion had been born, taken seed and spread its roots and branches. But at no time had contact been made with a god.'

'All on the dream of a drunkard,' mused Leth sombrely.

'Or the sincere and genuine effort of an individual seeking to make sense of Mystery. We do not automatically infer malice at the outset, rather that in our desperation to explain Mystery any one of us may be drawn to unreliable conclusions. Like you, Leth, my goal is Knowledge and Truth. But Mystery confronts us at every pass and is perhaps the natural state. Some answers may never be found, others only create greater and more profound questions. For many, many people the concept of Mystery without answers is too terrifying to bear. They seek reasons for their being, as do we, and sometimes it may be far easier and more comforting to put absolute faith in answers that do not bear serious questioning than to follow the path of Knowledge. The dream of a madman can be seductive. So can that of a genuine visionary, even though his dream may have been re-shaped by generations of other men seeing a way to power.'

'Still,' added Leth after a moment's contemplation, 'that does not explain the Sept's knowledge of the coming of the Child.'

'You are wrong. A dreamer dreamed a dream. Others embellished it. It became the core of a politico-religious faith. Then, as certain factors appeared to coincide with the belief, other factors were manipulated. The stage-management of your "assassination" attempt, for example. Who knows what else the Sept has stage-managed? Even the declaration that outlanders will join with the gods to oppose us, if seen in a clear light, is a generalization open to many interpretations. It does not necessarily refer to the Krai. And the Sept is so secretive: how do we know that the sacred words Grey Venger revealed to you were not written last week?'

Pader Luminis chuckled loudly at this, and the thought brought a smile to Leth's lips too. Then Pader added, 'Even if the Sept's founders were genuinely gifted crystal-gazers, that is not proof of godly favouritism. These are momentous revelations, but they are not evidence of divine communion.'

Leth nodded to himself, thinking, *Yes, for the gods are not gods. And I am the only one who knows it.*

How he longed to confide to Pader now. Did he dare? Into his mind sprang the memory of almost his last conversation with his dear mother, Queen Fallorn. He saw the stricken look upon her face, the tears in her eyes: 'Many times I wanted to tell you, and you will wish the same in future days. But I could not, and I knew I could not, and you will do the same. Even in your darkest hours, when your very soul cries to confide in someone, you must not do it. Not until the day comes – if it comes – when you will pass the casket on to your heir.'

The memory shook him, and on its tail came that of another voice, the warning voice of Orbus: 'Reveal the source of your wisdom and you will be rendered powerless. Others would seek access to your source by any means. You would lose me, and it would be a loss greater than you can calculate.'

He clamped shut his jaw. Orbus's voice continued to sound in his mind: 'Should you be the one, the one who does eventually destroy the Orb, then for your sake and the sake of your people and all that you hold dear, be absolutely sure of one thing: *that you know what it contains!*'

Leth grew aware that Pader Luminis was watching him. He swept back his hair, suddenly weary. 'Ressa, Pader. Is it possible that she was the mother of the Legendary Child?'

Pader Luminis bowed his near-bald head. 'Oh, this is disturbing. This is distressing. The poor child, she suffered so. But until we have the lost Child, or until Queen Issul returns and informs us, we can really know nothing.'

Leth scratched himself. He wanted to speak of the King without a Soul. The True Sept appeared to have at least some distorted inkling of Orbus's fall eons ago. But their credo seemed to have grown around the mistaken belief that it was he, Leth, King of Enchantment's Edge, whose soul was lost. But he could not pursue that issuc with Pader, not without revealing Orbus's existence.

'Tomorrow I am interviewing Venger in the small counsel room on the first level of the custodial wing. There is a listening-chamber there. It might serve us well if you secrete yourself within it and hear what Venger has to say.'

'Very good.'

Leth rose slowly, yawned and stretched. 'I am more tired tonight than I have felt in a long time.'

'I put a potion in your tea.'

'You did what?'

The little Murinean grinned. 'You will sleep well tonight, Leth, and be better equipped to deal with the problems the morning brings. But if I have done wrong, if I have offended you, please execute me now.'

Leth went briefly to his study. He opened the compartment in the wall and looked at the blue casket, the casket that was the Orb, that was Orbus's world, that was also Orbus. His eyelids were heavy, he was pleasantly drowsy, too tired to bring the casket forth. Tomorrow he would meet with Venger again, and then he would report the results of the two meetings to Orbus. But for now he wanted only to sleep.

FIFTEEN

I

Armed with the conclusions he had drawn with Pader Luminis, and refreshed and fortified by a night of deep and undisturbed sleep, Leth did feel better-equipped for another meeting with Grey Venger when he rose the following morning. The previous day he had approached his adversary feeling nervous, daunted, even – if he would admit it – afraid. Not of Venger himself, but of what their meeting could portend. And the revelations Venger had subsequently thrown at him, plus his own sudden cognition of Ressa's terrible role, had cast him into ever greater turmoil and shock.

But today he was clearer. Venger was not the giant he had been. Leth could view his pronouncements in a more proper perspective. To some extent Venger was even discredited, and this gave Leth some heart. Venger was not himself aware of it, and his fanatical, blind belief in himself and the creed of the True Sept likely ensured that he never would be. But that was not necessarily an obstacle. Leth saw that he needed to draw him out, to discover whether he was genuinely in possession of information in regard to the Legendary Child which Leth could use, or whether in fact the True Sept's beliefs were founded partially or entirely on falsehoods, superstitions and amended scriptures – or, as Pader Luminis had put it, 'the dreams of a dreamer who may not have known that he dreamed'. If any of the latter were shown to be the case, then Venger's and the True Sept's role in this intricate business might be as good as over.

Voluble in his rhetoric, Venger had yet withheld a great deal yesterday. More exactly, he had given the impression of withholding.

Perhaps he had nothing more to give, but Leth had to be sure, one way or the other, before he could dismiss him. To this end Leth felt it desirable to let Venger bask in the semi-illusion that he still had control. Like any man, Venger was at his best when he believed himself respected, perhaps even feared, and most of all needed.

Leth went first to his childrens' chamber. They were awake, Galry leaping up and down upon his bed, shouting, ignoring the demands of his nanny, Mistress Flenda, for calm. Jace was playing quietly with her doll. Little Lir was curled in her cot, sleeping still, or pretending to do so.

At the sight of his father Galry stopped jumping and ran to leap into his arms. 'Daddy! Daddy!'

Jace looked up and smiled – again Leth was reminded so strongly of Issul. Taking her doll she came to him with her arms raised. Balancing Galry on one hip Leth lifted Jace onto the other.

'When is Mummy coming home?' asked Jace.

'Soon, my sweet.'

'But when? I want to see her. I miss her.'

Leth gazed into her wide, limpid green eyes. 'And I know she misses you, my darling. Both of you. And I know she is doing everything in her power to speed her journey back to us.'

He turned, intending to carry them to breakfast.

'Uncle Leth.'

He turned back. Little Lir had stirred and was kneeling up in her cot. Her elfin face was slightly tilted, her dark tousled curls falling over her forehead, her eyes deep green and bright. 'Uncle Leth, why do you say that?'

'Why? Because I believe it to be true, Lir.'

'But you don't know it.'

He looked at her in some surprise. She was two years old. He had never heard her speak so before.

'Aunt Issul might be dead.'

'Lir!'

Galry and Jace set up a barrage of protest. 'No! Don't say that! Mummy isn't dead. She's coming home, isn't she, Daddy? Isn't she?'

'Of course she is,' replied Leth tensely. 'Lir, what makes you say such a thing?'

Lir became interested in the fluted rail spanning the rim of her cot. 'I have heard people saying.'

'What people?'

'Servants. They think I don't listen or understand them, but I do.'

'I shall speak to the servants.'

'They say my Mummy is mad, too.'

'Do they?' Leth's brow creased. 'Do you know what that means?'

'Of course. She has lost her mind. And it's true, isn't it, Uncle Leth?'

Leth drew a long breath, disconcerted by the tiny child. She should not have been capable of understanding such concepts. As far as he had been aware Lir had command of no more than a few basic phrases and sentences. Uncomfortably he said, 'No, it isn't true, Lir. Your Mummy has been taken ill, but she should be better quite soon. I'm sure she will be. Now, we are all going to breakfast. Would you like me to carry you too? I think I can just about manage three.'

Lir gave a pout then shook her head. She settled back and snuggled beneath her covers again.

II

An hour later King Leth gave Sir Cathbo his final instructions and bade him farewell. Two companies of troops had still to ride south. Cathbo would lead the last company out of Enchantment's Edge, late in the morning.

Sir Cathbo had been gone but a few minutes when Leth was told that Lord Fectur waited outside. He suppressed a groan. He had wanted to avoid Fectur, at least until after he had spoken with Grey Venger again. His concentration was sharp and he felt ready for Venger. It nettled him, but he acknowledged that his hope of staying clear of Fectur had really been unrealistic from the outset.

Fectur entered as though hurled from a ballista, his voice loud and forceful. 'Sire, I was expecting word from you last night, or at the very latest first thing this morning.'

'I don't know why, Fectur. I gave you no reason.'

'You agreed to apprise me of details of your meeting with Grey Venger.'

'And so I shall, when the time is right.'

'I think that is now, Sire,' said Fectur, uncharacteristically displaying his agitation. 'I am Master of Security, after all, and this is an issue of highest value to the Crown.'

'My business with Grey Venger is not yet concluded, Fectur. When it is, and I am satisfied that I have all the relevant information to hand, I shall summon you. Meanwhile, if you will excuse me . . .'

'I happen to know that you have confided in another. It would have been proper to have come to me first.'

Leth stiffened. 'Pader Luminis was, in my opinion, the man most qualified to provide me with the answers I sought after last night's meeting. My judgement was not misplaced, nor was it anyone else's concern.'

Momentarily he wondered whether Fectur had approached Pader Luminis directly, whether he had with veiled threats or subterfuge drawn from him details of their conversation. But he satisfied himself that it was more likely that one of Fectur's spies had simply reported the meeting. If Fectur knew what had been said his approach now would have taken a different turn.

'Sire, in a matter as important as this the Lord High Invigilate has every right to be fully informed. I take great exception to your decision to exclude me from yestereve's interview, and consider your failure to consult me afterwards indefensible.'

'And I take exception to your interfering!' snapped Leth, his temper breaking. 'You will be informed and consulted at the proper time, Fectur, and not before. Do you understand?'

Lord Fectur took a deep breath. He thrust his jaw forward and linked hands behind his back. 'I understand perfectly, Sire. I understand also that it is perhaps your actions, rather than mine, that may be endangering the state at this time.'

Leth fought back his rage. 'What is that supposed to mean?'

'Simply that your judgement at present leaves some room for question. Perhaps not surprisingly, considering the pressure you are under. But of course, your enemies will not consider that.'

'You overstep yourself, Fectur!'

Fectur appraised him, his lips compressed. 'I merely advise

proper consultation. You are acting entirely on your own, more and more. It is not a wise course, and I am not the only one aware of it.'

'I am acting in the manner I judge best suited to the circumstances. I am not helped by the persistent attentions of persons whose motives I am not always entirely certain of. We will speak later of this, Fectur. For now, be good enough to step aside. I have a meeting to attend.'

All the good work done by Leth's night of sound sleep had been undone. He strode from that brief, unscheduled meeting with Fectur seething with anger. He felt himself in no state to deal effectively with Venger now, and halted outside the small counselling chamber where Venger waited. He closed his eyes, breathing deeply and gathering his thoughts before entering.

'The King Without a Soul, Venger. You say his soul – my soul, as you put it – has been cast away. Do you know where, or how?'

If Venger was aware of Leth's inner fury he gave no sign. 'Your soul was cast away at birth, Leth. So it is written, for the gods judged you unfit to house such purity. Without a soul you should not have lived, yet the power of your malevolence is such that you did.'

'Then where is the Soul now?'

'The One God sealed it in a crucible of shining adamant, and guards it in his sanctum high in his fortress in Enchantment.'

'And if it was returned to me, what then?'

'That cannot be!'

'Is anything written that tells of what would happen?'

Venger's hard eyes narrowed. 'It cannot be.'

'What is the name of the One god who guards it?'

'Seek not to draw secrets that may not be drawn, Leth. The One God is the One God. That is all you may know.'

'I detect a conflict here, Venger. You say that the Legendary Child will be supreme over all, but also that the land will become the domain of the One True God once again. Is this not a contradiction?'

Venger straightened his spine, folding his arms upon his chest. 'The One God is the father of the Child.'

'They are to rule together?'

'As one,' replied Venger, 'in Unity. The Child will be among us to reveal the way of the Father.'

His arms had tightened; Leth sensed his discomfort. There was something here that Venger was not sure about, or did not want to speak of.

Fearful that he might wholly alienate Venger if he pressed the point, Leth shifted to a different tack. 'Let us talk of the Krai for a moment, Venger. They storm nations, emboldened by the patronage of a god. Is it the One True God who favours them?'

'The Krai are outlanders, ranged with others to combat your evil, just as it was written.'

'But what is their connection? Do they, or their god, seek the Child? If so, why?'

Venger shifted in his seat. 'They have their reasons. It is not for the Grey Venger to reveal.'

'Is that so? Or are you simply unwilling to admit that you do not know?'

Venger thrust himself erect, his eyes ablaze. 'The Grey Venger has secrets! Fantastic secrets! The One and True Sept knows all! But to the King Without A Soul some things may never be imparted!'

'The True Sept has attempted illicit contact with the Krai,' said Leth. 'That is a crime in itself, enough to condemn you and your followers to death as spies.'

'I have told you, I have no fear of death at your hands, Leth. My death will not harm the True Sept. We are as water, ever elusive to the grasp of one such as you.'

'Very good. But I hoped and believed that our mutual aim was to work together to find a way to restore the Sept.'

Grey Venger gave a cynical laugh. 'Do you think the Grey Venger is so easily gulled, Leth? You have no intention of restoring the True Sept. Why would you?'

'My intention is to save Enchantment's Edge. I will do anything in my power to accomplish that.'

Venger shook his head with a haughty and contemptuous smile. 'It is far too late for that. Far too late. Already it has begun. It cannot be stopped now. You are doomed, Leth, as are all who have listened to you.'

Leaving the chamber of counsel King Leth turned from the main corridor and passed along a passage leading eventually towards the residential wing. A blue gonfalon upon a wall twitched then billowed as he passed, and Pader Luminis stepped out from behind it. He closed the small portal at the back of the gonfalon, checked that it was concealed, and fell into step beside Leth.

'You heard all?' asked Leth.

Pader nodded. 'It is a jumble. Vaguenesses and evasions. It is impossible to know whether there is anything there that can be genuinely relied upon. Venger does give the impression of having more to give, but it may be an act. I don't doubt that he believes everything he is telling you. It is the belief of a lifetime, of generations. For him it must be true, for it shapes his world. As a child he would never have been permitted to question it; as an adult he is no longer capable. But there are intriguing aspects to what he says. You should speak with him again later, I think. In the meantime I shall apply myself to the Arcane College to seek information on the One True God and the King Without A Soul.'

'I am beginning to suspect he knows nothing more about the Legendary Child.'

Pader scratched his nose. 'It is possible. Or he may be waiting.'

'For what?'

'Something more from you, perhaps. Or a sign from the Child itself.'

'He speaks of the King's Soul being sealed in a crucible within Enchantment,' Leth mused, half to himself. 'Is it possible that there is something in Enchantment that might aid us?'

'We do not lack for tales of Enchantment's marvels, but in the end what good do they do us? A lost soul within a crucible of adamant? Perhaps, but it is beyond our reach.'

They parted and Leth continued on towards the royal apartments, wanting to spend some time with his children again.

The day passed; Sir Cathbo departed Enchantment's Edge with his detachment of élite troops. Leth watched them go with a tingling in his stomach. Could they accomplish anything? Sir Cathbo's instructions were precise. His task was to harry and hinder, make lightning strikes and vanish, in a manner similar to that of the Krai to date. To anger Anzejarl was the goal, to use his own methods to goad him in the hope that he would make an uncharacteristic move. It was just possible that what could not be achieved by an army on the wide field of battle might be done by a smaller, mobile force which never struck in the same place twice.

There was no chance of actually defeating the Krai by this

method; it was a testing time, nothing more. Leth needed to try Anzejarl's defences and reactions, and gain firsthand intelligence as to the deployment and discipline of his troops. A small, highly mobile force should achieve that.

Or were his men riding to their deaths? Leth felt the weight of their lives upon him. Was it Anzejarl who had goaded Leth into uncharacteristic action? Were his intelligence units already apprising him of the movements of Sir Cathbo's troops? Was he even now preparing to snare them?

Leth paced his chamber, his head bowed, profound apprehension and nervous exultation warring within him. He felt now, with deepening certainty, that he was on the edge of something. Or beyond, in fact. He had stepped over, committed himself. It was as though he had until now been poised upon the battlements of one of the highest towers upon the great outer wall of Enchantment's Edge, and now the stone was no longer beneath his feet.

Had he stepped over, or been pushed? He was unclear, but he knew he was not quite falling. He was suspended above the great forest, which was like a swelling sea so far, far below. He was borne upon the wind, with nothing beneath. At any moment he could plummet to certain death an infinite distance below, yet ever terrifyingly close; or he could somehow command the wind, or himself as he rode it. Yoke the forces that had both propelled him from the Edge and now bore him up. Or be destroyed by them.

Leth gave an anguished cry, pressing his hands to his temples. 'How? How? I am but one man!'

He sank to his knees. 'The gods toy with me! They seek my end!'

He was slipping, then; the unseen wind no longer willing to bear him, the ground far below pulling him to it. He glanced back. Upon the grey battlements his enemies watched. The creased white face of Prince Anzejarl, jewel-eyed and expressionless, a mysterious red-headed beauty at his shoulder; Grey Venger, tensely exultant, a bony fist raised. And a short distance off, not so very far from the others: Fectur.

'No! No! You will not destroy me!' Leth saw his children, Galry and Jace, further along the parapet. They were calling him. Issul stood a way behind them. Issul, Issul. *She had to be alive!*

Leth scrambled breathless to his feet, banishing the images of his foes from his mind, clinging only to the thought of his children and their mother. There was a knock upon the door. Leth quickly recovered himself, stood firm. 'Enter.'

His head steward, Ardenmor, came in. 'His Excellency the Lord High Invigilate instructs me to inform you that the assembly awaits you in the Hall of Wise Counsel, my lord.'

Leth frowned. 'I have no meeting scheduled, with Fectur or anyone else.'

'That was his instruction to me, my lord. He did add that I should stress that your presence is eagerly awaited.'

'Who else attends with Fectur?'

'I am not informed. I simply bear the message.'

Leth quickly left the chamber and went to his office. There he checked with his secretary, fearing for a moment that his memory had played him false or his staff had failed to keep him informed. But his first impressions were borne out: he had no meeting scheduled at this time.

Curious, Leth made his way directly to the Hall of Wise Counsel. He entered through the main double door at the rear of the hall, rather than passing on to the side portal which was by custom the monarch's entrance and which led directly to the dais upon which the Seat of the Sovereign was set. As he passed through the doors he stopped short in shock.

About forty persons occupied the Hall of Wise Counsel. They were dignitaries, members of the Crown's Advisory Committee, men – and some women – of very high station. The heads and deputies of all the recognized factions were among them, with the exception of the True Sept, indicating the extraordinary nature of this convention. Pader Luminis was noticeably absent. Around the walls were positioned a score of guards from the Security Cadre.

All rose as the King came in, though they did so without hurry, almost casually, and their faces as they turned towards him were almost uniformly solemn, even stony.

Leth's gut twisted, but he strode forward. 'What is this?'

Fectur rose and stepped forward. 'Sire.' He performed a deep bow, his eyes never leaving Leth's face, a chill, fulsome smile upon his lips. With one arm he gestured towards the Seat of the Sovereign.

Leth hesitated, then moved past him and ascended the three steps to the dais and seated himself. He felt vulnerable and alone; no other person occupied the dais, as would have been proper. Even

Fectur remained upon the floor. Leth scanned the faces arrayed before him. He saw and felt only coldness, with the exception of Doctor Melropius who looked tense and uncomfortable, and one or two senior knights.

'This is highly irregular,' he said, addressing all. 'I was not informed of any assembly. Would you mind telling me what this is about?'

'It is an assembly convoked under exceptional circumstances,' replied Fectur, still standing. 'Convoked as a matter of urgency, in response to a matter of unusual concern. As you see, a majority of the Governing Council is present, as is the Crown Advisory Committee and as are senior representatives of the citizenry.'

'Well, please enlighten me as to the reason. It seems that all are informed but the King.'

Fectur considered the marble mosaic in front of his feet for a few moments, then looked up. 'Considerable debate has passed between our members, severally and *in toto*, over the past days and nights. A single issue concerns us. I will be candid and to the point: we, the assembled, representing the government and people of Enchantment's Edge, are gravely troubled by the manner in which you, our King, have chosen to exercise your responsibilities in recent days. Our nation lies beneath a dark cloud of conflict, and we consider that you have not acted to its or our best advantage. Serious doubts have been raised as to your state of mind and ability to rule.'

The words slammed into Leth like a battering-ram. For a moment he felt himself pushed back in his chair as if by a mighty, unseen hand. His lungs had constricted, he clenched his fists upon the arms of his chair. An unspeakable rage surged within him, but at the same time it was checked by a raw, gut-churning fear. No words came for some moments. His blood pounded in his skull and he saw nothing but Fectur standing below him, bland, complacent and utterly sure of himself.

I know what this is, Fectur! Curse you, you will not succeed!

He could scarcely believe they had gone so far.

'There is nothing wrong with the state of my mind!' he finally stammered, and was aware of how inadequate those words were.

Fectur clasped his hands before him and pushed forward his chin. 'How I hope that may be so, Sire. But your conduct of late . . . well, you are under immense pressure. We all accept that. You require rest. Your own physician, Doctor Melropius, has expressed as much to me. He tells me, however, that you have ignored his advice and refused medication.'

Leth switched his glance to Melropius, who sat hunched in embarrassment, one hand to his brow. Leth imagined the scene: Fectur approaching Melropius, brimful with solicitude for the King. And Melropius, innocent that he was, expressing his concern, never for a moment suspecting that his words would require him to stand witness against Leth.

'Is that not so, Doctor?' Fectur enquired.

Melropius flushed deeply and could not raise his eyes. 'Th – that was my – that is, I said as much to you, my lord. But I was not—'

'Thank you, Doctor.' Fectur grasped the lapels of his gown and placed his feet well-apart. 'King Leth, I speak as the voice of all assembled. You have been found to be in dereliction of your duties. The unanimous decision of this Assembly is to declare you unfit to rule. I hereby list all faults, defaults and omissions of which you stand accused, and to which you will be required to answer. One: that you have—'

Leth exploded, thrusting himself to his feet. 'This is outrageous! Fectur, I have warned you already, you have overstepped yourself! Desist immediately, or you will pay dearly. I will have you flayed alive! All of you – you are committing an act of treason!'

'You are wrong, Sire,' said Fectur smoothly. 'Under the powers invested in me as Lord High Invigilate, Master of Security for the Realm, Deputy to the Crown and Protector of the Crown and the People, I have every right. My primary duty is twofold: to ensure that the stability of the nation is not threatened by any means, and to attend myself by all means at my disposal to the safety and welfare of the incumbent monarch and his or her immediate heirs. As we stand at this moment, I see the nation threatened on many fronts. I see also that your health is a cause of no little concern, that your judgement shows all indications of being severely impaired, that in short you are yourself a threat to our beloved nation and to yourself. Sire, I have taken counsel and received support. I am temporarily relieving you of your right to rule and installing myself as Regent in your stead until such time as you are adjudged fit once more.'

Leth's jaw fell wide. He stared dumbly at Fectur, shocked beyond expression. Fectur returned his stare blandly. Leth's legs had turned warm and watery; he knew only that all was lost and that his hatred for Fectur radiated from the innermost core of every fibre of his being.

'You have the right to reply, Sire. I will, if you will permit me this time, define the charges which have brought us to this lamentable decision.'

Fectur waited. Leth cast his eyes across the assembly. A variety of expressions met him: cold, wolfish, hostile, just a few showing sympathy or disquiet. He noted again the fact that the guards in the hall were all Fectur's men, and realized that he was trapped. With cunning and deceit Fectur had led him here, had in fact let him pave the way to his own downfall. Leth could see now how he had engineered it. From the viewpoint of Leth's enemies and detractors he had allowed himself to occupy an indefensible position, a position of which they could, with full support, take advantage. Fectur would have kept the heads of the factions informed of all Leth's major decisions; whispered in influential ears, encouraging misgivings, expertly sowing the seeds of doubt even in the minds of Leth's closest advisors. He had waited, secretly manipulating, secretly hoping, until the time came when he could make a decisive move. Leth fulminated silently and emptily to himself. Could he survive this? It would take quick and agile thinking, absolute command, and more. Much more.

'Sire, will you permit me to continue?' asked Fectur, his voice a purr.

Leth slowly, shakily, seated himself. 'Proceed.'

'The charges are as follows. One: that you have weakened the position of the Crown and contributed to the instability of the Realm through your blind adherence to the Deist Edict. Two: that you have repeatedly failed to heed the advice and appeals of the members of your Council and Advisory Committee, and have furthermore acted *against* their recommendations, bringing danger and instability to the realm. Three: that you have demonstrated weakness and indecision in dealing with the encroachments of our common enemy, the Krai, and have permitted them to enter the realm unopposed—'

'Fectur, this is madness!' stormed Leth, unable to contain himself.

'It is not I who am mad, my lord,' replied Fectur smoothly. His eyes met Leth's and calmly challenged him. Complacent, he continued, 'Four: that you have secretly consorted with a known criminal and terrorist, a man who but recently attempted to murder you, and who has sworn vengeance against both yourself and the State for the lawful executions of his sons; further, that you have wilfully held secret all details of your dealings with this man. Five: that in instituting, against the will of the government, a Declaration of Emergency, you have effectively silenced all voices but your own, and therein held menace against democratic opinion.'

'You know my reasons for declaring Emergency. And under that very ruling you are, at this moment, placing yourself at gravest risk. All of you! This assembly is unlawful. It is a flagrant attack upon the Monarchy.'

Edric of the Far Flame spoke up. 'On the contrary, Sire, it is a lawful attempt to save the Monarchy, and the Realm.'

'Under Emergency any defiance of the Sovereign carries the most severe penalties. I had hoped never to have to invoke such a ruling, but you are leaving me with no choice.'

'Sire, the ruling carries no weight at this time. While we acknowledge without question your status as sovereign, we no longer support your actions or your position as ruler.'

Leth looked at their faces. They knew they had him.

'As your Protector, Sire, I have, in consultation with all relevant persons, come to the conclusion that it is you who are acting unlawfully, or at the very least irresponsibly,' said Fectur. 'Which brings me to the two final charges. They are, six: that you have declared yourself to be in possession of extraordinary knowledge concerning the gods of Enchantment, knowledge which you have declined to place at the disposal of others. And seven: that you have acted irrationally and extremely, abusing your position as Sovereign – albeit without true malice, while the balance of your mind is disturbed – and that your actions constitute a very real threat to the Realm. We acknowledge extenuating circumstances. You face extreme pressures, possibly more than any man should have to bear, and we are sympathetic. Nevertheless, we adjudge you unfit for rule, and relieve you, temporarily, of that office.'

'You cannot do this!'

'It has already been done, Sire. I am – for the next few days at least – Regent and Plenipotentiary Absolute. During that time you may rest and recuperate, freed of the ropes that bind you and the stones that bear you down. We hope that your recovery will be swift, and that you can perceive that this action is not taken lightly, but in a spirit of right and proper concern for yourself and our cherished Kingdom. We assume you will wish to take time to consider the charges and present your defence. To that end I present my scrip, with signatures. All details are listed. For now, Sire, I have provided an escort to see you to your apartments. I will join you there presently.'

Four knights of the Security Cadre stepped towards the dais. Leth felt his spirit leave him. The soldiers in the room showed implacable faces. *All Fectur's men!* Hand-picked, obviously. He had the authority to order them to defy Fectur, but he knew they would ignore him and hence his utter hopelessness, the final humiliation, would be exposed for all to witness. The eyes of the faction heads shone, gluttonous at his humiliation. Only Melropius and the few knights of the King's Army remained on his side, but their hands were plainly tied. Again Leth berated himself for his blindness.

Yes, Fectur, he thought, this was the only way. You could never have got so many behind you had you simply tried to overthrow me. Nor would they have sanctioned violence. But to declare me insane, and to have the evidence here to point to! Ah Fectur, how I hate you even as I admire you. Yours is a rare and devious intellect. What tragedy that you must target your brilliance against me. Were you of a different cast we could work so well together.

He rose, his legs hardly supporting him, and stepped from the dais. Fectur's knights closed around him. As he passed the Lord High Invigilate he paused and inclined his head towards him. 'There will be a reckoning for this, Fectur. Make no mistake.'

SIXTEEN

I

Issul rose with the first light of day. With her three remaining companions, Shenwolf, Kol and Phisusandra, she had passed the night at an inn, the Green Ram, in the township of Crosswood, the same inn in which she had stayed on her way to Lastmeadow. It seemed a lifetime ago.

Crosswood was busy. Many folk were on the move, heading north for the security – so they hoped – of Enchantment's Edge, driven from their homes by fear of the encroaching Krai. Issul had questioned some and learned of the fall of Wizard's Lea. There were rumours that the Krai army was now assaulting Giswel Holt. Crosswood itself had suffered a slooth attack. Everybody was afraid.

It was a chill, grey morn. The four took breakfast together, then Kol made off to fetch their horses from the stable at the rear of the inn, while Phisusandra settled their account with a nervy, bleary-eyed landlord. Issul and Shenwolf sat together at a table in the common-room.

'We have been a good company,' observed Issul. 'I shall be sad if I must part with these two when we reach Enchantment's Edge.'

Shenwolf nodded. 'I do not think either has definite plans for their future. Certainly, neither Kol nor Phis claim to have close families awaiting them. Kol's only relatives were murdered by the Krai when they attacked his home; Phis seems to be a wanderer. Perhaps they will stay. Their surprise will be great when you reveal your identity, but I have no doubt that they have come to love and respect you first as a loyal friend and brave companion. That is worth much, I think.'

'It is, and I thank you for your words. But if they stay, they will inevitably be drawn into war. They may prefer another course.'

'They have already been drawn into war. I think they know that there is now no other way.'

'And you, Shenwolf? What will you do?'

'You know my plans. I am a soldier in the King's Cavalry. I will serve my King and his young Queen to the best of my ability. If I can I will help rid our land of its invaders.'

'I have never asked you about yourself before. Where are you from?'

The young soldier gave a quick, almost diffident smile. 'A long way from here. My home is beyond the forest. It is a quiet place, generally peaceful.'

'And what brings you here?'

His brow clouded momentarily. 'Simply that word arrived of King Leth's summons to arms. We are remote, but we are your subjects even so. And I had always dreamed of coming to the capital.'

'But your skills – surely you did not gain those living such a quiet life?'

'Well, perhaps not so quiet. Peaceful it is in the main, yet there are bandits to deal with, sometimes ogres, vhazz, occasional mercenary bands who consider our location ideal for their own purposes and seek to take it from us without asking. My father taught me martial skills from birth, both armed and unarmed. He taught me to hunt and to track, and how to survive in the wild pursuing brigands who have attacked a nearby village or stolen our cattle.'

'So you have left your family to come here. And what of a sweetheart? Is there not a comely maiden back there pining for her lost love?'

Shenwolf lowered his eyes. 'Ah no. Not now. There is no one.'

Issul studied his face. Youthful, not quite handsome, but engaging and open. She sensed a slight evasiveness in his manner, and thought she had seen, just fleetingly, a look of sorrow cloud his eyes. She wondered if perhaps her questions were intrusive, and decided to enquire no further for now, yet she was intrigued to know more. Shenwolf glanced up and met her eye, smiled quickly and looked away.

Phisusandra appeared. 'The bill is paid and Kol waits outside with the horses.'

As they rode slowly out of the town Issul felt a poignant excitement grip her spirit. In just a few short hours she would come in sight of the towers and spires of her beloved Enchantment's Edge, high upon the soaring scarp. By nightfall she would be within its walls, safe within Orbia with her loved ones again. The thought warmed her. Leth would be waiting. Jace, Galry. How would they respond when they saw her? How had Leth explained her absence to the children? She had so much to tell them. Now, all that had happened during the previous days seemed almost like a dream.

She felt a slight heaviness descend. No matter what she had been through, no matter her joyful return, the crisis that faced Enchantment's Edge was far from past, had in fact hardly even begun. She glanced around her at the forest, fearful just for a moment that unseen foes lurked in ambush among the dark and mist-swathed trees, determined to thwart her homecoming. Yesterday she and her companions had passed the spot where the Krai had attacked and kidnapped her. No traces of the skirmish remained; she had only been able to guess the precise location. But she had thought back then, as she did now, to that day, and had wondered about the child, Moscul, her unnatural nephew. He had escaped her. Where was he now? She shivered, recalling the terrible moments of his birth, the knowing look in his eye when she had spoken to him outside Ohirbe's home. What was he? What was he doing?

Her fury rose as she thought of Lord Fectur, the way his men had interrogated Ohirbe's family without her permission and made off with the mysterious ivory piece that had been given to Moscul by the stranger in the woods. She bristled at the recollection. *How dare he!* She intended to confront Fectur as a priority upon her return. *Fectur, prepare yourself well. There will be a reckoning.* She promised herself that.

The day wore on, still grey, a little blustery, but no longer as chill. Phisusandra, Kol and Shenwolf sang for much of the time as they rode. Sometimes Issul joined in, enjoying the easy company of these men, her friends, and for just a few moments actually forgetting that she was Queen. There were many people upon the road, some on horseback or with pack animals or carts, most on foot, often bearing their entire belongings on their backs. There seemed no end to them, and their numbers impeded progress. Issul wondered at the crowds that must already have thronged to Enchantment's Edge.

The four stopped briefly at midday to eat and to rest their horses in a clearing beside the way. A group of travellers were there before them, congregating about a fire. Issul listened for a while to their chat, but learned nothing new about the Krai. She gazed towards the trees and the unseen mountains of Enchantment far beyond.

I have entered Enchantment!

It was like a dream. The mysterious bright oval of the Farplace Opening, her sudden transition from the Krai camp to the tower chamber, the blazing mountains outside, the swirling coloured air, the three strange children who were Triune, and their bizarre, extraordinary conversation . . .

I have entered Enchantment!

And she knew, much as she feared the thought, much as she tried to reject the idea, she knew that a little piece of Enchantment now resided within her. Was that what Triune had given her? Whatever it was, she felt she could never rest now. Not with that memory, the knowledge of having been within the unknown land. The Krai camp lay razed in the wilderness, the Farplace Opening entombed beneath it, and it was a mystery she might never leave alone. Much as she yearned to return to her home there was within her, contrastingly, a tug in the opposite direction, back the way she had come, to the Farplace Opening, the way to Enchantment. She knew that she had to return there.

As she dwelt upon this Issul grew aware of the tone of the conversation around her. There was tension among the people with whom she sat. Their words had become sullen and resentful. Criticisms were being levelled against King Leth and the manner in which he was said to be handling the crisis. Issul bit her lip and kept silent rather than draw attention to herself. But the criticisms became jibes and poisonous denunciations, and when an elderly man declared Leth a base coward she could hold back no longer.

'The King is no coward!' She declared angrily. 'He is doing everything he can to save our country. Only a fool would march out now to meet the Krai.'

'Oh, is that so?' The man looked at her with cynical surprise. 'And who might you be, missie, to know so much?'

'Someone who takes no pleasure in finding herself among ingrates who readily take refuge behind the King's shield yet can do nothing but insult and deride him.'

A dark-haired woman spoke up. 'Easy for you to say. Obviously you have not lost your home to the Krai, nor seen your friends and neighbours murdered. Where was the King's shield then, when it was most needed? There was not a soldier in sight.'

There was a low chorus of agreement at this.

'You are from Wizard's Lea?' enquired Issul in a softer tone.

The woman nodded, her mouth twitching, too emotional to speak further.

'I know you must have suffered greatly. But I also have experienced much at the hands of the Krai. We are together in this, all of us. It helps no one to blame King Leth.'

'He should have sent his soldiers!' said another man, and turned to Shenwolf. 'Where were you? Why did you not come to save us?'

Now Issul realized that the comments had been chiefly aimed at goading Shenwolf, who again wore his blue tabard bearing the royal coat of arms.

Others echoed the man's words. 'Where were you? Where was the King? Why were we sacrificed?'

Shenwolf looked thoughtfully from one to the other. 'You were not sacrificed. For my part, I have been fighting the Krai elsewhere. My companions also. Many of us who rode out have not returned, nor will they ever. We cannot be everywhere, and my friend Jace is right, it would be unwise for King Leth to attempt to meet the Krai in open battle. They are strong and have powerful allies. We must bide our time.'

'Bide our time!' spat one man. 'That is the action of a weak and indecisive leader.' He rose angrily to his feet and stabbed a finger at Shenwolf. 'Why are you here, then? Why are you not now fighting the Krai? Are you afraid? Do you call yourself a soldier when you do not even dare to fight?'

Shenwolf gazed steadily into his eye but took the taunt in silence. Issul began to speak but the man butted in, grabbing a staff and thrusting its end towards Shenwolf. 'Is that the truth, soldier? Are you afraid? Are all the king's men afraid?'

'Losses are inevitable against an enemy as powerful as the Krai,' said Issul angrily. 'Wizard's Lea was not sacrificed, but we knew it could not be defended. We sent warning and the promise of shelter weeks ago, to you and to the nearby villages.'

'We?' said the woman. 'We? Who are "we"?'

'The King,' said Issul quickly. 'Envoys were sent out. It was well broadcast within the city-castle.'

They did not want to hear. The man with the staff was shaking with emotion. 'Cowards! Skulking behind walls!'

He thrust his staff at Shenwolf. It would have struck the young soldier upon the breastbone with some force, but he fended it with his hand.

'Fight me!' snarled the man. 'Fight me! Or are you afraid of me, too?'

Issul glanced around at the other travellers. They were mainly elderly, or women and children, but their mood was becoming ugly and there were enough of them to constitute a mob. She stood, as did Shenwolf and the other two.

'Plainly you do not wish us here. We will leave.'

The man with the staff swung at Shenwolf, who stepped lithely to the side. The blow went wild. He grasped the staff, twisted quickly and pulled it from the man's grasp, then cast it to the ground.

Issul motioned him away. She backed off, Kol and Phisusandra beside her. They mounted their horses, watched by the group which had now fallen into a sullen silence and seemed a little uncertain of itself.

'You people,' Issul called. 'You will be made welcome at Enchantment's Edge. Every one of you. The King will turn no one away, not even those who deserve only his disfavour. But come peacefully. Troublemakers will be arrested and dealt with harshly.'

She put heels to her mount's flanks and rode back onto the way, watched by puzzled, haggard faces.

Midway through the afternoon the cloud broke up and at last, rounding a bend, Issul saw in the distance before her the vast towering scarp. She brought her horse to a halt, her heart pounding as she peered into the far, high distance and, yes! there at the crest, the high walls and the towers behind them, shimmering in the sunlight. She turned to Shenwolf, smiling with tears in her eyes. 'I am home!'

He returned the smile. 'It is a good feeling, is it not?'

As they passed on none of them took notice of a bent figure at the wayside. It was one among several, poorly garbed, nondescript. A woman, advanced in years, heavily built and leaning upon a staff. She wore a long dress of dark fust and a worn and faded green shawl pulled up over her grey hair. Scored upon the flesh of her left cheek were the marks of deep fingernail scratches where she had once, not long ago, struggled with a child in the woods, and lost him.

Arene watched the Queen as she rode away. She recognized her as the young beauty who had pursued the Foulborn in the forest and had been knocked down and carried away by the Krai. The subsequent influx of soldiers, frantically searching the region, making enquiries everywhere, had quickly told her that the woman must have been of major importance. Through listening, observing and questioning she had learned that it was the Queen of Enchantment's Edge herself who had fallen victim to the Krai. The soldiers did not know her fate, and Arene had not elected to inform them.

But what did the Queen of Enchantment's Edge know of the Foulborn?

Arene nodded to herself as she watched Issul ride away down the forest road. The Queen was alive and had returned. She would hunt the Foulborn again, as her destiny predicted. It all could have been prevented so easily, there beside the pond, had not the impudent young stranger intervened. But his intervention, also, was surely destiny, that part which affected her own, to which she was necessarily blind. Such was the way of things. So many possible paths; she could never have been open to them all.

Arene had not seen the face of the young soldier at Issul's side as they paused upon the way, for his back had been to her. Had she seen him she might well have wondered.

She observed thoughtfully until the little party had passed out of sight around a bend. Then she leaned upon her staff once more and hobbled on, bound like all the others upon the road for the great city-castle that was now not so very far away.

II

The Krai prince Anzejarl cantered up the grassy slope on his black stallion, the beautiful Olmana at his side on a chestnut gelding, her long burnished-red hair blowing in the breeze. They came to a halt upon the crest and gazed down the long shallow valley where the bulk of the Krai army was encamped. Rows of blue and white tents stretched into the distance, a strong wooden palisade enclosing them. Anzejarl rested his hands upon the pommel of his saddle. He looked towards a nearby lake-side. Tall, lumbering, grey-skinned trolls were gathered there, more than one hundred in number. They squatted by the waterside, lazed beneath the trees, rolled upon the dusty earth. Here and there a squabble broke out between two or more of the creatures. Brief flurries ensued, then broke up, the creatures parting with snarls, beating their chests and making threatening gestures. Anzejarl spurred his mount and rode down to put himself among them.

As he and Olmana approached, the trolls looked up, one then another, then more. Gibbers passed between them and they became subdued. Their ugly faces watched the pair, their brutal eyes blinking stupidly. Some licked their chops or scratched at parasites on their thick skins, but none moved towards the two who, with their horses, would ordinarily have been seen simply as fresh meat.

Anzejarl's nose wrinkled in disgust at the pungent reek that came from the trolls. He passed among them uneasily, stroking and patting the neck of his nervous horse. He was still not fully accustomed to the fact that he commanded these bestial things, that they were cowed and submissive in his presence. In fact, there was much that he had not yet grown accustomed to, and he wondered if he ever would.

The trolls stood eight or nine feet tall, were ropily muscled, hard-skinned with a sparse covering of short, coarse hair, long of limb and immensely strong. They were rare creatures, typically holding to small family groups, half-a-dozen strong at the most.

But they had come out of Enchantment in a horde, obedient to Anzejarl's call.

How did he summon them? He knew only what Olmana had told him. She had given him a gift, so she described it, soon after she had come to him in the Krai capital, Zhang, and seduced him. First she had given him the gift she called Awakening: she had awoken him to emotion, human feelings, something quite alien to the Krai. She had placed rapture upon him, given him new vision, made him experience joy, wonder, sometimes sadness or anger, even fear. She had opened his eyes to many things, and when he had seen she had made him *want*.

And most of all he had wanted her.

When her seduction of him was complete and she had turned him upon his own family, she had offered more. The means to summon and command trolls and slooths – with a hint that other things might follow. But the means by which she had accomplished this was a mystery. She told him she had to put something inside him, that it was done while he slept. By this time Anzejarl was wholly in her thrall, and more, had come to trust her unquestioningly and, just as importantly, to need her. So he awoke one morning and knew the harsh guttural tongue of trolls and the piping calls of slooths, though at that time he had never laid eyes on either. And he did not know how he knew it.

Olmana took him to a bare mountain peak on the edge of Enchantment and revealed to him the words to call into the wind. Days later the creatures of Enchantment were gathered before him outside the walls of Zhang.

A huge, almost white and hairless troll loped forward and placed itself before Anzejarl as he brought his horse to a halt. 'Do you bring us news of man-flesh, Prince of the Krai? Does warm blood and fat gore await us?'

Anzejarl nodded sombrely. 'Very soon, Gulb. Very soon.'

'We hunger for the battle.'

'As do I,' Anzejarl lied, for he had tired of war. Even victory brought him little joy now. It had become . . . almost routine, and Anzejarl had begun to crave new and indefinable excitements. He nodded ruefully to himself. These thoughts, these *emotions* . . . before Olmana he would not have known them. All had been duty, all necessity and nothing more. But now, at her behest, he ravaged nations in search of a child he knew nothing of.

Two days earlier Olmana had become excited. 'I sense him! He is free!' she had exclaimed. 'Anzejarl, we must move swiftly now!'

Anzejarl dug into the pouch at his waist and brought forth a wad of green *ghinz* leaves. He stuffed them into his mouth and chewed, closing his jewel-eyes for a moment to savour the rich narcotic as it chased through his over-sensitized nerves. He looked down at the squatting troll. 'Be patient, Gulb. Very soon you will taste human flesh again.'

He turned his horse away and walked it from the monstrous horde, Olmana following.

'What are your plans, oh Prince?' she asked, her green eyes twinkling as they passed beneath the trees.

In his mind Anzejarl shrugged. 'Duke Hugo is an impatient man, unlike his cousin the king. I think he does not like to be cooped up in the castle of Giswel. I think the sight of my army camped before him is too much for him to bear.'

She smiled to herself, but she was restless, he knew that. Olmana was a woman given to temperament, and in recent days he had seen changes in her. She was impatient and demanding, more so than before. It was the Child, her goal. For whatever reason, the Child was of absolute importance to her, and she seemed sure that she was now virtually within grasping distance of it. But yet she feared something. Did someone else seek the Child? Was she in danger of losing it? It was beyond Anzejarl's capacity to say, for Olmana confided nothing more than her obsession, her unswerving need to locate the mysterious Child.

Anzejarl watched her aside as they rode. She was beautiful. Far too beautiful. His eyes travelled from her shining bronze-red hair, over her slim arms, her full breasts swaying beneath the loose velvet blouson she wore, her slender thighs spread across her horses flanks. Anzejarl felt his blood surge and knew that he loved her insanely, that she could never love him in the same way, that she controlled him, had him totally under her spell, and he resented her.

Such a rush of emotions. It all but rocked him from his saddle. He spat free the *ghinz* and reached for more.

What are you, woman?

She was no ordinary female, he was certain of that. Olmana was of Enchantment. In his blind lust and love for her, he also, sometimes, feared her. In his dreams he had seen her change her form, become something quite monstrous and repulsive. In his dreams, when Olmana did whatever it was she did to allow him to command her creatures . . . And then he awoke and she was beside him, usually naked, and he reached for her, aroused by her in a way no Krai woman had ever aroused him, spending himself in pleasures so unlike the formal couplings he had known in his past.

She was his goddess. The way she played with his body . . . The way she played with his mind . . .

Anzejarl turned away, unable to bear the intensity. Desire . . . love . . . resentment . . . terror . . . wonder . . . And this was but a fraction of the whole. Was this truly what she had done? Awoken him to a realization of humanity? Was this all of it? The part of him that remained wholly Krai stepped back for a moment and observed curiously, detached and remote. How did humans live with such turmoil within them? The conflicts of desires and uncertainties, for all that they gave, were an agony.

Olmana's eyes were fixed upon the hillside ahead. A slight frown had clouded her pale brow. She might have been wholly unaware of Anzejarl's presence, and he wondered what she was thinking.

Two days earlier several slooths had flown back from the secret forward camp that Anzejarl had established deep in the forest. Some of them bore injuries; some had been burned. There was no way of knowing exactly what had happened there, for slooths were dim beasts who communicated only in terms of their immediate sensations, without a developed language. But it was plain that all had not gone to plan at the camp.

The news had thrown Olmana into a paroxysm of rage. She screamed at Anzejarl to dispatch a strong force to investigate and secure the camp. There was something there that she was fearful of losing, something magical that she had had constructed underground. Anzejarl did not know what. At her behest his warriors had taken prisoners from surrounding villages to construct the camp and the magic chamber. But whatever was happening within that chamber had been kept secret from him.

Even before the slooths' return Anzejarl had had inklings that not everything was well with Olmana. She had seemed pleased with the progress of the camp itself but something else preyed on her mind and irked her intensely. He had watched her pacing up and down, muttering to herself, cursing. He had heard names fly from her tongue: Bartacanes, the Orb, the Triune. None made any sense to him, and he could not question her.

Olmana turned to him now with blazing eyes. 'We must move swiftly, Prince of the Krai.'

Anzejarl nodded and spurred his horse up the slope.

III

Leth seethed. He could barely take in what had happened. His mind rebelled against it, refusing to believe whilst knowing that it must. It seemed the most monstrous dream in which he struggled impotently, his greatest fears becoming real, his life taken from him as he watched, unable to move or respond. His whole body ached and burned with the knowledge of what had been done to him. He felt that he was going mad.

Why had he not foreseen this? How he railed at himself now. His errors were laid glaringly before him. He had been blind. He had not heeded the opinions of his counsellors. And never had he given thought to the possible, unthinkable consequences of that.

To declare him insane and unfit to rule! What outrage!

And he was snared and could do nothing.

It was a perfect coup, executed after careful and deliberate planning by Fectur. How long must he have been working towards this moment? How delicately must he have trodden? To what extent had he manipulated events?

All along Leth had been conscious of Fectur's disingenuosness, had wondered at his warnings, his heartfelt concern. Yet with guile and craft Fectur had actually been egging him on. Putting himself beyond blame Fectur had helped him make his own way down the path to his destruction. Leth had suspected something, but not this. Never this.

He was held in his apartments, guards stationed at the entrances. Fectur's men. Leth's household and professional staff had been removed and replaced: again by Fectur's men. Leth could communicate with no one who might give him aid.

He has declared me a danger to the state, sick and unsound of mind, my judgement impaired, unfit to rule!

Nothing else could ever have worked. But this way – the cunning! – to cast doubt upon the sovereign's sanity, to provide 'evidence' to support the charge while professing to act solely out of love and concern for both monarch and realm . . . All would know the real reason behind Fectur's action, but too many supported him, and what he had accomplished was, in essence, legal. It was a coup, full and absolute. Fectur had appropriated total power for himself.

Doctor Melropius had come to Leth minutes after he had been escorted from the Hall of Wise Counsel. He entered sheepishly, twitching with embarrassment, his forehead agleam with sweat, ears glowing scarlet.

Leth swung on him. 'Melropius, you must do something! This is insupportable!'

'Oh Sire, if I had only known! Believe me, I had no idea. When Lord Fectur expressed his concern for you and asked my advice—'

'Yes, yes. I understand that. I hold nothing against you personally. But what can be done? I have to get out of here!'

Melropius stood stiff and shamefaced. 'Lord Fectur has ordered me to bring you whatever medicines I deem necessary, Sire. I have herbal potions to help you sleep and to calm your nerves; stimulants to help your appetite—'

'Calm my nerves!' Leth exploded. 'Don't be a fool, man! Do you understand what you are saying? I have been overthrown! This is the most vile treachery, and you talk of calming my nerves!'

'Sire, I regret this, believe me.' Melropius was close to tears. He shifted from foot to foot. 'I will do all I can to help you. But these are Lord Fectur's instructions.'

'Do you believe me insane, Melropius?'

'No, Sire. Of course not. But you are under a great deal of strain—'

'Damned right I am! But can you not see, Melropius, that I will never be allowed to return? Fectur has no interest in passing power back to me. Why would he?'

Melropius stood open mouthed in shock. 'S-Sire . . . It-it-it is only a m-matter of time. A few days. A w-week or two, perhaps.'

Leth turned away. 'You have not seen, have you, Melropius?'

The door opened silently and Fectur entered. 'If you have given King Leth his medications, Doctor, you may leave.'

Melropius hurriedly departed, his bald head bowed. Leth glowered at Fectur, barely able to control himself. He was bigger, stronger than Fectur, and Fectur had entered without guards to protect him. Nor did he carry a visible weapon.

But Fectur was a master. He had instructed Leth in many forms of combat as a youth, as he had taught Issul. What he had taught had been a fraction of what he knew. With deepening anger Leth acknowledged that in this respect also he was powerless against Fectur. He acknowledged also that any assault by him upon the Lord High Invigilate would be further evidence against him.

'Well, you have it all now, Fectur. As you have presumably always wanted. What of me, though? I presume I will simply disappear now? How will you manage it?'

Fectur shook his head, tutting his tongue in mild admonishment. 'Tsk, tsk, Sire. It is not like that at all. I am concerned for you, that is all. Your refusal to see it is yet another symptom of your illness, I fear. But with rest and proper care I – and Doctor Melropius – believe you will recover in full and be ready to take up your right and appropriate station again within a very short time.'

Leth scoffed. In the Hall of Wise Counsel Fectur had spoken of Leth's 'temporary' removal from office, but from Fectur's point of view there could never be anything temporary about it. He would not willingly take second place again. His days would be numbered if he ever allowed Leth to resume sovereignty. He saw that as surely as he saw the stricken king before him.

But to simply kill Leth was out of the question. Fectur would have to bide his time. Close house arrest – or close medical supervision – would have to suffice until a suitable accident could be arranged. He would engineer Leth's end, somehow, just as with all the deviousness and resources at his command he had engineered his fall.

And the children, too!

That only came to Leth now. Fectur could permit no heirs to threaten his future.

Leth marvelled at him for a moment, even as he despised him. His moment had been perfectly honed and taken. Had Issul been here he could never have accomplished the coup. Even had he succeeded in bringing Leth down, she would automatically have assumed the throne in Leth's stead. But then Fectur would never have tried if he had believed that Issul could intervene.

Only now did the dark notion strike Leth. *Was* Fectur behind Issul's disappearance? Had he had her murdered? *Was Fectur in league with the Krai?*

Leth felt the blood of fury scald his cheeks and almost burst at his temples. Fectur was observing him closely, and presumably guessed his thoughts, for he said, 'Before you ask, Sire, I know nothing of the Queen.'

Leth stayed silent, not knowing what to believe. Fectur crossed to a table and took a pomegranate from a silver fruit platter. He picked up a knife and split the skin, laid half the fruit upon the tabletop, the knife beside it. He strolled away, picking at the hemi-shell of fruit with a little silver scoop, his back to Leth.

Leth glanced at the knife. Two steps and it was his. Two more and it could be deep in the flesh of Fectur's loathsome back.

Except . . .

It was what Fectur wanted. This was his challenge to Leth, and he relied on the King's state of mind to drive him to it. The fruit-moistened blade would never touch Fectur's skin; he was too adept, far too skilled. But the attempt would be the excuse . . . enough to have Leth restrained, placed in a cell, under restraint, where he could harm no one.

'You have come to gloat,' Leth said.

'Sire, it is not like that.' Fectur turned, his face betraying no disappointment but his eyes like stones.

'Then tell me what it is like.'

Fectur spooned out the last few pomegranate seeds and tossed the empty shell onto the table, ignoring the other half. He looked at Leth but said nothing.

'What have you done with Venger?' Leth demanded.

'He is where a condemned criminal should be.'

'Do not harm him, Fectur! I need him.'

'You need him?'

'*We* need him. Enchantment's Edge. He still has vital information to impart.'

'I have yet to be convinced of that.'

'Fectur, I gave him my word that he would come to no harm.'

'This man tried to murder you.'

'No. The assassination attempt was staged to bring about – as he and the True Sept believe it – the coming of the Legendary Child.'

'Or perhaps he is spinning you a tale to win his freedom.'

'No. He speaks the truth.'

Fectur pressed a last fragment of pomegranate between his incisors. 'It makes little difference.'

'It makes all the difference, Fectur! We do need the True Sept now. Venger must not die.'

'Sire, you are not well.'

'*Don't patronize me!*'

Fectur stood with infuriating blandness, waiting. Leth said, 'He will not be executed, Fectur. Do you understand?'

'I understand that you are perhaps overtired, Sire. It is better if I leave you now to rest.'

He took from his robe a scrolled parchment and put it on the table. 'For your reference, this is the list of offences and omissions of which you are accused, to which I referred in the Hall of Wise Counsel.'

He turned towards the door.

'Your triumph will be short-lived,' said Leth.

Fectur paused. 'How so?'

'Can you defeat the Krai and their god? Or are you perhaps in league with them?'

'I am not, be assured of that. But a change of policy may be called for. Now, Sire, you must rest.'

'I want to see my children,' said Leth suddenly.

Fectur hesitated, then gave a curt nod. 'I will have the Prince and Princess brought.'

When he had gone Leth paced the room in distraction. How could Fectur dispose of both him and his two children without losing the vital support of his allies? Somehow, he was convinced, Fectur would contrive the means. And it would be soon. As soon as he reasonably could.

Most probably it would be Leth first. As Regent Fectur could then take his time over dealing with the children. A year, perhaps two or even more, and then another tragic accident. Something in their food, most likely. The simultaneous deaths by the same cause of one or two of their attendants would add gravity and authenticity.

But did Fectur have a year or two to spare? What of the Krai? What had he meant by 'a change of policy'?

Leth went to his study, bolted the door and took out the blue casket. He flipped open the lid. The dazzle of blue flooded him and he found himself in Orbus's world.

'Orbus! Orbus!'

There was a delay, then the familiar sounds as the bent figure hauled itself out of the mist. 'Ah, Leth. I did not expect you so soon. A few moments later and you would not have found me.'

'Why? Where do you go? Where *can* you go?'

Orbus chuckled to himself. 'It is just something I have been experimenting on.'

'You speak as though you are leaving.'

'How can I leave myself?'

Leth closed his eyes, striving to think clearly. 'Orbus, I need your help. I am desperate.'

Quickly he recounted all recent events to the bundled god-creature. 'I have been rendered powerless, Orbus. I can do nothing. Whatever Fectur tells the people they will believe. He may even parade me before them to reassure those who are loyal to me that I still live. But he has taken everything and will certainly dispose of me at the earliest opportunity.'

'What will it take to regain your power?' enquired Orbus.

'A massive vote of confidence, a revolt . . . I do not know precisely.'

'Fectur's death?'

'In itself that would not be sufficient, not as things currently stand. It would throw the kingdom into anarchy, or open it wide to the Krai.'

'But you have supporters? Powerful supporters?'

'Of course. But the war takes their attention and they cannot divert themselves to my cause – not to a direct confrontation with Fectur. He holds immense power, Orbus. I have badly understimated him.'

'So it seems. This is grave. Most grave.'

'Can you do anything?'

'Me? I am a prisoner in my world as you are now in yours. I do not see how I can act to help you.' He fell silent.

'Then I am contemplating the end of all I stand for and all I and my forebears have worked to achieve.'

'What else have you learned since we last spoke, Leth? You were to meet with a man and discuss the Legendary Child.'

Leth told him of his discussion with Grey Venger, of the True

Sept's claim of duplicity in arranging Venger's assassination attempt upon him. He told him of his sudden conviction in regard to Ressa and the creature upon Sentinel's Peak and the outcome of that violent and tragic meeting. Orbus seemed interested in this, even a little agitated, and paid particular attention to Leth's description of the creature. Presently he said, 'It is true. Your fears may be confirmed, for if the poor girl was inseminated by one of my kind, the normal human gestation would not be a factor.'

'But you said earlier that it had not been possible for a god to impregnate a human woman.'

'I said it was not possible in my time. Eons have passed, the world will have changed incalculably.'

'What of the One True God who will rule supreme alongside the Child?'

'I cannot say at present. But it seems you may have an unlikely ally now.'

'What do you mean?'

'The True Sept consider you to have no soul. They have said they cannot allow you to die by ordinary means, at least until they have achieved their aims. If that is so, then they are surely bound to aid you now.'

'Grey Venger is imprisoned. Fectur could well have him executed, may already have done so.'

'But the Sept . . . if its members know what is afoot, will they not intervene?'

Leth put the heels of his palms to his eyes, striving to think clearly. 'I don't know. I simply don't know. Orbus, this prophecy of the King Without A Soul . . . does this not refer to you?'

'It would appear that it may. But the True Sept does not know I exist. Hence they must continue to direct their attentions to you.'

'But from where has the notion of the Soulless King come?'

Orbus slowly shook his great head. His reply, when it came, was not what Leth wished. 'You should return now, Leth. I will give myself immediately to investigation of this.'

'Orbus, wait!'

But the ragged figure had lifted his staff. Leth was cast from Orbus's world, back to his own study. There was a knocking and the muffled sound of someone calling. 'My lord! My lord! Are you there?'

It came from beyond the door of his study. Someone, a woman, was at the door. Half in a daze he rose and crossed the chamber, drew back the bolts. His children's governess, Cascane, stood there; a guard, Fectur's, was behind her. She quickly curtsied, a strained look upon her face. 'My lord, I was told you wished to see the children.'

'Yes.' Leth peered around the door. Galry and Jace were in the chamber beyond, lounging at a window. Jace glanced around, saw her father and ran towards him, arms outstretched. 'Daddy!'

He stepped forward and took her in his arms. 'Thank you, Cascane. That will be all.'

The governess curtsied again. Her cheeks were pale, her nose red, eyes moist. 'I'm so sorry, sir,' she said quickly, then turned, sobbing, and hurried away. The guard followed her.

'Daddy, what is in here?' asked Galry, pushing past his father into the study, the door of which Leth had left open.

'It is not for you,' said Leth.

'I want to see. I have never been here before.'

Jace pointed. 'Let me see! Let me see!'

She wriggled against Leth and he put her down and she shot through thc door. Leth followed them in.

'What is this?' asked Jace, rushing around in wonder, gazing at everything. 'And what is this? And what is this?'

'What is all this blue?' Galry asked.

For the first time Leth became aware of the colour in the chamber. Something of the blue mistiness of Orbus's world seemed to have escaped into his study, noticeably toning the air.

'And you, Father, you are surrounded by it,' said Galry. 'Is it magic?'

Leth looked at his hands. Sure enough, a blue aura clung to them, enhanced, it seemed, by the vague blueness that hung in the air. He felt vaguely discomforted.

'Daddy what is this?' asked Jace. 'It is lovely. What is inside?'

'Jace, no!'

She was at his desk and had the blue casket in her hands. In his distraction he had neglected to put it away.

'Put it down!'

'I want to see inside.'

'*No!*'

It was too late. His little daughter freed the catch and opened the lid. Leth was lurching forward, hand outstretched to stop her. The world flashed sudden blue. He staggered forward a few more paces. Galry was crying out in sudden alarm. 'I can't see! I can't see!'

Leth grabbed Jace, who was also rubbing at her eyes. Her hands were empty now. He turned. Galry had his hands over his eyes, shrieking. 'I can't see!'

Leth sprang to his side and hugged him to him. 'It is all right, Galry. Don't be afraid. It will pass in a moment.'

He stared around him, into the endless blue, at the high, high walls that were never close nor far away. The children, their vision gradually clearing, gazed also.

'Where are we?'

Galry, trembling with fear, began to cry. Jace, too young to grasp so much, just stared wide-eyed.

Leth stood, holding them both. 'Orbus!'

There was no reply. He waited a short time, infinitely fearful, then called again. 'Orbus!'

The silence moved around them. Leth felt inklings of the soul-chilling fear he had felt when first entering this lonely place.

'*Orbus!*'

'Daddy, can we go back now?' said Jace.

Leth took a few paces forward. 'Orbus, where are you? Answer me!'

But Orbus did not answer. Leth recalled his words of a short time ago: 'a few moments later and you would not have found me'.

What had he meant?

'*Orbus!*'

Had he left? But Orbus himself had said, 'How can I leave myself?'

Yet there was no response. No matter how Leth called. Nothing except the silence of the endless blue. As if the god had indeed forsaken its world.

And if the god was not there to raise the staff of freedom, there was no way to leave.

SEVENTEEN

I

Duke Hugo of Giswel waited edgily in the pre-dawn dark. His mind was alert, he was convinced he was doing the right thing, but his gut had knotted with tension. It was the waiting. Waiting for sufficient light. Straining through the silence, never knowing. That was what was so unbearable.

Over the previous days he had observed Krai movements minutely. The cordon of enemy troops surrounding Giswel Holt had diminished significantly. Elements had made off northwards; there had been no further attacks by the deadly slooths. The force that remained was powerful, but the cordon was not so tight as to prevent Hugo's spies from stealing from the castle and bringing back up-to-date intelligence on Krai numbers and movements. Hence Hugo was informed about the massive encampment beside the Whispering Lakes a league or so to the north. It was here that Prince Anzejarl's main army rested, and the troops that were leaving the force outside Giswel Holt were marching to join it.

Hugo had become convinced that Anzejarl's army was making ready for a major push north to assault Enchantment's Edge. The numbers left outside Giswel Holt were sufficient to contain Hugo's men and a deterrent against any large-scale offensive action on his part, but Hugo now believed he had identified an area of weakness. His agents had reported that to the east of the castle the Krai were stretched thinly a short distance forward of an area where it appeared a tunnel was being mined. From the rear that area was virtually undefended. A determined charge by sufficient mounted soldiers, launched from close quarters, could smash through the Krai forward defences. Hugo's men could then continue the assault onwards to the tunnel area. With success they could cause great damage while incurring minimal losses and, with infantry protecting their rear, withdraw safely back to the castle.

Hugo was acutely conscious of the need to buoy the spirits of the people and troops of Giswel Holt. They had been cooped up in the castle for days now, with the Krai siege troops sitting patiently and quietly outside, doing nothing but watch and wait, as though never doubting that Giswel Holt was soon to fall. There had been two slooth attacks initially. Casualties were relatively light, damage minimal, and there had been nothing more for some days now. But the fear those attacks had engendered was insidious, corroding the will of the folk of Giswel. Something was needed, a drama that would boost morale and show the audacious Krai to be not invulnerable.

Hugo had thought about it long and hard. His plan ran counter to the orders of his cousin, King Leth, but Leth was not here, nor could he know the precise circumstances. Communications between Giswel Holt and Enchantment's Edge had recently ceased: the risk of carrier pigeons being shot down or caught, their messages read by the enemy, was too great. But Hugo had persuaded himself that, were Leth at Giswel Holt, he too would not let this opportunity pass.

Hugo's remaining dilemma had been one of timing. Should he wait for the main Krai army to depart, or strike now? On the face of it the latter seemed unwise, likely to bring the retributive wrath of the entire Krai force on his head. But there was no way of knowing how quickly Anzejarl intended to march north, and in the meantime the Krai might spot the flaw in their defence and plug the gap. Hugo reasoned that, in effect, were Anzejarl to throw his full weight against Giswel Holt, he would ultimately be no more nor less effective than with the siege force now in place. He could not smash the castle by force, at least not quickly. He was more likely to starve it into submission, whilst battering and undermining it over many weeks. So Hugo opted to strike without delay.

He knew he lacked the manpower for a decisive blow, but believed that this way he might make the Krai stumble a little in their course. He had to do something. Let Anzejarl know that he was not facing a passive enemy, and also reassure his own people that he, their Duke, did not fear the Krai.

The methodical approach of his enemy unsettled him; their

silence was unnatural. No jeers and taunts were thrown from the host outside Giswel Holt's walls; at night no campsong drifted from around their fires. Just silence, watchful and grating. A massed, ordered silence that preyed upon the nerves.

So Duke Hugo had crept forth in darkness from a concealed sally port beneath Giswel Holt's eastern wall. Twenty knights and fifty heavy horse had accompanied him, with one hundred foot soldiers following in support. The horses' hooves were muffled, the men carried much of their armour wrapped in cloth to prevent noise. Now the cloth and muffles were removed, mail and plate donned. The fires of the Krai twinkled through the trees, the closest less than fifty yards away. Just a short while longer, enough for the oncoming dawn to reveal the precise location of their quarry and salient features of the land around.

Duke Hugo mounted his horse. He could discern the silhouettes of the thick tree-trunks around him, dense and opaque, tendrils of grey mist wreathing ghost-like between. He glanced around, to the knights on either side of him, the heavy horsemen and invisible foot soldiers beyond. All were looking to him for the word. His throat was dry, his palms damp. The pre-dawn was without a sound. He raised his helmet and placed it upon his head, adjusting neck and cheek-guards for comfort. There was a hint of glimmering pale gold light low at his back through the trees. Ahead he made out the dim shapes of Krai tents across the rough bare ground beyond the trees. Hugo unsheathed his sword and held it aloft. He drew back his lips, glanced about him once more to be sure his men were ready, then roared, 'Forward for Giswel, for Enchantment's Edge! Forward for freedom! Charge!'

They galloped forth in two columns, each of two files, fanning out once they broke free of the trees and weaving between the sharpened stakes and caltraps the Krai had laid for defence. Hugo's spirit soared; he felt his fear, smelt it in his sweat. The din of his charging men was deafening. Krai guards were coming alert now, rushing to meet them, but in disarray, without formation. He swung his sword, brought it down to take a Krai head from its shoulders. More came at him. It was the first time he had met them face to face. He took in their white, wrinkled visages, grim-set but emotionless and still mute as they fought, as his men ploughed into them, striking them down. It was too simple. He thundered past a tent. Two Krai rushed at him with spears. He brought the first down with another blow, swerved his horse to avoid the second, twisted about in the saddle, struck once, twice. A fountain of blood spurted high and the Krai slipped writhing in death to the ground.

The air was thick now with the clamour of conflict, the screech of steel on steel, the yells of Hugo's men, single staccato barks of command and occasional laboured grunts from the Krai. Hugo peered about him as he surged on. His men were in the thick of it, hacking, stabbing from their saddles, while the foot soldiers came from behind, pouring a bloody wave into the enemy. As far as he could see the scene was the same.

To his left a knight was in difficulty, hemmed in by four or five of the enemy. Hugo swung around and charged. A Krai fell to his blade, then a second. The knight broke free, spun his mount and barged a Krai warrior to the ground.

'Onward!' yelled Hugo. 'Before they can swamp us! Yaaah!'

The knights and horse soldiers of Giswel pounded on, through the basic camp, striking down any who came against them, making for the slope behind. From there it was a short gallop to the right, through a small copse beneath the lee of a low cliff, and down again to the area of excavations that marked the mouth of the tunnel the Krai were constructing, presumably in an attempt to undermine Giswel Holt's walls.

Hugo risked glancing back. The infantry were fully engaged, most of the horse troops had broken free. Bodies littered the ground, Krai and human, but many more Krai. Now, as planned, he veered right, followed by three-quarters of his mounted force. The remainder, following the battle-plan devised the previous day, spun about and charged back down the slope to put themselves among the Krai who were running from east and west to aid their stricken comrades.

Hugo grinned, his sword high. It was all going so well!

An arrow sighed past his head, then another. He ducked low to his horse, urging it to its best speed, and shifted his shield to his right shoulder. He had anticipated archers and knew his men would be relatively exposed on this brief stretch. But there could be relatively few bowmen, visibility in the pre-morn was still restricted to less than thirty yards, and the copse was just a short way ahead. That and the cliff would provide cover until the men of Giswel Holt charged down to the mine. There they would be among Krai again, and no arrows could fly.

He reached the trees, their welcome dark shade enclosing him. They were sparsely spaced, there was hardly need to slow his pace. His knights were with him, his ears filled with the thud of their horses' hooves, the jangle of harness and armour. Fleet dense shadows pounded through the sombre wood. He roared his ebullience, rejoicing in the kill, the savage splendour of his bloodied blade. So far as he could tell he had lost but a handful of men.

He veered towards the cliff. A little way further on it broke onto a grass slope. Then the mine at its foot . . .

At that moment Hugo knew that something was wrong. Little more than a fleeting impression at first, an awareness of something moving between the trees. Then a grey shape, darkly mottled, swift and bulky. Another, and another. He heard a cry to his left, and something not human. From the corner of his eye he glimpsed one of his knights upon the ground with his mount. A monstrous shape was upon him; pounding him with massive fists. Then another knight went down, two of the things leaping upon him.

Something sprang out of the cliff face into Hugo's path. He swerved, striking out with his sword. He just had time to see the bestial face, lank powerful limbs and overlong body, then his blade struck into thick grey flesh. The creature emitted a dismal howl. With difficulty Hugo wrenched his weapon free.

Now others were dropping from the trees and high rock. Their guttural roars filled Hugo's ears. He knew bewilderment, an awful sinking feeling in his gut. The cries of his men, the terrified screams of their horses pierced him like barbs. A pair of the troll-things were careering towards him. He tried to veer between them. One reached out long arms to seize his horse's head, yanked it around. The horse fell, catapulting Hugo from the saddle.

He hit the ground hard, rolled, came up kneeling, his vision fuzzed, a throbbing, blazing pain in one shoulder. A troll rushed at him, raising two arms, hefting a cudgel. Hugo lunged, piercing its belly. The troll bellowed its agony and twisted away, its movement wrenching Hugo's sword from his grasp. He stood as another troll swung its cudgel. He blocked the blow with his shield but the force of it sent him staggering backwards. Now Hugo felt panic for the first time. Terrible, cold, clamouring. Another horse was felled close by, its rider slamming into the earth and lying still. Hugo ran to him and grabbed his fallen sword. He whirled, striking out at random. A mighty cudgel blow hammered into his shoulder. With an agonized yell he tumbled to the ground, somehow managing to keep hold of the sword, his whole being vibrant with pain. A gigantic troll towered over him, swiping with an axe. Feebly Hugo raised his shield, but his arm was numbed and would not obey him. The troll's blow came around inside the shield. Hugo staggered to his feet, stared uncomprehendingly at the stump of his arm where it ended above the elbow, rhythmically pumping the bright fountain of his lifeblood.

He raised his sword, struck at the troll, became aware through a haze of terror that his blow was wild, that he was faint, his legs would not support him. He was upon his knees, the world rotating in a blur of greenwood and hazy red. Something colossal rammed him, sent him flying, now beyond pain, rolling, coming to rest upon his back. He was cold, very cold. The troll was upon him. Strange, he no longer feared, was more fascinated. Its hideous grey face, long canines bared, sinking into his belly. There was another troll now. He was a feast. And cold, ripped and flung, unbearably cold.

The world was turning strangely white. He struggled to regain his feet, against the unbearable weight pressing down, glimpsed the blood spraying from his arm. His head sagged back, too heavy to bear. The creatures feeding on him and he wanted . . . he wanted . . . He cried out his awful final distress. He stood in a wide green meadow dotted with wildflowers. A figure was before him, her arms wide.

Hugo frowned, confused. 'Mother, why are you here?'

He was glad to see her, though he did not understand. It had been so long. Years. He was a boy again.

'Mother, it is dangerous.'

She shook her head, smiling warmly, delighted at the sight of him. Such a long, long time . . . She came towards him. He had never thought to see her again. He did not understand, but he knew there was no danger now. He was glad. So glad. He ran forward to leap into her open arms.

Prince Anzejarl was sitting down to breakfast in his pavilion when the news was brought to him by one of his commanders. He showed no visible reaction but within himself he knew a strange mixture of emotions as he learned of the deaths of the Duke of Giswel and his men.

'Were there survivors?' he asked.

'The majority of foot soldiers and horsemen involved in the initial attack fought their way back to the castle,' replied the commander. 'Of those that came on for the mine, more than half were killed or injured by the trolls. The others managed to escape. But it was a masterful plan, my Prince. The trolls performed excellently.'

'Injured?' queried Anzejarl. 'The trolls took prisoners?'

The man shook his head. 'They ate them. A few they dragged away for later.'

'Then they still live?'

The commander gave a shrug. 'You might call it that.'

'It would be useful to question these men,' said Anzejarl. His commander looked doubtful. Anzejarl turned to Olmana, who shook her head.

'It would not be advisable,' she said. 'You command the trolls but you would be on dangerous ground were you to try to take their meat from them now. There is a certain primordiality, a sacred and inviolable ritual, which must be observed. The trolls of Enchantment have won a battle, their passions run deep, mingling with instinct. No, Anzejarl, you would excite passions that even you cannot control were you to attempt to take their prizes from them. What could be learned from these prisoners, anyway?'

'King Leth's intentions, possibly.'

'I would doubt it.' She rose and came to him, draping her arms about his shoulders. 'Rejoice, brave Prince. The Duke of Giswel is dead. In a short time now the castle will surely fall.'

But Anzejarl could not find it within him to rejoice. Not because the concept was still relatively knew to his psyche, but more that he could find small cause for celebration at the deaths of so many brave men. For some reason he found this unsettling. As with so much else there were deeper aspects to his feelings these days, powerful undercurrents that he could not fathom.

The commander departed. Anzejarl sat on in silence.

'You are troubled?' whispered Olmana.

'I feel so many things.'

'You are still adjusting, still Awakening. But come,' she pressed her lips to his neck. 'Olmana has ways of comforting your troubled soul.'

'Behind it all, within this dark jungle of emotions, there lies a void. I feel an unknown. Unanswerable, even unaskable questions assail me. I contemplate emptiness.' Anzejarl put his white hands to his face. 'Is this part of it too, Olmana? The Awakening? Is this a feeling of being human?'

Olmana took his hands, kissing him and drawing him to his feet. She backed towards the soft palliasse of their bed, bringing him with her, lowering herself to the cushions and pressing her lips to his thigh. 'You are still growing, Anzejarl. What you sense is what has still to be filled. Let me take your mind from these things.'

He moaned with the pleasure of her kisses and her touch, yielding to her even though they had spent themselves in loving only an hour earlier. She drew him down to her, her fingers slipping beneath his garments, seeking, her warm lips touching his. Anzejarl closed his eyes. For an instant, through his pleasure, he glimpsed her in another guise, as he had seen her in his dreams. He recoiled, just momentarily, his eyes opening, staring into hers. Did his dreams tell him something, he wondered. Her lips were on his again, her tongue slid into his mouth, her body pressed against him, her fingers closing around his hardness. He could not resist her. With her free hand she peeled aside her silk gown, took one of his hands and placed it upon her naked breast. He had forgotten what he had seen, had forgotten that he knew that she was not all – or was indeed much more than – she seemed. He could not help himself.

II

Later she woke him. 'There are things we should discuss.'

The light from outside the pavilion told him the morning was well-advanced. He felt easier now. She had done what she had said. He was sharp and untroubled, his mood of earlier dispelled. He barely recalled the doubts and uncertainties that had plagued him.

'Enchantment's Edge,' she said.

'You want to move against it now?'

'Why not? Giswel Holt is no longer a threat. You can leave the siege force in place. The soldiers will not sally forth again so briskly. But now we must move swiftly. The Child is not far away, and I will not lose him.'

He saw and heard her passion as she spoke those words.

'Does Leth have him?'

'That I have yet to determine. I sense only the life of the Child. What of the forward camp, Anzejarl?'

'I have had no word, but it is early. The warriors will not have arrived there yet.' He risked a question. 'Olmana, what is this child you seek?'

Her eyes flashed. 'That is for me to know. Do not become too curious, Anzejarl. Be warned it is a trait the the Gift bestows, but in this instance at least it is one you will do well to disregard.'

He took the rebuke in silence, eased himself from the cushions, stood and dressed. His gem eyes followed Olmana as she moved about the tent. She was agitated. Strange, that her equilibrium seemed to suffer as a result of restoring his. As though she had given something of herself to restore him, and in doing so was temporarily reduced.

He wanted her again, but she turned and faced him. 'What of it? Can you march immediately?'

He nodded. 'I will give the order.'

EIGHTEEN

I

Lord Fectur, High Invigilate and now Absolute Regent of Enchantment's Edge, took proud stock of his day's achievements. It had taken precise planning and much hard work to arrive at the immensely gratifying position he now occupied. He acknowledged that Fortune had aided him, and was the more fortified and reassured for that. All else notwithstanding, he could never have overthrown Leth had not luck sided with him in his endeavours. No matter the support that he, Fectur, had gathered, no matter the doubts voiced so volubly by so many on the matter of King Leth's decisions – in themselves they would not have been enough. To have been able to demonstrate persuasively that the King was no longer in control of himself was one thing – even if most persons tacitly acknowledged that it was largely a pretext. To have himself installed as Regent – to have taken control of the throne! – was another matter entirely. It had required that extra boost, the validation of Fate.

Fectur was mightily pleased with himself. But he was not so foolish as to anticipate a smooth ride ahead.

A dominant consideration nagged: the Queen.

Her disappearance had been most fortunate. He could hardly have planned it better himself. There seemed little doubt now that she had been captured or murdered by the Krai. Troops from the Security Cadre, as well as Leth's men, had scoured the forest where her ambush had taken place, and found nothing. What tracks were visible had led away deep into the forest towards the west before they became obscured. As the Queen's body had not been recovered it seemed reasonable to assume that she had been taken – alive or dead.

If the latter, he had nothing to fear. But the possibility of the former remained a spectral threat. What if the Krai made contact, demanding terms for her release? Could he keep it quiet? Or contrive by some means to ensure that the Krai did not succeed in returning her? At any cost, she could not be allowed to return. She would undo everything; all he had achieved would be as chaff in the wind.

He briefly consoled himself with the knowledge that for the Krai negotiations of such a nature were unheard of. Their campaign to date had consisted solely of warfare and conquest. They showed scant interest in the overtures of their adversaries, irrespective of the incentives offered. Not a single monarch or envoy of the overrun Mondane Kingdoms had succeeded in establishing useful communications with Prince Anzejarl, or even his subordinates, prior to conquest. But to Fectur's knowledge the Krai had never before held such an important hostage. Would it change anything? No word had been received at Enchantment's Edge, leading him to assume not. But Fectur needed to make contact with Prince Anzejarl if he was to survive. He believed he had, almost within his grasp, the leverage to break the Krai prince's customary silence. But he could not permit any negotiations over the Queen.

Fectur wondered about Anzejarl's motives. Was he content simply to raze, plunder and subdue? It seemed not, for Fectur accepted now that there was almost certainly a link with the Legendary Child. It was as good as established that Anzejarl had the support and protection of a god, implying a deific interest in the Child. It was a daunting thought. Could Fectur really hope to sway a god from its chosen path? He would have to be utterly sure of the god's motives. Even he balked at this. Was it possible to know the mind of a god?

Perhaps, he thought, for he had a few of the right kind of indications.

Fectur returned his mind to his most immediate concerns. Leth was his first and most pressing problem. Disposing of the King – utterly necessary, demanding swift action – was something of an obstacle. An accident, perhaps a spectacular suicide while the balance of his mind was disturbed, would serve. It had to be carefully and convincingly managed in order to retain the loyalty of a strong majority of supporters. But there were important matters to attend to before he could terminate Leth. Most urgently, Leth's outburst at the Special Assembly, his outrageous assertion of knowledge of Enchantment's gods and of Enchantment itself. Though Leth had spoken in the heat of the moment, that in itself was not reason to dismiss his words. The contrary, in fact. Impassioned, he had given every impression of having blurted out far more than he had intended. And the words he had spoken carried resonances that were potentially too momentous to be disregarded without serious investigation.

Was it possible that Leth held a great secret, was somehow party to extraordinary knowledge?

The thought had not left Fectur alone. '*The gods as you claim to know them do not exist. You, or those who went before you, have created them. Those beings that do exist within Enchantment, though they may as well be gods, yet know nothing of you. Nor would they care if they did.*'

The words of a madman? Fectur had never considered Leth mad. But the implications . . .

Had Leth communed with gods?

How else could he know anything of Enchantment? Or was if bluff? Had he spoken simply to quiet the faction heads? It was a perilous ploy, if so. And no, Fectur was convinced from Leth's manner that he had unintenionally let the words slip, or at least had not given proper consideration to their impact.

As one the faction heads had turned on Fectur, demanding the truth. They wanted Leth brought before them to explain himself. Fectur had temporized, using the planned overthrow of the King to divert them. He had promised a full enquiry but then, with Leth ousted, had declared him to be in no fit state to meet them. He could not stall them for long. They were impatient, clamouring. They were not oblivious to the fact that Fectur wished to get to the King first.

But how? If Leth had secrets he would not give them up willingly. In Fectur's dungeons, of course, it would be a different story, but there was a certain protocol to be observed. Fectur's position was not one that invested in him the authority to commit torture upon the royal person. Not yet.

He had given much thought to Leth's behaviour of late. Almost at the same time as his accession to the throne the King had taken to shutting himself away in his study whenever an opportunity offered.

More so in recent months. It was a place to which Fectur lacked access. Fectur had initiated covert enquiries, keen to discover – unknowingly like Issul before him – whether Leth was engaged in magical studies. But his efforts drew a blank. No teacher was found, nor any evidence of Leth's having installed the associated paraphernalia of esoterica. Leth always went alone to his study. His voice had been heard within, but no other person had ever come out.

Symptoms of withdrawal and depression, perhaps? The burden of his responsibilities bearing too oppressively upon him? Fectur shook his head. He was not happy with that.

There was also the matter of Leth's insistence upon meeting with Grey Venger, his excitement over the Legendary Child and its connection with the True Sept. And his infuriating secrecy regarding the content of his conversations with Venger. What had he said now? That Venger's attempt upon his life had been a sham to bring about the advent of the Legendary Child? And that the Sept and Grey Venger still had vital information to impart?

Fectur mulled over all this. He had to know everything, rapidly, by whatever means necessary. Hence he was unable entirely to rule out torture upon the King. As a last resort. Or perhaps more effectively upon the sweet little Prince and Princess. He was greatly skilled, after all, and could deliver the most terrible excruciations without leaving an incriminating mark. In fact, the threat to the childrens' welfare might be sufficient in itself to loosen Leth's tongue. The priority would then be to ensure that neither Leth nor his infants could blab about it to others – or at least that they would not be believed.

Yes, he would take that path if need be. First, though, he would have a little chat with Grey Venger.

II

Venger had been housed in the lowest level of the palace of Orbia, in the warren of passages, cells and grim, hopeless chambers that comprised the dungeons of Fectur's Ministry of Realm Security. Here men and women languished in terrible solitude in tiny, cold, lightless locked cubicles or iron cages. Some were forgotten, others were destined for unimaginable attentions. Most accepted that they would never leave that place. Many prayed that they would soon be allowed to die.

Grey Venger occupied a cell set somewhat apart from the others, though not so far as to deprive him of the sounds of the sufferings of his neighbours. He was chained to the wall by wrists and ankles, spreadeagled naked against the harsh stone.

His head was slumped upon his taut chest as Fectur entered. He looked up, squinnying his eyes against the dazzle of the Lord High Invigilate's torch. Fectur set the torch in a bracket upon the opposite wall then turned and surveyed his prisoner.

'I think we have things to discuss.'

'I think we have nothing to discuss, Lord Invigilate Spectre, Oppressor of the Righteous, Corrupter of the Good,' sneered Grey Venger, his eyes glazed. 'I think there is nothing, absolutely nothing, that the Grey Venger has to say to one as low, insignificant and contemptible as you.'

'Now don't be like that,' replied Fectur, not in the least discomposed. 'After all, I am sure we have much to exchange. In the light of the changes that have occurred I think you will find yourself much more willing to talk to me.'

Venger's vision focused. 'What changes?'

Fectur waited on a half-breath. Venger knew nothing of the abrupt shift in the balance of power at Enchantment's Edge. It was perhaps expedient to keep him guessing. 'Oh, just one or two things, the nature of which I may reveal to you in due course. It all depends on yourself, of course, as I'm sure you can appreciate.'

Grey Venger produced a pained, mocking smirk. 'This is all as I had anticipated; you know that, don't you? I did not trust Leth's word. Never. I knew that if he failed to get all he wanted then this was what I could expect. But it truly makes no difference to anything. I would not have come if it did.'

Fectur considered this. Could he make use of Venger's conviction that Leth was behind his betrayal? He kept it in mind.

Venger's eyes were narrowed and hard. 'Do what you will, Great and Mighty Spectre. It will bring you nothing. No amount of pain you inflict will affect me. Never will you know the satisfaction of hearing me beg for mercy. You will learn nothing of what you want to know. The Grey Venger is far above creatures such as you. Some things you can never comprehend.'

Staring deep into Grey Venger's eyes, Fectur saw the truth in the first part of that statement. The noble art of torture would be wasted on this man. He had lived a life so attuned to denial that he was probably no longer capable even of feeling pain. Or if he felt it he would rejoice in it. For a moment Fectur was lost for words.

'You would give so much to be like me, would you not?' said Venger with satisfaction. 'But you could never. No, not one like you. I am beyond you. Far beyond.'

Surely there are tortures that would suit this man?

Fectur smiled grimly, his anger barely contained. 'We will see.'

Venger smiled once more, and for a heartbeat Fectur felt the unbearable certainty that the other man knew his thoughts. He shifted his weight, linked his hands behind his back. 'I had hoped we would speak of the Legendary Child, further the progress you have made with King Leth.'

Venger scoffed. 'Speak further? When Leth has broken his word and thrown me here, given me to you like a man throws scraps to a starving hound? There is nothing more to be said, High and Mighty. Leave me, or do your worst. It will avail you nothing.'

Fectur wetted his lips with the tip of his tongue. 'Believe it or not, Venger, it brings me no pleasure to see you here. I am a servant of the Crown, bound to adhere to the King's wishes. He has given up on you. His orders to me are to extract whatever you know, by any means. I advised against extreme measures, but King Leth has lately taken to disregarding the advice of even his closest confidants. But it does not mean that you and I cannot talk. I consider you to be of tremendous importance at this time. The True Sept also. I would rather see you walk out of here than be carried out in a shroud. And you, I am sure, wish in your heart to be witness to the events your people have prophesied for so long.'

Venger watched him. Fectur clenched his jaw. He was walking on fragile ground, for he knew almost nothing of what had passed between Grey Venger and King Leth. Yet he had to know whatever Venger knew, and if torture was not the medium then perhaps his enemy would respond to another approach.

'You believe I wish in my heart to witness your doom, and the doom of all like you?' said Venger. 'Yes, you are correct in that at least. My one regret as I am chained here is that I may not witness the deaths of the Unbelievers. But the Grey Venger has played the part that was his to play, and nothing else matters now. The One True God will acknowledge my devotion when his power is restored.'

Fectur had stiffened imperceptibly. 'Our doom? How is this?'

'It is as I have told Leth.' Venger grinned. 'Or did he not inform you?'

Fectur seethed. There was so much here, he was convinced. But he could not reveal his ignorance. Venger would toy with him. But what was this One True God?

'Leth has told me,' he said. 'I simply seek clarification. And that which you have not yet given up. I have already said, Venger, the King is persuaded that you have more to give. He grew impatient, hence you find yourself here. But I am drawn to wonder whether the King treads an optimal path just now. Hence I offer you a lifeline.'

He watched for a reaction, no matter how minute, and saw it, the tiniest glimmer of interest in Venger's dark eyes.

'You do not know whether to believe me. That is understandable. But I assure you, if I were following King Leth's orders you would be flayed meat by now.'

Venger rattled the chains that bound him to the wall. 'Unclasp me, Fectur.'

Fectur looked again, deep into those distant eyes. Then he stepped to the wall and stretched up to release the bolt on one of Venger's manacles. He watched as Venger unclasped the others and rubbed and flexed his sore wrists and ankles.

'I will leave you now, Venger. We will speak again later.'

Venger's face betrayed his surprise, but Fectur took himself from the cell. Let Venger dwell on that! And in the meantime, before he could confront Venger again, he had to learn more, for he was in danger of revealing his ignorance. Unnacceptable! He would not permit Grey Venger that pleasure.

Fectur perceived two courses open to him. First, he could approach the King and persuade, cajole, threaten, demand until he learned precisely what had passed between him and Venger. And if somehow he still failed to gain what he wanted he would turn to Pader Luminis. Neither Leth nor Pader were likely to tell him all, but interviewed separately they would provide pieces of a picture that he could fit together. Certainly they would furnish him with far more than he presently had. Then, more sure of where he stood, he could return to Grey Venger.

At the end of the dim corridor that led from the dungeons a portal opened and a bulky figure strode hurriedly towards him. As he drew closer Fectur recognized an officer from his Security Cadre. The man came on with unnatural haste, his shoulders high, then slowed. His face as it came into Fectur's light was drawn and troubled. He spoke as though gagging on his words. 'My lord, it is the King. He has vanished.'

Fectur almost shuddered. He fixed the officer with a deadly stare. '*What?*'

'The King, my lord. He cannot be found. Nor the Prince and Princess.'

'They are under supervision in the royal apartments.'

The officer swallowed. 'I know, lord. I am in charge of the detail. They have not left, yet neither are they there any longer. I have no explanation. The entrances were guarded and they did not leave. But my men have searched everywhere.'

'You have let them escape?'

'No, lord. That is what I am trying to say. They have not left, yet they are not there.'

Am I betrayed from within? The thought made Fectur dizzy. Who would dare? He could not conceive of it. But a red rage swelled within him and he could barely keep himself from striking the man dead on the spot.

He threw himself towards the exit. 'Take me there!'

In the King's apartment Fectur bellowed orders. 'Cordon off the apartments! Isolate the wing! Search every chamber, every cupboard, every nook! Search again! Keep searching till they are found!'

He rounded upon the officer who had brought him the news. 'Bring me the wretches who guarded the entrances!'

He was told that Leth had last been seen entering his study with his children. When nothing had been heard for some time the guards had grown suspicious. Eventually they had knocked upon the door, received no answer, and informed their commander, who had entered the chamber to find it empty.

Fectur scanned the study. There was only one window, a double-slit, too narrow for even a child to slip through. 'There is a secret passage here. Find it.'

Frightened soldiers shifted furniture, lifted rugs, peered behind arrases, pressed or hammered or prised wall-blocks and flagstones. A secret storage compartment was discovered in one wall, in which were manuscripts, valuables and other personal items, but no exit was found.

Was there magic involved? Fectur stood beside Leth's desk, his fingertips unconsciously settling upon the lid of a jewelled blue casket resting there. Had Leth prepared for this moment all along?

There was nothing visible to indicate magic. No apparatus, nothing. Outside of Enchantment Fectur knew of no means by which a man and two children might be magically transported between locations. But there *was* magic here. Fectur sensed it almost subliminally, a susurration along the fine hairs of his skin, a psychic breath ruffling the edges of his consciousness. The shadows in the corner of the chamber seemed unusually tinged with blue.

How had Leth done it?

He seized a chair and hurled it across the chamber. 'Find them! Find them or you will all fly from the battlements!'

Outside, six soldiers of the Security Cadre waited, pale and nervous. It was they who had guarded the two main entrances to the royal apartments. They swore before Fectur that the King and his two children had made no attempts to leave, nor had anyone entered. Fectur stared into the eyes of each of them and knew that they spoke the truth. They were terrified. They knew what they faced. The crime was too blatant. No person aiding the King in his escape would have stayed around to face the Spectre's wrath.

The children's nanny, Cascane, was brought. She was incoherent in her terror, but it was plain that she knew nothing. Fectur stormed back into the study and stood impotent with rage beside the desk where the blue casket rested. His soldiers cowered before him. They had searched and searched, then they had searched again. The apartment had been turned upside down.

Nothing.

How? How had Leth done this?

And where had he gone?

NINETEEN

I

Issul swept past the Lord High Invigilate's astonished chief secretary and burst into Fectur's office without pausing to announce her presence. Fectur sat at his desk, and at the sight of him her pent-up fury was checked, just for an instant.

He had his eyes tightly closed and was hunched forward in his seat, fists bunched upon the surface of his desk, grey hair in disarray, long spikes and strands radiating wildly from the sides of his head. His face was set in a taut, rancorous grimace; his brow and fleshy nose were blistered with tiny gleaming beads of sweat, his skin a mass of vivid red blotches. Momentarily she thought he had been struck by disease.

Fectur's eyes flashed open as the young Queen entered. He grunted, coerced a flicker of a smile onto his grim visage and slowly heaved himself erect, apparently with some effort. 'My Queen.'

'Fectur, what have you done?' Her anger returned, tempered just a little by curiosity. This was Fectur, the master of iron self-control. She had anticipated his discomfiture at her return, but to see him thus, all but a-tremble, openly the victim of his emotions, took her unawares. On a very few occasions in the past she had seen the red welts appear when his anger or frustration grew great, but this was something of a different order. Here was a man in the grip of powerful demons.

She almost felt sympathy. Almost. But as, in the early evening, she had passed through the city gate and up the magnificent azalea-and conifer-lined Sovereign's Boulevard to enter the Palace of Orbia, she had gained her first inklings of recent events here. She had sensed that something was wrong the moment she had arrived at the city gate. It was revealed in the faces of the soldiers when she announced herself, their initial confusion when she had demanded a guard of honour to escort her to the Palace. It was unspoken, sombre, furtive, and it permeated the very air of Enchantment's Edge. Something. Intangible, indefinable. A gravity, a shadowy expectancy, a brooding imminence. Something.

In disquieted tones the captain of her guard had told her of the King's sad decline as they rode, of the Lord High Invigilate's ascent to the position of Regent. Issul's hackles rose further with every fresh word he spoke. And through her rage and disbelief had come a fear. How powerful had Fectur become? Did he have the support of the government and army? Somehow he had contrived Leth's downfall in order to seize control for himself, that much was obvious. But legally, now, with her return, he must relinquish sovereignty to her. Would he do so? Did he need to? Or was she about to confront her own demise?

Her stomach had knotted. Was everything lost? Whom could she rely on? The fabulous towers stretching above her now seemed ominous and chill. But she would not shrink. For her family and the realm she would face Fectur and learn the worst.

'My lady, welcome. Welcome back,' said Fectur now, through his teeth. Fists still upon the desktop he gave a stiff bow.

'What have you done, Fectur? Where is the King? Where are my children?' She had run straight to the royal apartments, seeking Leth whom she had been informed was under medical supervision, and Galry and Jace. She found none of them, and her questions had brought only garbled replies from her staff and Fectur's guards, who were disconcertingly in evidence. She was breathless now, frantic with concern.

'What have I done? My lady, have you not been told? It has been my sad duty to assume the office of rule whilst the King recuperates from an illness that has gripped his mind. Might I say, my lady, how delighted I am to see you returned to us safe and well. We have been so concerned. Our troops have searched everywhere and we had, alas, all but given you up. I look forward to hearing of your adventures.'

Fectur could barely speak. It was evening, the dusk closing in upon the city-castle. Only two hours ago he had been in Leth's study, dealing with the impossible fact of Leth's disappearance.

Distracted, fulminating, disbelieving, he had returned to his office. He brooded darkly, questioning over and over again how Leth could have achieved this, wondering what it would mean for him, Fectur, now. He would rise above it, somehow. He would not be swayed from his course. But it was a severe, debilitating blow, complicating his plans beyond calculation.

And then, just minutes ago, a quaking lackey had brought the news that the Queen was approaching the Palace. Impossible! Unthinkable! Fate, Fortune, which earlier had seemed to smile so warmly upon him, had now conspired to bring him down. He had barely moved since the lackey retired. He was locked into himself, a welter of conflicting impulses and emotions. He could scarcely order his thoughts into a coherent pattern.

Issul stared at him. His mouth twitched, his eyes would not focus on her face. He was despicable to her eyes, but her fear and apprehension had not yet receded.

'Where is the King, Fectur? Where are my children?'

'My lady, I am at a loss to explain.'

'A loss? You?' Now another species of fear yawned in the pit of her stomach. 'Fectur, if you have harmed them . . .'

'I have not. The King was in protective custody. He had requested that your children be brought to him, with which I gladly complied. Subsequently they – all three – vanished.'

'Vanished?' There was a rushing sound in her ears; her stomach dropping, her knees threatening to buckle.

'Every effort is being made to locate them, but somehow the King has achieved the impossible. He has escaped from a chamber from which escape was not possible. Not by ordinary means. My lady, if you know of any secret way—'

She shook her head. What was he saying? Were they alive, or had he secretly had them murdered? She struggled to remain standing, heard her breath coming in short, deafening gasps.

'Or of any magical practice the King was involved in?'

'No, nothing.' Her thoughts flew back months, to the seeping blue lucency beneath Leth's study door, and the bluish aura around him the night before she had ridden for Lastmeadow. Her own enquiries had revealed nothing, yet was it possible that Leth had foreseen what was coming, had found a way out? *Oh, Leth, my babies, my darlings, be safe. Be safe!*

She blinked back tears. Could Fectur be lying? Yet he was

thoroughly thrown by something. It had to be a combination of – to his mind – disasters. Not just her return. Or had she returned just after he had committed the unthinkable? 'Fectur, their welfare is your responsibility.' Her voice was feeble, shaking.

'I am wholly aware of that. I am sparing no effort.' Now his cold carp eyes met hers. 'My lady, I do not wish to alarm you, but I am afraid . . . the King, he was distraught . . . he asked for the children . . . I saw no harm. But I fear he may have . . . in the state he was in—'

'*Never!*' She screamed, her fingers curling, outraged. 'You are responsible, Fectur. You! Only you!'

'I have acted at all times in the best interests of the realm.'

She inhaled deeply, steeling herself, forcing back the terrors that rose to rob her of all reason. 'There is much to discuss, Lord Fectur. I want a full report, within the hour. I want to know precisely how my husband came to be overthrown—'

'My lady!'

'I will have a full report, Fectur. Every detail, every ruse that was employed to undermine his authority.'

'You have it wrong. It was not like that.'

'Additionally you will convene an urgent Assembly tonight in the Hall of Wise Counsel. All ministers, nobles, knights, generals, faction heads and officiers will attend. Before them you will declare the termination of your office as Regent and your resumption of your former station. You will announce my formal investment as Sovereign in temporary stead of my husband. Is this wholly understood?'

Fectur slowly straightened. She held his gaze, the silence building like a scream between them. Finally he gave a single, curt nod. 'Quite, my lady.'

I have him! Issul almost shuddered with relief. All could have been lost in that moment, but she knew now that he lacked the support to defy her openly. How he had succeeded in removing Leth she could not imagine, but quite plainly he had achieved it without overtly threatening the integrity of the Crown. With her return he could but yield – to fight another day.

'Moreover, I wish to know all that has been learned of the Krai movements and anything else relevant to our situation.'

'Of course.'

'And you will explain to me, here and now, how it was that

you came to defy me by sending your own men to Lastmeadow to interrogate the peasant-woman Ohirbe and her family.'

'Defy you? My lady Issul, there was no defiance, I assure you. You requested an escort for the woman—'

'I expressly forbade you to interrogate her!'

'I feared for your safety, my lady, and as subsequent events have demonstrated, my fears were far from groundless. It was wholly in order that I should take whatever precautions I considered necessary to clear your way.'

'To the extent of sending Commander Gordallith, one of your most senior intelligence officers? To the extent of having him strike terror into the hearts of simple folk with warnings of what might befall them if they spoke to any other?'

'It is possible that in his endeavours to ensure your safety Gordallith may have gone a little further than was strictly required.'

'I think not. I think he followed his orders to the letter.'

'For all we knew these persons might have been kidnappers, conspirators against the throne, in the pay of our enemies . . . anything! You declined to divulge anything about them, yet insisted upon placing yourself at their mercy with only a minimal guard. I would have been remiss had I not acted to secure your welfare. As it is, the King berated me in no uncertain terms for my failure to overrule you.'

Issul glared at him, the heat rising again to her cheeks. 'You know—' she began angrily, then halted. It was futile. Fectur could glide smoothly around her, ever able to cite as evidence in his favour the fact that she had been ambushed and almost killed. She should wait, then, until she had all the facts. But if she found he had acted illegally . . .

She could not think clearly. A scream persisted at the forefront of her thoughts: *my babies, Leth, what has happened to you?*

She held out her hand, palm up. 'Gordallith took something from Ohirbe's husband's cousin, the man called Julion. I will have it, now.'

Fectur's thin brows lifted quizzically.

'Do not push me, Fectur!'

'Ah,' said Fectur, a forefinger raised. 'You must be referring to this.'

He stepped across to a cabinet behind his desk, opened a small compartment and drew forth a small white object upon a leather thong, which he passed to Issul.

Intrigued, she turned it over in her fingers. It was ivory, as far as she could tell. A little stained and ingrained with age, no larger than the terminal phalanx of her thumb. It was beautifully, intricately carved and shaped, representing an abstract form, vaguely animal-like, but unidentifiable. 'What have you learned about it?'

'It appears to be a trinket, nothing more, of curiosity value only. We have discovered no special properties. Apparently it was given to the child whom you suspect to be the Legendary Child – given by a stranger in the woods.'

Issul studied him, suspecting more, but his face was blank. The welts upon his skin were dissipating; he seemed to have accepted the inevitable and regained his customary command of himself. She remained wary, despite her triumph. 'If you know more, Fectur, tell me now, for I will find out soon enough.'

'There is nothing more.'

Issul studied the little carving a moment longer, then slipped it into a pocket in her tunic. She turned and called over her shoulder, 'Shenwolf!'

From the outer office the rangy figure of Shenwolf stepped through the door, glanced first to Issul, then stiffened to attention and bowed his head tersely to the Lord High Invigilate. Fectur observed him with narrow-eyed bemusement, shot with indignation that someone – a common trooper – should be invited into his private office without his prior permission. 'Who is this?'

'A brave and loyal soldier of the 1st Battalion of the King's Light Cavalry. His name is Shenwolf. Through his efforts – initially his efforts alone – I was saved. He will be accorded the highest honours. It is solely through his courage and heroism that I am able to stand before you now.'

Fectur's grey eyes travelled over Shenwolf, taking in every detail, despising him. Tall, lean, young, perhaps handsome in a rough and undefinable way. A firm jaw, bright, intelligent eyes, resolute and good-humoured. There was a powerful rapport between Issul and Shenwolf, this he detected instantly. The way the trooper's eyes had gazed at the young Queen as he entered, the way they so plainly longed to return to her now. Were they lovers? If not, what would it take to bring them together? Fectur considered. It would be the Queen who would demur, certainly not the soldier; but she was impressed by him, this much she had already made abundantly plain.

Fectur filed the notion away in a secure compartment somewhere in the back of his mind, for future consideration. Possibilities would suggest themselves. He was resigned to the fact that he had to begin to plan again, for the future. His immediate aspirations lay in tatters about his feet. How it galled, but he could not stand against Issul, at least not yet. Not directly against the Crown.

But if she were shown to be an adulteress . . .

Yes, he could make use of this. He was down, temporarily disadvantaged, but not beaten. Far from that. Nothing was unsalvageable. The future beckoned, and his shadow extended there.

'I said, "it is through Shenwolf's courage and heroism that I am able to stand here today," Lord Fectur,' repeated the Queen.

Fectur's mouth twitched. 'Allow me to express to you my overwhelming gratitude, and that of the Realm, Shenwolf. Our precious Queen is returned, safe and well, and for that we give unqualified thanks. You will not be forgotten.'

'Now, about your business, Fectur. Have the Assembly convened by midnight at the latest.'

Outside, Issul strode down the corridor from Fectur's office, trembling, wanting to scream, needing to weep, unable to think of anything but her children and Leth. Would she see them again? Would she ever know their fate?

She spoke quietly, in an unsteady voice, to the young cavalryman at her side, 'Mark him well, Shenwolf. There stands an enemy perhaps more vicious and determined than any other I may face.'

II

In the dark silent hours Issul stood at her window and gazed across the barely discerned rooftops, the straining, crowded towers of her beloved Enchantment's Edge. She looked past the city walls, to the void beyond the scarp, and she felt nothing of the elation that had gripped her earlier in the day as she had ridden with her three companions up the climbing road towards the city gate. Dawn's first pale tints had yet to illumine the eastern sky; Issul could see nothing but the innumerable lantern-lights and little communal fires of the city-castle, the dense starclouds so infinitely far above, and the far-off glow of the weirdlights of Enchantment.

I have seen you, she said to herself, and her pulse quickened. *I have been within you.*

She had been within a mysterious tower inside Enchantment, had spoken with a threefold child-being which called itself Triune. She had gazed upon bright, blazing mountains and watched the shifting, changing colours of the air. And still she was no wiser. As if Mystery might be the natural state.

Her heart swelled. Tears streaked her pale cheeks. To return here and find such turmoil and uncertainty, such betrayal, mistrust, anger, fear. Her children gone, her husband gone, Enchantment's Edge being torn apart from within even as it was assailed from without. And she had returned with nothing. No answers, no way through the darkness. She felt more desolate now than in even her darkest moments in captivity.

The night had gone well, in its own manner. The Assembly had convened in the Hall of Wise Counsel at midnight. Issul had occupied the Seat of Sovereignty, Lord Fectur and one of the senior knights upon her right, Pader Luminis and the Commander of the King's Forces upon her left, the assorted nobles, ministers, grandees, sundry officiers and faction heads of Enchantment's Edge ranged before her. It was an impressive turnout at such short notice, which both pleased and concerned her. If she had their support, all would be well. But if the majority put themselves against her she could be rendered powerless. She had tried studying their faces to gauge the mood, but could read little in what she saw.

The ceremony was brief and to the point. Lord Fectur stood and formally welcomed the Queen, expressed his heartfelt gladness at her safe return. His manner was subdued. With the minimum of words he renounced sovereign authority in her favour. Issul had suppressed a bitter smile, wondering how much those few words were costing him.

When he had done she addressed the assembly briefly. She gave them her thanks for their loyalty and spoke of her intention to rule resolutely and justly in her husband's stead, and to respond to the current crisis in the manner she believed Leth would approve. Leth's disappearance had not yet been made public, and for the present she left it at that. Re-seating herself, she scanned the faces before her and saw scepticism, indignation, disappointment on a significant number, but many were with her and when she departed the Hall she was buoyed by the sound of rousing cheers.

Once alone again her fears had mounted. She could not sleep, though she was exhausted. Too many things lay upon her mind, and how she missed Leth, how she missed Galry and little Jace. How she feared for them.

Be safe! Be safe! Be safe!

As she gazed towards the distant lights she fingered the little carving absent-mindedly. Was Fectur being truthful about this? She was inclined to believe so, for he would surely not have handed it over so readily had he discovered anything of interest. But if the carving lacked significance why had the stranger made a gift of it to the Child? Coincidence?

She would probably never know. The Child had vanished. The old woman also. And the identity of the stranger who had given the gift would almost certainly never be learned.

Issul heaved a desperate sigh, racked by waves of despondency and guilt. She had brought disaster upon her world; without her the Legendary Child would never have lived. And still she knew almost nothing about the Child.

There was a soft knock at the door. Issul dabbed at her eyes with a silk chiffon, gathered her gown about her and went to answer.

'Pader,' she smiled wanly, genuinely pleased to see the little Murinean. 'Thank you for coming. I need so much to talk to you.'

'And I you.' Pader Luminis stepped lightly into the room, the steward who had brought him fading back into the depths of the royal apartment. 'But what is this? Issul, my child, my bright young Queen, you are sad. Your eyes are pools of sorrow, your brow clouded with worry, your cheeks deprived of colour, your lips adroop with remorse. Come. Come now. We can hardly talk when you are like this. Oh, look! Oh my, what have we here?'

Following his gaze Issul glanced across the chamber. A brilliant shower of radiant golden stars danced in a column before the window. Countless, they spun, twirled, darted and suddenly flew in a bright plume straight towards Issul. She stepped back, lifting her hands. The stars were transformed into a score of tiny finches, multi-hued and loudly chirruping. Their fluttering wings stirred the air as they encircled Issul, playing upon her loose hair and gown.

Issul laughed. She spun, trying to follow the movements of the tiny birds, reaching out to try to touch one. The finches became stars once more, shimmering blue this time. They whirled in a cloud, floated to the window and were gone.

Issul smiled, clasping her hands. 'Pader! Oh Pader, how I love you!'

'Ah, sweet child, that's better. It gladdens my heart to see a smile light your face once more. Now come, let us sit. I am anxious to learn of everything that has befallen you since you took leave of Enchantment's Edge.'

'And I rely upon you to tell me all that has happened in my absence. I return to find Fectur as Regent, my husband and children gone. Pader, how is this? What has happened here? But wait! Before you attempt to answer that, there is something I must tell you. A confession. Will you listen, Pader, and promise not to speak of what I say to any other? You are the only one I can trust.'

'Only I?' Pader clicked his tongue, adjusting his robe to sit. 'I think that is not so. What of the dashing young cavalry man who has seen you home, and your other two companions? From what I hear they have proved themselves worthy of your trust?'

'Shenwolf? Yes, he risked his life again and again to save mine. We have become . . . good friends. I think I can safely say that. Certainly he has earned my trust. But in truth I know very little about him. His background, his past . . . He shies away from my enquiries. Phisusandra and Kol have also proved themselves.' She smiled briefly to herself, remembering their faces when they had entered the city with her and finally learned her true identity. It had been a moment to savour. 'Yes, all three are good, brave and loyal men. Even so, as Leth is not with us, what I have to say now I dare impart to no one but you.'

'Then I am honoured.'

Issul's look became sombre and inward. 'Pader, my sister Ressa gave birth to a child.'

Pader's wrinkled head, which had bowed slightly in an attitude of attentiveness, came up sharply. 'Ressa? Issul, what are you saying? I know of no child.'

'I know. I know. Just listen. You know she was attacked, as was Mawnie. The full details were never made known. Our parents put out the story that they were mauled by a bear. But you were told, about the creature.'

Pader nodded.

'You weren't told everything, Pader. I knew more, but I told no one. Not Leth, not Mawnie, not our mother and father. Ressa made me swear.' She hesitated a moment, frozen in the horror of recollection. 'I was at her bedside just a couple of days before she passed away. She had been in a feverish, unbroken sleep for some time. But she woke, suddenly, and looked at me, and said, quite clearly, "Iss, when my baby comes, tell no one. They will be shamed. Tell no one."

'I took her to be in a delirium. We knew nothing of a pregnancy, and there were no signs. Duke Hugo was courting her, was besotted with her and had let it be known that he intended to ask for her hand, but even so . . . I began to say something, something to do with Hugo, but she grasped my hand, fiercely. I can feel it now, burning hot, and the intensity in her eyes. "It is not Hugo. No one must know, Iss. No one, but especially not Hugo. Promise me. Swear to me that you will never tell a soul. And promise me you will take care of my baby. Take it somewhere, in secret. Look after my child, Iss, dear Iss, but let no one know. I am trusting you, you alone. Not Mawnie, no, never tell Mawnie. Do you promise?"

'What else could I do?' said Issul to Pader Luminis. 'It made no sense. She was fevered and deluded, but I promised, to calm her. She gripped my hand even more tightly, then closed her eyes and slept again. Two days later she was dead.'

Issul paused, gathering the courage to continue. 'On the day before Ressa's funeral I went to her room to be with her one last time. She lay upon her bed, draped in her funeral gown, so peaceful, too young and beautiful. I stood there and wept silently, enraged at a world so cruel as to permit such an injustice as this. I spoke to her, a few final parting words, and was about to leave. But as I turned away . . . Pader, it is so painful to describe. As I turned away, she moved. Ressa moved. Pale and still and dead, yet her body gave a twitch and then was suddenly convulsed. Her back arched; something shifted beneath her gown. She seemed to be undergoing a most terrible, terrifying struggle, yet her face remained serene and lifeless, her arms limp at her sides.

'I do not know what I did, Pader. I was transfixed, I think, rooted to the floor. Ressa's poor body writhed and bucked, her legs . . . *splayed*. It was terrible, Pader! Terrible! Terrible!'

Pader Luminis took the young Queen's hand in his, calming her with soothing words yet barely able to contain his own feelings, so shocked was he at what he was hearing. Leth's fears had been borne out.

'And then the blood,' continued Issul, her face haggard. 'Dark blood, soaking through her pale gown, so much of it, soaking the bed beneath her. And Ressa was still. Nothing was moving. I don't know how long I stood there, just staring, sobbing, so terrified, not knowing what to do. And then, a sound. A thin, tiny cry. And the smallest movement, almost nothing at first, beneath her gown where the blood still spread between her lifeless thighs. And the cry again. I did not know . . . oh, I was so frightened. But I stepped forward, so afraid, and reached for her gown, lifted it, exposing her, not knowing what I would see. And there it was. I could not . . . I didn't . . . a baby, perfectly formed, so small, smaller than any child I had ever seen. A boy, impossibly. Pader. How? How? Ressa's son!'

Issul's voice had risen to a querulous contralto, and now she broke down, the tears streaming freely down her cheeks, her hands rigid before her face.

Pader sat in numbed, troubled silence, grappling with the images she had presented. Presently he rasped, 'You are saying, this child, this baby, was the result of Ressa's having been raped upon Sentinel's Peak? But that happened just weeks earlier.'

'It was an unnatural child, Pader. It had given birth to itself, three days after Ressa's death. There was no indication – she did not swell, nor lactate. Yet there it was, a tiny baby boy, human in every respect, except . . .'

'Except?'

'Oh, I don't know, but its eyes. The way it looked at me, intelligently, as though it knew me. As though it was fully aware. But I was distraught, I hardly took anything in. I gave no thought to the father at the time. Only afterwards did I admit to myself that it must have been that monstrous thing on Sentinel's Peak.'

'You are positive it is not Hugo's?'

'If it was, he knew nothing of it. I observed him, then and since, and I am convinced. I have even, on occasion, made oblique references in his presence. He made no response whatever. And even if I am wrong, there is no explanation for the mode and manner of its birth. But no, it was the offspring of that thing upon the Peak.'

'What did you do?'

'I minded Ressa's request. Innocently, I suppose foolishly, I took the child and hid him in my own rooms. Fortunately he slept for much of the time. When he woke I gave him goat's milk. I wanted to tell someone. I desperately needed help, but I was confused and could think only of Ressa's insistence that no one know.'

'But what of Ressa's body? The blood?'

'I went to my father and told him I had found her thus. He was stricken with horror when he saw, and of course there was no explanation. I longed to tell him, but did not dare. It would not have helped. Between the two of us we removed the bloodstained bedding and clothed Ressa in a new gown. Not even my mother knew. Father did not want her to suffer. He has never spoken of it since, not even to me. He has shut it out.

'Immediately after the funeral I returned to Orbia. It happened that one of my staff had a sister who had just given birth to a stillborn child. Her name was Ohirbe. It was she whom I went to see at Lastmeadow. I went to her, disguised as a woman of wealth and some status, and arranged for her to take the boy and raise him more or less as her own. Understand, Pader, I knew the child to be unnatural. I also knew something of the tale of the Legendary Child, as propounded by the preachers of the True Sept, but I was not a follower of the Sept, and could not believe this could apply. It was far-fetched, impossible. Perhaps I simply did not want to believe it. The baby, unnatural though his birth was, was my nephew. I could not admit his existence, but I had promised to keep him safe. This seemed the best way. Only now have all my worst, half-realized fears come true and I can see that I acted wrongly, yet still I know so very little.'

'And did you meet the Child, in Lastmeadow?'

'Yes, and he knew me. He had seen me only at his birth, but he knew me. Pader, has there been any word from the True Sept in my absence?'

'You have not been told? King Leth visited Overlip. He spoke with Grey Venger there and persuaded him to come here, to Orbia.'

'He was here? Venger?'

'And is now. Surprisingly, he came as a guest, for constructive talks, acknowledging the fact that what is happening now precludes his remaining hidden. What he has told Leth is far from comforting. But now he resides in the Lord High Invigilate's dungeons, against Leth's wishes, and who knows what Fectur has done to him?'

'The gods! Fectur told me nothing of this. He was to have brought me a full report this evening, but he excused himself on a pretext and a promise to present his case first thing in the morning.' She rose and hurried to the door, passed through her apartment to the main entrance and summoned the captain of her personal guard. 'You will go immediately to the dungeons of the Ministry of Realm Security. Upon my authority you will secure custody of the prisoner, Grey Venger, and take him to the guest's apartments. Guard him well and let no harm befall him. Take sufficient men and if you meet resistance taking him from the cell, mount an armed guard about him. I will join you as soon as I can.'

Back with Pader she enquired about Leth's discussions with Grey Venger. Pader told her all he knew, and as he did so Issul's last desperate hopes that they might not be dealing with the Legendary Child were finally dispelled. And still she knew so little. And the Child, Moscul, her nephew, was gone. In her grasp, then gone.

'What are we to do, Pader?'

The Murinean ran his hand over his pate, shaking his head gravely. 'I do not know, dear Issul. I truly do not know.'

Issul stood in renewed agitation, walked towards the window, then halted half way. 'What do you make of Fectur's account of Leth's and the children's disappearance?'

'He has not spoken of it to me directly. I am told the King has "escaped", or more mysteriously, simply vanished with the Prince and Princess while under guard in your apartments.'

Issul nodded.

'Prior to your return it might have been in Fectur's interest to permanently remove Leth, and his heirs. Even so, it is highly unlikely that he would have acted so swiftly. He would have been very foolish to have committed murder at this time, even disguised as accident. It would seriously undermine what has been a quite brilliantly executed coup on his part. No, he is not by any reckoning a foolish or impetuous man. He should have been carefully biding his time, consolidating his position. Furthermore, I think there was much he wished to learn from Leth.' Pader slowly shook his head. 'He has backed down almost graciously now, wrongfooted and embarrassed not only by your return but by his inability to explain the disappearances.'

'Then how, Pader? Magic? Your magic, the illusions you produce so effortlessly, can something of the kind have been used to transport Leth and Galry and Jace? Or to conceal them?'

Pader Luminis smiled sadly and shook his head. 'No, child. I have told you before, what I produce are fripperies. They cannot be sustained for more than a few moments, and they take years of study and practice to produce. King Leth has never seriously studied magic. Yet magic, I am quite sure, is at the heart of this. Something more powerful than anything known to us.'

She looked at him curiously. 'You know something?'

'It may not help you. But I spoke with Leth on more than one occasion in recent days. He had become deeply worried, tense, distracted and mistrustful of almost everyone. We spoke of many things, largely related to the scourge that has befallen Enchantment's Edge, and the many baffling forms it seems to be taking. Like you, Leth was keen to discover all I might know about the Legendary Child and the gods of Enchantment. On the way to attend a Special Assembly he said something which, whilst not particularly odd given the circumstances, did strike me as portentous. He told me that he might come to me with an unusual request, and that if he did I should not question him about it. Subsequently, only hours before Fectur moved against him, he did come to me in my private apartment. He said he feared the inexplicable, and would not elucidate. But he said, "Pader, if anything should happen to me, there is something you must do.' And he took me to his study and showed me something which he said I was to pass into your hands under specific circumstances, if you ever returned.'

Pader hesitated.

'Pader, what? What was this thing?'

'I will have to show you. I believe – hope – it is in the study still, but I lack the authority to go there.'

Issul grabbed a shawl. 'Quickly. Show me.'

Inside Leth's private study there was no evidence of the rigorous searches that had taken place just hours earlier. As far as Issul could tell nothing had been removed, though she was not familiar enough with the chamber to be sure of every article.

'Strange,' mused Pader as they entered, his eyes upon Leth's workdesk. 'Leth took the object from a secret compartment in the wall over there. He told me that, were I ever to have to find it, that was where it would be. Yet it is here, upon the desk.' He raised the blue casket almost reverentially in both hands, gazing at it, then at Issul. 'Child, he told me that should anything happen to him I was to take this and ensure its safety, and give it to you if you returned.'

Tears stung Issul's eyes. 'He believed I would return?'

'He hoped beyond hope.'

'But if I didn't?'

'I was to safeguard it and pass it to Prince Galry upon his accession. "This casket is more precious than you can imagine, Pader," he said. "It is fragile, mysterious, wonderful, and perhaps to be feared. It is also easily destroyed. It must be protected at all costs, for it is perhaps the means by which we will be saved".'

Wonderingly, Issul took the casket. It was light in her nervous hands. 'What does it contain?'

'The King would not say. He told me it cannot be opened, save by the right person at the right time, but if it comes to harm we will be lost.'

'He knew? He knew something was going to happen to him?'

Pader gave a shrug. 'Perhaps a premonition, or simply a reasonable precaution. He was highly emotional and plainly suspicious of something, or someone. But . . . I do not think even he knew what, or limited his suspicions to any single individual. My Queen, this is truly a rare and extraordinary object. I sense . . . I sense its nature, its power. You must safeguard this as you would your own children.'

She flinched at that, and Pader looked away, regretting the choice of words.

'Can you tell me anything more, Pader?'

'Leth offered nothing more, and forbade me to ask further.'

Tentatively Issul tried the catch on the casket, but as Pader had predicted the lid was fast.

'Let us hope that the King – and your children, too – will quickly return to us. Then the mystery may be explained.'

Issul held back the lump that swelled in her throat. She turned the casket over in her hands, examining its outer casing. 'Of what is it made?'

'Uncommon material, some sort of shell or keratinous substance I think, set with stones I cannot identify. There can be little doubt that it originates from Enchantment.'

'Enchantment?' Her eyes widened. *What can this thing be?* She clasped the casket to her bosom. *Oh Leth, I am so alone! Why did you not say more? Leth, my babies, where are you? Where are you?*

Quickly she removed her shawl and spread it upon the floor, then, kneeling, placed the casket at its centre and carefully wrapped it in the fabric. 'Pader, no one must know of this.'

'I swore as much to Leth. He bade me warn you, or whomsoever I eventually passed it on to: its existence must always remain a secret.'

Issul stood. She glanced towards the door. A shadow had settled there. She all but gasped at the sight of the figure in its frame. 'Lord Fectur!'

Fectur's eyes were slits, flicking from the bundle in her arms to Pader Luminis to Issul. Issul's heart raced. What had he seen? What had he heard?

'What do you want?'

'Your men have removed a prisoner from my custody, apparently on your authority.'

'That is correct. I am told that Grey Venger came here voluntarily, a guest of my husband.'

'He is a dangerous subversive, a madman, an assassin.'

'*Ahem!*' Pader Luminis cleared his throat. 'It has been established that the assassination attempt upon the King was a sham. The plan was not to murder the King but to establish conditions permitting the advent of the Legendary Child, following prophecies contained in the screed of the True Sept.'

This was news to Issul. She flashed Pader a grateful glance. Fectur glowered, a sneer upon his thin lips. 'You place great trust in the words of a common criminal. I suspect him rather of bargaining for redemption.'

'It is irrelevant,' said Issul. 'He was the King's guest. Now he is mine. His incarceration was unnecessary and presumptuous.'

'He holds information that both King Leth and myself consider crucial to the wellbeing of the realm.'

'All the more reason to make available to him the hospitality normally accorded a respected guest.'

'I was making progress. I had released Venger from his bonds, gained his trust. He was on the point of opening up to me. Now I fear the information is lost.'

'We will discuss this further when I have spoken to Venger. In the meantime you may relinquish all responsibility for him. I consider that done. Now, there is the matter of the report I asked for.'

Fectur ground his teeth. 'It will be done by morning.'

'Good. I will speak to you then. Thank you, Lord Fectur.'

Fectur's eyes went briefly to the bundle she was pressing unconsciously to herself. He seemed on the verge of saying something more, but bowed his head instead and withdrew. Issul released a long, pent-up breath. Her stomach and hands were damp where she clutched the bound casket. She exchanged a gaunt, haunted look with Pader Luminis.

III

They returned to Issul's chamber and for some minutes Issul listened nervously as Pader recounted all that had taken place in her absence: the renewed attempts to have the Deist Edict repealed, and Leth's declaration of Emergency (which, under Fectur's auspices and pressure from the factions, had now been withdrawn); the slooths' attack and the Krai's encirclement of Giswel Holt; Leth's conversations with Grey Venger, the King Without A Soul and the Legendary Child; Fectur's briefly triumphal overthrow of the King.

'Was there any justification, Pader, in what Fectur did?'

Pader slowly kneaded his jaw with one hand. 'He acted, strictly speaking, within the law, I am afraid. But the case against Leth was tenuous; he was quite viciously and calculatedly exploited.'

'But was he sick?'

'I believe not. He was, though, exhausted and severely distracted. Your disappearance, combined with everything else, affected him badly. And . . . something else. I think now it must have had something to do with this.'

He nodded at the blue casket which lay upon a table at Issul's side.

'What does Fectur know about this?'

'As far as I am aware, nothing. He searched the chamber and must have seen it, but attached no importance to it.'

'Did he see us, Pader? Did he hear?'

'I pray not.'

Issul sat in silence, her head spinning. Finally, after profound consideration, she made the statement: 'Pader, I have been to Enchantment.'

Pader stared at her in sudden consternation.

'It is true. I was captured by the Krai. There was an underground chamber, and within it a strange thing, a Farplace Opening.' She related her experience within the tower chamber, her encounter with the three white-haired, blue-eyed children who called themselves by the single name of Triune.

Pader stood and paced the room, his head bowed and brow furrowed in deepest contemplation. 'I am astounded. A way into Enchantment?'

'And a way out. But for what?'

'And you were held, you say?'

'I could do nothing. I was helpless. I have no way of knowing whether I could have survived outside the tower.'

'And it was the Krai who built the bunker where the Farplace Opening is lodged?' said Fectur.

'But Krai were not permitted to enter. Once the chamber was built they were excluded. I am sure they did not know what was in there. And Triune claimed to have "acquired" the Farplace Opening or the tower, or both, from the god which aids the Krai.'

And, she thought, Triune had said that something of Enchantment was now hers. And what else? *In the dream you may not always be the dreamer. The dream may not be yours. Or it may be, and it may become real, now or soon or never. All things may be.*

Pader was gripping his jaw now, shaking his head in utter abstraction. Issul's eyes went to the blue casket resting at her side. 'Pader, there is such mystery here.'

TWENTY

I

The dim ghost-light of early morning found Issul awake upon the bed she shared with Leth. Sleep had continued to elude her and she hovered on the fitful border of wakefulness, tormented, mystified and deeply afraid. For the present she had avoided meeting with Grey Venger. She recognized that she was in no fit state to deal with him, and also required a fuller picture of the situation, which would be provided by Fectur's forthcoming report and another discussion with Pader Luminis.

Issul thought about Mawnie. She had visited her bedchamber briefly upon returning to Orbia. Mawnie had been asleep, sedated. Doctor Melropius reported that her condition had not improved. When awake she was unpredictable, sometimes violent, and in her lucid moments had no recollection of what was happening to her. Issul had held her hand for a few moments, but was too pressed to remain. Gazing at Mawnie's pale, sleeping face, virtually the mirror-image of Ressa's, Ressa in her death-sleep, Issul had almost recoiled, suddenly fearful, the memories flooding back. A dreadful unknown confronted her.

Lir, Mawnie's and Hugo's little daughter, was sitting cross-legged on the end of her mother's bed. Issul extended her arms to embrace her but Lir rolled away, slid from the bed and hid herself beneath, from where she obstinately and silently refused to be extricated.

Issul dwelt now on Mawnie's dementia. What was it she had blurted out in her delirium, prior to Issul's departure from Enchantment's Edge? 'It was me. Truly. It was me he wanted. In the woods. In the woods.' Poor Mawnie had kept the dreadful memory of the attack and Ressa's rape and murder buried for so long. Finally, inevitably with hindsight, she had cracked. Ressa's death, Mawnie's doomed marriage to Hugo, his subsequent disappointment and heartless rejection of her . . . She had been building to this, becoming dissolute, seeking solace where none was to be found. Issul racked herself, anguished that she had not done more to help her sister.

Before he had left earlier in the night to conduct researches at the Arcane College, Pader Luminis had been at pains to try to set Issul's mind at rest. She was not to blame. Firmly but gently he had bade her understand this. She could not hold herself directly responsible either for Mawnie or the advent of the Legendary Child and the disasters that were befalling Enchantment's Edge. But Issul's doubts would not be quelled. Somehow, if she had acted differently . . .

Issul threw herself upon her side. She stared at the mysterious blue casket on the cabinet beside her bed. *What is this thing? What is its power, its nature? . . . 'Perhaps the means by which we will be saved'. A magical blue casket. How?*

'Safeguard this as you would your own children.'

She thrust herself up, crying out. Pader's words echoed relentlessly in her mind. *My children! What am I doing here? I should be up, doing something, searching for Galry and Jace!*

But she remained as she was. What could she do? The search continued throughout Orbia for the King and their children, but Issul entertained little hope now that they would be found. Something had taken them, and whether they lived or died she was persuaded that no amount of human searching was likely to reveal them.

Her eyes returned to the casket. She felt anger, at Leth, at the casket itself. Why could not Leth have been more explicit in his instructions to Pader Luminis? He should have given an indication. Anything. What did he know that had prevented him revealing more?

The casket had to be linked in some way to Leth's and the children's disappearance. She found herself fearing and loathing it, wanting to smash it even as she wanted to take it to her and protect it from a violent and uncertain world in which it was so fragile.

Around and around went the thoughts in her head, like a storm, with no order. Was this what Leth had gone through? And Mawnie? An external madness, a chaos, that worked its way inward, infecting the mind . . . She thought of Fectur, wondered again what he had seen, what he might even now be plotting. Issul's swollen eyes ached. Her breast was constricted with a soundless, ceaseless shriek.

She lay back again. Her eyes were on the raftered ceiling where shadows shifted uneasily in the subdued amber light cast by the flame of a single candle. She had one other thing to consider now: the little ivory carving. She had shown it to Pader. If there was anyone in Enchantment's Edge who could tell her anything about it, other than the stranger who had given it to Moscul, it would be he. Even so, she had not expected much. Fectur would have passed the carving to Pader and the Arcane College for examination, and plainly had learned nothing of value. But to her surprise Pader had been forthcoming.

'I told Lord Fectur that this was unusual but without value,' he said.

There was an inflection in his voice and an arch look in his eye.

'Do you know something more?'

'The carving resonates a subtle aura not dissimilar to that of the casket. It is almost certainly from Enchantment.'

'But you made no mention of this to Fectur?'

'I wished to speak first to the King.'

Issul smiled to herself.

'There is one other thing,' added Pader Luminis. 'The carving is hollow. It is what is within it that generates its aura. I cannot guess how it has been sealed inside, nor would I wish to liberate it until I know more.'

'Are you able to discover more?'

'Frankly, no. At least, not with the resources presently available to me.'

'Is it harmful?'

'I do not know. It is yet another of Enchantment's mysteries. I would say that, while it remains sealed within the tusk, it can exert virtually no effect. One wonders whether perhaps that is the reason it was sealed in there in the first place.'

'This was given by a stranger to the Legendary Child.'

'That is very interesting. I would say, sweet Issul, that if you wish to learn more, short of taking the possibly perilous route of breaking open the tusk, you should locate the stranger and ask him.'

'The stranger has never been seen again, Pader.'

Issul lay still as a breath of breeze stirred the candle-flame and the shadows quivered among the beams. *Ask the stranger, who has never been found, who is now long gone.*

She did not know how long she lay there, but she became aware suddenly that she must be sleeping. For she was having a dream, and in the dream she was gazing across the chamber, and a strange figure was standing there, bulky yet indistinct, seeming to hover before one wall.

'Who are you?'

The figure, which was turned towards the window, now brought itself around to face her. She could see no features. It was a vaguely mannish form, hunched and stooped, and gave the appearance of great age. It was clad in long, ragged, ill-fitting robes and strips of cloth, and leaned with two bound hands upon a thick staff. The head was huge, a bundled mass of rags, ribbons and bindings, and all around the figure hung a pale bluish luminescence, which somehow failed to cast light upon anything.

'Who are you?' Issul repeated, sitting up.

For some moments the figure was silent, then in a cracked, muffled, hoary voice it said, 'I? Who am I? It is a good question, but a complex one. I find myself, in the light of epiphany, forced to redefine my own understanding of who and what I am and have become. But for ease of communication, for you, for now, I am Orbus. I am the Orb and the voice of the Orb. The Orb of Orbia.'

This answer was so extraordinary as to reinforce Issul's belief that she was dreaming. She stared at the strange figure in baffled silence.

'Do you not know me?'

Issul shook her head. 'Should I?'

The bundled creature slowly nodded to itself. 'Good. Leth heeded my instructions, then.'

'Leth? You know Leth?'

Orbus made a wheezing sound. 'Of course.'

'Do you know where he is? And my children?'

'Your children?' Orbus raised a tattered hand. 'Ah, now I see. They are the cause. Of course. Yes, I know where they are.'

'Where? Are they safe? Can I see them? The cause of what? Have you harmed them?'

'Stop! Stop!' protested Orbus, twitching his other hand which held the staff. 'Always the way with you in the formed world! A babble of questions, never waiting for answers.'

'What have your done with them?' Issul screamed.

Orbus recoiled slightly, taken aback. 'I? I have done nothing with them. It is quite the contrary.'

'Then where are they?'

'They are here.' Orbus gestured towards himself, then to the blue casket upon the bedside cabinet. 'They are there. They are within.'

Am I dreaming? she wondered. 'I do not understand. Within where?'

Orbus gave a sigh. 'So hard to explain. Leth has broken the laws that govern my existence. Inadvertently, I suspect. He has introduced new elements and trapped himself within the universe, the world, that I have become. Your children also.'

Issul put her hands to her crown, shaking her head.

'I am not making myself plain,' said Orbus. 'I apologize, but I, like you, am also endeavouring to understand precisely what has happened.'

Issul stared at him. She had the impression that were she to approach and touch him she would find her fingers passing through empty space. Yet she did not doubt that he was real and that he stood there before her. And if she dreamed, the dream was also as real and meaningful a part of her existence as anything else. She tried to order her thoughts. 'Tell me again, what *are* you?'

'*I* am Orbus. I am my world. It is what I have become after long, long ages of solitude. I admit I am rather in a maze. You see, it is difficult even for me to comprehend, but I find myself obliged to accept that I have become something that I have always denied I could be. You look at me, what do you see? I am ancient and bent, my head is a bundle of rags, I know very little. Yet . . .' he emitted a profound sigh. 'I have *created* . . . I have become . . . I have given birth to . . . a fledgling world. A universe, in fact. What other conclusion can I draw, then? No matter what I have been, no matter what I have always believed, *I must be a god.*' He sighed again. 'It changes everything.'

Issul caught her breath. 'You – you are one of the gods of Enchantment?'

'Ah,' Orbus seemed to focus on that. 'Yes, let us use that as a starting point. Yes, once I was of Enchantment, was one of those beings whom you mistakenly term gods. This is a long tale, I warn you. It is one which ordinarily you would never be permitted to hear. But these are far from ordinary circumstances. Hence, if you are willing to listen I am quite willing to divulge.'

Issul nodded, enthralled, incredulous and filled with apprehension. As he had with Leth, Orbus recounted to her the history and nature of Enchantment, the evolution of its mighty denizens. He told her of his own defeat and dispossession, the severance from his soul and his eons-long imprisonment within the blue casket. 'For longer than I know I existed without consciousness of myself. But slowly, infinitely slowly, I became aware, discovered a recollection, a flow of memories of what had gone before and what I had been. And later, much later, I discovered that I had the ability to assume a form – the form you see before you. I began to explore the empty blue world that I had been transformed into. It is a strange concept and I can see that you have difficulty comprehending. But please, for now, just accept what I am saying. We are dealing, you see, with the absolute paradox of being, the mystical, ungraspable ramifications of existence, which defy intellectual comprehension. We are dealing with a world within a world within a world. It is a world which is both conscious and not. A mind within a mind within a mind. The world is I and I am it, and until now I was unable to enter the formed world which you inhabit. But now I am without. I am here and can no longer enter the world I have spawned, the world that is me and within me. I am excluded, no longer part of it. It has been invaded by your husband and children.'

'Invaded?'

Orbus slowly nodded. 'I will explain in a moment. But let me continue. You see, for ages beyond counting I was alone, with only memories and the commanding urge to *be* once more to sustain me. But I gradually discovered my world, my universe, my *self*, and I grew aware little by little that there existed another world, another reality, beyond the formed world, your universe, from which I had been cast. Much later I grew conscious of presences close upon the borders of my existence. I concentrated upon these and in time was able to reach out and speak into the consciousness of one. She was Seruhlin, a founding monarch of Enchantment's Edge. I willed her to my world, and eventually she came. She came into my blue existence. For the first time I learned of the form that I took in your world: the blue casket of Enchantment. I found that I could open and seal the casket at will, to permit one other being to enter. From that point a process was begun which has continued over many generations, involving every ruler since Seruhlin's time.'

'And always a secret,' breathed Issul.

'Always a secret. It had to be. I told Leth that he must never reveal this great secret to any other. My world is governed by precise laws, held in a fine and delicate balance. Now Leth has upset the balance. He has entered with your children at a time when I was not present. He has upset the balance. This is what I mean by invaded. I do not know the full consequences of what he has done, but it means that I am no longer a part of what I am. And he and the children are trapped within me.'

'Let me be clear on this. You are saying that you and the casket are one and the same?'

'That is so.'

'And you hold Leth and our children within you and cannot release them?'

'Not hold,' replied Orbus. 'Leth has been within many times and we have had long and mutually advantageous discussions. He came voluntarily, at my call, and at those times I was always present within. I could release him, and did so. But I have been researching and experimenting, always, and my most recent endeavours have involved attempts to externalize myself, to pass from my world into yours, the world I knew so long ago. I have had some success: witness my presence here now. But today Leth entered the blue casket when I was externalized. Worse, he brought others, and I have cautioned him again and again never to reveal the secret of the casket to anyone else. In bringing your children into me he has destroyed the balance that maintains my world. They are unnatural elements, alien presences, individuals that have evolved in another milieu. In bringing them Leth has sealed the portal. If I am not there to free him he has no means to leave my world. But he prevents my return. I, who am my own god, am cast out of my world.'

'I still do not understand,' said Issul. 'How are you prevented from returning?'

'My world cannot accomodate more matter than it is formed to contain. A universe is composed of a finite amount of matter, energy, light and space, all of which are mutually interactive. It can contain no more, other than through the infinitely gradual process of natural generation. I had created the means to enable my world to accept but one other being from yours at any one time. Had I been present when Leth chose to enter with the children he would have found it impossible. But I was absent, which enabled them to take my place. Now that they are there, my return would cause a clash of cosmic energies far greater than you can imagine. I would be annihilated, with everything that is within me. Even this, the formed world, might be destroyed as a result. I speak of divine energies, Cosmic pre-mind, awesome Potentia. I speak of the energy of becoming and un-becoming. We are but specks of insignificance within Mysteries such as this.'

The candle-flame wavered. Beyond the indistinct figure of Orbus the lights of far Enchantment glowed in their flux of colour. Issul sat absorbed in her thoughts. 'How, then, can they return?'

Orbus slowly shook his huge, ragged head. 'I do not know if they can.'

She swallowed. 'There must be a way.'

Orbus was silent. Issul said, 'Can they survive within your world?'

Orbus inhaled deeply. 'I think there is sustenance.'

'Think?'

'Very slowly, over a long, long period of time, I have absorbed elements into myself. Leth brought me things, as did his forebears. They have helped to bring my world to life. I do believe that the basic elements necessary to support life are here, within me.'

'Then you have expected this, or something like it?'

Orbus hesitated. 'No. I have experimented, that is all. I am, if you wish, a Creator, largely blind to what I may have created. I have had the most profound understanding lately that there is life within me. I sense it, though I have never seen it. I do not know its forms. I have endeavoured to communicate, but to no avail. Perhaps, as both world and Creator, my purpose prevents my having direct contact with whatever dwells within me. But, definitely, there are other existences.'

Issul blinked back tears. *My babies, what unknowns do you face? Will I never see you again?*

She pushed back her hair from the temples. 'There has to be a way of getting to them.'

'I do not know it, if there is. But the formed world has changed since my dwelling-time in Enchantment. Enchantment itself has changed. Leth made it plain that my former adversaries are greatly advanced. Who knows, then, what might be possible now?'

'Within Enchantment.'

'Within Enchantment, where also lies my soul.'

She stared at him. 'The Orb's Soul?'

He slowly nodded. She thought back to the evening Leth had referred to it, his reluctance when she had pressed him to know more. 'What can it do?'

'It can empower me,' said Orbus. 'I could exist again, as I was, in the formed world. And I would be more than I was before, I am certain of that.'

'Empowered? Enough to save Enchantment's Edge?'

'That would remain to be seen. But it is likely I could at least be influential upon the "god" who stands with your enemies, the Krai. I have learned much in my eons of isolation.'

'What of the Legendary Child?'

'Leth has spoken to me of this. The Child's role is unclear, but if it is the spawn of one of my old adversaries it can surely be no more powerful than I.'

'But you are not certain.'

Orbus leaned heavily upon his staff. 'Certainty, at this stage, would be inappropriate.'

'What of Leth and my children? If you are united with the Orb's Soul, can you free them?'

'I would be strong. If the Soul of the Orb is not enough in itself, then within Enchantment there must exist the means by which all this can be resolved. But of course, you are prevented from entering Enchantment. And I cannot stray from the vicinity of the blue casket.'

Issul scratched her brow. Was he being truthful? If he was truly a god, seeking revenge upon his former adversaries, what ultimately might he have in mind?

'You are troubled by me, are you not?' asked Orbus softly.

Issul stared at him. This was no dream, she realized now. And she had little choice but to confide in him, and hope.

'I know of a way into Enchantment,' she said.

'You do?'

Briefly she told him of the Farplace Opening and her experience when she had been drawn into it.

'Ah!' exclaimed Orbus. 'It is a long time since I have heard the name of Triune spoken.'

'What or who is Triune?'

'The Sundered God, broken and scattered. Defeated at about the same time I was. Triune was a single entity who chose to adopt a three-part form. When defeated her punishment was to be sundered for all eternity. Like me, she is deprived of the soul that will unify her.'

'And it is the other "gods" who have done this?'

Orbus nodded.

'Triune claims that she will soon be One again. Also that she has taken the Farplace Opening from the god who aids the Krai.'

'More and more interesting. But I suspect half-truths at best.'

'Then, what?'

'Until more is known, I cannot say. Think of what I have just related to you. The ultimate purpose of the beings you have termed gods is to reclaim the world which was all once part of the flux that is Enchantment. Enchantment diminishes. Infinitesimally. Leaving behind it the Mondane world, the world that you and your kind inhabit. The gods war constantly, perhaps not always wholly aware that the reason they do so is to generate the chaotic energies that keep Enchantment alive. So if Triune stands against the god of the Krai, she does so still with the ultimate aim of destroying your world. Still, something can perhaps be made of this.'

'Not wholly aware?' queried Issul. 'How is it, then, that you, who are one of them, know so much more than they? Are you so much wiser?'

A low, rasping chuckle sounded from within Orbus's mass of rags. 'I have had ample time to become wise. And I am now truly a god. Inadvertently they have made me so, and it changes everything. They have given me an understanding I could never have had before. They seek to regress, to turn the world back to what it was before. Do you think, now, that I could be part of that?'

Issul lowered her gaze, haggard. 'I no longer know what I think.'

'I want to help you, Issul, troubled Queen of Enchantment's Edge. I want you to have your husband and children back. I want you to overcome the menace that rises all around you.'

'Then tell me how!'

'I cannot, until I know. But the gods seek the means to reclaim all of the world. The first indication that they are succeeding will come in the form of Edge Riders.'

'What are they?'

'Phantasmal creatures that will come out of Enchantment, bringing with them a wake of destruction. Wherever they go they will leave chaos, paving the way for Enchantment to grow.'

'The Legendary Child?'

Orbus's great head swayed from side to side. 'He is a dark enigma that has yet to be understood. Linked in some way, I don't doubt, but he is not an Edge Rider. Everything you have told me, however, indicates that the Edge Riders will come. And I think they will come via the Farplace Opening.'

Issul caught her breath. 'That is its purpose?'

'One among several, I think.'

'Is it Triune who will control the Edge Riders?'

'How can I say without going there? You tell me Triune claims to be holding the Opening against the god who controls the Krai?'

'That is what I was told.'

'Then you must take me there. Together we must go to Enchantment.'

But if I leave here, thought Issul, I will be giving Enchantment's Edge to Fectur again. Playing straight into his hands. Giving him the freedom to do just as he wishes. And you, Orbus, how do I know if I can trust you?

Though she could not see Orbus's eyes – could not even tell if he possessed any – she sensed that his gaze was upon her.

'It is the only hope you have,' said the god.

And on the roadside at the foot of the colossal, soaring scarp of Enchantment's Edge a group had gathered around a camp fire. Most were sleeping, the fire dying low. But a single figure sat alone, huddled in a shawl, gazing to the myriad twinkling lamplights high above which marked the site of the great city-castle. Arene rocked herself slowly, her heavy arms wrapped around her bulk. Ah yes, young Queen, she thought to herself, I am almost with you. Your time has now come. I tried so hard to prevent all this. A single stroke would have done it. But it was not to be. Now you have no choice but to step forth and discover your destiny. Your time is upon you now, and ah! what a path lies before you! Issul, Queen Issul, how my heart bleeds for you.

The saga of *ENCHANTMENT'S EDGE*

continues in

Volume 2: *Orbus's World*